TRIALS AND TRIBULATIONS

THE ROBINSWOOD STORY - BOOK 3

JEAN GRAINGER

GOLD HARP MEDIA

Dedicated to my sister Barbara, a fine storyteller herself and one of the few people on earth that can make me cry with laughing.

CHAPTER 1

*R*obinswood, Co Waterford, 1950

'MAMMY, Poppy took my dough. She said she was awwowed and I said she wasn't and she hiss me with the wooden spoon.' Daisy's three-year-old flour-smudged face was indignant, while her twin sister, Poppy, grinned guiltily.

Kate swung around from the stove, where she was trying to make sure there were no lumps in the gravy, to face her daughters perched on stools at the large kitchen table. Jack, their brother, and their cousin Austina, both a mature four and a half, were playing peacefully with a piece of dough that had once been cream coloured but was now a grubby grey. She'd have to warn Sam not to eat the cake they were making for him.

She did not need this squabbling now, but there was nobody around to help her take care of the children. She knew Aisling had to go to the doctor, but today of all days? And where on earth was Mammy? She must have forgotten.

They had a large group of Americans booked in, the first big group they'd ever had at the hotel. The tourists were attending a summer school programme in Dungarvan on genealogy, but luckily one of the organisers had suggested Robinswood for the accommodation. They'd been managing to stay afloat, just about, since they opened Robinswood as a country house hotel last year, but if they could land big American groups, then that was going to be the making of them. Sam had gone to Dublin to meet with tour operators, and they'd visited and were impressed, so they had everything crossed. Sam's ancestral home was undoubtedly beautiful, and all of the guests so far had gushed about how much they'd enjoyed it. Kate always reassured her husband whenever he worried they had embarked on a self-destruct course of action, but the reality was the three-hundred-year-old mansion was also a money pit.

'Poppy Violet Kenefick, if I have to go over to you, I swear I'll find a very good use for that wooden spoon,' Kate snapped.

Her mother was always there to help with the baking and the preparation for the guests, and it wasn't like her not to turn up. Kate felt a pang of guilt mixed with frustration. Maybe her parents were being pushed too hard. She forgot sometimes how old they were getting, and she'd said as much to Mammy last week.

Isabella had told her she was being ridiculous, that she and Dermot were as fit as trout. All the same, Kate tried to make it a bit easier on them, but there was always so much to be done and Isabella knew the house better than anyone alive. Her mother had spent near a lifetime as the housekeeper on the Robinswood estate, followed by several years running a house in Dublin, only to return to the even more arduous work of helping her daughter and son-in-law drag the big old house out of almost dereliction and transform it into a sumptuous hotel.

Before she had time to reprimand them again, Daisy and Poppy were back thick as thieves. They had their own language – nobody had the faintest idea where they got it – and they spoke to each other incessantly, chatting and giggling in a kind of gibberish that they both appeared to understand perfectly.

Jack, their brother, was a different personality, more like his father, quiet and sensitive. He trailed after Sam all over the estate, blissfully happy when his father was herding cows or tilling fields. One thing was sure, he wasn't being raised as if the title he would one day inherit exempted him from hard work even at that young age. Everyone on Robinswood earned their keep, so being the ninth generation of the family to inherit the family seat had no bearing on how he was reared.

Kate thought with frustration of her sister-in-law lounging about upstairs. Everyone except Lillian pitched in. Kate wished she could ask her to mind the kids or set the tables or something, but she would just refuse. She didn't even mind her own child, let alone Kate's. Lady Lillian, as she called herself, was too good for skivvying as she saw it. *Stuck-up cow*, Kate fumed. How was she going to do everything herself?

To Lillian, neither Kate nor any member of the Murphy family would ever be anything but the former staff of this house. Kate knew that she never saw her as family, more an example of a servant getting ideas above their station. Kate hated the off-hand way her sister-in-law spoke to her parents, Dermot and Isabella, and as for the dismissive tone she used with her, well, she really was a nightmare.

'Mammy, can we eat the skins?' Daisy asked as Kate began furiously peeling the Bramleys for the apple tarts. Just as she and her sisters had done when they were little girls, the children loved dipping the tart skins in the sugar bowl and crunching through them.

Kate had an idea – she'd bring the children down to her mother. Isabella was probably at home tending the flowers for the altar in the parish church, oblivious to the fact that her daughter was near collapse up here.

'You can. Then when we get this all in the oven, we'll take the bicycle down to the farmhouse to Nana Bella, will we?'

They squealed with delight. They loved Kate's bike. She'd had a big box trailer fitted to the back of it, and all four children fit in it. Her mother had nearly had a heart attack when she saw it, but the Kenefick children and their cousin Austina couldn't get enough of it.

She put six loaves of soda bread in the big Stanley range. It still gave her pleasure to see it; it had been worth every penny. Not only

3

was it a fantastic oven – and she could cook on the hob as well – but the fire heated the water, so for the first time, there was hot and cold water in the bedrooms upstairs. It was a real selling point for Robinswood, how luxurious they had managed to make it on what could only be described as a shoestring. Aisling's husband and her father, along with Beau, Lillian's husband, all worked the estate with her and Sam and were between them the handiest group of men you could meet. Kate and Aisling joked about how they chose them for that very reason.

She took off her apron. The loaves would take forty minutes, just enough time to pop down the avenue to the farmhouse where her parents lived and where she and her sisters had grown up, drop the kids with Mammy and get back before she burned the bread.

'Right, down to Nana,' she said, lifting them each from the big bench that ran the length of the twenty-foot table that dominated the sunny basement kitchen. A pang of guilt hit her at the thought of foisting four lively little ones on her mother, but she had no choice.

She made a quick check that everything would be all right while she was gone. The strawberries were hulled and sitting in a bowl with caster sugar and the potatoes were peeled, but she had yet to do the vegetables.

She loved the kitchen at Robinswood. It had been a dark and dreary room years ago, but her father had broken through the walls to create large windows and dug out a courtyard to the rear of the house with steps up to the garden level, so now it was like a sun trap. Kate remembered her mother sitting there, having a well-earned cup of tea mid-morning when Kate was a child, and now she did the same.

As she hoisted the children into the box on the bike leaning against the kitchen wall outside, she gave them each a cuddle. The girls were live wires, to put it mildly, and their arrival had been a surprise. She'd had to come to terms with not just a toddler but a pair of newborns as well. By then though, they were back in Robinswood. Her sister Aisling and Aisling's husband, Mark, had come over from England to work with them, her parents were always on hand, and Beau and Lillian and their little daughter, Austina, were around too. Though

Lillian was as useful as an ashtray on a motorbike, Beau was a great help on the estate, and all the children adored the large black American.

Austina gave Kate a squeeze as she popped the child in beside Daisy. Kate smiled at her niece. She was a sweet little girl, thankfully taking after her father more than her mother, and she and Jack were inseparable. They'd both be starting at the village school in September, in the baby and infants class. Jack would be the first Kenefick to attend the local school and Austina the first mixed-race child, so they would both be little groundbreakers. Sam was fine when Kate said that there was no way on earth she was ever sending her children to boarding school, as had been the norm for every generation of Keneficks, but Lillian had been appalled at the idea of Austina attending the local school. She had assumed Austina would have a governess and at age seven would go to a British prep school as a boarder, as she and everyone she knew had done.

To the Murphys, Beau was just another member of the family, but the villagers had only recently stopped staring. Most of them had never seen a black man before, and the idea that he was the husband of Lady Lillian, the snooty little madam that had looked down her aquiline nose at them all her life, was gossip they couldn't have dreamed of.

The anticipation of the trip on the bike elicited squeals of delight. They had turned heads at first around Kilthomand, Kate pulling the children in the trailer, but now people were used to them. She might have the title of Lady Kenefick, but she was still just Kate Murphy. Her dark curly hair flew loose when by rights it should have been tied up modestly, she wore her signature blood-red lipstick, even if she was only popping to the shop, and her effortless chic and curvaceous figure were the envy of the parish.

'Did you bring Nana Bella a bun, Mammy?' Poppy asked, pointing to the buns wrapped in a clean tea towel.

'I did, pet. She'd love a bun to have with her cup of tea, and seeing her four favourite little people in the whole world will make her day.'

Kate really hoped Aisling would get back soon; she needed the help so badly. She checked the big clock in the yard. Half past four. The group of ten Americans had a bus of their own that was coming from Dublin and were due to arrive around seven. They would fill the hotel. The beds were ready and the rooms looked beautiful; Aisling had ensured they did before she left. Her sister had a great knack of adding little touches – bud vases, an old book from the library, little trinkets – about the rooms to give the guests the impression that they were private visitors at a home rather than a hotel. The little things planted about the house served as great talking points too when people came down to dinner.

'Right, you lot, let's go. I'll be back in time to give Granda and Daddy and Mark and Beau their tea.' She pedalled out of the yard.

She thought the Robinswood grounds looked spectacular as she sailed down the sloping driveway. The ocean far below stretched off to the horizon, and the old stone wall to her right enclosed the orchard where she and Sam played as children. Surreptitiously, of course. If his mother, the previous Lady Kenefick, had known he was climbing trees with the staff children, she would have had a stroke. Paddocks that supported their herds of cattle and sheep rolled to the sea, green and fertile.

All of the outbuildings, of which there were many, were in the process of being converted into accommodation as well, and they'd only last week decided to have a thatcher come to thatch the roofs. Kate had read somewhere about the numbers of Americans who had family, or at least roots, in Ireland, and now that the war was over and money more plentiful, they would all want to visit. Already one could fly to London or even Amsterdam, and according to the article she read, it was only a matter of time before people would be able to fly to New York...and more importantly, from New York to near Robinswood. And what would be more fun than to stay in a thatched cottage, just like your ancestors lived in, except with all the modern conveniences? Sam thought she was crazy at first, but her father had backed her, and so the project was going ahead. The trouble was getting enough men to do the work. There was so much work in

London, and the bright lights of the city and the prospect of good wages was emptying the towns and villages.

Kate sighed as she cycled past the sheds. They would be done by now if only they had the skilled labour. She couldn't blame the people who left, she supposed. Hadn't she and Aisling taken off in the middle of the night to join the British army back in 1940, not a word to anyone? London was so exciting, so vibrant – not words anyone ever used to describe the sleepy village of Kilthomand.

The idea was that Robinswood wasn't a hotel in the conventional sense; more it was a stately home that could be booked by a group or a family, or basically anyone who wanted to or could afford to play at being aristocracy. It had been restored not just to its former glory but far in excess of it. The cut limestone house on four floors with red sandstone edging was a beautiful place to live, and she knew how lucky they were.

Sam could have stayed in the RAF after the war – he was well decorated and would have risen up the ranks quickly, the wheels of promotion oiled by his title undoubtedly – and they could have had a nice house in one of the better suburbs of London, but he didn't want that and neither did she. Robinswood was home for both of them, though his childhood there was upstairs while hers was definitely downstairs, but they both loved it equally and wanted to raise their family there. And if that meant baking loaves of soda bread and dancing attendance on God knows who, then so be it.

CHAPTER 2

$\mathcal{K}$ ate leaned the bike against the gable wall of her parents' farmhouse and let herself and the children in. Instantly, she felt shocked. The sour smell of unemptied bins and the dirty dishes on the table were utterly unfamiliar. Her mother's kitchen always smelled of baking and laundry soap, but today it looked like nobody had tidied up all week. The curtains were closed in the middle of the day as well, which was unheard of. Something was wrong.

She ushered the children back outside into the sunshine. Worried, she scanned the fields around the house. She heard the sound of chopping and ran around to the yard behind. There was Beau, chopping firewood, his muscular frame swinging the heavy axe over his head.

'Oh, Beau, could you watch the kids for me?' She knew she looked panicked. Isabella had never taken a day off in her life before.

'Of course.' Beau smiled his big easy grin, the one that made Lillian fall for the black GI during the war.

'Daddy!' Austina ran into her father's arms, and he picked her up and cuddled her.

'Thanks. I need to go up to Mammy, but can you keep them out here?'

'No problem. But, Kate, is everythin' all right? You lookin' worried,' Beau said in his slow Southern drawl that three years in Ireland had done nothing to change. He set his daughter down and picked up a twin in each arm as Jack and Austina clung to his legs. He could carry all four of them around the house, and they loved it. The twins rummaged in his shirt pocket for a barley sugar, as he always had a few sweets on him. He tickled them and they squealed with giggles.

'Yes…well, I hope so. I don't know… Thanks for minding them. I won't be long. Be good for Uncle Beau, children.'

She ran distractedly back inside and climbed the stairs, ignoring the dirty kitchen. Her mother had drawn back the curtains and was sitting up in bed.

'Mam? What's wrong?' Kate asked, approaching the bed.

'No, stay over there.' Her mother raised her hand.

'What are you on about? For God's sake, you're scaring me now.' Kate tried to joke.

'Sit there.' Her mother indicated the chair at her dressing table. The bedroom had hardly changed a bit since Isabella and Dermot got married, and Kate and her sisters knew growing up that it was their parents' private place. They knocked before entering, and in a busy house with hard-working people as a wife and mother herself now, she knew how precious that space was. The bed was covered in a lovely patchwork quilt Kate remembered Mammy making when Kate was small, stitching each colourful panel lovingly onto both sides of an old woollen blanket. One side was all pinks and greens, and the other blues and yellows. There was a large dressing table and a heavy oak wardrobe. Kate knew her mother was a beautiful woman, not just in the way that every little girl thought her mammy was lovely, because with Isabella, it was more than that. She always told them of her Spanish blood, how her granda was a Spanish sailor who fell in love with a Galway girl and broke his poor mama's heart by never returning to Spain.

Kate looked most like her – the same flashing eyes, skin that took the sun easily, the same dark curls and voluptuous curves. Aisling was dark too but more slight and with straight hair, and Eve looked like Daddy, tall with dark-red hair and creamy skin.

'I want you to listen, and don't go making demands or telling me what to do,' Isabella said.

'Mam...' she began.

'Kate, I mean it, no hysterics. I wasn't feeling well, very tired all the time, sure I've hardly had the energy to do the housework.'

Kate felt awful. She'd been driving her mother too hard. She opened her mouth to speak, to apologise, but Isabella held her hand up to silence her.

'So I went down to Doctor Grahame this morning. He needs an X-ray of my chest to confirm it, but he's fairly sure it's TB. Now, don't panic. I fully intend to recover, and I'll do whatever it takes. I haven't told your father yet, but he had it as a child, so he's immune. But you all need to stay away, and for God's sake, keep the children away from me.' She struggled to catch her breath, and Kate noticed it then, the sheen of perspiration, the gauntness in her mother's cheeks that wasn't there a month ago.

'But you don't know for sure...' Kate began, silently pleading with God, the universe, anyone.

'Kate, love.' Her mother's voice was sad now, sad and tired. 'I know. And the doctor was almost a hundred percent certain. You know too. It's TB.'

The words hung between them, palpable and poisonous like the virus ravaging her mother's lungs.

'No.' The word came out as a strangled sound. Kate didn't recognise her own voice.

'Now, listen to me. I know it's not great news. Of course it isn't. But they have all kinds of treatments for it now, and isn't that Doctor Noël Browne up in the government making fantastic strides opening sanatoriums and all the rest of it. So I'll go where I need to go and do what I need to do, and I'll beat this thing.'

'Will I go and find Daddy?' Kate asked, suddenly feeling like a child again, not a grown adult and mother of three.

'Do. I hadn't the energy to go looking for him when I came home. I walked back from the village. I should have asked someone to collect me, but I'm so used to it, I didn't think. But yes, get Der for me. I need him.'

Those words. Kate swallowed the lump in her throat and bit back the tears. Her mother needed her to get her husband, the man she'd been married to for over thirty-two years. For Kate and her sisters, their parents' relationship was the best example of how to do marriage. Dermot and Isabella were utterly loyal, they laughed together, and they held each other in the utmost respect and regard. Isabella had stood by Dermot through thick and thin.

Once Ireland was free, they went on to raise their daughters, never undermining each other. When Lord Kenefick died, leaving nothing but empty whiskey bottles and debts, they packed their few belongings and went looking for work, leaving the only home they'd ever known, but it didn't even put a crack in their marriage.

They were the ones who'd held Eve up when her husband of only a year was killed, they were the ones who'd supported Aisling as she loved Mark, a man who had served time in Dartmoor prison, and they were the reason Sam and Kate were back in Robinswood. And now it was Kate's turn to support them. She could do it.

'I'll get him now, Mam. You just relax there. Beau has the children.'

Isabella nodded and smiled. 'Don't bring them near me, love, and stay away yourself too. I couldn't bear it if...'

'I won't, Mam. We'll solve this like we solve everything, all right?' Kate tried to infuse her voice with positivity and hope.

She got on her bike without saying a word to Beau, who was in the yard pushing Austina and Jack on a swing Dermot had made for them while Daisy and Poppy picked flowers in the garden.

'Don't pick Nana's flowers!' she called. 'She needs them for the church.'

She pedalled back in the direction of the house. Sam and Mark were in the long meadow repairing fences all day, but the big old Ford car was in the stable yard, so she hoped her father wouldn't be far away. She abandoned the bike and ran in search of her father. Relieved, she heard him whistling in a stable.

Winston, the big grey gelding they used for ploughing, was standing patiently as Dermot examined his hoof. 'Ah, Kate,' her father said as he looked up, glad to see her. 'Just the girl! Can you pass me those pliers there?' He pointed to an upturned barrel with a selection of tools on it. 'Poor old Winston needs to be shod really, but that will have to wait till Thursday because Tommo Keane can't –'

'Mammy needs you. She needs you to go down to her – now,' Kate interrupted.

Something in her voice made her father look up. 'What's wrong?' he asked, his blue eyes raking her face for a clue.

'Mammy just wants you.'

Dermot lowered the horse's leg and stood up. He was tall and broad, a powerfully built man. Now that he was past sixty years of age, his dark-red hair was showing signs of grey, but it was still full.

'Take my bike. I'll walk down. The children are below.'

'Is she hurt?' he asked.

'No, she's in bed, but she asked me to find you.' Kate hoped he wouldn't cross-examine her further.

Dermot passed her and took the handlebars of the bicycle. He gazed at her quizzically for a second but then pedalled away.

Kate walked back to the farmhouse but this time didn't go in, looking instead for Beau. She'd have to manage somehow. The bread was in the oven, and regardless of what was going on in their lives, the Americans were coming and expected to be treated royally.

Kate saw Aisling with Beau as she re-entered the yard. 'Hi, Ais,' she said as the twins ran to her.

'Mammy, Uncle Beau showed us a nest and there's ickle eggs in it and he said that someday soon ickle birdies will come out,' Daisy said excitedly.

The twins' diction left something to the imagination, and really only Sam and she knew what they were saying all of the time, but when Kate told Isabella of her worries, her mother had assured her that Eve couldn't say R's until she was five and Kate herself had a lisp until she went to school.

The three Murphy girls believed their mother knew everything. Being without her was unthinkable, but TB had been ravaging the country for years, leaving death and chaos in its wake.

Kate glanced up at the bedroom window; the curtains were drawn again.

CHAPTER 3

Kate and Aisling let Beau get back to work and the sisters walked together back to the main house. Aisling was full of news. The doctor had been really nice and listened to Aisling's concerns about her infertility. She suggested sending both Aisling and Mark for tests in Dublin, and following on from that would perhaps offer her some supplements or hormones to help her conceive. Apparently, there was a doctor in America who was even experimenting with conception outside of the womb. It was very early days, but at least someone was doing something rather than just saying it was God's will.

'She asked about my monthly cycle, something Doctor Grahame never even mentioned. I told her that it had never been regular, and she said that was most likely the problem. So maybe if there's a way of regulating that, then I might be able to get pregnant.'

Kate wished she could share in her sister's enthusiasm, and she tried her best to put a smile on her face, but it felt like a big black stone was sitting in the middle of her chest.

'I hope so, Ais, I really do,' Kate said as the children ran ahead.

'She said it's more common than you'd think, people having trouble conceiving. And sometimes even when people have a child, they can't have another.' She lowered her voice. 'Maybe that's what's happened with Lillian and Beau?'

'Maybe, but I'd say she just hated being pregnant.' Kate was never going to give Lillian the benefit of the doubt.

'You don't think she's deliberately stopping it, do you?' Aisling asked, again in a murmur.

'Well, I wouldn't put it past her, and it's not like she'd have Father O'Connell looking suspiciously at her,' Kate said with a sigh.

Father O'Connell, the curate and a very zealous Jesuit, was often heard giving sermons on the evils of birth control. 'It is flying in the face of God,' he would bellow, 'to interfere with His divine plan for selfish reasons.'

'I know. I hate it when he goes on with that, feeling like everyone is looking at me, blaming my English husband and his heathen ways no doubt.' Aisling sighed.

'Don't mind him, that big eejit,' Kate said furiously. 'It's nothing to do with him.'

Aisling cast a sideways glance at her sister. 'Are you all right, Kate? You seem a bit...I don't know...'

It was Mammy's story to tell, but Kate longed to share her grief and worry. 'I'm fine, sorry. I was just down with Mam, and she's a bit under the weather, and I'm worried about this group. If this goes well, we could really be onto something, and without Mam to oversee everything, I'm afraid I won't be able to do it all. I usually greet the guests upstairs, as you know, but how am I supposed to do that if I'm in the kitchen? It would be fine if you and I could stay downstairs, we'd manage fine, but...'

Aisling linked her arm. 'Hey! I've an idea. Why don't we ask Lillian to do the Lady of the Manor bit, and you and I manage the food? Look, we've been catering in that house since we were knee-high to a duck. We'll be grand. And she'd love nothing more than to be swanning about upstairs being all toffee-nosed talking about her ancestors on the walls. And sure we can rope the lads into the kitchen if needs be. Mark can't cook to save his life, but he's great at washing dishes, and Sam and Lillian can play Lord and Lady of the Manor in the drawing room.'

Kate smiled. It was a genius idea. 'What would I do without you?' She gave her sister a squeeze. 'Lillian will love that idea, that her job is to just be her snooty self. Sam would rather be out mending fences or milking, but I suppose they are not just paying to stay and eat at Robinswood – they want to rub shoulders with the Lord. You better ask her though. She'd say no to me just because she could, but she likes you a bit better.'

'Only marginally,' Ais said with a grin.

'Indeed.'

After arriving back, they set about getting the children fed and washed while simultaneously preparing dinner. Kate was preoccupied, as she was worried sick about her mother and unable to share the burden. She saw Sam return and head to their rooms to prepare for dinner, and she left everything simmering and went to join him. She needed a hug.

She and Sam had converted an annex to the house into their own private quarters, complete with two bedrooms, a bathroom, a kitchen and a little sitting room, and while originally it was meant to be a temporary measure, they found they liked it. It was warm and cosy and private. Beau and Lillian's rooms were on the third floor, their bedroom jokingly called 'the half acre' because it was so impossibly big, and Austina slept in a room off theirs. Lillian had suggested redecorating the old nursery where she and Sam had slept as children, but Beau had been adamant that it was too far away, being on the second floor and at the other end of the corridor.

Lillian did love Austina, there was no doubt about it, but Kate had inadvertently heard Lillian pleadingly tell Beau that she wanted her raised as a young aristocratic lady, not as a wild ragamuffin. Kate had been furious, knowing the reference was to how she and Sam were raising their children, but when she told her mother and Aisling, they both burst out laughing.

'That Lillian is deluded if she thinks the toffs over in England will welcome our brown little girl with open arms,' Isabella had remarked wisely. 'Austina is part of Robinswood and of this community where she is loved and accepted, but even Lillian with all her mad notions knows the fate that awaits her child in the big bad world. No, Kate darling, you are stuck with Lady Lillian, and everyone, including her, knows that.'

It was a small price to pay, she supposed, and for the most part, Lillian behaved. Beau took no nonsense from her. He loved Lillian and treated her with the utmost respect as his wife, but he was not one for airs and graces.

* * *

AISLING KNOCKED on Lillian and Beau's bedroom door and heard the imperious voice call, 'Enter.' She walked in to find Lillian seated as usual in her gold brocade Queen Anne wingback chair beside the rosewood coffee table. She spent hours there, reading or writing letters or simply surveying the estate through the large double-bowed windows.

'Yes?' Lillian raised her eyebrows.

'Lillian,' Aisling began, trying to keep her voice neutral. Lady Lillian, as she would rather be called, made her nervous. 'Kate and I were talking, and we had an idea. Well, I had it really,' she said, remembering to keep Kate out of it. The pair were like red rags to a bull together.

'What?' Lillian prompted, as if she had a very important engagement and Aisling was delaying her.

'Well, our mother isn't feeling well at the moment, and we have this large group of Americans in tonight. So I was hoping that you could take Kate's place in greeting them and telling them about the house and all of that and she could stay down in the kitchen.'

Lillian's face was inscrutable. 'As the hostess?' she said eventually.

'Well, yes, I suppose so. You and Sam know this place better than we do, all the people in the paintings and so on, so you'd probably do a better job than Kate anyway on that score...' Aisling knew she was laying it on a bit thick, but she needed Lillian to agree.

The other woman sighed theatrically as if this really was the most audacious imposition. 'Fine, I'll do it,' she said wearily.

'Do what?' Beau asked as he emerged from the bathroom, a towel wrapped around his waist. 'Oh, hi, Aisling! I'm sorry. I didn't know you were here.' He smiled sheepishly.

Aisling averted her eyes as he pulled on a robe.

'So do what?' he asked.

'Kate can't cope with the guests tonight, so they've asked me to play hostess,' Lillian explained.

'That's great! You know all about this place, and you've got the right accent and everythin'.' He grinned and kissed her cheek. 'We should have thought of this before.'

Aisling was as amazed as always to see how relaxed Beau was around Lillian; everyone else walked on eggshells for fear of offending her.

'So you gals going to cook up a storm downstairs?' he asked.

'That's the plan, though I normally wait on the tables, as you know, and Kate will need me more in the kitchen now than before, so I'll have to master the art of being in two places at once before seven o'clock.'

'How about I do it?' he asked. 'I can get myself dressed and ready in ten minutes. I might need some pointers, but it can't be too hard, right?'

'No, Beau, you don't need to do that...' she began. 'You should be at dinner with Lillian as her husband...'

'Aisling, it's fine. Y'all need to stay in the kitchen now that your mama isn't well, and I can wait on them. Besides, these people are Americans. Having a black man serve them is normal, but if they are from my part of the country, they would not accept me as their equal. Sit at a table with me and eat dinner? No way. This is better.'

'But, Beau, that's not right...' Aisling objected.

'Aisling.' Lillian cut across her. 'Beau is happy to wait tables. He understands these things. Now, I must get ready.' The clear implication was that Aisling was dismissed.

Beau's chocolate-brown eyes locked with Aisling's, and he smiled.

Words were unnecessary. Beau knew who he was, what he was worth and how much his family loved him. He could not be hurt by people who only saw the colour of his skin.

Aisling had no idea what part of the United States the guests came from, but she hoped it wasn't the South. The stories of lynchings and the racism and abuse suffered by black people there set her teeth on edge.

'Thanks then, both of you. You can leave Austina in the kitchen with Kate's three. We'll get them to bed after preparing dinner.'

* * *

SAM AND LILLIAN ALLOWED BEAU, resplendent in an old footman's uniform dug out of a suitcase in the attic and pressed in time for the event, to open the door. Sam was in black tie, and Lillian looked stunning in a floor-length cream sheath dress, her blonde hair held in place by an exquisite mother-of-pearl comb. Beau gave his wife a swift kiss on the cheek before letting the guests in and whispered, 'Showtime,' with a grin.

The driver was an affable man, and once he got over the shock of seeing a black man, he helped Beau bring in the luggage.

After the guests were shown to their rooms and checked in, Lillian and Sam welcomed them into the drawing room for a sherry or whiskey before dinner, and the small group marvelled at the beautiful space. They had splashed out on the peacock-blue wallpaper with gold motifs, and Sam's mother's new husband, Lord Perry Goodall, had donated some furniture and a large gold vase from Framington Hall, his ancestral seat in England. The overall effect was breathtaking.

Dermot had sanded back the floorboards and varnished them since carpeting was way beyond the budget, and though it had been back-breaking work, they now gleamed a lovely dark oak. Some old rugs in the attic had been pulled back from the brink of moth domination and were on the floor.

Lillian was playing a blinder. She caught Beau's eye, and he gave her a surreptitious wink as he passed around a silver tray of drinks and canapes.

One of the ladies engaged him in conversation. She was silver haired with intelligent blue eyes and wore many jewelled rings. 'You're a long way from home,' she remarked as he offered her a sherry.

'Yes, ma'am, I'm from Georgia.'

'I thought I recognised the accent. Whereabouts you from?'

'Near Savannah, ma'am,' Beau said as he topped up her sherry glass.

'Beautiful city, Savannah. I grew up in Augusta, but my father moved us all to Chicago when I was seventeen. I cried bitter tears, I can tell you, and even though Chicago is my home now, has been for close on fifty years, my husband and I always took our vacations in the Blue Ridge Mountains.'

'It's a beautiful part of the world, ma'am, no doubt about that,' he said with a smile. 'Sometimes I miss those big open skies.'

'I'm sure you do. Though the place you are now isn't so bad.' She winked, glancing around at not just the lavish house but the rolling parkland outside. 'And if you don't mind me asking, how come you wound up here?'

'No, ma'am, I don't mind at all. I was in the services when I met someone in London and fell in love, and, well, when the war was over, I came back to her.' His voice held no hint of either defiance or deference; he just was who he was.

'Well, good for you. I hope it worked out? So many wartime romances don't.'

'It worked out very well, ma'am, but then my lady is a very special person.'

The older woman patted his hand. 'I'm glad.'

Beau continued to circulate.

One by one as the group assembled, they marvelled at the house and asked Sam and Lillian a lot of questions about the family, the construction and their new business adventure. Lillian knew who was in each of the Kenefick portraits and regaled the group with tales of great uncle Herbert who ran away with the cook's daughter, much to everyone's delight. She neglected to mention how history was repeating itself under their very noses as Lord Kenefick's wife slaved over saucepans in the kitchen and Lady Lillian's husband served the drinks. She explained the significance of crests, and told them stories of her father's many horses, immortalised in oils around the room. There had been many more paintings of course, much more valuable ones too, but her father had lost them in card games or sold them to pay his gambling debts. There was a rather odd-looking painting of a bowl of fruit hanging where once a Gainsborough hung. Sam never took any notice, but Lillian could have told them of Renoirs and even a Monet that now adorned some wiser person's drawing room. She conveniently forgot to mention them to the guests, however.

Sam smiled at her as she waxed lyrical about the Kenefick family but in particular about her father, Austin, after whom her daughter was named. Lillian had always had a fraught relationship with her mother, Lady Violet, but she'd adored her hapless, hopeless but ultimately lovable rogue of a father. Lillian added that certain dose of snobbery that people seemed to enjoy, and Kate was glad to have her there for that if nothing else. Sam was not as poetic on the subject of his lineage but was happy to discuss farming and building, which the men enjoyed.

Kate made sure everything was going smoothly, popping upstairs occasionally to collect glasses and empty plates. She made herself as inconspicuous as possible. They had not yet worked out how much to reveal to guests about the family dynamics. Sam was for being honest, but Kate thought that it might take some of the magic away.

The group seemed lovely, and they all had Irish roots. Some of their people, they explained, left Ireland in the 1700s, others much more recently, but they all wanted to see and experience the land of their forefathers. Kate thought they would enjoy meeting Dermot, who was an expert on Irish history. Nobody would ever know now that her gentle, well-read father was once one of the IRA's most feared assassins and that his position as groundskeeper of Robinswood allowed him access to information that did untold damage to the crown forces that had occupied his country for almost 800 years.

He still didn't talk too much about those days, back in the early 1920s, when he and his best friend, a German-born Irish man called Oskar Metz, wreaked all kinds of holy hell on the Royal Irish Constabulary, the dreaded Black and Tans and the vicious Auxiliaries. He enjoyed that his country was at last at peace and didn't, like some of his former comrades, relish reliving those dark days. Though he never discussed his past, the girls were under no illusions. Their father was not a man to be trifled with. The War of Independence was not a war in the sense of those they learned about in school. It was guerrilla warfare, and it required nerves of steel and total dedication. They knew that their lovely, gentle father had killed people and that he felt no remorse for it. He was quite clear: the Black and Tans, the Auxiliaries and the British Army were the enemy. They had been asked to leave Ireland, to let the Irish live in peace in their own country, but for 750 years they steadfastly refused. Each generation of oppressors was more ruthless than the one before. They treated the Irish people appallingly, with a total disregard for human rights and dignity, and so there was only one language they understood. Whenever the subject came up, Dermot Murphy was firm. The British brought their brutality and violence, and it was met with an ardent savagery in return, the force of which was reserved for those defending their homes and families.

As Kate left the drawing room with a brimming tray of dirty dishes, a woman came through the doors. She was in her forties, dressed most extravagantly in a ruby-red gown and matching gloves. Her blonde hair and blue eyes reminded Kate of one of those china dolls. She completely ignored Kate and brushed past her, striding to stand beside a tall man, presumably her husband. Kate watched as Beau offered her a drink. She looked him up and down and then said, 'No, not that. Get me a gin and tonic, one cube of ice, a slice of lime.' And arrogantly turned her back to him.

They had decided that a whiskey and sherry reception as a preprandial cocktail was enough, and anyway, they had no tonic water, so Beau spoke gently. 'I'm sorry, ma'am, sherry or whiskey is what we are serving right now. Or I could get you a cup of tea or a lemonade if you'd prefer?'

The woman stood with her back to Beau, not even turning around, and her husband, a slim man with a pencil-thin moustache and dark oiled-back hair pulled out his wallet. He thrust a five dollar bill at Beau, throwing it on the tray. 'Boy, just get the lady what she wants.' He then turned to continue the conversation with the man to his right.

The conversation in the room slowed to an awkward silence. Beau stood there for a long moment before speaking. 'Sir, we do not serve the drink your wife ordered at this time. As I said, we have sherry, whiskey, lemonade or tea. Dinner will be served shortly in the dining room, and after dinner, some additional drinks are available.'

The man, oblivious to the embarrassment of his countrymen, swung around. 'What did you say to me, boy?' His brow was furrowed.

Kate fought the urge to panic. They needed this business so badly, but they could not stand by and allow someone to speak to Beau like that. Sam caught her eye – it appeared he'd had exactly the same thought. He looked to be at the brink of intervening, but his sister put her hand gently on his arm, throwing him a warning look.

'I just explained –' Beau began.

'Listen to me, boy. I do not take instructions from niggers at home, and I sure as hell won't do it here in Ireland!' His eyes glittered dangerously.

Sam glared at Lillian, shrugged her hand off his arm and started to cross the room, but before he got there, the woman with the silver hair intervened. She walked with a cane and hobbled to stand before the man with the moustache. 'Sir, I think you need to adjust your tone.' Despite fifty years in Chicago, she still had a softness to her accent that was unmistakably Southern. 'We are guests in this house, and this nice man from Georgia has served us graciously since we got here. Please do not continue to embarrass the rest of us with your uneducated attitudes.'

23

Kate thought she might have imagined it, but the others seemed to move a little behind the woman in a gesture of solidarity. The man and his wife appeared to stand alone.

'I think an apology might be in order?' the elderly lady suggested mildly.

The woman in the red dress looked uncertain. She glanced at her husband, who spat, 'Kenefick, get me a car. We're leaving. You can choose to elevate this monkey to the level of a gentleman if you want to, but mark my words, you'll regret it when he robs you blind and tries to force himself on your wife.'

Sam crossed the room, standing before the couple and beside Beau. 'Get out of my house and off my property. Beau is not just a member of staff, he is also family, and I will not tolerate anyone speaking to him in such a manner. I'll drive you to the village, and you can make your own arrangements from there.'

Kate suppressed a smile. Though this was not how she would have wished her first big group booking to go, she was proud of Sam and knew that the other guests supported his decision. She was stunned that Lillian said nothing.

Being stranded at this hour of the night in Kilthomand would be tricky. *Let this odious man and his haughty wife see how they get on*, she thought. Very few people had private cars, and the next bus was not until the morning. Mossy would have closed the post office, so communication with the outside world would be off limits as well. She'd give anything to see the pair of them in all their finery standing full of indignation in the village square with nowhere to go. Of course, they could make trouble for them, but it was worth it to defend Beau.

'Fine,' the man barked, and then turned to Beau. 'Get our luggage.'

'Don't worry, I can take care of that,' Sam said pleasantly. 'Would you like to pack your things, Mrs Baxterville? Then we will take them to the car presently.'

'Laurence, it's late and dark... Is there even another hotel in this place?' Mrs Baxterville had suddenly realised the precariousness of their situation, but her husband was too far in to back down now.

'Meredith, get your things,' he hissed. 'I will not stay another second under this roof.'

'Very well,' Sam said, almost grinning now, as Beau started offering more drinks to ease the tension. The smiles of gratitude and light conversation he had with the other guests left nobody in any doubt whose side they were on.

Sam sidled over to where Kate stood. 'Get Mark to bring the car around. He can drop this pair in the square.' He gave her the tiniest of winks and went back to mingling.

Kate ran down the back stairs to the kitchen and filled Mark in on the events upstairs. Of Dermot there was no sign. Mark hooted with laughter as Kate explained how first the older lady and then Sam faced the Baxtervilles down.

'They'll be lucky if Father Mac has left the chapel open,' Mark said in his soft English West Country burr. 'They could say their prayers until the ten o'clock bus in the morning.' He chuckled. 'Or maybe Mrs Moriarty would take them in. She keeps travelling salesmen and the like in her two spare rooms, doesn't she? Of course they'll have to risk recruitment to the Legion of Mary.'

Mrs Moriarty, a local widow, did indeed provide accommodation of a sort, but it was nothing of the Robinswood standard. Besides, the woman was dodged by everyone these days because her devotion to the Virgin Mary was manifested by her press-ganging anyone who stood still to join the Legion. Mark, a Church of England man, and Beau, a very devout Baptist, were her main targets, as in her mind at least, the conversion of those two heathen Protestants would be worth untold reward in the next life.

Dermot had had to be most blunt when she cornered him after Mass the previous weekend, saying he definitely would not join the Legion of Mary and to please stop asking him. And Aisling had come home from Lacey's hardware and draper's the prior week with the news that somehow she was now a member, despite never actually agreeing to sign up.

'That would be just the job for him, good enough for him.' Kate giggled.

'Look, if you can manage down here, I'll drop them to Dungarvan. At least they can stay at the hotel, though it's a bit of a comedown from Robinswood. It would be nice to abandon them, but we'd better not, I suppose, on our first big night.'

'All right, Mark. You're right. Poor Mrs Moriarty would have a heart attack if you turned up at this hour with a pair of Americans. They are really horrible though, so don't do them any favours. If you saw the way he spoke to Beau and the way his wife looked at Beau like he was something she scraped off her shoe...' Kate shook her head. She knew from stories Beau had told them and from Lillian's exploit in Mississippi after the war just how hard life was for black people in Southern states, but to witness it first-hand was deeply shocking.

She had no more time to think about it, or about what was happening below at the farmhouse with her parents, as she and Aisling managed the entire dinner. Beau waited on the tables perfectly. The previous week, Dermot and Mark had fixed the old dumb waiter that had not worked for years, so at least they could send the food to the dining room in that rather than have Ais and Beau running like hares all over the huge house, but it was still a lot to do for just three people. Sam would have been happy to help, but his role was to dine with his guests, and it ruined the magic if he was gathering dishes. And it would never enter Lillian's head to do anything but sit and be served, even after the incident with Beau, which she seemed able to overlook.

Kate had made the soup that afternoon – cream of root vegetables – and she knew it was delicious as it was her mother's recipe and foolproof. The soda bread was light and tasty, and the butter was their own, churned in the dairy every Monday morning. The leg of lamb was roasted and served with fresh-from-the-ground vegetables. The new Stanley range was fantastic, but it would take some getting used to. Dessert was apple crumble and custard or strawberries and cream. The apples fell in profusion in the Robinswood orchard and had for centuries, so each autumn since she was a child, she and her sisters had the job of picking them, making sure there were no slugs and then wrapping them in newspaper to be stored in the cellars to keep them fresh.

She whipped the custard until it was a creamy yellow and poured it into the antique jugs arranged around the large dish of crumble. She'd enjoy a portion of that with a cup of tea late that night when the dishes were done and the guests were all asleep. She wished she or Aisling had time to go and check on Jack, Austina and the girls, but she couldn't leave the kitchen. Sam said he'd excuse himself every so often to look in on them, but she hoped he'd remember. Now that they had guests, and more bookings every day, they needed to take on some more staff as well as someone to watch the children.

She thought of her parents in their bedroom, trying to come to terms with the devastating news. The family relied on them so much. It was now time for her and Sam to really take the reins and give them the time they needed, but how they would manage Robinswood without them was a total mystery.

CHAPTER 4

*E*ve looked radiant as she emerged from the car Bartley drove. They were a little early. Kate knew her sister's great news, that her first child was on the way, but she wasn't showing yet.

'Come in, come in.' Kate welcomed them into the Robinswood kitchen. Dermot had asked Eve and Bartley to come down for a visit. Kate and Aisling knew he wanted to talk about the situation with Mammy, but they didn't want to write or tell her on the telephone.

They had tea while they waited for their father to arrive in from the estate. Aisling appeared, and Bartley went out to the yard to talk to the men, leaving the sisters some private time.

'How are things here?' Eve asked, casting admiring glances all around. 'It looks amazing. I don't know how you do it all.'

'Some days neither do we,' Aisling joked.

'Any time you want to send some of those students of yours down, feel free. We need all the help we can get,' Kate added. 'How's the school going, by the way?'

Eve sat down, having hung her coat on the nail behind the door. Her copper curls were tied up in a ponytail, and she wore a rust-coloured dress and a light-blue cardigan. She looked nothing like her thirty-one years.

'From strength to strength really. We are turning people away, but the trouble is, when they finish with us and are ready for a job, they all seem to want to go over to England. The success of our students, how they all get good jobs after leaving us, means we are totally oversubscribed. We're renting houses along the terrace beside us and using them for the students, but it's not ideal because we are constantly being called in there for something or another. They used to stay in the house, but there are too many of them now and it wasn't working for any of us. We have forty students in this latest group, boys and girls. The houses we are renting are really expensive too, so I don't know what we'll do. We were just talking about it on the way down actually.'

'And are the boys in the rented houses too?' Kate asked, surprised.

'They are not indeed.' Eve grinned. 'Do you think we don't have enough problems? No, the lads are packed like sardines in the loft space of the workshop. Only girls in the houses, but as I said, it's far from ideal.'

'And how's Elena?' Aisling asked, cutting a slice of gingerbread.

Elena Hamilton-Brooks was a wealthy Dublin widow for whom Dermot and Isabella worked when the Keneficks left Robinswood in 1940. She and her husband, Thomas, had taken Eve in as well when Jack, Eve's first husband, died. The two women were now firm friends.

'She's doing well but spending more and more time in England. She misses Georgie and Arthur when they're away at school, so she stays in England to visit them on the weekends, and she spends a lot of time with her sisters. To be honest, she'd have moved back there if it wasn't for us and the school. She feels like she got me into it and can't desert me at this stage.'

Eve and her husband ran a training school for young people emerging from the care of the churches, orphans mainly, and Eve trained the girls as house staff and Bartley trained the boys in building, farming, gardening and so on with a view to them getting a decent position. So many of them had failed to get work once it was discovered where they came from, and the state would no longer support them, so the two women had set the school up during the war. It was how Eve met Bartley.

'Well, with the little one on the way, how much longer can you keep it going either, Eve?' Aisling asked gently.

'I know, but we do such good work. They come out from us so much better – more skills, more confident. It's been hard to get it to this stage, so I'm slow to walk away.' Eve shrugged. 'Anyway, enough about that. How are things here? Is Mammy feeling any better? Daddy said on the phone she was feeling rotten, but there's a desperate cold going around. Sure I'll pop down to her in a bit.'

Kate caught Aisling's eye over Eve's head as she went to fill the teapot; both knew that Eve would not be going anywhere near their mother.

* * *

DERMOT SAT at the head of the table in the kitchen of Robinswood, and Kate felt her heart lurch at the sight of him. He was trying to find the words, but they knew by his face that the results of the X-ray confirmed what Mammy knew. Aisling and Kate hated keeping things from their sister, so at least now Eve would know, though she looked so content it was hard to burst her bubble.

It was lovely to see her happy again after so much pain. She'd married Jack O'Neill ten years ago, but he was killed tragically when they were less than a year married. Poor Eve had been heartbroken for so long, and her sisters had feared she would never really live again, but one day Bartley Doherty turned up in her life and it was as if a light switched back on inside her.

They were an unusual match. Bartley turned heads wherever he went. He was the seventh son of a seventh son, a traveller and an expert tradesman. Some people in Kilthomand would call him a tinker, but Dermot and Isabella always had great time for the travelling people, so they were treated with respect at Robinswood. There was something otherworldly about Bartley. He knew the healing properties of plants, and he could relate to animals in a way not even Dermot could. He was also an expert farmer. He wore a copper bangle on his wrist and had black curly hair, barely tamed. Even his clothes were unusual, as he opted for leather and moleskin rather than cotton and tweed as would have been the norm. But for all his strangeness, there was something serene about him. His dark, almost-black eyes had a way of making people feel like they were the only one in the world when he spoke to them. He was from Ulster and had the distinctive Donegal lilt to his accent, but he'd grown up all over the place. His mother died when he was young and the state deemed his father unfit to care for the fourteen children of the family, on no other evidence than the fact that he was a man, and so the children were split up and sent to various institutions.

'Right. So I asked you all to come here because I have something to tell you and I wanted you all to hear it together,' Dermot began, and Kate recognised that voice, the no-nonsense voice he used when he expected to be obeyed without question. Bartley, Sam and Mark had joined them too.

'Mammy wasn't feeling well, so she went down to Doctor Grahame a few days ago. He sent her up to the hospital in Dublin on Tuesday, and they confirmed it – she has TB.'

Kate could see that underneath the stoic exterior, her father was devastated. Sam had mentioned how off form her father had been for the last few days. She thought about the gossip mill in the village once the news got out. There was a terrible stigma still about TB, and there would be a few who would sniff and say how it was a wonder Isabella Murphy got it, she up in the big house, considering it was seen as a disease of the poor.

'Now, we don't want anyone making a fuss. She's had an X-ray, and she'll have to go on a waiting list to go to the sanatorium up there. Hopefully, they've caught it early and she'll be cured.' Dermot smiled, the same smile that fixed cut knees or sister squabbles for as long as the girls could remember. 'She said to tell you that she'd love to see the children and all of you, but we don't want to risk infecting them or any of you. In fact, Dr Grahame wants to see you all just for a check-up, so make sure you go to see him before the week is out. Lillian and Beau and Austina as well. I've had it as a child, so I'm fine.'

Kate blinked back a tear. The last thing her mother needed was anyone being maudlin.

'Is the sanatorium the right place?' Eve asked Bartley quietly, and all eyes turned to him. Though he had no formal medical education, they had all consulted him at one time or another over the years. When all the children came down with chicken pox, Bartley made a paste for the spots and they instantly stopped itching. When Mark had bouts of depression, brought about by his experiences during the war, it was to Bartley he turned, and a combination of his healing hands and the tinctures he made up seemed to return Mark to his sunny self. Any sick animals on the farm were also treated by him, in almost every case successfully.

Bartley thought for a moment. 'Doctor Noël Browne is the new Minister of Health, and I know Isabella has great time for him. With good reason, as he's a great doctor and a TB survivor himself. He thinks sanatoriums are the way to cure it. Also, there's a new drug called streptomycin and it's having some success, but TB is a hard disease to treat.'

Bartley was not the kind of man to dismiss modern medicine even though he was an expert in herbal cures. He'd explained to Kate when the children got an infection that he could help alleviate symptoms certainly, but that penicillin was a remarkable drug.

'But Daddy said there's a waiting list. Surely the sooner they begin treatment...' Aisling was struggling to keep the panic out of her voice. Though she knew what the local GP had said, she'd hoped the Dublin consultants would diagnose something else. Having the dreaded tuberculosis confirmed was still a shock.

Kate reached over and took her sister's hand.

Sam's brow was furrowed. 'Mark, remember there was that chap, the flight commander, the one with the red curly hair? Remember him? He was at Biggin Hill with us – Gordon or Gardiner, something like that. Didn't he go to some place in Switzerland with TB and was cured?'

'I don't remember him, though I have heard of people going to Switzerland. They say the mountain air there is good,' Mark replied.

'You *do* remember him,' Sam insisted. 'He was the chap that got that old crate of a Lancaster back, crash landed on the apron, remember? He bailed out before the whole thing went up in flames?'

'Do you mean Greelings?'

'Yes, him! He got TB in '46. Poor chap had been through enough already. But his family sent him to Switzerland to some clinic, quite famous apparently, and last I heard, he was fine.'

'Good for him, but he's the son of Greelings Investment Brokers. That place would cost a fortune.'

'To hell with what it costs. We'll raise it if we need to. We have to save her, we just have to,' Sam said vehemently, and Kate had never loved him more.

Isabella was not just Sam's mother-in-law, she was in so many ways the mother he'd never had. Lady Violet was ineffectual when he was growing up, as she was married to a man who had deeply disappointed her and stuck in a draughty house in a country she despised. It was Isabella who'd cuddled him, looked after him when he was sick, made him bread and jam when he came in from the garden muddy from play. He loved Kate's mother entirely independently of his wife.

'It's in Davos,' Bartley said. 'Thomas Mann wrote a book about it, *The Magic Mountain*. They have a lot of success.'

It struck nobody as odd that he knew about this. Kate caught his eye. Deep was how she would describe him, the total opposite of Eve's first husband, Jack, who was full of fun and teasing. Jack could talk for Ireland and could charm the birds from the trees. The only thing the two men had in common was that they both adored Eve.

'How much would it cost?' Eve asked Bartley.

'I've no idea,' he said solemnly.

'She might not even agree to go abroad,' Aisling said. 'You know how stubborn she can be, and whatever about Daddy being apart from her when she goes to Dublin, how will she feel about being in separate countries?'

'Ais, your mother is fully determined to get well, and I know that woman better than I know myself. If she sets her mind to something, it will happen, and if she has to go to the ends of the earth, then so be it.' Dermot shrugged, and a silence descended as everyone absorbed the news.

'Will I get you a cup of tea, Dad?' Eve asked, rising and placing her hand on his shoulder.

He was the strong one, the one who could solve everything. It was Dermot especially who physically and emotionally held Eve together when they put Jack in the ground, taking her heart with him. It was Dermot who agreed to come back to Robinswood and help Sam and Kate, and it was he who gave Mark the benefit of the doubt and a job when Mark and Aisling reconciled after Mark served a sentence in Dartmoor. Dermot was a capable man, and his family meant everything to him. It was hard to see him so broken.

'Thanks, love.' He patted her hand on his shoulder and gave a weak smile. 'Look, we'll get through this, like we've weathered many storms before. She's made of tough stuff, my Bella. This won't beat her.'

TB was the terror of every town, village and home in Ireland and had been for decades. The death rates were astonishing, and for most people, especially the young or old, and despite the random nature of infection, it still carried a huge social stigma. Kate wondered where her mother had caught it.

'So, Daddy...' Eve placed the teapot on the table and poured him a cup. Being the eldest and also the one who had stayed at home when Kate and Aisling ran away to join the WAAF during the war, she was the one he was most likely to listen to. 'Will we look into the place in Switzerland?'

He exhaled slowly and raggedly. 'We'll try anything, and if you say this place can cure her... But there's the matter of paying for it.'

'We don't know what it would cost, but Dermot, if we have to sell land, then we will. We'll do whatever it takes, and Charlie Warren is dying to get his hands on the river meadows so...' Sam said.

Whenever they were very tight for cash in the past and Sam suggested selling some land, Dermot had immediately vetoed it. They were business partners – it was a term of their agreement when they moved back in 1946 – and Dermot, after years of watching while Sam's father, Austin, frittered away the family fortune along with chunks of land, helpless to stop it, now held onto it like a drowning man. This time, however, there was no such objection.

'Right, Sam. Let's make an enquiry. I'll go down to Dr Grahame now. He probably knows about this place, or if he doesn't, he'll know someone who will, and we can take it from there.'

CHAPTER 5

*L*illian picked up her wedding photo and smiled. They'd been so happy that day. She and Beau had married in the spring of 1948 in the registry office in London. He was a man of deep faith, something Lillian found a little disconcerting if she were honest. She tried to explain to Beau that mentioning 'the good Lord' all the time and quoting from the Bible wasn't exactly the done thing in polite society, but he had been most blunt in his response. 'I hope to spend eternity in the Kingdom of God, with you by my side, so I'm more interested in the done thing there rather than in whatever you call polite society.'

It was just one of the many ways they were different.

There was no Baptist church in Kilthomand. The nearest one was in Waterford, and he went there every Sunday, rising before dawn to be in time for the service. He usually borrowed Kate's bicycle and headed off on the sixty-mile round trip. Sam had told him any number of times to take the car, but he always went by bike. He read his Bible every night and said prayers with Austina as well. Lillian was nominally a member of the Church of England, all fine for weddings and funerals and so on, but it wasn't part of her life. During the war, when she first met Beau, it was just another thing about him that made him unusual, but now his religion bothered her.

She loved him, of course she did. He was handsome and kind and very funny, he worked so hard on the estate and Austina adored him, but she wished he'd make more of an effort to fit in her world.

She'd taken rather well to the role of hostess, and Beau was happy to play the footman. The reality was her husband preferred to wait on tables than be served and preferred the company of cooks and gardeners to that of dukes and duchesses, and while she'd rather he blended in with her set more, he just didn't.

Every time she tried to break into her social circle in the surrounding areas – old friends of her parents, women she knew from debutante balls and hunts when she was a girl, who were now married with homes of their own – it ended badly. If she managed to wrangle an invitation, on the rare occasions that she did, Beau was so unusual it usually went poorly. Not that he wasn't polite – he was, and he made conversation easily – but he had no idea what they were talking about and seemed not to care much either. She recalled their last disastrous foray into society.

Georgina LeVal, a rather dumpy playmate of hers from when she was a child, invited her and Beau to a supper one evening. Lillian was grateful for the opportunity and vowed to use dreary Georgina as merely a gateway into society, but unfortunately it was only her and her equally lacklustre weak-chinned husband, Edmund, and the evening was a washout. Beau didn't hunt, shoot or fish, he had no idea who was on the honours list – in fact, he didn't even know what it was – and he complimented the food and even offered to help clear away. Lillian had been mortified.

'Staff do that, darling,' she'd murmured as Beau began stacking plates.

'OK, if you say so, but I don't mind. I'm used to washin' up.' He'd smiled that big white grin, and Georgina blushed and Edmund offered Beau a cigar.

'No thank you, sir, I don't smoke,' Beau had responded, not realising this was the cue to leave the ladies and withdraw to the billiards room for brandy.

Lillian tried to gently explain how it worked as Georgina and Edmund busied themselves at the other end of the huge dining room, but Beau looked at her like she was insane. 'You want me to play a game with this guy? Without you? But he doesn't even talk 'cept to say things I ain't got no clue about.'

Lillian knew Beau well enough not to force it, as he would not be coerced, so they sat rather awkwardly in the drawing room until it was time to leave. She barely spoke to him on the way back, so he drove in silence.

That night, she'd cuddled up to his broad back and kissed the back of his neck.

He turned over and looked her straight in the face. 'You were ashamed of me tonight.' It was a statement, not a question.

'No, of course I wasn't. You're being ridiculous,' she said hotly, knowing he was right.

'You were. I don't fit in with people like that, Lillian. I try. I swear to you, I do try, but I can't say or do it right.'

She'd placed her hand on the side of his cheek, gazing deeply into his brown eyes. She loved him so deeply, but this was harder than she'd imagined. During the war, she'd liked the shocked glances she got when she walked down the street, her handsome black GI on her arm, but back here, in peacetime, it was much more difficult.

'But you don't try, not really,' she'd whispered. 'You know they have staff, so why would you clear up the dishes? And I know you don't drink or smoke, but couldn't you just go along with it, just to be part of how things are?'

Beau sat up and leaned back against the pillows. 'I can't do that. I would if I could to make you happy, but I just don't know the rules here and I ain't never goin' to learn them. I love you, and I…' He sighed. 'I wasn't ever thinkin' this was goin' to be easy, but when we go to stuff like that, I feel…I don't know…like somethin' in a circus. They stare at me and watch me eating, and I know they are just amazed that I can use a knife and fork. I don't drink, Lillian. Drunkenness is a sin, and I'm tryin' to live a righteous life. I know my God doesn't mean much to you, and that hurts me, it does, but I respect that you have a different way of thinkin' about that, so I just do my thing quietly. Life here at Robinswood, I love it, us all pitchin' in together. That's how I was raised, sweetheart, to work. I'm the son of a poor black man, my grandfather was born a slave, and I'm different from those people in ways I can't even count. And I don't just mean the colour of my skin. I mean everythin'. Sam doesn't make me feel like they do, you don't, the Murphys don't...'

'Well, of course they don't. They are servants...' Lillian snapped, instantly regretting her words.

The look he gave her withered her inside. He got out of bed and stood with his back to her, gazing out of the huge bay window over-looking the front lawn. Neither of them spoke for the longest time.

Eventually, he turned. 'I love you, but sometimes I feel like I don't even know you.' Wordlessly, he dressed, even though it wasn't yet dawn.

'Where are you going?' She knew she sounded pathetic, but she was in terror of him leaving her for good.

'To church.' And he left, closing the bedroom door behind him.

They'd patched it up in the following days, but the rift between them was ever widening.

Lillian sighed and went in search of her daughter. The family were all in the kitchen, the last guests fed, and they were enjoying the weekly Sunday morning fry-up together.

Austina, Jack, Poppy and Daisy were happily munching toast and jam at the kitchen table, blathering away together. The four of them were inseparable, and Lillian was glad her daughter wasn't growing up alone, though why she had to look like a street urchin all the time she couldn't understand.

Sam looked up from the newspaper. 'Edmund LeVal had a winner at Aintree,' he told her as she took a cup and poured some coffee from the jug on the table.

'Oh, really? Jolly good for him. His father had a way with horses too, as I recall – he and Papa were close. Georgina and I spoke about it a few weeks ago when we went to supper. It was nice to see Georgina again – I hadn't seen her since Cynthia Horesham-Smythe's coming-out do – and she married Edmund LeVal. He's one of the Surrey LeVals. I think you were at school with one of them, weren't you, Sam?' she asked, pouring cream into her coffee.

Sam put down his paper. 'No, I don't remember him from school, but he sent over his good stallion to cover the mares last month, which was decent of him.' He gave her a quizzical look. 'I thought you couldn't stand Georgina. Isn't she the one Mummy always made you invite to birthdays and you always kicked up a hell of a fuss? But yet you socialise with her now?' Sam caught Kate's eye as Lillian served herself brown sugar from the bowl Kate was holding.

'Oh, for goodness' sake, Sam, of course I see her. We are the same set. If you had your way, we'd be drinking pints of porter with the farmhands down in Maher's in the village,' she snapped, turning to Mark.

At least he was English. Not of their class, of course, but he had some kind of a clue, and she liked Aisling well enough – better than Kate anyway. All of the Murphys were a bit uppity now of course, now that they had their feet under the table at Robinswood. She tried to slap them down occasionally, but Sam had pulled her aside and most outrageously explained that Kate was Lady Kenefick, so it was her home, and Lillian was only there at her say-so, so she'd better behave herself. Lillian had been furious, but deep down she knew that the Murphys would never throw her out because even if they didn't enjoy living with the real aristocracy when they were merely playing house, they loved Beau and Austina.

'So, Mark, how was your week?' she asked pleasantly. He was a tall, rangy lad, very English looking, with fair hair and ruddy cheeks. It was hard to imagine him violently assaulting anyone, but apparently he had served six months in prison for it. Beau mentioned to her one night that Mark had had a bad time towards the end of the war. His squadron had been ordered to bomb some ships that they were told contained Germans attempting to flee but in fact contained survivors of the Nazi death camps. By the time the pilots knew the truth, it was too late. The experience had led to Mark drinking, distancing himself from Aisling and eventually assaulting someone who made an anti-Semitic remark in a pub.

'Good, thanks, Lillian. Looking forward to a day off. That one's working me like a dog, she is.' He grinned as Aisling gave him another slice of bacon.

'Ignore him.' Aisling smiled good-naturedly. 'That cottage hasn't seen a lick of paint for years and years, so we're going to smarten it up today. That's why you're getting your breakfast served up to you, Mr Belitho, so eat up and enjoy it. You'll need the energy.'

Aisling and Mark had taken over one of the numerous cottages dotted around the estate. They could have lived in the big house easily – there was more than enough room – but they wanted their own place, so Dermot, Sam, Beau and Mark had worked for a whole week to get it into habitable shape. The effort did not stretch to decorating, however, so Aisling spent her evenings sewing curtains and hemming sheets, and it was really coming together nicely. She had bought some buttercup-yellow paint for the second bedroom, the one they hoped would one day be a baby's room.

'She's a slave driver.' Mark grinned as Aisling playfully cuffed him across the head.

Isabella was in bed, where she spent most of her time these days. Lillian had been sad to hear of the diagnosis but had expressed concern to her brother about whether it was safe to have her on the estate, being infectious and everything. Sam had gone mad at her again. He'd barked at her that she had such ignorant views, how Isabella had decided to distance herself from them and the hotel by her own decision, that she was more than welcome to visit if she wanted to and that they should show a bit of understanding and compassion and even educate themselves about it before going off making rash pronouncements. He really was more like one of them than a Kenefick. She was just being practical, but apparently nobody saw that.

'How is Isabella, Aisling?' she asked.

'She's all right. We are waiting to hear back from the clinic in

Switzerland. Doctor Grahame had heard of it, but he didn't know anything further about it, so he asked someone he knew in Dublin to make enquiries. We are hoping to hear any day.'

'Davos, is it?' Lillian asked, buttering some toast while Kate wiped Austina's face and hands.

'Yes, do you know it?' Kate asked.

'Yes, I've heard of it, and as I understand, it is extremely expensive to go there.' Her implication was clear – the Murphys couldn't afford such treatment.

'We're going to sell the river meadows,' Sam interjected before she could go on.

'What?' Lillian was appalled. Bad enough that her father had gambled away parcels of the estate, but now Sam wanted to sell land to pay for a servant's medical treatment? It was an outrage, and she could not allow it. She thought quickly.

'Surely there is a better way. I know Mummy and Perry have some connections there. I just heard them talking about Davos and something about a relative of his working at that clinic. You should ask them.'

'I'll ring them now,' he said, shooting his sister a disapproving look.

'What?' she demanded indignantly.

Sam's eyes glittered with temper as he responded. 'What? Are you serious? You ask me what? We've all been worried sick about Isabella for weeks now, and you think Perry has some connection to the best clinic in Europe and you only mention it in passing? And only because you don't want to sell land? Land, incidentally, that is mine, not yours?'

Mark busied himself with his breakfast as Kate and Aisling cleared the dishes away.

Lillian bristled. Sam was the heir undoubtedly, but it was Kenefick land and he was merely this generation's caretaker. 'I don't want you to sell off *our* estate, of course I don't, but neither did I know she wanted to go to Davos!' Lillian exclaimed. 'How could I have known that?' she demanded of her sisters-in-law as Sam strode out of the room to the telephone.

'Well, it's hard to get in there apparently, so if we can use any influence, it would be helpful,' Aisling said, her voice placatory.

'Well, yes indeed, and if Perry can pull some strings, then maybe –' Lillian began.

'We could afford it?' Kate finished for her, her dark eyes flashing dangerously. She had shown restraint where Lillian was concerned in general, but she was so worried about her mam. For that entitled snob to say something so crass just pushed Kate off the edge.

Mark and Aisling watched as Kate stomped across the kitchen. She was furious that Lillian had sat on this information for so long.

'Well, Lillian, as Sam said, if we have to sell land, we will. Sam and I will sell *our* land, do you understand? We will save my mother because she is a wonderful person who deserves the best, and you deciding that we can't afford it, or objecting to what my husband does with the estate... You who incidentally hasn't a farthing to your name, looking down your nose at us! I've had enough. Honestly, Lillian, who the hell do you think you are? You swan about like it's the olden days and you have some kind of God-given right to be here, treating the rest of us like your slaves, contributing nothing, and now we are expected to endure this snobbish stupidity out of you as well?'

The entire group looked to the doorway where Beau was standing, home from church, taking in the scene. Lillian burst into tears and ran from the room as Kate stood there, seething.

Aisling gathered the children and took them outside to play, and Mark followed her, not wishing to be part of the conversation between Kate and Beau. None of them knew how he put up with his wife – she really was a pain – but he seemed to love her and defended her to the last. Nobody ever even said a teasing thing about her in his earshot, no matter how tempted they were.

'What was that about?' Beau asked quietly.

Kate stood with her back to him, the temper still coursing through her veins as she held onto the large Belfast sink.

She turned her head. 'Apparently your wife was aware that Perry had some connection to the clinic in Switzerland that we have been trying to get my mother into for the last three weeks. She only mentioned it this morning because she heard that we were going to sell land to pay for the treatment, which she objects to. Not that it's anything to do with her, by the way. And all of this while I was feeding her child and waiting on her hand and foot as usual. I'm sorry, Beau. I know she's your wife and everything, but I'm sick of the way she speaks to me and the way she talks about my family and the way she goes around here like she's the bloody queen of England and we are all here to do her bidding.' Kate was fuming.

'Thank you for taking care of Austina. I really appreciate that,' he said, his low voice rumbling as he stood beside her, watching as Aisling and Mark chased the children around the garden.

'I don't mind, you know that.' Kate sighed.

'I know you don't, but she is mine and Lillian's responsibility and you have enough to do. Come on, sit down. Let me make you a cup of tea.' He gently led her to the table.

They could hear Sam's muffled voice on the telephone in the hall.

'Sam's ringing his mother now, to see,' she said. 'If they tell us that a few weeks would have made a difference, so help me God, I'll swing for Lillian,' she muttered through gritted teeth.

Beau placed a cup of tea in front of her.

'Thanks.' Kate gave him a smile. She liked him so much, almost in proportion to how much his wife frustrated her.

'Lillian should have mentioned Perry knew someone before now. She wouldn't have thought it was useful information, I guess...' Beau tried to explain.

'Ah, Beau, will you cop on and stop making excuses for her for once!' Kate rounded on him, in no mood to hear his usual line in sticking up for her. 'She knows we are all out of our minds with worry. Mam is getting sicker every day, and my poor father doesn't know if he's coming or going. There's no room in any of the sanatoriums here, so we have to wait, and unless Lillian is blind and deaf as well as selfish, she would have known that.'

He didn't respond, and before she could go on, Sam came back in.

'Well?' Kate asked.

'One of the doctors there is one of Perry's godsons, a Doctor

Henry Carlin. He's going to make contact today and get back to us. They were devastated to hear of Isabella's illness and asked if there is anything else they can do.'

'Well, that's something. We'll just have to pray this godson is on good enough terms with his godfather to let Mam skip the queue.'

Sam sat down and Beau got him a cup of tea, pouring from the big pot he'd made.

'I suppose you had words after me and that's why she's gone sobbing upstairs?' Sam asked wearily. Both his and Kate's patience were wearing thin. Sam's mother had initially been dead set against allowing Lillian to move to Robinswood at all, insisting she should make her own way, but then she had Austina out of wedlock and rescued and married Beau. Her husband and baby became part of the furniture at the big old house, so Lillian just stayed.

'I gave her a piece of my mind. I just can't believe she knew Perry had a connection and never said. I lost my temper, I'm afraid,' Kate admitted.

'I wouldn't worry about it,' Sam said, placing his hand on hers. 'She'll calm down once she realises she'll have to cook her own food and look after her own child if she falls out with you.' He was the only one who didn't temper his opinions on Lillian around Beau. His sister had irritated him all his life, and as an adult, nothing had changed.

'Now, I promised Jack and the girls they could have a spin on the pony this morning, so I'd better stick to my word.' He kissed the top of Kate's head. 'I know it's hard, but try not to worry. Perry is on the case, and he's a good man to know, as we all realised a long time ago.' Sam winked at Beau, who smiled.

'He sure is,' Beau agreed. Perry had pulled in an old favour that managed to secure Beau's release from prison when he'd been wrongly accused back in the States. 'If anyone can help, it will be him. And I know they have such regard for Isabella, they'll do anythin' they can for her.'

Perry and Violet were an odd match – she was much taller than him for a start – but they were solid as a rock and they loved each other dearly. Perry had softened Violet, and she even came back to

Robinswood on occasion now without shuddering at the memory of all the years she was incarcerated there with an alcoholic gambler husband and no money. Perry was very wealthy and a shrewd businessman but had a kind heart.

Beau continued the tidy-up the girls had started before the big argument, and Kate worked companionably beside him.

'How was church?' she asked.

'Lovely. Very peaceful. And the congregation decorates the church so beautifully with the greenery. It's subtle but it kind of marks the seasons. The pastor is a nice man. He and I talk every Sunday after worship, and he's been a great spiritual support to me. I miss my church at home. All my family went there, and we would sing and get together after for lunch – it was like a family, my church, y'know? We lived our faith, Kate. It was an everyday thing. I guess it's different here.'

She handed him a dish she had just washed to dry. She was glad to change the subject from his awful wife.

'I suppose it is. I mean, we'd be more religious than the Keneficks or any of that crowd, I suppose, but people's personal faith is a quieter thing, more your own business. Maybe because practising our religion was banned for so long by the British or something. People are devout, but they don't discuss it much. The Church kind of rules the roost anyway about most things, but it seems to be more about the rules than people's own beliefs, if you know what I mean? Though nobody told Father O'Connell that. He's a right demon, denouncing people off the altar and the whole lot. I remember one summer, Aisling and I were about fourteen or fifteen, and we went cycling in skirts. He saw us and made some very thinly veiled remarks about young women who flaunted themselves on bicycles. Mammy nearly murdered us for making a show of her in front of everyone.' Kate chuckled, her good humour restored.

Beau laughed. 'I sure would have liked to have seen his face. He doesn't ever smile, does he?'

'Not that anyone has ever seen. Father Macintyre, the parish priest, is nice, but that curate is a piece of work. We used to think

Sister Bonaventure had a crush on him. She used to get all giggly whenever he came into our classroom, God help us.' She sank her hands into the soapy water. 'The things we used to be thinking about.' She paused, then asked, 'And is there singing and all of that in the Baptist church too, the same as Protestants, or is it more like us?'

'Well, I guess it's more based on scripture, y'know? We read from the Bible, and then the pastor gives a sermon, but it's different here than at home. Back home, people really engage, they shout out "amen" or "halleluiah", and man, do they sing. They raise the roof, and there's such joy and hope in that room, it's an emotional thing. But here it's much more kind of sedate, I guess. Still, I like it.'

'Is there a choir or does everyone sing?' Kate asked, interested.

'Both. The choir sings, but they lead the congregation, y'know?' He paused and smiled sadly. 'Y'know, in all the years, Lillian has never once asked me about my church? I've told you more in the last five minutes than I've told her in all the time I've known her.'

Kate finished the washing up, released the water and turned to him. 'It's not my business, and you know she and I don't get along, but is everything all right with you two?'

Beau towered over her, his muscular arms drying a large frying pan as he thought about her question. The pause dragged on, Kate regretting being so intrusive with every passing second. Beau was very friendly and charming, but he was a private man underneath it all. Nobody understood how he and Lillian worked, but they did – or at least they appeared to.

'Do you want to take a walk?' he asked.

The very last thing she had time for was a walk. Sometimes it saddened her that they were all so busy making Robinswood a success that they had no time to enjoy it themselves. The grounds and gardens were for guests to enjoy, the rivers and ponds too. She had harboured dreams of picnics with the children under the trees leading down to the Araghlin river that ran through the estate to the sea below, just as she and her sisters had done as children, but there was never any time. At night, she fell into bed, barely able to keep her eyes open. The

47

alarm clock went off what felt like five minutes later, and it was time to get up and do it all again.

Aisling and Mark had gone with Sam to the stables where the little pony was no doubt being trotted round in circles amid squeals of delight from the children. She made a snap decision. 'I'd love to. Let's go down to the bluebell wood, shall we?'

'Let's do it.'

They walked in companionable silence, and Kate wondered why Beau didn't check on Lillian. He knew she'd stormed out crying because of what Kate had said, but for once, he didn't go to her.

'We never know what's around the corner, do we?' Beau mused quietly as they crunched on the gravel path. A pair of squirrels played in a big old copper beech as they rounded the east wing of the house. They passed through the now-partially restored formal gardens and opened the gate into the north wall of the walled garden, its fruit trees groaning under the weight of their almost-ripe apples, pears, peaches and figs. The east wall was for plums and greengages. Though it was impressive it was nothing compared with the glory days of the house when she was a child. She recalled picking the red and white currants, and being told by her father to rush to open the southern door in the mornings to let the frost out.

She smiled at the memory of Benjy the pony getting in and eating all the red Bramleys, Mammy nearly had a fit. She only reminded Sam the other day about the day the Australians came, she must have been about ten, and they wanted to take cuttings of the Crofton apples to take back to grow out there. It seemed impossibly romantic to Kate and her sisters.

SHE WALKED COMPANIONABLY WITH BEAU. He was restful to be around.

'We used to grow pineapples in there you know.' She pointed at the glasshouse.

'Nobody in school had ever seen one, let alone tasted one, but Daddy grew them using the hot pipes from the boiler under a mix of manure and soil. But those were in the days when we had seven men and four boys just working the walled garden, and the formal gardens. Not to mention the men for the milking, and the grooms for the horses, it was a different time, Beau.' She sighed, suddenly bone weary. 'There were so many staff, there was enough money, Mammy and Daddy were in perfect health...' She heard the catch in her voice.

They stopped beside the red-bricked wall that caught the sun most of the day. On it were creepers and vines, and in the middle of the garden were the newly repaired glasshouses under which they grew berries too delicate for the vagaries of the Irish climate. The butterflies danced over the fragrant flowers, and the sun was warming things up. Kate leaned against an old wall, turned her face to the heat and sighed deeply.

'I'M PRAYIN' for your mama every day, Austina too. We pray the Lord will place his healing hands on her and make her well again,' Beau said with such sincerity and compassion that Kate felt herself well up.

From nowhere the tears came, bottled up under a veneer of coping since she'd heard, but his kindness, the hopelessness of it all, the upset with Lillian caused sobs now to rack her body. Beau put his arms around her and held her as she cried.

'It's hard, Kate, I know. I lost my mama, and it's a pain that never goes away. But Isabella is strong, and if Perry can get her into this clinic...' Beau reassured her as Kate accepted his handkerchief to dry her eyes.

'She says she's going to get better, but what if she doesn't, Beau? I'm terrified we'll lose her. And then trying to keep this place going in the middle of it all... I'm just so tired,' Kate finally admitted.

He sat beside her on a low wall, their backs leaning on a trellis, and turned his face to the sun too. He spoke without looking at her. 'I see that. What you and Sam are tryin' to do here, it's incredible. Really. And you guys have achieved so much already, and given us all a home in the process. We don't underestimate that...'

'Well, *you* don't,' Kate said wryly. 'You work so hard here...'

'Look, I know Lillian can be a little... I don't know. She says the wrong things sometimes, but she does appreciate it. Without this place, and without y'all makin' us feel like we are a part of something, life could be very hard for us, y'know? Austina loves your kids like her brother and sisters, and if not for me and Lillian, then, for her, we are so grateful. You think I don't know what life could be like for her, for us? We are insulated here, but that big bad old world out there, well… I see how they look at us. I can take it. I've lived with prejudice all my life. But my baby girl, she only knows love and acceptance.'

There was a quiver of emotion in his voice, but he went on. 'Someday, someone is goin' to call her an ugly word, or say something cruel to her about me and her mother, and that thought tears the heart out of me. But she's gettin' such a strong start here with y'all. I'll speak to Lillian properly, and she'll be better, I promise you. She thinks like it's twenty years ago, and she is just…I don't know…entitled to this or somethin', but I'll put her straight. You do not need this on top of everything else you are dealin' with, and I know if she keeps going, Sam will snap one of these days – I can't blame him – and she'll be sorry.'

Kate was astounded. Beau had never spoken like this about his wife before. 'Thanks, Beau. It would make life easier. We are so short-staffed, and she never lifts a finger. Sure, she plays the lady of the house, but she loves that. It was Mam and myself and Aisling who got the house in the shape it now is, and you have been such a help on the estate, and Mark too. I don't know what we would have done without you. We can't really afford to pay men – or women for that matter – the going rate, not yet anyway, but we do need the help to keep growing the business. We are making this work, we really are, but it's like turning a big old ship. It takes a lot of work and progress is slow, but we are turning this around. If only we had more people. And now with Mam out of the picture and Daddy half out of his mind with worry, we are really struggling. I don't know how much longer we can go on.

'It's such a pity we can't get Eve and Bartley's students. We wouldn't have to pay them as much as local people here because we could provide room and board as part of the job, but they all want to go to England. You can't blame them, I suppose.' Kate sighed.

'I don't understand it. This place is so beautiful.' He thought for a moment. 'Kate, I know you can't get the students to come here once they finish with Eve and Bartley, but how about while they are train-ing? Eve said they are runnin' out of space, and now that your mama is sick, I'm sure Eve would like to be here more. Could you suggest moving the school down here?'

Kate processed what he'd said. 'Beau, that's a brilliant idea!' she exclaimed. 'I never thought of it, but you're right. Eve will want to be here now, and Elena wants to go back to England, and we wouldn't have to pay them, just give them room and board. And we could give them some money when they finished to set themselves up and a reference and all of that. I can't believe we never thought of this before. Oh, Beau, thank you! I need to go back, talk to Sam.' She kissed his cheek, and he chuckled. Her eyes were bright. At last, some-thing might go right for them.

CHAPTER 6

*E*ve and Bartley stood at the door of Elena's red-bricked Georgian house as Sam and Kate pulled up the sweeping gravel driveway in their car. The two sisters embraced warmly, and Sam and Bartley shook hands.

'You two all alone here?' Kate asked, looking around for Elena.

'Yes, Elena is in England again, as Georgie has a piano recital this weekend,' Eve explained as she led them into the large comfortable house in the coastal south Dublin town of Dun Laoghaire. It was a substantial property by any standard but nothing on the scale of Robinswood. Sometimes Kate wished their home wasn't quite so big; it overwhelmed her.

Kate looked around. 'I love this house. It all looks the same. I can't believe I've not been here in years.'

Sam stopped in front of a family photo of a dark-haired man with a neat moustache and intelligent eyes, sitting next to his very well-coiffed wife and a boy and girl aged about three and five. 'Thomas. Seems so long ago, doesn't it?' he commented.

'Yes, it does. And yet so much has changed. That was taken shortly after Mammy and Daddy got here. Maybe one of them took the picture actually, as Thomas had his own camera. I must ask them.'

When Austin Kenefick died, leaving Violet with nothing but dry rot and debt, she'd packed up Robinswood, rented the land to a local farmer and took off for London. The Murphys were out, their home part of their employment deal, and it seemed like a dream come true that the Hamilton-Brooks family needed a gardener and a cook. As it turned out, it wasn't a coincidence at all. Thomas had been a British spy investigating links between the IRA and the Nazis. He knew Dermot was ex-IRA, and so the Murphys were targeted deliberately. Dermot had only found that out when it was almost too late. If it weren't for the intervention of Dermot's old IRA-friend-turned-German-soldier, Oskar Metz, things could have gone very badly indeed.

Eve put the kettle on as Kate and Sam took a seat in the kitchen and Bartley cut some tea brack.

'Oh, I love your brack, just like Mammy's,' Kate said, taking a bite of the delicious cake even before the tea arrived.

Bartley smiled, and Kate thought he looked like one of those gypsy men seen on the front of cheap novels, all dark curls and flashing eyes. His hair was tied back in a ponytail. He was clean-shaven, though his stubble was so black it looked almost blue. Today he wore a purple shirt and dark-green trousers, and Kate wondered where he could even buy clothes like that. She never saw anything like his wardrobe in any men's outfitters. She thought that she must remember to ask Eve, though Sam would rather go out in his pyjamas than dress so flamboyantly.

'So how is all at Robinswood?' Bartley asked, his melodic northern accent just as strong as it always was.

'Oh so busy. This is the first day off we've taken in years. Poor Mam is in bed all of the time now, and she won't let any of us near her, so Daddy is taking care of her. He goes from looking totally dejected to being like a briar, so we don't know how to manage him,' Kate explained as Eve sat and poured tea.

'There's a telephone being installed in the farmhouse next week,' Sam told them. 'It takes forever usually, but I managed to speed up the process by allowing the local under-twenty-one hurling team to use the brown paddock for training every Thursday evening. The trainer is Mossy the postmaster's son, the world's slowest human being and main arbiter of who gets a phone and who doesn't, but that favour sped the process up a bit.'

'Oh, thanks, Sam, that's wonderful. At least I can ring her now. I wish I could be there to help out, we both do, but we can't leave the school.' Eve looked relieved that she could now at least communicate with her mother.

Kate glanced at Sam, and Eve caught it. 'What?' she asked.

'Well, we came up to visit you obviously, but we wanted to put something to you as well, an idea. Well, it was Beau actually who gave me the idea, but anyway. You know how we are just run ragged trying to do everything, and now that Mammy and possibly Daddy too are not going to be around for a while, we are under even more pressure?'

'Yes, I do know, and if I could help, I would, or even send you help, but as I say, the moment they are trained, they want out of Ireland...' Eve began.

'No, that's not what I mean. You said that you don't have enough space here for all of your students, but we have tons of room at Robinswood. And you'd like to be nearer Mam even if you can't go to see her, and Elena wants to go back to England. So I thought maybe you would consider moving the whole school down to us? We could turn the old mill – you know, the one behind the lower stables – into accommodation for the boys, and there's that big old shed beside Mammy and Daddy's house that could be made into lovely quarters for the girls with a bit of work. You two could live in one of the cottages like Mark and Ais, or you're more than welcome to live in the big house if you'd prefer. You'd be near Mam and Dad, and the students could train in the hotel and on the farm. It would take the pressure off you two because Ais and I would help train them up as well, and Mark, Daddy, Beau and Sam could help Bartley with the boys, teach them all sorts of things. We couldn't afford to pay them, but we'll give them bed and board, and when they are ready to move on, they'll get a reference and a few bob to set them on their way.

What do you think?' Kate knew she was babbling, but she badly needed her sister to say yes.

Eve turned to Bartley. 'What do you think?' she asked.

But before he could respond, Sam interjected. 'Look, it's a big decision. How about Kate and I go for a walk on the pier, and we'll leave you two to talk it over. I know it's hard being put on the spot like this, so we'll get out of your way and pop back later on.' Sam was standing now and holding Kate's coat.

Kate tried to read Bartley, but it was impossible. He was inscrutable.

'Right, thanks for that, Sam. We'll talk about it,' Bartley said, seeing them out.

Kate hugged Eve. 'Please say yes. I need you,' she whispered in her sister's ear.

Eve smiled. 'We'll see,' she whispered back.

The walk on the pier seemed an eternity as Kate went over it all with Sam once more. 'It would just be perfect, the answer to our prayers,' she said for the fifth time, her arm through Sam's as they walked.

'I know. It was a stroke of genius, you and Beau thinking of it, but it has to be their decision. But yes, if they agree, it will be just wonderful. Getting the accommodation ready will be a problem though. I mean, that old mill hasn't even been opened for fifty years and that big shed needs an awful lot of work.' Sam was always the practical one; she had the ideas.

'Well, we'll jump off that bridge when we come to it,' she said confidently. 'Once we put our minds to something, we can do it fine.'

'If you say so, Lady Kenefick.'

She cuddled up to him as they walked. Then he stopped and turned to face her. Pleasure boats and the ferry to England dominated the harbour, but the pier was filled with people walking dogs, mothers pushing prams, little children skipping along, some licking ice cream. Nobody noticed the young couple standing in the middle of the pier.

'Thank you,' he said sincerely.

'What for?' She smiled, looking up at him and shielding her eyes from the midday sun.

'For everything. For following me to England, for marrying me, for my children, for making it happen that we live at Robinswood, all of it. None of the best things in my life would be happening if not for you.'

'Well, I *am* fairly fabulous, I suppose,' she joked and gave him a squeeze. 'Come on. Let's go and have a cuppa at the tea room, and then we'll go back, see if she's convinced him.'

He hugged her back and chuckled. 'Do you think it will be Eve wants to and Bartley won't?'

'He's so hard to read, I don't know, but I'd say Eve would like to come back. She couldn't before, too many memories of Jack. But now that she's happy again, I think she could.'

'Hmm... And of course having the handsome gypsy roaming about the place being all brooding and mysterious wouldn't be a terrible hardship on you and Ais either, I suppose?' Sam teased. He wasn't blind; Bartley turned heads wherever he went.

'I don't know what you're talking about!' Kate smirked. 'Sure aren't I married to the handsomest man for four counties?'

'Well, we both know that's not true, but thank you for the compliment.' Sam smiled lovingly at her. He still looked so young, tall and thin, with hair that would curl if he let it grow but he refused to. He looked like what he was – a handsome, solid, dependable husband and father – and his grey eyes crinkled into a smile every time he saw her, even after all these years. She'd known him all of her life and could still recall the pain of heartbreak each September and January when the time came for Sam to go back to boarding school. He'd hated it and so had she, and while there was never a whisper of romance between them until he joined the RAF in 1939 and she followed him to England without her parents' permission, Sam Kenefick was in her heart and always would be. He had nothing to fear from gorgeous seventh sons or anyone else, and he knew it.

They had tea and a sticky bun each, watching the boats out the café window. It was such a small thing to do, but she couldn't remember the last time they were alone and relaxed. Once an hour had passed, they started back.

Sam pulled into the driveway once more, admiring the colourful flowerbeds either side of the lawns planted originally by Dermot but maintained now by Bartley. This time, they went around the side and tapped on the French doors that led into the side garden. Dermot had enclosed it all years ago as a safe place for Georgie and Arthur to play, but they were both away at boarding school now, their carefree days of being loved and cared for by the Murphys well behind them. They still came to Robinswood for Christmas every year, and for a few weeks in the summer too, and the children adored Kate's parents like the grandparents they never knew. Elena and her children had become family, and though Thomas had proved to be duplicitous, he'd paid a high price for his behaviour.

As they came around the corner, they saw Bartley and Eve sitting together at the table, their heads close together. Eve had their father's copper hair, which hung in corkscrew curls down her back when she let it loose. She was much paler than either Kate or Aisling, who both took after their mother, and her eyes were emerald green.

'Well? Have you decided?' Kate blurted as Bartley got up to let them in.

'Have a seat,' Bartley offered, and Kate and Sam sat down. He sat once more beside Eve, and this time he held her hand. They were unusual in that there was no teasing in their relationship, but he treated Eve with such reverence, such love, it was heartwarming to see, especially since she'd been so sad for so long.

Eve looked from Kate to Sam. 'We have. We'd love to take you up on the offer. It would be a dream come true for us too.'

Relief. Kate could have cried, as it felt like a huge weight was lifted. Not only would Eve be there – Kate missed her so much and she was wonderfully capable as a housekeeper – but she would bring an army of girls who could learn everything they needed to know while simultaneously easing the workload.

'That's wonderful news.' Sam shook Bartley's hand while Kate hugged her sister. 'Thank you so much.'

'It's we who should be thanking you two,' Bartley said with a smile. 'Eve wants to be near her family, especially now with the baby on the way, and this place is just not practical any more. I think the experience our students would get at Robinswood would be so much broader than what we can offer here, so if you're happy to have us, then we'd love to come.'

'We'd love it.' Kate nearly squealed in delight. 'Are you sure Elena won't mind?'

Eve smiled. 'No, she'll be fine. I thought at one stage maybe something would blossom between her and Oskar, but no. They are friends and he calls round for tea sometimes, but that's all. There's nothing keeping her here except the school really.'

'How is he?' Kate asked.

Oskar Metz was her father's oldest friend, a fellow IRA volunteer who had gone back to Germany in 1922. Dermot didn't see him again until 1940, when he turned up as a Nazi agent looking for help from the IRA. Dermot refused, but the girls knew it didn't damage the men's friendship.

'He's fine. You know him – he doesn't say much. He bought a leather shop off Dame Street, makes belts and bags and things. We send some of our boys to him actually, and he trains them as leather workers, but he lives a quiet life.'

Sam smiled. 'I suppose he's had enough excitement to last him a lifetime.'

For some time after the war, Oskar worked at Robinswood, having deserted the German Secret Service in '43 in favour of helping Jews escape through the Black Forest.

'Does he know about Mammy?' Kate asked, knowing the news would be devastating for Oskar.

'No, I didn't tell him, though he was here for lunch last week. I didn't know if I should.' Eve seemed uncertain.

'I think we should tell him. Daddy needs the support, and they are best friends.'

'You're right. I'll tell him, will I?' Eve asked.

'Do. Daddy is so upset and trying to be strong for Mammy and all of us, but you can see this is killing him. We're waiting to hear back from Perry about Davos, if we can get her in.'

The rest of the afternoon flew by as they sat making plans. The training school was under the protection of a committee, so there was a bit of organising to be done, but neither Eve nor Bartley felt that anyone would object to the move as it made perfect sense.

It was a Sunday, so the students were all allowed to go into town or to the pictures, but they had to be back by six. They milled about outside on the grass, chatting and laughing in the sun. They seemed like nice young people, and Kate was excited at the prospect of their arrival.

All too soon it was time to leave, and Sam and Kate said their goodbyes with the plan in place. Bartley would come down the following week with a group of boys to get started on the accommodations. Sam would order the materials as soon as he could. The lease on the house next door was month to month, so they'd give their notice, and Eve and the girls would be down before the month was out. The girls could live in the main house for now. There were old servants' rooms in the attic and all they needed was a good clean. It would be a tight squeeze. Eve currently had twenty-five girls in her class and nobody'd been up there for years, but a bit of spit and polish, a few pounds on new beds and some bits and pieces to make it cosy and they would be right as rain for a few weeks anyway, until the shed conversion was finished.

Kate hugged her sister goodbye, whispering, 'Thank you, Eve. You've no idea what this means, and Jack would be so happy for you.'

Eve nodded. 'I know he would.'

CHAPTER 7

*V*iolet watched Perry's breakfast go cold and instructed the butler to have it kept warm until he returned. Dawson would normally never disturb His Lordship at breakfast, but Perry had left strict instructions that if anyone called from Switzerland, he was to be found at once, regardless of the time.

She hoped the news was good. Isabella Murphy was such an important part of Samuel's life. There had been a time – she could admit it now – that she resented her former cook, but she knew Samuel loved Isabella and that she was such a good influence on him. Violet had been horrified when she discovered that her son, Lord Kenefick, had taken up with one of the servants' children, but it had all worked out so well. Kate was an incredible girl, such a power-house, and together with her family, she was turning that draughty old pile Robinswood into a thriving business.

Violet shuddered at the memory of all the years she had endured there, Austin drunk or racing most of the time, the children away at school. How many hours had she spent just looking out the window of her bedroom, on the endless sickening green, the howling wind rattling the rotting frames?

Getting out of the godforsaken pile was the best thing she'd ever done, and when Samuel told her he wanted to go back there with Kate Murphy and turn it into a hotel, she'd told him straight that she thought he was mad. But against all the odds, they'd managed it. Dermot and Isabella had been invaluable, and the place had provided a home for Lillian and Beau and little Austina as well, insulating them from the inevitable cold shoulders they would have been subjected to had they returned to England and Lillian's set of so-called friends. It was most unfair that Isabella should contract that dreadful disease. It was rampant apparently, particularly in the poorer parts of cities and towns where people lived in cramped conditions, cheek by jowl. But Isabella and Dermot lived quite comfortably in the farmhouse they'd inhabited for over thirty years, apart from the brief hiatus when she'd had to leave. A local woman had died recently, according to Samuel, and she and Isabella were both on the flower-arranging committee for the church. As part of her many talents, Isabella had green fingers, so her blooms were in much demand. The word in Kilthomand was that this woman claimed she had hay fever and never admitted it was TB. She'd probably infected Isabella and who knew who else? It really was a dreadful disease. Violet's feelings towards her former housekeeper had rather taken her by surprise.

Violent never enjoyed having the Murphys as servants – not deferential enough, she always thought – and as a result, relations had been strained. But that was all water under the bridge now. The Murphys were family and were back in their beloved home, and she was mistress of Framington Hall with all the grandeur of one of Britain's truly great houses as well as all the comfort of every modern convenience.

Perry was fascinated by gadgets and inventions, and so when any new device or machine came on the market, he usually bought it. The housekeeper told her the story of how, back in the twenties, in one week he ordered a pop-up electric toaster for the kitchen, a vacuum cleaner and a washing machine. Cook had cried for a week, thinking eventually if His Lordship continued, there would be no job for her at all. Mrs Dillingsworth had to gently explain to Perry how, while the staff were very grateful, they'd just as soon do things the old way, but

Perry was having none of it. He addressed the entire staff, a weepy Cook in the corner, and told them that everyone's job was safe, but that Framington was going to move with the times.

Of course, he also presented Cook with a huge bunch of flowers to say how sorry he was for upsetting her. That was the kind of man her husband was. He was charming and funny and ever so thoughtful, but he always got what he wanted in the end. It was one of the things she loved about him. After so many years with Austin, who was, well, so utterly hopeless, she had found a capable man. She'd married someone who could make money and hold onto it, who wasn't a fool for every tip on some old nag he'd heard down in the pub, and it was a very attractive trait.

Perry was determined to get Isabella into this place in Davos, and he would, by hook or by crook. Of course, they would be more than happy to foot the bill, but not because the Murphys had worked for her for so long. No, she wanted to fund it as a gesture of, well, love and support, she supposed. And she didn't want Samuel to have to sell the valuable river meadow either.

But fundamentally, she wanted Isabella to survive. They all needed her, and she could see that clearly now.

She smiled at the memory of her old self. How shallow and brittle she was then. Austin was so much better at dealing with the working classes, and she'd never had to do it, she supposed. Growing up in India – her father was posted there – she knew nothing but deference and adoration from servants, so to find herself with the Murphys, especially Dermot, was a rude awakening. He was polite and did what he was asked to do, but he was not reverent or submissive as she was used to. Nobody in Ireland was, truth be told. The people there didn't ever really accept the class structure and resented the families who lived in the big houses.

All those years, when Ireland waged a brutal war of attrition on Great Britain, Dermot had been in the IRA apparently. While she'd had no idea, she suspected Austin was only too well aware of his groundsman's affiliations. That would be just the sort of nonsense that Austin would have got a kick out of. So often she despaired of her late husband. He had actually sympathised with the rebels, despite being a decorated officer of the king, believing that nonsense that Ireland should actually be free. At the time, she saw it as treasonous, but now that Irish independence was a reality, she supposed it wasn't so bad. She sighed. Ireland was beautiful but so complicated and unwieldly. She was happy to be back at home where she belonged.

Perry came into the breakfast room, a broad grin on his face. 'Henry's come good. I knew he would – he's a decent lad. His father is an oaf, but he takes after Delia's side more than his. Anyway, despite the waiting list, he's going to make a place for Isabella. They'll take her as soon as we can get her there.'

'Oh, darling, you're a marvel. This is simply wonderful news. We must telephone Samuel right away.' Violet got up and hugged him. He was a good five inches shorter than her and had a bald head, but she loved every inch of him. And not just because he'd helped Lillian to get Beau out of some dreadful institution in America, or because he loved and accepted Austina open-heartedly, but because he loved her, really and truly. And while she enjoyed the trappings of his wealth, she could honestly say she would love him if he had nothing. He was a deeply good man.

'I thought you might like to do that while I finish my breakfast?' He smiled and rang for Dawson.

He was doing it so she'd get the credit, she knew.

'Thank you, Perry. I'll do it right now.' She hesitated. 'What should I say about the fee?'

'Say nothing, old girl. We'll cover it, of course, but maybe just say Henry is letting her in as a favour? I don't want them to feel beholden or anything like that, and we certainly don't want Dermot to be offended.'

'I think if it's to save his wife's life, he'd just be grateful, but I'll do as you suggest. He adores her. I've never seen a marriage like theirs,' Violet mused.

Perry pretended to be indignant. 'Until you and I got married, I hope you mean.'

She laughed. 'Well, yes, of course, but we're hardly spring chickens in the first flush of youth now, are we? They've been together forever.'

'As will we be, Lady Goodall,' he replied with a wink as Dawson appeared with his kippers.

'Of course we will.' She kissed the top of his bald head.

She went out into the entrance hall, an enormous but welcoming space with a twelve-foot-diameter marble table on which was placed a Chinese vase, tall as a man, filled with fresh blooms every three days. It was an extravagance, especially in winter when the flowers had to be imported from sunnier climes, but it was such a lovely feature. Generations of Goodalls, immortalised in oils around the walls, watched the comings and goings through the ten-foot-wide front doors from their gold frames, secure in the knowledge that all was well with Framington Hall. She passed the suits of armour, there since the Hundred Years' War in the fourteenth century, and opened the door of her husband's study, where a telephone was installed. She was hoping she could reach Samuel, though he was so rarely in the house – he worked on the estate constantly – but if not, Kate would do.

She sat in Perry's leather seat behind his walnut desk and rang Robinswood. As the call was put through by Mossy, who seemed to find the whole process bewildering despite being the only telephone exchange in their part of County Waterford for years now. As she waited, she could visualise the scene in her former home. The black and white tiles of the entrance hall had been scrubbed by the Murphy girls to reveal their lovely stark contrast, and the large – and to her mind, ugly – black marble fireplace also shone. In winter, they set a large fire there, but in summer, the hearth was full of dried pinecones and varnished logs to make an attractive display. Robinswood was enormous, but it was no Framington Hall. The Irish house was cold and draughty, with rooms so big no amount of furniture could fill them.

'Good morning, Robinswood. Lady Kenefick speaking.'

Violet smiled at Kate Murphy referring to herself as Lady Kenefick, a title that had been Violet's for so long. She knew Kate didn't give a hoot about titles, but Samuel had explained how it was necessary for her to play the aristocratic card in order to attract the tourists.

'Kate, dear, it's Violet,' she said. Kate would have only ever referred to her as Your Ladyship in the past, but those days were gone, and good riddance.

'Oh, good morning, Violet.' Kate's voice was warm. 'How are you?'

'Very well, my dear. I'm ringing with some news. Perry had a telephone call from his godson, the doctor in Switzerland, and he's agreed to find a place for your mother. She should leave for Davos as soon as possible.'

There was a pause and then Kate spoke again. 'Oh, Violet, thank you.'

Violet was surprised to hear Kate crying, her voice choked with emotion. It was so unlike her. She was usually stoic in the face of all adversity.

'Of course. Perry was determined to make it happen, and you know Perry when he sets his mind to something.' Violet smiled. 'Now, how soon can you get her there?'

Kate recovered enough to answer. 'Well, we'll do it as soon as we can, but then there's the cost. Have you any idea of the fees for that place? I mean, we will raise it, but do you think they'll want it all up front or...'

Violet knew she would have to choose her words carefully. The Murphys could be so prickly sometimes, but she really wanted to do this, and selling the land was the last resort.

'Perry's godson is pulling some strings. Put it this way – he probably owes him a favour or two, so I think there won't be a bill, and any other expenses, Perry and I will cover happily.'

'Look, you're so kind and we do appreciate it, but we can manage, and we'd rather not be in debt –' Violet heard that same old Murphy pride and stubbornness. Kate was her father's daughter all right.

'Kate,' Violet interrupted gently, 'please hear me out. We are family now, and goodness knows that was a rocky road we all had to travel. But here we are, and you and Samuel and your parents have given Perry and me so much. We are grandparents and we love your children. You've given Lillian and Beau and little Austina a home, and even before all of that, I will be honest, Isabella raised my children. Your father saved us from bankruptcy so often over the years by refusing to follow Austin's silly plans, instead making wise decisions to keep the estate running on a shoestring. So if anyone is in debt, it is I. Besides, Samuel told me of the plan to sell the river meadow, and we'll avoid that if we can. Please let me do this Kate – please. We can arrange a flight from Dublin, and she could be in the sanatorium within days, beginning to recover.'

Silence crackled on the line, and Violet hoped she hadn't offended her daughter-in-law. She was trying to do the right thing, but so often in her dealings with the Irish family in the past, that had been misinterpreted.

'Let me talk to my parents. I'll get back to you.' She heard a slight catch in the young woman's voice. 'I really appreciate it, genuinely.'

Violet exhaled in relief. She realised for the first time she'd been holding her breath. 'Good. You do that. And please make them understand this is just a gesture of, well, of love and family solidarity, nothing more or less, and we need never refer to it again.'

'Thanks, Violet, you're very good.'

She was just about to say her goodbyes when Kate said, 'One moment. Can you say hello to Poppy and Daisy, Grandma?'

Violet saw herself blush in the mirror opposite Perry's desk. She had called her own grandmother just that – Grandmother. Violet remembered an austere woman in black lace. Her own mother had died before Lillian and Samuel were born, and Austin's mother was utterly allergic to Ireland and, as a result, rarely saw her grandchildren, so she was not referred to much. But Samuel's children called her 'Grandma Violet', and they called Isabella 'Nana Bella'. Perry was 'Grandpa Perry' and Dermot was 'Granda'. She was surprised by the thrill of joy and pride she felt when she heard Jack or the girls refer to her by such an affectionate name.

'I would love to,' she said.

The girls told her their news, about a kitten born to Sooty the kitchen cat, how Jack cut his knee falling off a swing, how Austina was able to ride the little bicycle Perry had bought her and Jack a few weeks ago, and how Nana Bella had a pain in her tummy from eating too much ice cream so she was in bed but that the doctor was going to give her medicine to make her all better.

Violet chatted happily with her granddaughters on the other side of the Irish Sea and realised she was at the happiest juncture of her life.

* * *

EVE and the girls had arrived from Dublin. Eve was just about to go upstairs and Aisling was writing a list of things she would need to pick up in the village for dinner when Kate called them. 'Girls, we need to talk.' She closed the kitchen doors, and for the first time in weeks, it was just the three of them.

'What's wrong?' Eve asked, worried. Her bump was showing now, and that was something else Kate wanted to talk about. Eve shouldn't be working as hard as she was, but that was for later.

'Nothing. It's good news. Perry – well, Violet rang, but Perry has got Mammy into that place in Switzerland, and they are saying it's free, but I don't believe a word of it. I'm sure they are paying. They want to fly her from Dublin tomorrow.'

'That's wonderful.' Aisling had tears in her eyes. They'd all been strong for their mother, as she would not want them moping about, but the fear of losing her was something they all felt keenly.

Their father crossed the courtyard outside the kitchen.

'We'd better bring him in, tell him,' Eve said, nodding in her father's direction.

She went outside and called Dermot. He followed her moments later and took his dirty boots off at the door, walking in in his socks. 'So what's going on?' he asked.

'Sit down, Dad, have a cup of tea,' Kate said gently.

'You're scaring me now. Just tell me.' He looked at each of his daughters in turn. Kate and Aisling cast a nervous glance at Eve.

'Right. Well, remember a few weeks ago, we mentioned that place in Switzerland? Well, it turns out that Perry knows a doctor there. It's in a place called Davos, and it's meant to be the best place to go for a cure. So Sam asked Perry to see if he could get Mammy in there. It's very hard to get in and it costs a lot, but anyway, one of the doctors there is Perry's godson and he agreed to find a place for Mammy. She can fly over there from Dublin tomorrow. Violet and Perry want to take care of any bills. Though she said this godson was doing it as a favour, I don't think that's true. But anyway, she says she owes you and Mam for all you've done for her and Perry, and for all of us, and they want to do it.'

The other two watched their father's reaction. He was a proud man who had fought to free his country from the likes of the Keneficks. He believed that Ireland was the best country on earth, and though he was the finest man they knew, he was as stubborn as a mule. The only one who could get him to change his mind about anything was their mother, and even she struggled when he dug his heels in. They would not be able to convince him otherwise if he refused this offer – they knew that.

'Have you told Bella?' he asked quietly.

'No, we didn't want to say anything until we knew it could happen,' Kate said.

'And they'll cure her, do you think? This place in Switzerland?' He sounded so vulnerable.

'Well, it's high up in the mountains, and the air is really clean.' Eve was gentle but firm. 'Bartley read a book about it. The patients are put outside on balconies for hours every day to breathe the air, they get really good nourishment and treatment from the best doctors in the area, and they seem to be able to restore people to health. There are new drugs too, ones they may not have here in Ireland, that they can give her. I know you'd rather she was here, or at least near us, but if this is the best place, then we must send her there.'

'Will she go, though? You know what she's like...' Dermot said, and the girls heaved a silent collective sigh of relief. At least he hadn't dismissed the idea out of hand and insisted that an Irish hospital was every bit as good – or something daft like that.

68

'She might not go for us, but she'll do it for you. You know if anyone can convince her, it's you.'

He looked round at them. 'And this is the best place for her? You're sure?' he asked Eve.

Their father was the decision-maker in the family; he was always the one who knew what to do. Seeing him helpless, uncertain, was deeply unsettling.

'I think so, Daddy,' Eve said, placing her hand on his.

'And you two agree?' He addressed Aisling and Kate.

'We do,' they said together.

'Right.' He stood. 'This is great news. Perry and Violet are very good to organise it. I'll go down to her so.'

'Will we come?' Eve asked. Their mother had seen them, but only from the door. She didn't allow anyone but Dermot inside for fear of infection.

He smiled, the first smile in weeks. Instantly, his face lost the exhausted haggard look he habitually had these days. His hair was still the colour of a wet fox, thick and wavy, and fell over his high forehead when he didn't oil it back. He was tall and well built and strong as an ox.

'Well, there's strength in numbers, I suppose, and you know she might refuse. She's a big advocate of Dr Noël Browne and thinks he's doing great things for TB sufferers, but maybe between us all, we can convince her.'

They walked together down the avenue to the farmhouse and let themselves in.

'Bella!' Dermot called. 'It's me and the girls.'

'I'll come down,' they heard her reply, followed by shuffling in the bedroom overhead.

Kate got a shock when she saw her mother, and she knew by her sisters' faces that they did too. They'd only seen her from the landing, and she'd always been in bed. Now, as she came through the door into the kitchen, they could see how much weight she'd lost. Her once curvaceous figure was thin. Her dark curly hair was loose around her narrow shoulders – nobody outside of the family had ever seen her hair down, she always had it tied back – and her cheekbones jutted in a way they'd never seen before.

'Well, to what do I owe this mass visitation?' she asked sceptically. 'All of you over there by the door, keep your distance.'

They didn't answer but did as she instructed, letting their father speak. If their father was stubborn, their mother took obstinate to a whole other level. How their marriage worked was a mystery because they were as strong as each other and both iron-willed, but somehow it did.

'Bella,' he began, 'I know you might not want to go, but please hear us out. Perry has found you a sanatorium in Switzerland...'

CHAPTER 8

The guests had been fed breakfast and were all gone out for the day, and the bedrooms had been changed, so Kate sat down with a cup of tea in the sunny courtyard before starting the lunch preparations.

Eve and her girls had proven to be nothing short of a godsend. The young people, generally aged sixteen, came to Eve and Bartley's school for a period of three months. In that time, they learned all they needed to be gainfully employed in service, or in the case of the girls, how to be good wives and mothers. Institutional life had taught them discipline, and they were remarkably self-sufficient, but the skills the Murphy girls had learned at their mother's knee were notably absent, so Eve started from scratch. By the time the three months were up, they could all cook, sew, knit, clean, bake, churn butter, preserve fruit and vegetables, tend a kitchen garden and keep hens, ducks and geese. Now that they were living with the three little Kenefick and Austina, they were also learning how to care for children.

At the end of the three months, Kate and Sam would give them some money to get themselves set up. The same arrangement went for the boys, and it was working like a dream.

Beau, Mark and Sam were delighted with the help, especially now that Dermot was distracted with Isabella so ill. Dermot stayed in a hotel near the clinic for ten days when he brought Isabella to Switzerland the previous month, but the doctors encouraged him to leave her to their care and eventually he agreed. He hated being away from her, but he knew she was in the best place.

They had worked non-stop to get the accommodations ready, and now the boys and girls were staying in two separate buildings on the estate. The mill where the boys lived was unrecognisable. It looked a little like a military barracks, with rows of single beds and a locker beside each one. The boys had made their own lockers and beds, and they'd even managed to construct a shower and toilet block with hot pumped water and everything. Downstairs was a large kitchen and dining room.

The girls' quarters were prettier and a little less utilitarian. They had converted the old shed behind Dermot and Isabella's farmhouse, and now they had a series of little rooms, two girls to a room, and each one had matching bedspreads and curtains. They too had toilets and showers and a kitchen, and they'd done most of the work in decorating it themselves.

Eve and Bartley took two rooms upstairs in the main house. They were smaller than most of the others but overlooked the mill, so they could see the boys' quarters from their bedroom window, which suited them perfectly. They had a little parlour too, with a wireless and a sofa and a small bookshelf. They had a gas ring and a kettle, and though they took their meals with the others, they could make a cup of tea in their own little nest in the evenings.

Elena had pretended to be cross with Kate when she came down for a visit soon after Eve and Bartley moved, for stealing not just her teachers but her best friend as well, but Kate knew she didn't mean it. Eve had been right; Elena was considering selling up in Dublin and was happy for Eve that she could finally go home.

Bookings were coming in fast and furious, and while it was intense, it was good to stay busy so they couldn't mope about their mother, and the students were so helpful, the pressure was considerably reduced. The girls and boys catered for themselves – it was all part of Eve and Bartley's plan to deinstitutionalise them – so while the family began each morning with breakfast in the big kitchen, the students cooked for themselves in their quarters.

Having Eve's girls made such a difference. It was an inspired idea to move the school down. The boys were a great help on the farm as well. Bartley and Eve followed the same pattern they had in Dublin, but now there was so much more scope for learning, and the students were generally very receptive. They knew that this time in the school was their ticket to a better life, and only the odd foolish one didn't take advantage of it. In the mornings, they were supervised as they went about the various tasks – inside the house for the girls, apart from caring for the poultry and the kitchen garden, and all over the estate for the boys. In the afternoons, then, were lessons. The boys learned to drive as well as woodwork and metalwork and every aspect of farming, while the girls learned first aid, baking, cooking, laundry and childcare. By the end of the three months, all of the students left with a glowing reference, skills that would qualify them for several positions and ten pounds in cash. The girls made each person, male and female, a new suit of clothes, and Kate and Sam bought each person a pair of good shoes. They got the bus from Kilthomand, usually to Dublin, and from there travelled to England or America. Over the years, Eve and Bartley had received many letters – from Chicago and Liverpool, some even from Australia and one in Singapore – from former students, thanking them for giving them a start in life. It was deeply gratifying work.

Kate got up at five thirty each morning to have a large pot of porridge ready, served with honey, followed by boiled eggs, toast and tea. Aisling, Eve, Bartley, Mark, Sam and Beau all filed in at six on the dot, and they breakfasted together. Lillian didn't surface until after ten, looking elegant and cool. She still shopped in London and seemed to always have new clothes and jewellery. She usually ate in the dining room with the guests, which she saw as part of her role.

Once breakfast was over, the men left and would not be seen again until lunchtime. So much of the estate had been neglected under Austin's poor stewardship and then abandoned in the war years, and they were gradually reclaiming the farm back from nature – cutting ditches, building walls and fences, tending to the new herds of dairy and beef cattle, the flock of sheep and the goats, ploughing fields and sowing and reaping crops. The list of jobs was endless, but Bartley and the others instructed the boys gently, and they picked everything up quickly.

Mark was an expert woodworker, so he took over the training in everything to do with wood. He and five of the boys were in the process of making beautiful outdoor furniture so guests could sit on the lawn and enjoy afternoon tea or a drink before dinner.

The estate looked lovely. The tree-lined avenue allowed dappled light through the canopy, and livestock and crops were everywhere. Kate had to admit the house too was really lovely. The revenue from the guests – they were full most nights – was being ploughed back into the business. Mark had done a temporary job on the windows, so they weren't as draughty as they were after years of neglect and woodworm, but the next big project was replacing them. They hoped to tackle it the following summer, but it would mean closing the hotel temporarily, something they were loath to do.

The rooms on the third floor were operational now as well, so they could take up to twenty guests a night. Beau was happy outside, but he did a splendid job each evening as a footman, and she had to admit Lillian was good too in her role as hostess. What had started out as a favour had become her position, and it was working. The girls waited on tables now as well, so they were much better able to cope.

If only Mam was well, then everything would be great. But as of yet, there was no good news from Davos.

CHAPTER 9

*A*isling sat on the side of the bathtub in their little cottage and cried. She'd just got her period again. It had been ten days late so she'd been hopeful, but now she was bitterly disappointed. She was sure that this time she might have conceived. She and Mark had gone to Dublin for tests, and the doctor there said that they were two young healthy people and that while there may be something stopping her conceiving, it was not immediately apparent.

Mark didn't really understand how she felt. He wanted to have children, he said that, but he also said that if it never happened, then he'd be fine with it. She knew he said it to make her feel better, so that she wouldn't think she was a failure, but it just made her sadder. She longed to have a baby of her own; the need was so strong, it felt like a physical pain.

Watching Kate with her three and Eve blooming with every passing day made it worse. It wasn't their fault, and she wasn't jealous of them, not in the way that she wished she had their children or begrudged them their happiness, but she just wanted a child of her own.

She dried her eyes and went downstairs. Mark was already gone;

he and Beau were taking the bullocks to the mart, so they had left at dawn.

She saw the lad from the post office, his bag slung over his shoulder, and went outside.

'One for you, Mrs Belitho.' He grinned.

'Thanks, Kevin,' she said, her heart lifting a little as she took the flimsy letter. It was from Mammy. She wrote to each of her daughters individually each week, claiming there was nothing else to do anyway.

Aisling made herself a cup of tea and sat at the table. There were no guests for dinner. Although they had another large group in, they had plans elsewhere this evening, so Kate and Sam gave everyone the night off.

She was glad to be alone. Getting her period up at the big house would mean she'd have to hide her bitter disappointment. It wasn't that she couldn't talk to her sisters – she could – but she didn't want to make them feel guilty that they had what she wanted. It was stupid probably, but it was how she felt. They both knew she was trying and it wasn't happening, but she did her best to stay positive and upbeat, even with Mark. The only one she confided in honestly was her mother. She ripped the letter open.

DEAR AISLING,

How are you, pet? I hope you're doing all right and that things aren't getting on top of you too much? I know you don't like to talk to the girls about the baby thing, but now that I'm over here, I'm worried you're bottling everything up. You were always my deep thinker!

Life here is falling into a very strict rhythm. As I told you in the first letter, they are determined to send me home as fat as a butterball. They're never done feeding us here, and they think we are little sucky calves with all the milk we have to drink. But I have to say, they are very kind and it's an amazing place. It is beautiful, like nowhere I've ever seen. The mountains are so close, they are right beside us and reach up beyond the clouds. We thought we had mountains – well, they are nothing like these. The farming here is amazing. The animals all wear little bells round their necks for fear they'd *get lost, and the farmers drive them up and down the mountains all the time. It's fascinating to watch. The houses look different too, like the picture books. Remember that Hans Christian Andersen book you had as children? Well, the houses look like that, all timber fronted and with high-pitched red roofs. If I wasn't here battling it out with the old TB, you'd say I was in a fairy tale.*

The treatment is that we have to sit out on the balcony for two and a half hours every morning, another two and a half hours in the afternoon and another hour and a half in the evening. I'm reading books and writing letters by the new time. The only bad thing really is the ice-cold showers, but it's all part of the treatment. Doctor Carlin, Perry's godson, wasn't here when I arrived, but he landed yesterday and he's a very nice lad. He's only about thirty, I'd say, and he reminds me of your dad when he was younger, same red hair. Anyway, he says that Perry warned him he was to cure me, so he said he was making me a special priority. He was only joking, of course, as everyone here is treated so well, but he's a nice boy and at least he speaks English. Every language of the earth is to be heard here, Ais, I'm telling you. The nurses are mostly Swiss or German, and the doctors are from everywhere.

Dermot left yesterday and that was hard. He stayed at a hotel nearby for the last week and a half and spent most of every day with me. We started doing crosswords together to pass the time. I tried not to be too maudlin when he left, but you know us, like two peas in a pod. We don't like to be apart. Mind him for me when he gets home, and don't let him go into himself – you know how he gets. Send him up to Oskar in Dublin if he gets too miserable, and he'll talk sense to him.

I keep asking them how long the treatment is. There's a woman I meet every day on the balcony, and she's been here for the last eleven months. I really hope it will be quicker than that, but they won't say. They just keep saying to do what they tell me and let the treatment work. It's very vexing, I can tell you. I have worked all my life, and this sitting around doing nothing all the time is driving me daft.

Anyway, enough about me. I hope the doctor in Dublin was helpful, and that you'll have some good news soon, pet. Be sure to talk to Mark too. Tell him the truth about how you really feel rather than pretending everything is all right. It's the only way. Don't let secrets or half-truths come between you, even if it's not an easy conversation to have. Mark loves you very much, Aisling, and you've been through a lot together. You can weather this too.

Write back with all your news. I love getting letters. I can just see you cycling that mad bike of Kate's with the box behind it down to Mossy and he all questions about me. That fella's nose will get him into trouble one of these days. Tell everyone I'm fine but can't wait to get home and that I miss you all, and give all the little ones a big hug from Nana Bella.

I love you, my darling girl. Everything will be fine, I promise.

Love,

Mam xxx

AISLING READ and reread the letter. It wasn't as good as having her mam there, but it was the next best thing. Her mother was right – she'd have to tell Mark how much this was affecting her. His depression was what was stopping her. He still had nightmares sometimes, and while he was unrecognisable from the broken man who'd come home from the war, he was still fragile. Working outside, the comradeship Sam, Beau and now Bartley provided and her love had brought him back from the brink of despair, but she didn't want to put too much strain on him. She recalled the dark times, in the early days of his demobilisation. He wouldn't talk to her and drank too much, but he'd cleaned himself up, he didn't drink any more, and they'd moved back home to Robinswood.

And what solved all of that? She could hear her mother's voice in her head. Of course Isabella was right. Sitting down and telling the truth, being honest, not bottling things up – that's how she'd fixed her marriage. She needed to take her mother's advice.

Mark knew there was a problem, but he was reassuring and always said that even if they didn't have children, she was enough for him. She told him she felt the same, but that wasn't true. She wanted so badly to be a mother, and she should tell him that.

Looking around her lovely tidy little cottage, she sighed. She and Mark had everything they could ever want. A lovely home, great family and unwavering love for each other, but all she could see was the big gaping hole where their baby should be.

She folded the letter and replaced it in its envelope. Mark and Beau should have come home from the mart by now. She'd go and find him, make the most of the evening off. Mart day was an excuse for a lot of farmers to get their business done early and spend the rest of the day in the pub, but Beau and Mark were abstemious, so they got the business done and came right back. She laughed as they described the reaction they got the first day they brought cattle. An Englishman and a black American, and as if that weren't odd enough, they didn't drink.

She took her coat off the hook behind the door and let herself out, walking towards the big house. She loved her family, but she was so glad of their little home, tucked away behind the walled garden on the grounds of the estate. It was a little oasis.

She thought she might see if she could get Mark to come home for lunch. They could have the talk she'd been putting off.

She found him in the workshop as usual, covered in sawdust, showing a group of boys how to turn the legs of a table on a lathe. He stopped when he saw her at the door. 'Excuse me, lads. I'm just going to talk to my wife for a minute. Have a go yourselves there if you like. Mind you don't cut your hands off though, right.'

He walked over to her. 'Hello, beautiful girl. Are you going up to Kate now?' he asked, leaning against the wall and turning his face to the midday sun.

'No, we don't have any guests for dinner tonight. I was wondering if you could come home for lunch?' She spoke quietly. 'I need to talk to you about something.'

The look on his face broke her heart. The excitement, the hope. He thought she was going to tell him she was pregnant.

'I'm not pregnant,' she blurted, and saw the shadow of sadness pass where just seconds ago anticipation had lit him up.

'Of course I will. I can come now.' He pulled her into a hug, kissing the top of her head. 'Let me send those lads out to Beau. He needs help anyway. That new threshing machine is proving to be more trouble than it's worth – Beau spends all his day fixing the blooming thing.'

She nodded, not trusting herself to speak.

He dismissed his students and was back to her in a moment. He took her hand, and they walked back to their cottage. Neither of them spoke. It was one of the many things she loved about him, that he didn't need to talk all the time. She was the quietest of the three sisters, maybe being the middle one or something, but she enjoyed peace and calm. Mark was the same. He could be the life and soul of a party if necessary, but often they were quiet together.

The bluebells were blooming in the woods, and they walked along the path dappled by the sunshine through the leaves of the canopy overhead. A pheasant crossed the trail in front of them.

'Your dad would make short work of him.' Mark smiled.

'He would not shoot out of season!' Aisling admonished him, speaking to the pheasant she whispered, 'we only shoot pheasant between November and January, so don't worry, Mr Pheasant.' The bird disappeared in the undergrowth.

They let themselves in, and Aisling put the kettle on the gas and took out some soda bread, ham, cheese and tomatoes from the larder. Mark laid the table, and it wasn't until they were both seated that he looked at her, one eyebrow raised in a question. 'So what's going on?' he asked.

'Mark, I...I haven't been totally honest with you about the whole baby thing. I mean, we know there's a problem, but I was letting on that I was a bit disappointed, the same as you, but that's not how it is.'

'How do you mean?' he asked, his lovely open face concerned.

'It's all I think about, being a mother, and I'm so scared I can't, and that makes me feel so indescribably sad. I was afraid to tell you how I was really feeling because I didn't want you to worry and start feeling low again. So I pretended I was all right about not being able to conceive, but I'm not. It's killing me. I got my period this morning, and I was late so I'd got my hopes up, but...' Out of nowhere, the tears came.

Mark stood and went around the table, going down on his hunkers beside her. He rubbed her back and let her cry. Once she was able to speak again, he wiped her tears with the soft cotton of his shirt cuff. Gently, he turned her round, his rough hands cupping her tearstained cheeks. Their faces were inches apart, and his eyes locked with hers.

'I'm glad you told me, Ais, and I'm sorry that you felt like you couldn't, but I understand why. I'm all right though. I'm strong again. I'm who I was before, so please stop worrying about me going off the deep end – I promise you I won't. All that rage, that...I don't know, that frustration, has seeped away. I'm ready, willing and able to be a proper husband to you, so please stop treating me with kid gloves, that's the first thing. The second thing is I know. I have eyes and I know you, better than anyone, I think. I can see how this is tearing you apart, but I didn't like to bring it up. I thought before the tests that it might have been me, maybe I was firing blanks, as they say, and I was afraid that I was the cause of your misery.'

'No, at least we know the problem is mine. The doctor in Dublin was able to tell us that,' Aisling said.

'The problem is ours. Not yours. But at least now nobody is putting a brave face on anything. We have to keep talking to each other, Ais, you know that better than anyone. If you'd not forced me into telling you about all that stuff that happened in the war, God knows where I'd be now – dead or in jail for life probably. But you saved me. I love you so much, and honestly, you're enough for me. I'd love kids, of course I would, but if it's just you and me forever, then that's all right too. You are all I need, but I understand that for you, that's not the case –'

'You are enough, I don't mean that,' she interrupted. 'I just... I can't explain it, Mark. It's like a big hole in the middle of me, and only a child can fill it. Seeing Kate with her three and Eve's bump growing every day... I'm so happy for them, of course I am. It's not that I'm jealous, or maybe I am, but it's not that I don't want them to be happy. I just want to be happy too...'

'I know you do, sweetheart. I know exactly. But there are other options we can consider, you know?'

'Like what? We're seeing the doctors in Dublin, and they don't think there's anything wrong, but clearly there is. You're fine, we're doing what we're supposed to...' She coloured while discussing their lovemaking in such clinical terms. 'Nothing is working. Every month, the same thing.'

'We could adopt a child?' he said quietly.

She stopped, a wave of irrational pain washing over her. He'd given up. There was no point. She couldn't do what women had been doing since the dawn of time. She could not conceive a child.

'I want our baby, Mark, yours and mine, not someone else's.'

'I know that, but if it doesn't happen, could you consider it? So many babies born that need to be loved. Maybe we could give some little soul a home, be parents that way?' She knew by his face that he was aware that he was treading on thin ice.

'I don't know, Mark, I honestly don't. I never... I just hoped that...'

'And we'll keep trying, of course we will, but it's just something to think about, isn't it?'

'I suppose so,' she said, though inside she had no enthusiasm for the idea. She knew it would be the charitable thing to do, as Mark was right – there were so many children in need. But she wanted a baby. She wanted to carry it and give birth and have that little boy or girl look like Mark, or look like her. She didn't want a stranger's child.

CHAPTER 10

*L*illian had the taxi drop her at the opposite end of the street from where she was going. No need to attract unwanted attention. The building on Whitmore Street in North London was unobtrusive, and the woman who had founded it had come under fire for her views on female reproductive health, but Lillian knew how widely her services were used. Marie Stopes had been a lifeline for so many women. Lillian remembered a friend giving her a copy of Stopes's book *Married Love* when she was a teenager, total contraband of course in her very strict girls' school, but it was eye-opening.

She glanced at her watch. Beau and Austina would be having lunch now at the big dining table in the kitchen with everyone else. She wished things had been better between them when she left yesterday, ostensibly to visit her mother and Perry and catch up with some old chums, which is why she couldn't take her daughter. What would he say if he knew the real reason for her visit? If only Ireland wasn't like someplace from the dark ages, all priest-ridden and old-fashioned, she could get what she needed without this trek across the sea. But that was impossible, so she found herself once again at Whitmore Street.

Stopes's clinic was free, so one met all sorts there. Lillian knew her set used the service just as enthusiastically as the common girls from the East End with their bright-red lipstick and short skirts. One couldn't risk visiting the family doctor, even in England.

Back during the war, some of her friends used French letters to prevent accidents, but Beau wasn't that sort of chap. She had to practically beg him to sleep with her when they first got together, him insisting he wanted to wait until they were married. Eventually, her feminine advances won out, but only a handful of times. Now that they were married, however, it was a different story. He was a wonderful man and she adored him, and that side of their relationship was very happy, but she just could not bring herself to have another child. She loved Austina – she was a lovely little girl, and Beau was a kind and caring father – but she was happy with how things were. Motherhood in all its messiness wasn't something she relished. When she'd had Austina, she'd had to fight hard to keep her. Once Violet saw Lillian was determined, she had paid for her to stay at a very nice nursing home where the staff cared for the baby and did all of the functions of care necessary. But the new system in Robinswood, where everyone was expected to work like donkeys, would not allow for wet nurses or nannies, and she just couldn't do it. Nobody understood, she knew, but she wasn't raised to be a skivvy, and it didn't sit comfortably with her.

Beau had been most unfair when he said she was not pulling her weight following Kate's entirely unwarranted and unfair attack. What was he talking about? Didn't she have dinner every night with tedious tourists, entertaining them with tales of the big house? But apparently, even that wasn't enough. He wanted her to take over care of Austina, as well as Kate and Sam's children, while Isabella was ill, and then he suggested that she offer to teach the students something. Did he not understand? She had nothing to teach. Flower arranging was a class she had to take at the Swiss finishing school she attended for a year when she was seventeen, along with deportment and piano, so when he asked her what she could do to help Kate and Sam out, it was all she could think of.

He was so much more on their side than hers, and it really hurt. And when he wasn't singing the servant family's praises, he was going on about 'the Lord'. Honestly, sometimes he was just too much.

She wondered what their future held. She'd fought so hard for him – he was all she wanted – but there was a distance between them, an ever-widening chasm, and she had no idea what to do about it. During the war, things were easier. Everything was so immediate, and nobody knew if they'd live to see another day. And so because of that, life had a certain excitement. Peacetime seemed just drudgery.

The colour of his skin was the least of it. It was what people saw, of course, and if she were honest, she quite enjoyed the looks of shock she got when she walked down the street on his arm. But their differences went much deeper. He didn't fit in her world, and she had no idea about his. What she saw of his country appalled her, the way people like Beau were treated. His mother and father were dead, his brothers scattered to the four winds. She was his family, she and Austina, and she wanted more than anything to fix their fractured marriage but had no idea where to even start.

Stop lying to him for a start. She heard the voice in her head. But he wouldn't understand. He wanted Austina to have brothers and sisters, he wanted them to have a big family... But then what? Live in a cottage, in a grace-and-favour house on her brother's land? Live like servants? She had no way of earning money, Sam had inherited everything, and Beau was a farm labourer. She supposed when Perry and her mother died, they'd leave them something... She felt a pang of guilt at the mercenary thought.

She entered the building and gave her name – not her real name, of course – and went to the waiting room where she did not make eye contact with the two other women there before her.

After a few moments, a woman in a nurse's uniform popped her head round the door. 'Mrs Elton?'

Lillian almost missed her call. She'd given that name when she made the appointment because she saw it on the cover of a magazine beside the telephone. 'Er...yes, that's me.' She stood up and followed the nurse.

The room was sterile and the chair hard. A youngish woman with a blunt fringe and short, very dark hair entered. She wore trousers and a fitted jacket under her white coat.

'Mrs Elton, nice to meet you.' She shook Lillian's hand, then sat at the large desk, opening a file and writing in it while speaking. 'So you'd like a permanent solution to birth control, I understand?'

'Yes.' Lillian confirmed.

'And have you been using any form of birth control up to this?'

'Um, yes, well, I was using a diaphragm.'

'And that is no longer satisfactory?' The woman looked up, her face open and uninhibited by the subject matter.

Lillian felt herself blush. 'No.'

'Can I ask why?' The woman's gaze was most disconcerting.

'Well, I…my husband…he doesn't know that I…um…'

'Oh, I see. Your husband is unaware of your efforts at birth control, and so you thought a permanent device would make the deception easier?'

Lillian wished the ground would open and swallow her. That was exactly what she wanted. Beau didn't know she used a diaphragm – she was discreet and quick – but she lived in terror of him finding out. If she had one of those rings she'd read about inserted permanently, he would never know and it would stay there and she could pretend to be as mystified as he was that she wasn't having another child.

'Yes, I suppose so,' she mumbled.

'Well, I can't help you, I'm afraid. We don't do those here. There is a ring available, but frankly, the risk of infection is high. I understand your predicament, and I sympathise. Many men are simply not willing to discuss their wives' reproductive rights. But an IUD would not be wise for you at this stage. I understand you live in Ireland?'

Lillian nodded.

'Well, you see, contraception is illegal there as far as I'm aware, so if you were to run into any problems – infection, rupture, even inflammation – and you needed medical assistance…well, you can see how tricky that could be.'

Lillian stood. This had been a total waste of time. She was mortified.

The doctor stood as well. 'I'm sorry I can't be of more help. It is your right, you know, to decide if or when you want to conceive, but in this case, the cap is the best we can offer.' She gave a sympathetic smile.

'Thank you for your time,' Lillian managed, and shook the woman's proffered hand.

She stood on the footpath and flagged a taxi. 'Liverpool Street,' she said in clipped tones.

She would catch the train to Framington and spend the night with her mother and Perry before going back to Ireland in the morning. She'd have to catch the boat from Southampton, but at least Perry would have his car take her to the dock.

She seethed in the back of the taxi. She had been sure it was just a matter of popping the damned thing in and that would be that.

* * *

'So who did you see today?' Violet asked as the butler and footman served dinner to her, Perry and Lillian.

'Oh, you know, just the usual crew...' Lillian answered vaguely, but she noted her mother's eagle eyes. Why did Violet know everything?

'I *don't* know actually. Who are you still in touch with?' Violet's tone was light, though the words had a razor edge.

'Oh, Jinty Ludlow, the Carrington-Knowles girls, Pippa Huntsworth, you know. We arranged it last month.' Lillian went on without a breath. 'So, Perry, Mother tells me *La Violette* is in Antibes awaiting your arrival?'

Before Perry could begin talking about his favourite thing, his yacht, the real-life Violet cut across him. 'Really? Because I ran into Claudia and Pippa Huntsworth in Harrods just last week, and she said that she hadn't heard from you in over a year. She was asking after you.' Violet raised an eyebrow.

'Well, Pippa wasn't there, but I thought you just meant which group. Anyway, what does it matter who I met for lunch? I'm more interested to hear about the Antibes trip. I bet it's going to be terrific.' Lillian turned once again to her ally Perry. She did love her stepfather, not just because he'd been invaluable in her retrieval of Beau from America but because he softened her mother's harsh attitudes.

'Well, *La Violette* has had her bottom scrubbed...' Perry said with a wink, and Lillian giggled but Violet wasn't letting it go.

'Such a pity you didn't bring Beau and Austina. We'd have loved to have seen them.'

'I know, and I'm sorry, but things are so busy at Robinswood and Beau is stuck in the middle of it all, and apparently he's been invited to preach at his church of all things. I've no idea what it entails, but he seems to be very flattered and is planning his sermon or whatever, so he's busy with that as well.' She took a bread roll and began to butter it, giving it her full attention.

'And when is that happening?' Violet asked.

'Oh goodness knows, he may have told me, but I've forgotten...' Lillian said dismissively.

'But you and Austina are going surely?'

There it was again, that edge. Lillian longed to yell at her mother that she hadn't been so welcoming of Beau when she first discovered he was black, and that once Lillian was pregnant with Austina, it was her mother who suggested she be put in a home for mixed-race children, so it was a bit rich her suddenly becoming Beau's biggest fan.

She gritted her teeth. Perry was on her side, but his loyalty was always to his wife, so if she reared up on her mother now, she would lose his backing for certain.

'No, Mother. I am C of E, as you know, and Beau is a Baptist, and therefore, I do not attend services there, any more than I go to Catholic Mass or Buddhist temples or any other religious services.' She tried to nail a smile on her face, but inside, her blood was boiling. Something about her mother just got on her nerves.

'But he is also your husband, my dear. I thought you would support him if it means so much to him, and surely he'd love to have his daughter there?'

'Yes, well, it's too far, and those services go on interminably – she's too young.' She hoped her tone conveyed her lack of enthusiasm for further debate on the matter.

Dawson saved the day by approaching Perry and murmuring something in his ear.

Perry addressed them both. 'I am frightfully sorry, my dears. I'm being called away, a telephone call I've been waiting on. Please excuse me.' He stood up and left. Did Lillian imagine a conspiratorial glance between Perry and Dawson? Dawson had been the butler at Framington Hall for over fifty years and showed no signs of retiring. He was as loyal to Perry as Perry was to him.

Lillian and her mother sat in silence for a few moments. The game trophies gazed glassy-eyed from over the mantles at either end of the vast dining room. Lillian would have preferred to have dinner with one of the elk, or deer or whatever they were, than her mother, but they were alone and she had no means of escape. She should have gone straight back to Ireland, but then she would have had to tell Beau even more lies. She told him she wanted to see her mother before Violet and Perry took off for the South of France for two months. The reality was Lillian could happily go two years without seeing her mother, but Beau seemed to have some overly sentimental attitude to parent-child relationships and saw nothing odd in her suggestion. The fact that Perry and her mother had visited Robinswood only a few weeks ago didn't seem to enter into it.

He hadn't offered to accompany her, for the first time ever, and while she was relieved given the purpose of the visit, it stung at the same time. She was terrified he was going off her. They didn't seek each other out the way they used to. Austina was always there, and so often Beau fell asleep on her little bed as he read her stories at night and Lillian ended up sleeping alone. In truth, if things continued the way they were going, she would have no need of the device she'd been trying to procure today.

'You know he left so we could have this out, so we might as well get on with it,' Violet said matter-of-factly. 'What is going on?'

'What?' Lillian tried to infuse her voice with bored disdain.

'You know perfectly well what. We are not blind. Things are not right between you and your husband. I think you are trying to make Beau into something he's not, Lillian, and it will backfire.'

'I don't know what you're talking about,' Lillian snapped, pouring herself some more claret.

'Lillian, you do.' Her mother's voice was softer now. 'Believe it or not, this is born out of concern for you, and for Beau and Austina. You love him, I know you do, and he loves you, but he is never going to fit into the mould you've made for him – he can't. I was there when you suggested that you both attend the Hunt Ball at Beechcourt. I saw his face and so did you.'

Months of frustration welled up inside her. 'So I must change, is that it? I must adapt to suit Beau because he wants to be a farm labourer and a God-botherer? I must forget who I am? Does nobody see my side in any of this? Sam is happy as he got everything. He's Lord Kenefick, and he and Kate swan about, issuing instructions and ultimatums to me! I am trying, I really am, I am doing my bloody best. I talk to the dreary guests every night, but it's still not enough, is it? I'm stuck-up, lazy Lillian, so lucky to have landed the saintly black man, and I'm so sick of it, Mother. I really, really am.' Tears stung her eyes but she blinked them back. She would not cry.

Violet got up, walked to where she sat and took the chair beside her. 'What were you doing in London today?' she asked quietly.

'I was at a birth control clinic, if you must know.' Lillian saw her mother's shocked face. 'No, I wasn't there to have anything taken care of, as we so politely say. I just wanted a more permanent answer. I don't want another child, and I wanted to make sure it didn't happen.'

Violet exhaled. 'And Beau has no idea, I take it?'

'No, of course he doesn't,' Lillian snapped. 'It's probably against his religion, almost everything is.'

'Do you still love him?'

Lillian was taken aback by the question. He mother's class and generation saw love as an optional and not altogether helpful element of a successful marriage. Lillian frequently marvelled at how Perry had changed her.

'Yes. I do. But this life...being beholden to Sam and Kate, never having nice things or going anywhere fun. He doesn't even drink, he has no interest in my friends, and we have less and less in common... He gets on better with the Murphys than with me. Sam is the same. It's like everyone has gone over to their side and I'm alone on ours.' Lillian found herself voicing her darkest fears to the woman she'd hardly ever confided in.

Violet covered her daughter's hand with hers. Lillian looked at it, old with age spots now, an enormous diamond and gold band on her ring finger. Violet had no idea what it was like.

'When I lived there,' her mother began, 'I hated it. Truly, I did. Austin adored you children, but he treated me as if I were some silly old bat, going on endlessly about having no money. I wasn't raised that way. We were not aristocratic, as you know, but my family was well off. I had all I ever wanted, and growing up in India, well, it was delightful. I thought I was going to have more of the same, better even. After all, the Keneficks were titled and wealthy. I had no idea all that awaited a fresh-faced bride was a crumbling old house in a cold, damp country where the natives hated us.'

Lillian turned to face her mother, who went on. 'When he died, I felt nothing but relief. I could get out! Until I had to face the reality of his debts. I knew it would be bad, but I'd no idea just how bad. When I left, I had barely enough money to rent that small house on Hampstead Heath, remember? I couldn't imagine how I was going to survive. Samuel was totally engrossed in the RAF and Kate Murphy, and cared little for his mother, and you were living the high life, drinking and going to nightclubs, demanding money I didn't have.'

Lillian coloured, recalling the conversation her mother had had with her, demanding she mend her ways or get out of her house.

'When you brought Beau home, I really thought that was the last straw. I was sure you were just doing it to shock me, and it worked. I'd never even spoken to someone of his race before. But do you know something?' Her eyes met Lillian's.

'What?' Lillian asked, finding herself interested in what her mother had to say.

'I found out all the prejudice, all the feelings of superiority, were entirely wrong. Beau Lane was then and is now a fine man. I could see that he loved you, and more importantly, that you loved and respected him. Against all the odds, you were determined to have him. And when Austina was on the way, well...again I thought, what on earth next? But you were determined to keep her, and in that case, you were right and I was wrong. You moved mountains to get him back from America, you and Perry, and now you're telling me that things aren't good with you two?'

Lillian desperately needed someone to talk to. The reality was she had no real friends. She'd been shunned by her set once Beau was on the scene, and while she knew other aristocratic families in Ireland – those that were not driven out by the Irish when she was a child – they were acquaintances. The Murphy girls were thick as thieves, the three of them, and Isabella too. Everyone loved Beau, as he was lovable, unlike her. Nobody at Robinswood would understand, and so that left her mother.

'It's not that. Well, it is, I suppose. I love him, I truly do, and he is such a good father and loves me too. But it's like we aren't speaking the same language. He's so religious for a start. I mean, really, what on earth is someone supposed to do with that? It's like I'm losing him and I don't know how to get him back.' Lillian sighed.

'Respect his beliefs maybe?' her mother suggested mildly. 'Look, we were never religious, but you have certain beliefs from when you were a child. Religion is not just faith for people like Beau. It is his connection to his culture, his people. Just as you are clinging to yours, not making friends with the Murphys, wanting to establish connections with other big houses, it's all you know, all you've ever known, and so you cling to it. You say Beau makes no effort to come into your world with you, and he doesn't, I agree, but do you make any effort to go into his?'

'No, but I wouldn't be comfortable there. And I'm sure that as much as they all love him, they sure as hell won't love me,' Lillian said glumly.

'Who cares? Beau loves you. Austina loves you. How about if you offered to go to his church with him?'

'I could, I suppose. Not regularly, but I could go once or twice. But it's bigger than that...'

'In what way?' Violet poured them each a cup of tea.

'Well, and I know I sound like such a snob, but I suppose the future frightens me. We are only at Robinswood because Kate and Sam allow it, and I don't think they'd throw us out as they love Beau and Austina – they'd have evicted me ages ago if it weren't for them. Beau is a farm labourer. I don't mind that as such, which is odd, but everything about my marriage is odd. He works with Sam and Mark and now this Bartley, who is a tinker's son, would you believe, and they all work together, but I don't know how or who to be. Aisling and Eve are Kate's sisters, and they were raised in service to us. So they know their place and are happy there. I wasn't raised like that, and it feels like there is nowhere I fit. We don't have any money, we live off my brother, and he doesn't like me, so any day I'll do or say the wrong thing, like I always do, and then what? I've no skills, Beau is black – what would we do?'

Violet placed her hand on her daughter's in a rare display of affection. 'When I left Ireland, I was in a similar position. All I knew was being a lady. I was raised to be one just as sure as those cows are raised to be milked.' She gestured to the lush green pastures beyond the formal gardens where Perry's sizeable herd munched happily. 'I landed in London, virtually penniless, and it was so hard. I felt everything you feel now, that I didn't belong anywhere and I had nobody on my side. I just felt old, useless, washed up. But something happened. Actually, I got kidnapped with Kate and Aisling, but after that, Kate suggested I get a job. My initial thought was, the audacity of the girl, has she forgotten who I am? But she said I could get my own job, my own house, and although it would not be what I was used to, it would be mine and I would chart my own destiny as it were. As you know, I began work the following week, and that was how I met Perry, convincing our class to provide housing on their land for the millions who found themselves destitute after the Blitz. And I'll tell you something – I loved it.'

Lillian gave her mother a smile. She remembered those days, when she and Violet were at constant loggerheads, but all that time, her mother was having fun.

'I met new people, I made friends, and I'll never forget Samuel and Kate's wedding. The Murphys came over – remember? – bringing all kinds of delicious things from Ireland, and we made a feast. I made sandwiches and cut cakes, and Isabella and I washed up together afterwards. I started to see people for who they were, not what class they came from, and it was eye-opening. We miss so much when we live in the ivory towers, Lillian, clinging to a life that wasn't even all that great to begin with.'

'But you managed to get into an even higher ivory tower after-wards,' Lillian couldn't help pointing out, glancing around the sump-tuous dining room.

'I did. But I will swear on my life this is true – I was drawn to Perry not by his wealth, but by his spirit. And initially I'll admit there may have been a mercenary element to it, but now, and this is with a hand on my heart, if he were a pauper, I'd be right by his side and we would manage. I've been at rock bottom, and I survived, so I can do it again if needs be. I know I can.' She pointed a finger at her heart. 'In here, I know I can do anything, and so can you. But in order to embrace the future, you have to let the past go.'

A long silence hung between them.

'So you think I should pull on some overalls and scrub the floors like the Murphys do?' Lillian suggested with a wry smile.

'Why not? Why should they get chapped hands and sore backs and you don't? Because you are Austin Kenefick's daughter? Because you had a public school education? Because you shopped at Harrods or Fortnum and Mason? These things are not who you are. They are just experiences. What if you sat down with your brother, just the two of you, and told him the truth? You are worried for the future and want to stay at Robinswood – but not at his discretion or as a burden, but as a fully paid-up member of the staff. Tell him you'll pull your weight, and really do it. You never know, you might enjoy it. I loved my job in the end. Then you suggest to Beau that you go to church with him, once in a while is fine. Take an interest in something that matters to him. And take care of Austina, but the others too. Take all four of the little ones on a picnic some day, and let Samuel and Kate have some time alone together. These are all things you can do, so focus on that, not what you can't.'

'Do you think it's just that simple?' Lillian asked suspiciously.

'I think it's a start.' Violet sipped her tea. 'And the most important thing is to tell Beau the truth. Tell him you don't want another child when everything is so uncertain. Ask him to be patient, and let him see how, over time, you meant it when you said you'd change. And tell him what you need from him. It's not all you, Lillian. It takes two people to make a relationship work, not just one. You spend your days in that bedroom, filling in time. Trust me, in the kitchen, the girls are gossiping, laughing, sharing – it's much more fun. I learned more about life in those war years when I worked at the housing committee than I did in the decades before it.'

'What if I am useless?' She knew she sounded young and vulnerable and hated to hear it in her voice, but it was how she felt.

'Fiddlesticks. They will teach you. Isabella is in Switzerland, so they are down a person. You can't make a soufflé or roast a perfect leg of lamb, but you can peel potatoes and wash dishes, and over time, you'll learn from them. And you know something? They can learn from you too. They don't know things you know, so hold your head up, Lillian. You are no better nor no worse than anyone else.'

'I could try, I suppose?' she said uncertainly. 'Beau and I had an argument. He and Kate were talking about me, about how lazy, how entitled I am. And maybe they were right in a way, but he's supposed to be on my side, not theirs, and I lashed out at him because it felt like they were all ganging up on me. He's been sleeping in Austina's room for a few weeks now.'

Violet sighed and patted Lillian's hand. 'He's caught between you and them. And yes, he's more like them. He was raised to work, and you were not. This marriage wasn't ever going to be easy – you are very different in many more ways than the obvious – but if he's worth it to you and you're worth it to him, then you can fight for it. But as I said, there needs to be an open conversation. You need to tell him the whole truth and expect nothing less in return.'

'And if he doesn't want to fix it? What if I'm not worth it to him?' she asked, that hint of little girl still there.

'Well, then that's another hurdle to overcome. But let's do one at a time, shall we?' Violet gave her daughter a smile.

'I'll give it a go. Though the idea of peeling potatoes repulses me, I won't lie,' Lillian said, regaining some of her habitual froideur.

Perry came back, almost on cue, and beamed when he saw the women had moved beside each other. 'All well?' He smiled and winked at Lillian. She knew then in that moment with total certainty that Perry and her mother had discussed her and this was the solution.

CHAPTER 11

*E*ve groaned. She'd just sat down, but someone was knocking on their door. Bartley was in the bathroom down the hall, cleaning up after the day, and she'd just made a pot of tea and had cut two slices of apple sponge. She'd hardly seen her husband all week, as he was so busy with the vegetable garden, and she missed him.

She opened the door to find one of the students there.

'Hannah, is everything all right?' Eve asked. The girl was quiet and timid, and she felt a wave of panic.

'Yes, Miss Doherty. I just wanted to speak to you and Bartley for a moment about a personal matter.' Eve could tell that the speech was prepared. She looked at the girl, with her curvy figure and hazel eyes. She would be a beautiful woman if she could ever shake off that hangdog aura so many of those raised in care had.

'Can't it wait? Bartley is in the bathroom...' Eve felt bad trying to get rid of the girl, but she was six months pregnant now and exhausted after the day's work.

'Not really, Miss Doherty. I...I have some information for Bartley, and I wanted to deliver it myself...' The girl's cheeks were flushed, and Eve realised she'd rather do anything else than intrude. It must be important.

'All right then, come in.' Eve stepped aside and allowed Hannah to enter. 'Cup of tea?' she offered.

'No thank you, Miss Doherty. I'll just wait.'

At first, the students had called her Miss Murphy, and when she and Bartley married, they switched to Miss Doherty. But they only ever called Bartley by his first name.

'How are you enjoying it here?' Eve asked. The current crop of students had only been there a week; the previous group were all in employment.

'Oh, it's lovely. And the bedrooms are so pretty, and it's all...well... I've never been anywhere like it,' Hannah gushed.

Eve knew she was telling the truth. The girls came from St Basil's, which was a Protestant home for girls born out of wedlock or orphaned. Eve had visited a few times with Elena when they were setting the whole thing up, and it was the epitome of dreary, all dark walls and a smell of disinfectant. It broke her heart to see the little girls there, years of drudgery ahead with nobody to love them. It could not have been more different from her own upbringing, and it made her want to do even more for these girls.

'Good, I'm glad. And we're not working you too hard?' Eve smiled.

The girl gave her a grin in return. 'No, Miss, we don't work half so hard here as we did in St Basil's. And the food is lovely here, and we can go for a walk in the gardens, and Miss Kate even said we could go to the pictures one night in Dungarvan.' The girl's eyes glittered with excitement at the prospect of such a glamorous outing.

'Yes, we usually do a trip to the pictures, so we'll have to see what's in,' Eve said, wishing Bartley would hurry so they could hear whatever the young woman had to say. She wanted to change into her nightie and slippers and put her feet up.

Eve struggled to find more conversation. She never asked the students about their families or their backgrounds. Some of them knew where they came from, more didn't, but either way, it was a sad story.

'What part do you like best so far?' Eve asked.

The girl's face lit up again. 'I like it all, but today Miss Kate had an errand to run, so she asked me to give the little ones a bath. I did, and I loved taking care of them. They are so sweet, Jack and the girls, and Austina is so clever for such a small girl. She can read better than me and everything, and she's not even five.'

Eve never stopped marvelling at the need to nurture, even when the girl had close to no nurturing herself. She'd watched over the years as the girls took on birds with broken wings, lame rabbits, lost puppies and kittens, all helped and encouraged by Bartley. He really was an incredible man, so gentle, so in touch with all of nature, so intuitive. There was something otherworldly about him for sure, but she never felt excluded or left out – he gave himself entirely to her, held nothing back. But sometimes when she watched him making his potions from herbs, or tending to an animal, she heard him speak in low tones to himself, his own language, his cant, the language of the travellers, and he seemed very far from this earth.

'They are little dotes,' Eve agreed. 'Though Daisy and Poppy are a right handful at times. They are born mischief-makers. Kate found them putting her best lipstick on the dog last week.'

Hannah giggled as Bartley appeared.

'Ah, Hannah, isn't it?' He made a point of learning all the students' names the day they arrived.

'Yes, Bartley.' She coloured and looked at her shoes.

Eve could see why. With his long dark hair hung down his back, wet from the shower, freshly shaven and wearing a loose white shirt tied with a drawstring rather than buttons, which hung loose over brown trousers, he was breathtaking. His eyes, almost black, seemed to be ringed in eyeliner, his lashes were dark and thick, and his complexion was the colour of the autumn leaves, golden under his clothes while his arms, neck and face were tanned a dark brown. He wore a copper bangle and a metal symbol on a piece of leather cord around his neck. Men hardly ever wore jewellery so he got some odd looks. His dress and long hair caused quite a stir when he first arrived in Kilthomand, but they accepted him now, just as they accepted

Mark and even Beau. Besides, the travellers were the friends of the farmers. They came around each year to help with the harvest, they mended pots and pans and anything else that was lying about and broken, and in return they got a few shillings and could stay for the summer and graze the long acre on the side of the road. Eve and her sisters used to love to see them coming, with their brightly painted wagons and their wild-looking children. Kate always said she'd run away with a tinker, but instead, she took the Lord of the Manor, and Eve, the sensible older sister, had got the gypsy. Life was funny.

'Hannah wanted to tell you something,' Eve prompted, and Bartley sat down, not wishing to intimidate the young woman further by standing over her.

'Go ahead.' He was gentle.

Hannah looked to Eve, and Eve gave her a nod of encouragement. It was a common thing with the girls that they were afraid of men. They grew up in an entirely female environment – women teachers, women housemothers, other girls – and when they first met Bartley and the boys who trained beside them, they were usually tongue-tied.

'I... My name is Hannah Woods, and I was allowed to visit my brother before I came down here. He...' The girl's face flushed beet-root now. 'Well...he's in a borstal, and he used to take care of me. That's how I ended up in St Basil's. But he's getting out now and everything, and he's not a bad person or anything.'

'Go on, Hannah, it's all right,' Bartley said with an encouraging smile, his pearly white teeth visible.

'Well, my brother, Desmond is his name, I write to him every week, telling him my news, and I wrote to say I was coming here. I was so excited. Anyway, when I went to visit him, he said he was friends with a lad called Isaac Doherty in the place they are being kept, and he told him I was coming here. When he mentioned you, Bartley, the boy said you might be his brother.'

Eve watched Bartley's reaction, shock turning to incredulity. The family had been split up when Bartley's mother died and the authorities thought his father would not be able to cope, so the boys were sent to various institutions and the girls other ones. Bartley had never seen his siblings again, and she knew it hurt him.

'Where are they?' Bartley asked, his voice husky.

'St Patrick's in Tipperary, near Clonmel,' Hannah said quietly.

'Thank you, Hannah.' Bartley stood up, and the young woman moved towards the door.

'Goodnight, Miss Doherty, Bartley.' But as she turned the handle, she thought of something else. 'He's getting out too, I think, same as Dessie, at the end of the month. So if you want to go...' She nodded and let herself out of their room.

Eve went to Bartley once the door was closed and put her arms around his waist inasmuch as she could with her bump in the way. His arms encircled her, and he rested his chin on her head, neither of them speaking for a long moment. Then he led her to the sofa and sat her down, taking her shoes off and rubbing her slightly swollen ankles. It was summer and the day had been hot.

'Well?' she asked.

'I do have a brother called Isaac...' He thought for a moment. 'He'd be sixteen or seventeen now, I think.' He sighed. 'Last time I saw him, he was only a baby, six months or something. I wonder how he knew I was his brother?'

'Well, there's one way to find out,' Eve said. 'You could visit him.'

'I will.' Bartley's eyes shadowed at the memory of their family being forcibly broken up. He was the seventh son of a seventh son, and there were fourteen children in his family. It was believed in the traveller world that Bartley by virtue of his birth order had second sight. He never confirmed or denied it, but Eve suspected it to be true.

The tinkers that came knew of him by reputation and brought their sick to him, believing completely in his skills. Bartley saw everyone who came but never made any claims.

'Maybe he knows about the others?' Eve suggested gently. Bartley never spoke in any detail about his family because it hurt him to do so, and Eve didn't want to intrude but desperately wanted to help.

'Maybe.' He rubbed her tired feet and thought. 'The day they took us, I was fourteen years old. We were camped on the banks of the Shannon, and there were about ten or twelve wagons. Mammy was dead about a month, and we'd burned her caravan, the one her father had made for her when she married. We were in two wagons, my da and us boys in one, all nine of us, and the five girls in the other. My eldest sister, Maggie, was doing a good job taking care of us. My da drank a bit but not so much that we hadn't food or anything.' His gaze was on the flickering flames of the fire, his thumbs rhythmically rubbing her feet. He was back there, she could see it.

'He drank because he was heartbroken. My parents were a love match, not the usual arrangement. Her father wanted her to marry someone else, but she begged him to have my father instead. Only that he was a seventh son himself, he'd have had no chance, but because they believed he had the sight and because my ma was my granda's favourite child, he agreed. They were both sixteen. But how he loved her, Eve! I can still remember it, him standing, watching her as she cooked or looked after us kids – he would often just stare at her. She was a beauty, my ma...' His face softened.

He turned to look at Eve. 'She looked like you. Gorgeous copper hair, green eyes, freckles across her nose. Her hair went all the way down her back – I remember watching her brush it by the fire at night.'

Eve smiled. 'Tell me more,' she whispered.

'Well, she got sick, and even my da couldn't cure her. It was her time. She died in his arms, and he sobbed like a baby. Cousins, aunties came from everywhere. They helped him, taking care of us and all of that, and we were doing all right, but it wasn't enough.'

Eve saw the flash of pain, even all these years later.

'They came, the priest and the guards, telling my da it would be best, that we'd get an education, make something of ourselves. He'd had a drink and was in such a fog of grief over my ma anyway, he...he hadn't the strength to fight for us. They took us that day.'

The darkness had fallen by now, and the curtains were still open, the small room only illuminated by the fire. She longed to put her arms around him but didn't want to disturb the atmosphere.

'They sent me to Cork. On my own. I think they knew I was the seventh son, and the church never trusted our ways. I never knew where the others went, if they kept them together or separated them. I'm sure the girls went one place and the boys another, but other than that...'

'What was it like?' Eve asked gently. This was unchartered waters for them. She knew he'd been in an institution, but he didn't talk about it.

He looked at her, and she could see he was weighing up whether or not to tell her. He inhaled. 'It was no place for any child, Eve.'

'Did they hurt you?' she asked gently.

His gaze never left hers as he nodded slowly. 'When I got out, at sixteen, I tried to find them, to find anyone. Eventually, I found a camp, and one of my uncles was there. He told me that my da was dead, and that he'd nearly gone out of his mind once he sobered up and realised that they'd taken us. He tried to get us back, but he was a traveller and couldn't read or write, and they wouldn't even open the door to him. He tried different priests, anyone, to help him, but it was no good. In the end, he couldn't take any more, and he took his own life.'

'Oh, Bartley, I'm so sorry. Your poor da...' Eve had tears in her eyes now.

He nodded and held her hand. 'I tried to find them, my brothers and sisters, but nobody would tell me anything. So I stayed with my uncle. He taught me all about woodworking and metal and all of that. And the plants and animals – well, I remembered that from before.'

'Did your da teach you, or did you just know?' she asked.

'He taught me, but I was born knowing it too – it's hard to explain. I'm the last in the line of seventh sons, but it does mean something. When I saw the job in Elena's school advertised, I knew that it was going to be right for me. I'd never applied for a job before. When I went there that first day, I was so nervous, but inside I knew it was right for me. And then I saw you, and you had such sadness in you, but you looked so beautiful to me. I knew then why I was there.' He looked around their little rooms.

'My life was very happy until I was fourteen, then it was awful, worse than you could ever imagine, and I'll never tell you because I wouldn't put those pictures in your head. But when I met you, Eve, and I finally managed to screw up the courage to ask you out, that's when I came home. You're my home, and I can't tell you how grateful I am. And now we're having a little baby of our own. I...I'd love my ma and da to meet you, to meet the baby.'

'They can see us,' Eve whispered, sitting up and putting her arm around his shoulders. 'They can see me and you and they'll see our baby too, and they'll be looking over us.'

Bartley turned his head and locked eyes with her, a single tear running down his face. 'They'd love you,' he said. 'A priest a few years ago, when I got back to my uncle's camp, told me my da was in hell because he took his own life. It was his anniversary, and I wanted a Mass said for him and my ma...' His voice sounded raspy now, infused with hurt and pain, and all Eve wanted to do was take it away.

'Your parents are in heaven, Bartley. They are together like they always wanted to be, and they are up there, along with my Jack, and they are watching over us and keeping us safe. That is the truth, so don't you mind some old priest...' Eve's eyes glittered with fury. How could a man, supposed to be a follower of Jesus, be so cruel?

'Are you sure?' He looked at her, and she saw that lost little boy again.

'Absolutely sure.' Eve cuddled up to him. 'When Jack died, I thought if I could just climb into the grave after him, that was all I wanted to do. How could he be gone? I was in such a dark place. There was no light, no way out. And only for Mammy and Daddy I might have decided to end it all too, but Daddy promised me if I could just hold on, breathe in and out, put one foot in front of the other, that one day I'd smile again, that life would be good again. I didn't really believe it or anything, but I had no choice, I suppose. But he was right, and slowly – so slowly, Bartley – my broken heart healed. And then, when the time was right, Jack sent me you. And now we are here, and soon we'll be a family, and all the hurt is healed. God is watching us,

Bartley, he is, but he's got a lot of people to care for, so I think he's given the job to your parents and Jack.'

Bartley smiled. 'That's a nice idea,' he said, and kissed her. 'Will you come with me to visit my brother?' he asked.

'Of course I will.'

CHAPTER 12

*A*isling propped Kate's bike against the pole outside the draper's shop and went in.

'Ah, Aisling, how are you?' Sean Lacey asked, and she gave him a bright smile. Nothing, not even the sight of Sean Lacey, could dampen her mood.

He smiled back in that creepy way he had, and she wondered how she could ever have had feelings for him. He'd humiliated her when they were younger, making her believe she was his girl and then carrying on with others behind her back. The embarrassment of the night at the dance years ago when Kate and Jack, God rest him, confronted Sean was as vivid as if it had happened yesterday. It was why she left for England with Kate.

But time had gone on, and she'd returned to Robinswood while Mark was in prison, and Sean had been so kind. When he drove her from the boat in Rosslare to Robinswood, she had foolishly confided in him. Mark was due to come to her once he got out, and she had waited and waited but he never came. Little did she know at the time that Mark had turned up in Kilthomand but Sean had told him some cock and bull story about him and Aisling being back together and how she'd be better off without him. Poor Mark believed him and had left again, without ever seeing Aisling. If it hadn't been for Sam and Mark's friendship, and Sam going over to England and figuring it all out, she might have lost her lovely husband forever. She had good reason to hate Sean, but she just didn't care two hoots about him any more.

As a rule, the inhabitants of Robinswood avoided Lacey's drapers, getting everything they needed in Galvin's in Dungarvan instead, but today they were stuck. Austina and Jack had done a colouring job on the good tablecloth, and they had a big group in for dinner. Sam and Beau were gone off in the car to look at some machinery they were thinking of buying, and the bike was all that was available, so Lacey's was the only option.

Kate had offered to go, but she was in the middle of making a beef Wellington. Since she was a much better cook than Aisling, it made no sense to have her leave.

'I need a cream tablecloth, the biggest one you have,' Aisling said brightly.

Sean continued to smile but it didn't reach his eyes. Mrs Delaney and Mrs O'Brien suddenly found they had an enormous interest in a basket of oddments beside the counter.

'Righto, let's see if we have anything suitable for the big house. I presume it's for Robinswood and not your cottage?'

Did she imagine it, or was there a slight emphasis on the word 'cottage'? As if she would be ashamed of living in a little cottage as opposed to Lacey's big double-fronted house on Kilthomand's square? Sean was deluded if he thought for one second she'd any regrets about Mark. Though it was none of his business, she replied, 'Yes, for Robinswood, that's right.'

He held her gaze a fraction longer than necessary and then turned to the shelves behind the large mahogany counter. He looked older. Still the narrow face, the thin shoulders, the same tape measure around his neck, but definitely older. He'd never married, despite the amorous adventures in his youth, and everyone said he was still obsessed with Aisling. Eleanor Conlan, the girl he'd been kissing behind Aisling's back all those years ago, was still sniffing around him, though everyone knew the shop and the house were the lure there, not weaselly Sean Lacey.

He gazed at Aisling on Sundays at Mass because he could. Mark was Church of England and so didn't go with her. Her husband was not a violent man and had eschewed all forms of aggression since his time in Dartmoor, but sometimes she'd love it if Mark just gave that sleeveen one puck that would land him into the middle of next week. She didn't tell Mark how Sean behaved; Mark had a criminal record, and being an Englishman to boot in a country with a long memory, it was best to stay out of trouble.

Sean took a tablecloth off the shelf. 'That one is eight foot long by four foot wide. Is that big enough for you?'

'Give me two of them,' Aisling said, grinning, and extracted her purse.

She saw Mrs O'Brien and Mrs Delaney exchange a glance. This was great gossip, Aisling Murphy smiling brightly at Sean Lacey. Everyone knew he was still sweet on her and regretted deeply losing her in the first place by fooling around with that Eleanor Conlan. Aisling Murphy was a beauty – all those Murphys were – and Eleanor Conlan couldn't hold a candle to her.

The Murphys had always been respected, though Dermot and Isabella tended to keep to themselves, but now that half the village was employed at the hotel and the other half were supplying something or other to them, everyone was totally behind them.

Sean was not a popular person in Kilthomand. His mother, who ran the draper's shop before him, was a mean-spirited woman who'd raised a real mammy's boy in Sean. He was shrewd and loved making money, so not getting the Robinswood business, especially when all other businesses in the village were flourishing as the hotel went from strength to strength, really hurt him. He'd lost Aisling, and he'd lost the respect of the village once they found out what he did to Mark, whom everyone loved because he scored the winning point in the hurling final against Carrickonbride, the neighbouring village. To see Lacey lose out on the money too was something that delighted Kate in particular. She deliberately got the Galvin's van to park in the square several times when they were delivering all the sheets, blankets, curtains and other drapery for the hotel. It drove Sean mad.

'They're one pound, fifteen shillings each,' he said.

'Fine.' Aisling extracted the money, and ignoring Sean's outstretched hand, she placed the money on the counter and then took the cloths.

'You seem very chirpy,' he remarked.

'Sure why wouldn't I, Sean? It's a lovely day.' Aisling smiled again as he handed her the change from his cashbox. Not one to splash out on a newfangled cash register, Sean operated his shop as his mother had done before, out of a tin box with a hunting scene on the lid.

'I suppose it is,' he agreed, and this time the smile did reach his eyes.

She went to the butcher to buy two steaks. She was cooking steak and onions with mashed potatoes and garden peas for their tea, her husband's favourite. She and Mark normally ate at Robinswood, but she wanted them to have a special night, just the two of them. She hugged herself with glee. She'd been to the doctor and it was confirmed – she was pregnant! She didn't want to tell Mark until she was sure, but the doctor had examined her and was very sure. Her belly was still flat, but she felt different. Her breasts were tender, and she felt nauseous at the smell of things that previously hadn't bothered her. She wished her mother was there to talk to. She hadn't told anyone – Mark should be first to know – but then she'd tell Kate and Eve and everyone else.

She got her few last bits and pieces, put everything in the box on the bike and set out for home. As she cycled past Lacey's, Sean was outside, sweeping the path in front of his shop, and she caught his eye. She waved and he waved back as she cycled on, although she quickly averted her glance. Nothing and nobody could put a dent in her good humour today.

Mark, Bartley and the boys had spent the entire day cutting trees and chopping them for firewood. The voracious fires at Robinswood in the wintertime needed constant feeding, and the timber needed months to dry, so they cut in the summer and stored the wood in the big barns. Mark had walked home, exhausted.

She had drawn him a bath and kept the dinner warm in the oven. 'Do you want me to scrub your back?' she called up the stairs.

'Lovely,' he called back, and she skittishly ran up.

Immediately, he looked strangely at her. Putting his blond tousled head to one side, he said, 'So what's up?'

'Nothing,' she replied, but she couldn't keep the grin off her face. She was wearing her yellow dress with the little red roses on it. She'd made it herself and knew Mark loved her in it.

'There is something. You're behaving very oddly.' His soft West Country accent blurred his 'r' sounds.

She'd planned to tell him over dinner but couldn't keep it in. She perched on the rim of the big roll-top bath with the brass claw feet. It was far too big for their tiny cottage bathroom, but it came out of the big house and Aisling had fallen in love with it, so Mark plumbed it in for her, even though they had to walk around it to get to the toilet.

'OK,' she said slowly, a grin crossing her face. 'Well, how would you feel if I told you that you were going to be a daddy?'

The dawning realisation spread across his face. 'Are you sure? Really?' he asked, astonished.

'I went to the doctor this morning, and she confirmed it. January, she thinks.'

'Oh, Ais.' Mark could barely speak. He reached for her, his strong arms soapy and wet. She giggled and then screamed as she toppled into the bath with him.

'Oh my God, are you all right?' he asked, worried.

She was soaked but didn't care. She kissed her husband, a long loving kiss, and then whispered, 'I've never been better.'

* * *

LILLIAN BRACED HERSELF, took a deep breath and entered the kitchen. Kate and Eve were washing up, and the children were playing on the swing outside where they could be seen. The more she thought about acting on her mother's suggestion, the more she hated the idea, but she was this far now, so she might as well try.

Both Murphys looked up as she entered. It was rare to see her in the kitchen.

'Um...well, I was wondering if you needed any help, with um... well, anything,' she said.

The sisters looked appalled. What was wrong with these people, she thought. If you didn't help, you were wrong; if you offered, they looked like you'd suggested they be led to the gallows.

'Well...ahem...we were just washing up, so we're almost fin –' Kate began.

'Shall I put those away?' Lillian interrupted, pointing at a pile of crockery.

'If you want to, then of course...' Eve said, recovering.

Lillian didn't reply but began moving the plates from the large table to the dresser. As she crossed the kitchen carrying a large tureen, she tripped on an uneven flag and stumbled. In an effort to save herself from falling, she let go, and the tureen flew out of her hands, breaking into smithereens on the floor.

Kate and Eve ran over. 'Are you all right, Lillian? Did you cut yourself?' Eve asked.

And while the words were kind, Lillian couldn't help but notice the glance the sisters shared. It said it all about what they thought of her efforts at helping.

They swept up the shards and she excused herself. That had been, as she suspected it would be, an unmitigated disaster.

Up in her bedroom, she resisted the urge to write to her mother and tell her just how foolish her suggestion was as she knew it would be pointless. Violet would just tell her to try again, and there was no way she was going to do that.

Beau came in as she seethed. He was oblivious, of course, and absentmindedly kissed her cheek before heading to the bathroom to get cleaned up.

'Ugh.' She grimaced. 'You smell of cows.'

He guffawed and came back to stand before her. 'Well, I started out as a mechanic, but now I'm a farmer, so I guess smellin' of cows is part of the job.'

'Well, it's horrid,' she said with a shudder.

'As I recall, you used to like the smell of oil and grease when I was in uniform,' he murmured, his arms encircling her waist.

It was true. She had loved the working-man smell of him, though she would never admit that to anyone. But that was different. The smell of engines was one thing, but the odour of manure and sour milk was something else entirely.

'Oh, get off me, Beau, and get washed up.' She pushed his chest away from her.

'OK.' He smiled, then walked into the bathroom. 'Hey, Lillian, could you listen to my sermon? I'm almost ready to preach, I think, but I could use a set of fresh ears for any parts that don't work,' he called as he ran the bath.

She'd used her mother's money to build a bathroom off their bedroom, so they had their own facilities. Mother had complained as usual – honestly, that woman was so penny-pinching, even now when she was positively loaded – but finally Lillian convinced her that she could not be expected to share with the guests.

Now was her chance to offer to go, to support him. Her foray to the kitchen had ended in disaster, but perhaps this part of the advice would work better. Besides, she wanted things to be good between her and Beau again even if she couldn't care less what the Murphys thought.

'I'll go if you want me to,' she said, leaning on the doorjamb as he lowered himself into the warm water.

Instead of delight, she was sure she saw a shadow cross his face. 'But do you want to?' he asked.

'Well, I'm not of your faith, but...' She was flustered now. Why was this so hard? 'But I am your wife, so if you want me to go to support you, then I will. I mean, I don't believe in it, you know that, but appearances matter, so...' She shrugged.

He looked crestfallen. 'It's OK, Lillian, you don't need to go. You're off the hook.' He took a bar of soap and began to wash.

She wished she could just walk over, touch him, explain that her offer came out wrong, but she couldn't. 'Very well, as you wish,' was all she could manage.

She retreated to their bedroom to prepare for dinner.

* * *

THE NEWS of the baby was greeted with delight in Robinswood. Aisling had written to her mother and was waiting on a reply, but her father was over the moon, as were the whole family. Everyone knew that Aisling and Mark longed for a baby, and it had been looking increasingly unlikely as every year passed. Kate and Eve squeezed her in delight. One of the many payoffs for the hard work they all did was to have their families grow up together in this idyllic place.

Beau walked in in his footman's uniform just as she'd broken the news. 'I'm sorry,' he said, clearly feeling like he was intruding.

'No, Beau, come in, come in! Aisling has some good news.' Eve waved him into the kitchen.

'I'm going to have a baby,' Aisling said with a smile, and Beau's face broke into a huge beam.

'Oh, praise the Lord! I'm so happy He has bestowed this blessing on you and Mark, Aisling, I truly am. This is wonderful. Congratulations.'

'Thanks, Beau. Mark will probably tell you later anyway, but we're so excited.' She took the teapot from Kate and brought it to the table. 'Tea?' she asked him.

'Y'know, I will never understand you Irish and your love of tea. Back in Georgia, people only drank tea if they were sick or something, or weak, but y'all drink gallons of the stuff. I don't get it.' He chuckled.

'Well, if you were here during the war, you wouldn't say that,' Eve said. 'We only got one quarter of the English ration. Daddy always said it was a penalty for our neutrality. Tea was honestly like gold dust, so now that we can, we are splashing out.'

'Sit down. I'll make you some coffee,' Kate said. Knowing how he loved it, she'd ordered some for him.

'You got coffee?' he asked incredulously.

'Specially for you, Beau.' She grinned.

'So when is your big sermon?' Eve asked as she heaved herself down onto a seat. She was becoming uncomfortable now with only four weeks to go. Everyone wanted her to take it easy, and she was, compared with the girls, but there was so much to be done and they were already down one pair of hands in Mammy. Lillian's offer to help was a one-off it seemed.

'First Sunday next month. And I'm so nervous. It's so different here, y'know?'

The three Murphy sisters looked at him. His handsome open face was longing for reassurance.

'Well, we don't really, since Father Mac would have a stroke rather than let any member of the congregation speak at Mass, but I could see how it would be nerve-racking all right. Will there be many there, do you think?' Kate asked.

'That's the thing, I don't know. The church is little, and it's usually half full, but I dunno if a black American preachin' will draw more people to take a look or make everyone stay at home. I'm thinkin' the second one.' He stirred sugar into his coffee, a luxury he'd missed during the severe rationing. Though it was still going on in Ireland, it was nothing like as bad as it was during the war, and there were rumours that rationing was going to come to a complete end next year. 'Lillian offered to come but I told her not to. It's not her kind of thing, y'know?' Beau shrugged. 'I could imagine just her and me, and me preachin' to her about stuff she don't believe anyway...'

Eve glanced at Aisling and Kate, then asked, 'Would you like us all to come, Beau? I mean, I know we're the wrong religion and all for that, but we are a crowd, and if it would help, we'd love to hear you.'

He thought for a moment. 'You'd do that?'

'Of course! You're family, and we'd be going to Mass anyway, so we'll just do our duty in your church for a change,' Kate said matter-of-factly.

Beau looked overwhelmed. 'Well, if you wouldn't mind, then I'd love it.'

'Why don't we see if Sam can borrow another car? Then we can all go. I can't guarantee that Daisy and Poppy won't shout out something totally inappropriate, but if you're willing to risk it, then we'd love to come.'

'Great. At least you guys will fill up the church,' Beau said, then sipped the coffee gratefully.

Outside on the lawn, Lillian and Austina were playing with a bright-pink ball. Lillian had taken her from Hannah, who loved minding the children.

Beau stood, picked up his cup and excused himself. The girls watched as he crossed the lawn to his wife and daughter. Austina ran into his arms, and he lifted her up, swinging her around much to her delight. They could not hear the conversation between him and Lillian, but the body language was not good.

'What's going to happen with them, do you think?' Aisling asked quietly.

'Who knows?' Kate was pensive. 'She's such an odd fish. I thought she seemed better when she came back from London, whatever she was doing over there, but since then, she's been so strange. I know she's not driving us cracked any more, but still, it's peculiar. Beau is such a lovely man, and look at little Austina – she's such a sweetheart. They deserve to be happy. Do you know she told me that she thought the new furniture for the drawing room was a bit unsuitable, that she was sure it was the best we could afford but if I'd have waited and asked her or Sam, they would have chosen something more fitting. Like no matter how much money I had, I'd never have class, that's what she was trying to say.'

'I suppose it must be lonely for her, not having any friends. She's neither staff nor gentry now so...' Aisling said.

Kate turned to her. 'Ah, Ais.' She turned back around and started filling the dresser with the newly washed dishes. 'She's a disaster. I mean, I know we wanted her to help, but Daisy and Poppy cause less destruction. We need help from Lady Lillian like we need a hole in the head. The one time she did try, she was like a bull in a china shop. She's neither use nor ornament.' Kate started to laugh, but the look on Aisling's face stopped her in her tracks. Her sisters' expressions told her all she needed to know. The kitchen window was open and Lillian had walked over. She'd heard every word.

Eve and Aisling blushed, and the colour drained from Kate's face. She turned. 'Lillian, I'm sorry. I didn't mean –' she began.

'I think we both know you meant every word, Kate,' Lillian replied icily, and walked away.

The three girls were speechless. Kate had given her sister-in-law an earful in the past, but this was different. Eve tried to look on the bright side. 'Look, she's not exactly been diplomatic where we're concerned either, has she? I mean she definitely still treats us like we work for her, so maybe if you go and apologise and, you know, clear the air a bit?'

Kate looked at her older sister. 'Yes, I'll just go up and say, "Sorry for calling you all the names under the sun, but you are a bit of a cow so it was probably fair, so let's just put it all behind us, shall we?" No, this is bad. And she'll tell Beau, of course, so he'll be even more torn between us and her. Oh God… Me and my big mouth.' Kate groaned.

Neither Eve nor Aisling had any words of consolation.

CHAPTER 13

*D*ear Kate,
    I got your letter this morning, and I have to admit I burst out laughing. I know I shouldn't, but I can just picture it – you off on one of your rants and herself listening to it all. God love you, child, that mouth of yours gets you into trouble.

Burn this letter for God's sake when you've read it, will you? So what to do? Look, she is Sam's sister and you are stuck with her either way, so you'll have to make some kind of peace with her. But I wouldn't go crawling because she thinks she's superior to you anyway.

I've been thinking about how to deal with her, and the most effective person at dealing with her mother was Dermot back in the day. Lillian is very like her mother, or how Violet used to be anyway – to be fair, she's much better now. But that same haughty way of going on, like we were something she dragged in on the sole of her shoe.

Your dad was never rude to her, but he never once kowtowed to her either. He addressed her as an equal. It drove her mad, of course, but she could not intimidate him, no matter how hard she tried. I'll suggest you do the same with Lillian.

There's no point in getting Sam or Violet or anyone to intervene. You need to fix this yourself. So I'd go up to her room and say something like

'Clearly we have some problems. We need to sort them out because if we are all to live here together, then it must be in harmony, and this atmosphere isn't good for anyone. So how can we find a way to do that?' That way, you are not taking the blame, nor are you putting the blame on her – you are both taking responsibility.

I hope this helps. I wish I was there. I'm rightly fed up of this place, I can tell you. It's beautiful and all of that, but I'm sick of the sight of the place. I've had enough snow-capped mountains and goats with those bloody bells round their necks to last me a lifetime.

It's fantastic news about Aisling, isn't it? Please God all will go well. Mind her and Eve, don't let them do too much, sure you won't? You are devils for work, but you didn't lick that off a stone, I suppose. She told me about having to buy tablecloths off that eejit Sean Lacey. He never got over her, you know, but he's another one to watch. I wouldn't trust him as far as I'd throw him.

Eve told me that she and Bartley are going up to Tipperary this week to visit his long-lost brother. I'm happy for him that he's found someone in his family, but I just hope he and Eve aren't opening a can of worms. They don't put people in a borstal for nothing. Especially with the baby so close now, she doesn't need any dramatics.

The doctors say that while I'm not improving as fast as they'd like, I'm not getting any worse, but I won't be getting home any time soon. I'm eating for Ireland, but I can't put up weight. I haven't told your dad what they've said. You know what he's like – he'd be over here again, and while I'd love to see him, there's nothing he can do. How is he? He writes every day and says he's fine and not to worry about anything, but I do worry. He's deep, that husband of mine. I miss you all so much, but I miss him like a limb cut off. We're together so long now, I don't think either of us functions well without the other.

Anyway, write back soon, telling me how you get on with Lady Muck, and give everyone a big hug from me.

Love, Mam xxx

. . .

KATE REREAD THE LETTER, and partly out of paranoia and partly because her mother told her to, she threw it in the range. The last thing anyone needed was for Lillian to somehow see it. Though it was unlikely – she'd hardly been seen since the day she overheard Kate.

Kate's face burned in shame. She should not have said what she did, but her mother was right. Going to apologise would give Lillian the go ahead for full-on supercilious condescension. She could not let her sister-in-law get the upper hand, but she needed to fix this. Beau knew obviously; he was very quiet these days. His sermon was next Sunday, and there had been no more talk of them going. She told Sam everything, but he just laughed. He agreed completely with everything she said and refused to see that it was a terrible situation.

'But if not for her sake, then for Beau and Austina, shouldn't we try to...I don't know...do something?' she'd asked as they lay in bed.

'Look.' He turned onto his side and looked down into her face. 'It was unfortunate that she overheard you, but you didn't tell any lies. She is useless. She was an entitled brat as a child, and nothing has changed. Yes, Beau is a lovely chap, but he's miserable with her. You can see it. I've tried talking to him, so have Mark and Bartley, but he won't discuss it. You hit the nail on the head. Beau was a novelty, a way of shocking everyone, and she fell in love with the idea of him. But now that the war is over and everything is back to normal life, she sees she married a poor black mechanic with no means to keep her in the style she is accustomed to. She's not willing to change, and so it's ultimately doomed.'

'Do you think the marriage will end?' Kate asked, horrified at the thought that she may have accelerated it.

'I can't see how he would leave her. He's a devout Christian and believes marriage is for life. He loves Austina and would never give her up. But would she leave him?' Sam shrugged. 'I wouldn't put it past her.'

'But where would she go?' Kate was worried now.

'Back to Mother and Perry, I suppose? Perry would convince my mother to let her in – he's got a soft spot for her inexplicably. And she'd get to live the life she feels she should have. But who knows?' He rolled onto his back and settled her head on his shoulder.

'It's hard for her though. I feel so mean. I know I was right, but it was still horrible for her to hear that. I wrote to Mam and asked what I should do, and she suggested talking to her in an open way, as equals, the way my father used to talk to your mother years ago.'

Sam chuckled. 'I remember it well. Your father would not show her the deference she felt she was due. It drove her mad. "Austin!" – he mimicked his mother's querulous tones – "Servants in India loved us, they longed to serve us. Seeing their masters happy was enough, but what on earth is wrong with these Irish? We are paying them, giving them homes, and still they border on insolence."'

Kate slapped him playfully. 'Seriously, though, we should do something, or at least I should. I think I'll do what Mam said and try to reach some kind of truce with her. I'd hate to see them separate.'

'OK, if you want to, but don't you dare grovel to her, do you hear me?' Sam responded before drifting off to sleep.

* * *

THE FOLLOWING MORNING, once the guests were fed and the rooms done, Kate decided to approach Lillian. She took off her apron and made sure her hair was tidy. She wore her second-best dress. She didn't want Lillian to think she was dressing up for her benefit, but neither did she want to seem shabby. Lillian always dressed immaculately. She glanced at her reflection in the mirror over the kitchen sink and took a calming breath. She smiled at the terrific racket coming from the poultry pen and decided she'd rather be out there than face her sister-in-law, but it had to be done.

Aisling and Eve were dealing with the rooster who'd become so aggressive he was a danger. He'd be in the pot later that day, and that would put an end to his attacks. He was old and probably tough, but they'd cook him in buttermilk for long enough that he'd be tasty as anything. She'd begged them to get one of the men up to catch him, but they'd scoffed at her. They were raised on Robinswood, and they hadn't a squeamish bone in their bodies. That horrible bird had given them both plenty of pecks, so they were happy to end his days. The students were going to watch and learn.

Kate tripped up the huge staircase that split in two and formed two balconies overlooking the grand entrance hall. The steps were marble thankfully, so did not require carpet. They could never have afforded it. She walked down the west corridor, passing the oil paintings and side tables donated by Perry, mostly. The enormous floor-length windows, now scrubbed of years of grime, shed such light, dust motes danced in the corridor. The view of the western approaches to Robinswood were spectacular. The ocean sparkled azure in the distance, the formal gardens had been restored based on photographs of how they had been in the Edwardian era, mainly by Bartley and his students, and the lush green pastures of the estate stretched as far as the eye could see.

'This is your home and you belong here,' she told herself as she turned off the corridor down to the wing where Beau, Lillian and Austina lived. She squared her shoulders, took a deep breath and knocked on the mahogany door.

There was no answer. She knew Lillian was in there; she'd come down for breakfast and sat in the dining room with the guests as usual rather than in the kitchen with everyone else. Breakfast at Robinswood was a buffet of fruit and fresh-baked scones and brown bread, as well as the full Irish breakfast of bacon, eggs, sausages, black and white pudding and mushrooms, but Lillian only ever had toast and tea.

Since she'd overheard Kate ten days ago, she'd been seen only a handful of times. The house was large enough that you would not bump into anyone if you wished to remain aloof, and clearly that was precisely what Lillian wanted. Beau was quiet, just went about his work diligently and often was to be found back out on the land after dinner. Sam tried to get him to come in, and he always insisted he would but just had one more thing to do.

Austina spent her mornings with Hannah and the other children, either in the garden or the playroom, and then after lunch, she went to her mother, where she spent the afternoon. Hannah collected her for tea along with the others at 5 p.m. and then bathed them all. Austina went back to Lillian after her bath and was not seen again until morning.

Lillian never got any letters from anyone. It was as if she was a ghost in the house. She was rail thin and barely ate. She came down each evening there were guests and did her duty. She was charming and told her stories of the family, and to be fair to her, nobody would have guessed anything was wrong. Kate admitted Lillian was really good at her job, better than Kate could ever have been, and the guests seemed to like her. But once the guests were gone, she vanished back to her rooms.

The door remained closed, no sound from within. Kate knocked again, harder this time. Still nothing. What should she do? Turn the handle? Call out?

'Lillian,' she called, 'it's Kate. I'd like to talk to you.'

Still silence. *Oh for goodness' sake, this is ridiculous.* A combination of guilt and fury rose up inside Kate. She put her hand on the door handle, wondering if it was locked. It wasn't. She turned the handle and pushed the door.

Lillian was sitting in her usual beautiful wingback chair by the huge bay window. On a side table at her left were a book and a teacup and saucer. The bedroom they nicknamed 'the half acre' was tidy, the bed made, and everything was in its place. The room smelled of Chanel perfume and freesias, and Kate noticed the large bunch of the fragrant blooms in a cut-glass vase on the dressing table. The doors leading to the bathroom and Austina's room were closed.

'Lillian, I knocked and called, but you didn't answer,' Kate said, standing at the door.

Her sister-in-law turned to her, her face the picture of disdain. She was pretty in that she had delicate features and expertly coloured and cut blonde hair, for which she went to Dublin once a month, but Kate always thought she looked a bit like a cat.

'Yes?' Lillian asked, one eyebrow raised.

'Well, I wanted to talk to you,' Kate said, feeling already at a disadvantage.

'Why?' Lillian asked coldly.

Kate took a steadying breath. She would not lose her temper, no matter how difficult Lillian chose to be. 'Because we can't go on like this, being at loggerheads, and we all have to live here together.' She tried so hard to remember her mother's words.

Lillian didn't respond.

'And I just wanted to let you know that I regret that you overheard what I said. It wasn't fair. But that said, we do have some issues we need to iron out, you know, so that we can all live harmoniously here together.' Kate cursed her inner self, who was still twelve years old and beholden in every way to Lady Kenefick.

'I don't *need* to iron anything,' Lillian said in a bored tone. Ironing, either in the metaphorical sense or the practical, was not her forte. 'That is your department.'

'Oh, for God's sake, Lillian, you know what I mean. Are you going to live like this, like some Lady of Shalott up here in your tower, not engaging with any of us?'

Lillian turned, a slight smile playing around her lips. 'Kate, I have lived in this house for most of my life. You have lived on the grounds for most of yours. We were not equals then, nor are we now. You have married my brother, which makes you Lady Kenefick, but to me, you and your family are the servants. You seem to be anxious to change the dynamics of that relationship, but frankly, I have no aspirations in that regard.'

Kate willed herself not to blush. *How dare she, that stuck-up witch!* 'And Beau and Austina? You're happy to see them upset by this as well, are you?'

Lillian turned back and gazed out across the lawns. Kate wondered if she had struck a nerve. It was impossible to tell.

'My family is not your concern, Kate. You forget yourself. Now please run along and attend to your duties. This conversation is over.' Lillian sighed as if this were the most tediously boring conversation imaginable.

All of Kate's good intentions deserted her. How dare Lillian speak to her like that? The woman made her blood boil. Kate lashed out. 'You know Sam is only putting up with you because of them, don't you? He'd have you out in a heartbeat if it weren't for them. Things have changed, Lillian. You have nothing – do you not understand that? Now, we are happy to have you here, but you don't lift a finger to help, though the rest of us are going non-stop to make a success of this place. You behave like one of the guests rather than family, and you are making Beau miserable into the bargain. He's totally torn between loyalty to you and feeling like he fits in with us. You'll lose him, that's the way this is going, and then where will you be?'

Lillian fixed her with a steely glare. 'And this is your version of an apology, is it?'

'No, it bloody well isn't!' Kate exploded, not caring now who heard her. 'I'm not one bit sorry. Every single thing I said was true and you know it.'

'And so we are exactly where we were before you barged in here uninvited. Get out of my room please, and shut the door on your way out.' Lillian picked up her book and began to read.

Kate hadn't felt the desire to hit anyone since she was a child, but she could have cheerfully throttled Lillian. She marched over and grabbed the book from Lillian's hands, flinging it on the floor. Blood pounded through her veins.

'Have you forgotten' – Kate's green eyes glittered – 'that it was to me you came when you were pregnant and Beau was back in America? Not to your fancy London friends – to me. And when you needed to go and get Beau, where did you dump your child? Oh yes, with me again. When you had nowhere to go and no money, who put a roof over your head? Do you think it was Sam? Because you're mistaken. It was me who convinced him to let you stay.'

A voice inside her told her to stop, that she was making this a thousand times worse, but she couldn't help herself. 'I'm good enough for all your moments of crisis, but now that you are settled in like a cuckoo in a nest, I'm just the servant's child and not worthy of even a shred of respect? You are a pathetic person, Lillian, honestly just pathetic. Your precious father, whom you tell such warm and funny stories about to the guests, left you penniless. Whiskey and horses meant more to him than you. But still you live in this fantasyland where you are loaded and can talk down to me and my family. You're living in a dreamworld!' Kate ran her hands through her hair in frustration. 'Can't you see what's going on under your stupid nose? You are going to lose it all – your husband, your home, everything – all because you are such a stuck-up cow!'

The slap came as such a shock, Kate was speechless. Lillian had crossed the distance between them in one stride and hit Kate so hard across the face it stung. She put her hand to her cheek and stared incredulously at Lillian.

'What on earth is goin' on in here?'

They both turned. Beau, with Austina in his arms, stood at the threshold of the door.

Kate removed her hand from her cheek and knew from his expression it was inflamed. 'Maybe ask your wife,' she said as she walked past him.

CHAPTER 14

*K*ate hurried along the corridor, her hand to her hot cheek, blinded by tears. She couldn't put up with Lillian any more. This was all too hard. Her mother was gone, her father was distracted, and the whole thing seemed just too much to cope with. Maybe coming back here had been a terrible mistake.

As she entered the passageway that linked the downstairs with the main house, she bumped into Eve.

'Oh, Kate, I was looking for you. That rooster won't be pecking anyone else.' She chuckled. 'Listen, is it all right if we bring Isaac here? Once he finishes his time in that awful place, we thought he could get a start here.'

'Who is Isaac?' Kate asked.

'Bartley's brother?' Eve answered, sounding surprised that Kate had forgotten. 'He's due to finish his sentence at the weekend. The governor was very nice, and we told him that we'd be looking out for him from now on.'

Kate looked at Eve. She did not need this now. 'But is he staying here? At Robinswood?' she asked.

'If that's all right with you and Sam?' Eve looked oddly at her sister.

'We want to take him on, just like the students, train him up a bit. He's not had much of a start, but he's a good lad...'

After the strain of everything else, it was too much for Kate. 'Look, Eve, I know he's your husband's brother, but you can't actually say he's a good lad because you don't know him and he's just about to get out of prison. I'm sorry, but I don't think this place is a good idea. We don't know anything about him except that he's a criminal of some kind and –'

'Kate!' Eve exclaimed. 'That's not fair. Mark was in prison, if you remember, and Daddy and Oskar don't exactly have snow-white pasts, but you're going to judge this boy and not give him a chance?'

'Look, Eve, I'm not judging him, but I have children to consider, and the guests and the other students! I don't know this person from Adam, and neither do either of you!' Kate was furious now.

'You are being ridiculous! You've not even met him, and already you're judging him. I can't believe you sometimes, Kate, I really can't,' Eve snapped.

'Really? So me and Sam giving you all homes and jobs here isn't enough for you, is it?' Kate replied. 'You think you can just drag any old waifs and strays you find here in on top of us without even a word?'

'Oh, that's how it is, is it? We are all here at the favour of Her Lady-ship? Would you listen to yourself for a minute, Kate, and you might realise what a cow you are being! I didn't realise we're all to be so grateful for all you and Sam do for us lowly servants. Why, thank you very much, m'lady,' Eve said, her voice dripping in sarcasm and fury.

Kate stopped and looked at her sister, the woman she admired so much. Bad enough to be fighting with that stuck-up madam upstairs, but she couldn't fight with Eve. She was tired and upset, but this was stupid. 'I'm sorry, Eve. Of course bring him. I'm just... Look, it doesn't matter. Bring him, it will be fine.' She exhaled.

'Kate, what's wrong?' Eve too had forgotten her anger and now was concerned.

'Oh nothing, everything... Don't mind me. I'm grand.' Kate gave a weak smile and went to move on towards the kitchen.

127

'You're not grand.' Eve held her arm. 'Talk to me.'

Kate leaned against the cool stone wall of the passageway, resting her head against it and closing her eyes. 'I just had a massive fight with Lillian. She said some things, then I reacted – you know the way I am – and then she hit me and Beau walked in. Look, it's a mess. And then I met you, and well, it was just a case of wrong place, wrong time.'

'She hit you?' Eve was incredulous.

'Yes, but look, let's just move on. They'll be in for lunch soon.' Kate forced herself to leave the cool wall and face the daily grind. Eve let her go.

* * *

A WEEK LATER, Aisling tried to coax her sister out of her black mood. Kate suspected the hand of Eve. She knew Kate was really upset by everything that had happened, so had probably discussed it with Ais, and now this was the result.

'Come on, Kate. Mark will drive us in the new jeep. He's training tonight over at the pitch anyway, so he'll go for a lemonade to the pub with the lads after hurling and bring us back again. You need a break.'

Sam had managed to procure an ex-military jeep from an old RAF friend, and it was ideal for driving over farmland. It rattled the bones but did the job.

'I'm not in the form, Ais. Between that dragon upstairs and the letter from Mam, I couldn't concentrate on a film anyway.' Kate took a clothes peg from the bag between them as they hung the sheets on the line.

'Well, you can do no more where Lillian is concerned. She knows which side her bread is buttered, so she'll just have to let it go and so should you,' Aisling said, ever the voice of wisdom.

'Yeah, I know, but Mam?' Kate looked at her. 'If she's saying the doctors are not that happy with her, you may be sure she's made that sound better than the reality.' Kate finally aired what they had all been thinking.

'I'm worried sick too,' Aisling finally admitted. 'She wrote to me and to Eve as well, and though the rest of the letter was different, the sentence about her health was identical in all three. She obviously decided what she was going to say and said the exact same to all of us.'

'Did she say anything to Daddy, do you think?' Kate asked.

'I don't know. Should we bring it up? She says she doesn't want him over there, but she's so lonely, and if the diagnosis isn't good...' Aisling didn't want to finish the sentence.

'I feel like I want to go over there, or bring her back here or something. It's so hard just sitting by.' Kate's eyes filled with tears. 'What if she dies, Ais?'

'We can't think like that,' Aisling said, barely audibly.

'We might have to.' Kate wiped her eyes with the sleeve of her cardigan. 'And I think we need to talk to Daddy, the three of us, just sit down and talk it out. He might know more. He's her next of kin, and maybe they tell him things she won't tell us.'

'All right, we'll do it when Eve gets back from Tipperary. They are picking Bartley's brother up today from that place he's locked up at. I wonder what he'll be like? I hope she'll be all right.'

'Well, I don't think they let civilians wander among the general prison population, let alone heavily pregnant ones.' Kate smiled. 'She'll be fine. Sam said that Bartley decided yesterday he didn't want her to go, thought it might be too much for her, but she insisted.'

'I suppose she knows how much having at least one member of his family back in his life means to Bartley.' Kate lifted another heavy sheet from the basket and glanced at Aisling. 'So how's the morning sickness now?' Her sister had been a sickly shade of grey that morning.

'Subsiding, though I don't know why they call it morning sickness – it lasts most of the day.' She shook her head. 'But I'm not complaining. I just miss Mam.'

'Mam will see this baby. She will, Ais. We need her, and she's as strong as an ox, you know she is.' Kate wondered who she was trying to convince.

'I hope you're right. I lie awake at night, just thinking about her all the way over there, and sick and not getting better, and how it will be if...'

'Stop, Ais. We are only driving ourselves daft thinking like this. I was wondering, could we get the telephone number of that doctor, you know, Perry's godson, and talk to him ourselves?'

'I doubt he'd talk to us, only Daddy, I'd say. Maybe he has spoken to the doctors and didn't say anything to us. Especially with me and Eve expecting, he wouldn't want us upset.'

'Maybe. Look, you're right, we'll wait till Eve gets back. She said they might come back tonight, or tomorrow if it got too late. Bartley was worried we'd need the car, but we have that old wreck of a jeep. Though I think it's only fit for scrap, I suppose it does the job, just about. We'll sit down then, the four of us.' Kate tried to sound more upbeat than she felt.

'So will we go to the pictures?' Aisling was persistent. 'We've no guests for dinner, and that hardly ever happens, and we could do with something to cheer us up. Remember how we used to go to the pictures all the time in London?'

'And you think *In a Lonely Place* is the picture to cheer us up?' Kate asked.

'It's meant to be brilliant, and Humphrey Bogart is in it...' Aisling knew Kate had a soft spot for Bogie.

'He's old enough to be my father, but there's something about him.'

'Well, will we go so?' Aisling was persistent.

'Fine.' Kate gave in. 'I'll have to get Sam to put the kids to bed, but yes, Aisling, let's hit the high spot of Kilthomand.'

* * *

THE CINEMA WAS full despite the fact that the picture had been running for two weeks. Aisling and Kate took their seats, ushered in by none other than one of the dreaded Conlans. The young woman looked sour as she shone her torch to show them to their seats.

The picture was great. As the lights came up for the interval, Aisling needed the bathroom.

'Again? You only went as we were coming in?' Kate grinned.

'I don't know why, but I seem to spend my life in there these days,' Aisling grumbled as she squeezed past Kate's legs.

'Will I come?' Kate asked.

'No, no...stay and get us an ice cream,' Aisling insisted. The grouchy usherette was coming down the aisle with her tray of ice cream around her neck.

Aisling made her way towards the bathrooms, but the line was so long for the one toilet, she feared she might have an accident. Hopping from one leg to the other, trying her best to hold it, she waited in agony as each person took their turn. Nobody outside of the family knew she was pregnant yet, so she couldn't ask to skip the queue. Eventually, realising she was at least ten people behind, she made a decision. She slipped out the side and ran across the road to the parish hall. There were toilets at the back of the hall; she thought she'd run over, use them and run back.

The street was deserted, and the only lights were from the cinema and Maher's pub on the other side of the square. The hall was in darkness; she figured the Thursday night Legion of Mary meeting must be over.

She walked quickly around the back of the building and pushed the door of the ladies; it was open thankfully. She went to the toilet, ran her hands under the cold tap and wiped them on her skirt. Once outside again, she realised it was dark, but summertime dark, which was never quite pitch black. As her eyes adjusted to the gloom behind the hall, she heard a movement to her right. She spun around – who would be lurking? She shuddered. Maybe it was a rat. She was almost at the back corner of the building when a man, about her height and with a slight build, appeared in front of her.

'Sean!' she exclaimed. 'You nearly gave me a heart attack.'

Sean Lacey stood foursquare in front of her, barring her way. He was holding his shop's famous cashbox to his chest. He took it home every night to count his takings.

What was he doing there? She had not had any proper conversation with him in years, and she wasn't about to have one now. She just wanted to get back to Kate. 'Let me by, please,' she said with as much confidence in her tone as she could muster.

'Aisling Murphy commands me to move, I better do it so,' he said, a sneer in his voice. She smelled whiskey fumes. She'd heard he had become a heavy drinker, but he wouldn't drink to excess in the local pub, choosing instead to drink whiskey in the office over the shop while counting his money. Despite his words, he made no effort to move.

'Sean, I need to get back to Kate...' She tried to push past him, but he wouldn't let her.

'Kate, is it? The sanctimonious Lady Kenefick, looking down her nose at all of us and we all knowing what she came out of?'

Aisling realised he was drunk but not staggering. She suddenly felt afraid. 'Let me pass, Sean. My husband is in there, and if I don't get back, he'll –' she tried again.

'Your *husband*. That English criminal you married is not inside in the pictures – he's over in Maher's with the hurling team.' His face was closer to hers now, his breath making her nauseous.

'Well, he's picking us up, and the film will be over shortly.' Aisling tried to think. There was no way out the other side; the pathway around the back of the hall was overgrown with brambles since Danny Canty, who'd always cut it, was collared by Mrs Moriarty to attend her Legion of Mary meetings. Danny was a confirmed communist, the only one in Kilthomand, and though he had the courage of his convictions with anyone else, he realised his Marxist zeal was no match for Mrs Moriarty's dogged Catholic dedication, and so he gave the hall and anywhere she was likely to be a wide berth.

'It won't,' Sean said, moving closer, placing his cashbox on the ground and putting his arms around Aisling's waist.

For a second she was in shock, but then she tried to push him away. She struggled as he kissed her neck, his bristly chin rough against her skin.

'Come on, Ais,' he muttered. 'You know you want to. What was all that smiling at me and waving about the other day? Or are you just one of those women who likes to tease men? Is that what you are, Aisling Murphy?' She felt his hands roaming all over her back.

'Sean, let go of me this instant!' She tried to scream, but he clamped his mouth on hers. One hand held her head, the other had a vice-like grip on her waist. She tried to wriggle free, moving her head and pushing against his chest with her hands. But he was too strong for her. He shoved her, pinning her against the wall, and whispered in her ear, 'Your husband thought he could make a fool of me, thought he won the great prize of Aisling Murphy. Oh, he was the big man in Maher's tonight all right, but where is he now, Aisling?' His voice was raspy, his breath hot and sticky against her face.

'You made a show of me in this very hall, you and your sister, but I'm willing to forgive that because you and me were meant to be, Aisling. You should be with me, not that Englishman who thinks he can insult me in my own place in front of my own people!'

'Please, Sean, stop. I'm pregnant!' Aisling cried.

Sean's face twisted grotesquely.

'Sean, I...' She tried to protest, but he punched her in the stomach, so hard it winded her.

'Shut up,' he snarled.

Before she had time to realise what was happening, Sean pulled both sides of her blouse, exposing her. He grabbed at her bra with such force that he pulled it off and then roughly grabbed her breasts with his hands. His body was pressing hard against her. All she could think about was screaming, but no sound came. Her baby, she had to protect her baby!

She lifted her knee, managing to kick him in the groin. Instantly, he released her as he doubled over in pain. She used the moment to run along the back of the hall, away from Sean, but before she could get to the corner, he caught up with her, grunting, and grabbed her skirt. She heard it rip. Down, down... She felt herself falling on the rough gravel underfoot. Her face was pinned to the ground, his hand pushing her head. She felt something trickle down her face...tears, blood maybe...she didn't know. She only knew she had to get up, get away.

She rolled over, facing him now as he leered over her, a horrible smile on his face. She remembered the training she had received in the WAAF and immediately went for his eyes. Digging her nails into his eye sockets, she kicked him once more in the crotch, and as he howled, she dragged herself out from under him and ran blindly into the square.

She needed to find Kate. Her clothes were torn, and her face stung from where he'd forced her onto the gravel. She couldn't bear anyone to see her like this, she thought frantically as she tried to pull her torn and dirty clothes into position. It was pointless.

Mark. *He mustn't know.* If she told him what Sean had done, he'd surely kill him. Her darling gentle husband had a dark side – she knew he had, the war had seen to that – and though it was under control for almost three years now, she could not risk it. She'd have to get home some way, get cleaned up, hope nobody noticed. She couldn't stand anyone to know. Her father, her poor mother in a hospital in Switzerland… She couldn't bear their looks of horror and pity.

What could she do? She'd walk home. That seemed the only option. She placed her hands over her belly, whispering frantically to her unborn child, 'Don't worry, darling, don't worry. We'll be fine. We'll get home and have a bath, and we'll be fine. Please just stay where you are, please…' Tears were streaming down her face as she left the village behind and began the two-mile walk to Robinswood.

A car's headlights terrified her. Was he back? Had Sean Lacey got his car and followed her? She wondered if she should jump into the ditch before he saw her, but it was too late – the vehicle was pulling up beside her.

'Aisling, what in the name of God?' Eve jumped out, running to her sister. Bartley soon was beside her. 'What happened, Ais?' Eve held her sister's face, but Aisling couldn't speak.

'Sean… He had his cashbox…' Aisling knew she was incoherent, but her thoughts were a jumble.

'OK, get in. Let's just get home.' Eve bundled her into the back seat where, to her surprise, there was already a young man. He got out and had a word with Bartley before walking away, allowing Eve in beside Aisling. She was mortified. Her clothes were in tatters, and she pulled what was left of her blouse over her bruised body.

'Shh, Ais, it's all right, we'll sort this out,' Eve soothed, catching Bartley's eye in the rear-view mirror.

Bartley drove at speed. He dropped Eve and Aisling at the cottage, and after a quick exchange with Eve in which she instructed him to get the doctor and insisted they would be fine, he drove away.

Eve opened the cottage door. Nobody was there. She led her sister upstairs, not saying a word, and ran a bath. As she helped her out of her clothes, she asked quietly, 'Who did this to you, Ais?'

Aisling could barely get the words out. 'Sean Lacey. He was so calm, Eve. He'd been drinking but had his cashbox with him, the week's takings, like it was just the most normal thing in the world. And he just put it down, and he...' She couldn't say the words.

Eve's face was set in a grim line. 'Did he rape you?' she asked.

'No, I got away, but he wanted to. I kicked him and scratched his eyes, but... I told him about the baby, and he punched me in the stomach...' Hot salty tears stung the cuts on her face.

CHAPTER 15

*H*alf an hour later, Aisling was in bed, shivering despite
the tea and hot water bottle at her feet. She'd allowed
Eve to bathe her and dress her in a clean nightdress, but she could not
stop thinking about what had happened.

She'd managed to recount to Eve how it had come about that she
was behind the hall and everything that followed. It came out in
bursts, and then she would stop – was it a nightmare?

'What if he hurt my baby?' she'd asked her sister.

'We'll get Dr Grahame here as soon as Bartley gets back. I sent him
to find Mark and Kate and bring the doctor.'

'No!' Aisling almost screamed. 'We can't tell Mark! He'll go after
him, I know he will! He'll kill him and then hang for murder...'

'Ais, we have to tell him. You'll have to tell the guards and Dr
Grahame. Mark won't do anything stupid – we won't let him even if
he wanted to. Bartley and Beau and Sam will keep an eye on him.'

'I don't want anyone to know,' she sobbed. 'I'm so ashamed...'

'You have nothing to be ashamed of.' Eve put her hands on
Aisling's shoulders, and her green eyes blazed with intensity. 'You did
nothing wrong! It was him, that animal. If anyone should hang, it
should be Sean Lacey.'

Aisling gripped Eve's hand as they heard a car pull up outside. Eve pulled back the curtain.

'It's all right, it's just Bartley back. Mark and Kate are with him. It's all right.' Eve soothed her sister.

Aisling heard heavy boots take the stairs two at a time. Mark burst into the bedroom. He stood in the doorway, his huge bulk almost filling the space. 'Ais, what happened? Oh, my darling girl, your face! What happened?' Mark's expression was anguished as he crossed the room and knelt beside the bed.

Eve withdrew, allowing them some privacy. Downstairs, she filled Bartley and Kate in on what Aisling had told her.

'Oh my God, poor Ais! I should have gone with her... I offered to, but she wanted ice cream, so I got it. But the film began again and she wasn't back. One of the Conlans is the usher there, and I just thought Ais came back late and she wouldn't let her back into her seat. You know the way she is sometimes...' Kate was distraught. She felt responsible.

'You couldn't have known, Kate,' Bartley said quietly.

'But if I'd have gone with her...' She stopped, as if suddenly realising that a crime had been committed. 'We'll have to get the guards. We can telephone Sergeant O'Connell from the house. I'll go now...' She stood up. She needed to get out, get some air. She wanted to find Sam.

'Let's wait until Aisling's had a night's sleep. She was adamant that she doesn't want the authorities involved,' Eve said.

'But that's ridiculous! That monster needs to be arrested now! What if he absconds?' Kate was flabbergasted that Eve would even consider not reporting it.

'He won't go anywhere.' Bartley was certain. 'He'll deny everything and keep his house and business. He's probably banking on Aisling being too ashamed to tell. Look, I left a message with the doctor's wife. He was on a sick call, but she said he'll come here as soon as he can. I just think we should let Aisling and Mark decide what they want to do next. It's up to them.'

'But Dr Grahame is bound to tell the guards,' Kate reasoned.

'Look, we'll take this one step at a time. It's up to Aisling what she wants to do,' Eve said. She exhaled; her baby was kicking like crazy now.

Bartley saw she was struggling. 'Come on, sit down. You need to put those feet up.' He led her to the couch in Aisling and Mark's small living room.

'Where did you put Isaac?' she asked as he put some cushions on the seat before she sat down.

'I left him out when we picked Ais up. He's walking to Robinswood. He'll be fine,' Bartley said, soothing her.

'You think... Aargh!' Suddenly Eve doubled over, pain twisting her face.

Kate and Bartley stood there, frozen.

'Bartley,' she gasped, 'the baby...' A small puddle of liquid formed between her feet. 'The baby is coming...'

'Oh, Eve... Oh my God... Oh no... What should we do?' Kate was wild-eyed. She stood helplessly before her sister, horrified, as Eve leaned on Bartley for support.

'I want to be in my own bed...' Eve said, as the pain subsided only to rise again.

'OK, Eve, then that's where you'll be. Can you walk to the car if Kate and I help?' Bartley gazed into her eyes. She nodded.

Kate took one arm and Bartley the other, and they helped her out.

'Will I get Doctor Grahame? Or will I bring him here to Aisling first and then...' Kate was in such distress now, she could hardly think straight.

'No. I'll be fine with Bartley. He knows...' Another wave hit Eve and she had to stop and lean on them.

'Oh, Eve... Are you sure I can't do anything, send someone?' Kate asked as she helped Eve into the front seat of the car.

'We'll be fine, and Sam and Beau are above at the house if we need anyone. I'll send Sam down to you.' Bartley gave her a smile. 'You just take care of Aisling.' He led her away a little from the car as he went round to the driver's side. 'And don't let Mark out of your sight, Kate. If he goes after this Sean Lacey, it will end badly, so for his and for Aisling's sake, keep him here. Hopefully the doctor will be here soon.'

Kate nodded. Bartley was absolutely right. Mark could kill Sean Lacey if he got his hands on him. 'And you can look after Eve?' she asked dubiously. Bartley was a man of many skills, but childbirth was normally the domain of women and their doctors.

'I can. I've been with lots of women as they birthed. Traveller women give birth in their wagons, and it was considered lucky to have me there. I know what I'm doing, Kate, but if you want to, send Dr Grahame up to check on us after he's seen Aisling. We'll be fine. It's her first, so it takes a bit longer. We'll hopefully have good news in the morning. Just mind Ais and Mark. I'll tell Sam when I get back.'

'OK. Take care of my sister. And don't say anything to Daddy about Aisling for now. I'll speak to him in the morning. He's got enough to worry about.'

'Don't worry.' He gave her a one-armed squeeze and jumped into the car.

'I love you, Eve,' Kate whispered as they drove away.

Upstairs, Aisling and Mark were still in the bedroom, the door closed. She wondered what she should do. She felt like she should get the guards, have them arrest Sean Lacey – at least he'd be safe from Mark doing something stupid. She could understand if Mark wanted to kill him; she would happily choke him with her own bare hands for what he had done. She had never liked him, even years ago when he and Aisling were close. Kate used to tease her about him being such a mammy's boy. He was an only child and his father was dead years, so his mother had doted on him. He inherited the shop and one of the biggest houses on the square in the village, and he thought that made him something. He broke Aisling's heart when he cheated on her. She couldn't listen to the whispering and the gossip, so she went with Kate to London. How their lives had worked out, so differently from the paths they could have gone. Kate loved both her sisters equally, but those war years with Aisling in the WAAF created a bond between them that could never be broken.

Sean Lacey always knew he'd lost a prize in Aisling. When he tried to end her marriage to Mark by feeding him a pack of lies a few years ago, he'd almost succeeded – but he had failed again. This though... She knew he was a slimy little toad with an overinflated opinion of himself, but this?

She didn't doubt Aisling, not for one second, but they'd known Sean Lacey all their lives. He had sat beside Eve in second class, they made their first communions together, they went to the same dances, everything. How could he do that to Aisling?

She made a cup of tea that she didn't drink and sat in the little kitchen. It was 3 a.m. now, and she wondered if Mark and Aisling had fallen asleep. It was quiet up there.

The silence of the night was interrupted by the sound of a car. She looked out; it was Dr Grahame. As the elderly GP got out of his car, she saw Sam running down the lane towards the cottage. They both arrived at the same time, and Sam gave her a hug as she let them in.

'What happened, Kate?' the doctor asked. She tried to stay calm, but this man had fixed every sore throat, broken bone and infection that she or her sisters had ever had. Now he had to attend to poor Aisling.

As quickly as she could, she told him what had happened. His old face was grim as she recounted Aisling's ordeal.

'And you've contacted the guards, I assume?' he asked.

He would have been Sean Lacey's doctor as well, and his mother's before him. It struck Kate how it must be awkward to be a country GP knowing everyone's private business. She felt a wave of sympathy for the old man who'd looked after Aisling when she got the measles, or when she fell off the cranky donkey and was concussed.

'Not yet. Aisling didn't want to...' Kate didn't know what else to say.

'Right. She's upstairs?' he asked.

Kate nodded. 'Mark is with her.'

'Fine, I'll go up to her so.'

They watched him ascend the little staircase, and Sam drew her into his arms. He said nothing but held her tightly and kissed the top of her head.

'How's Eve?' she asked.

'She's fine. She was cracking a joke with me as we brought her into the house. I alerted Beau about what was going on, so he'll stay up, listen out for the children and be there if Bartley needs anything. But for a man about to become a father, Bartley seemed really calm. Rather him than me.' He gave a weak smile.

Sam had paced the streets of Cork while she had given birth to the twins in a private nursing home. He had no idea the time she'd had, being presented instead with two little bundles. She was going to tell him, give him a blow-by-blow account of how gruesome it all was, but what good would it have done? She smiled at his blissful ignorance.

'The travellers think it's good luck to have Bartley at a birth, being a seventh son and all of that,' Kate explained, 'so he's been at loads of them and helped out too as he got older. She'll be fine, I think. It's Ais... Oh, Sam... Poor Ais. She's so gentle, and for him to do that to her, I can't... Picturing her, on the ground, in the dark, it's like a horrible film playing over and over in my head. I should have gone with her... And she must be out of her mind with worry about the baby and everything. I just...' She could hardly express the combination of emotions that were threatening to engulf her.

'Shh.' Sam soothed her. 'You weren't to know. Nothing ever happens in Kilthomand, so of course you could never have expected anything like this. I do think we need to get the guards though, Kate. A terrible crime has been committed. I know Ais doesn't want to make statements and all of that, but he can't just get away with it.'

'I know, and she'll realise that too, but let's just give her time. Calling the guards now or in the morning won't make much difference.' She was struggling to make sense of it all. 'I would never have had him down as capable of this. I mean, I don't like him, never did. Even as children, there was something about him. But I...I just can't believe he would do that to Aisling. He loved her.' Kate was still trying to process what had happened.

'Well, they say there's a thin line between love and hate. And he openly despises Mark. I heard down at the mart that apparently Lacey tried to use his influence with the GAA as the local sponsor to get

Mark dropped from the team, but the only reason Kilthomand are as far as they are in the championship is because they have Mark. Who'd have thought an English lad would be lining out for Kilthomand in a hurling match? Everyone in the whole parish loves him because of it, so apparently the committee laughed Lacey out of the meeting. He didn't like it one bit.'

Their conversation was interrupted by the return of Dr Grahame. They both looked at him expectantly.

He looked grave and thought for a moment before he spoke. 'She's bleeding a little, and there is nothing else I can do at this stage. We'll have to hope that complete bedrest can save the pregnancy.'

'No!' Kate exclaimed. 'Please, Dr Grahame, Sam can drive her to hospital, or to Dublin even...'

'I'm so sorry, Kate. This is dreadful, really... I can't believe it happened. But her injuries are minor, a few cuts and bruises, and as I say, it's a case of just wait and see with the baby. Moving her anywhere wouldn't change a thing – if it would, I'd bring her in myself. She's sleeping now. I gave her something for pain and to make her drowsy.'

'Have you told her and Mark?' Sam asked quietly.

'Well, I told Aisling. Mark left as soon as I arrived to let me examine her. I assumed he was here with you.'

Kate felt a wave of panic. They'd not seen Mark since he and Kate arrived back. He must have slipped out the back when she was outside talking to Sam. She knew the murderous rage he must feel, but Aisling did not need a husband behind bars or worse. Bartley had warned her to keep him in her sights, and now he was gone.

'I'll go,' Sam said immediately. He knew exactly what Kate was thinking.

'Do you want a cup of tea, Dr Grahame?' Kate asked weakly as soon as Sam had gone.

'Thanks. I will if you don't mind.' He sat down wearily.

'Thanks for coming out,' she said, filling the kettle.

'Sure, Kate. Aren't I minding you since you were in your mother's womb? I delivered all three of you. I know Aisling's been going into

Dungarvan to the young woman there to help with the fertility, and she's right to. Women need other women for this sort of thing. With the best will in the world, I tend to say the wrong thing. I delivered Sean Lacey too,' he added with a deep sigh.

'How could he have done that to her?' Kate asked, placing a mug and milk and sugar on the table. She found some porter cake in the tin and cut him a slice.

'I don't know, but I'll tell you this. If she reports this crime – and he should answer for it, don't get me wrong – the whole place will have it, and you know this place for gossip.' He poured himself a mug of tea from the teapot she had placed on the table in front of him. The tea cosy was one that Aisling had knitted as a birthday present for Mammy when they were children, and Isabella had given it back to Aisling as a present when she and Mark moved into the cottage. It was all holes and dropped stitches, as Ais was only about eight when she made it, but it was much loved.

'I know. Mrs O'Connell could not be married to anyone better from the point of view of information,' Kate said darkly. Though the local sergeant was a quiet and honourable man, Frankie O'Connell's wife saw no issue around confidentiality. He told her as little as he could, but she was such an old gasbag, she managed to usually put two and two together, often making seven.

'Well, exactly. Now, I will testify to what I saw here tonight, don't worry about that, but I've been involved with cases before, and, Kate, I hate to say it, but it's very hard on the women. Lacey has plenty of money, and he'll get himself a fine lawyer up in Dublin who'll argue black is white and that either it wasn't him at all or it was consensual. Either way – and this is so wrong but it's how it is – the victim is nearly the one on trial.'

Kate exploded. 'What? But that's not right! Are you saying you think he'd get away with it even if we did go to the guards?'

'From my experience, yes, and on top of that, Aisling would be dragged through the ordeal of a trial, having already gone through this.' He ran his hands through his thick head of grey hair. 'I'm not going to tell any of you what to do, Kate, but I'm just giving you the benefit of my experience. If she was my daughter, I wouldn't, sickening as that is. It would only pile more misery on the girl, and I'd be very surprised if he served even one day.'

Kate felt deflated. All the furious indignation was gone. She knew Dr Grahame was probably right, and Aisling had endured enough. Dawn was streaking across the sky as the doctor finished his tea and stood up to leave.

'It feels like our world is coming apart at the seams. First Mammy and now this. I don't know how much more we can take...' She exhaled a ragged breath. 'Mammy wrote to me and the girls saying that the doctors aren't that pleased with her progress, and that they don't see her coming home any time soon.'

The doctor placed a hand on her shoulder and looked down into her face. He was a bear of a man, and age had not diminished his size. He had a grey beard to match his mane of hair, and she could see the deep lines around his eyes and mouth.

'TB is a killer, Kate. Your mother is in a great clinic, to be sure, and she's in a much better position than most around here, I can tell you, and if anyone can restore her to health, it will be them. But the thing is, a cure, like a medical cure, a drug that will kill the bloody thing, is still in the future.'

'We can't lose her. None of us, Daddy... We just can't!' She felt the hot tears prick the back of her eyes again.

Dr Grahame looked down at her, his kind eyes having seen it all before. 'Nobody can, Kate, that's the trouble. This new minister Noël Browne is on the right track though, getting rid of the stigma. For the love of God, anyone can get it, but people are ashamed and don't want to call the doctor for fear the neighbours might find out. At least if people weren't afraid to come forward early on, when there's some chance of catching it...'

'Did we catch Mammy's in time, do you think?' she asked, knowing he couldn't give her the answer she wanted to hear.

'I'm only a doctor, Kate. That's a question for the man upstairs.' He patted her shoulder and left.

She crept up the stairs, opening her sister's bedroom door as quietly as she could so as not to disturb her. Aisling was curled up in a ball, her eyes closed. Kate saw her dark hair spread out across the pillow, and she could see the bruising and cuts on her face. She pulled the curtains closed so the morning light would not wake her and gathered the torn and ragged clothes from the floor. Ais needed to sleep now, and they would deal with whatever was coming in the morning. She tiptoed out, pulling the door closed behind her.

She wished she knew what was happening. Hopefully Sam had found Mark before he got to Sean Lacey. Daddy was sleeping in the farmhouse on the other side of the estate, totally unaware of the horror of the evening before. If they followed Dr Grahame's advice and didn't report, maybe Aisling would rather that her father didn't know. Because, whatever about Mark, if Dermot Murphy thought that anyone had hurt one of his daughters in any way, let alone like that, well, he wouldn't walk away scot-free, that was for sure.

She wondered if she should go back up to the house. Maybe Sam was there? No, she thought, he'd come and find her. He knew she'd be worried.

At least Beau was there with the children, though she would need to get back soon to get breakfast started. They had twelve guests and it was now 5:30 a.m. She didn't want to leave – what if Aisling woke and found herself all alone? How was it that life went on, even when the most horrible things happened?

CHAPTER 16

*A*isling woke from a horrible dream. She was running away from something, but it was gaining on her. She was afraid, it was dark...

The shaft of sunlight that came through the gap in the curtains fell across the bed. She was alone. She went to sit up, and everything hurt. Her mouth felt dry and she tasted something metallic.

What had happened? Then it came back, in pieces at first. She was at the pictures with Kate and Mark... No, Mark wasn't there, it was just Kate. She... Oh God, she remembered. She had needed to use the toilet, she had crossed to the hall, Sean... Wave after icy wave of recollection. She felt sick and vomited.

The sound must have alerted someone downstairs, as she heard feet on the landing.

'Ais, Ais, pet, I didn't realise you were awake. I was having a cleanup...' Mark appeared. He looked pale and shaken, and she noticed as he went to help her out of bed to the bathroom that there were cuts on his hands.

She was crying, the bed covered in the contents of her stomach. As she allowed him to help her out of bed, she felt something between her legs – a sanitary napkin. What was that doing there? She had a

146

hazy memory of Dr Grahame. He had given her something, an injection... She wished she could think straight.

Mark helped her to the side of the bed and took off her nightdress, his hands trembling. He was as upset as she was. How much did he know? Aisling found it hard to think. He got a clean garment from the drawer and gently put it over her head, then sat her on the chair as he stripped the sheets and blankets.

'The baby,' was all she managed, her hands on her abdomen as if by the gesture she could hold her child inside of her.

Mark turned to her, his face ashen. He dropped the sheets and came around to kneel before her. 'Dr Grahame said there was a little bleeding, but we are hoping it settles down. Some women do get that in early pregnancy and go on to be fine, so I'm sure that's what's going to happen, sweetheart. You just need to rest, and I really think everything is going to be all right.'

'What happened?' she asked as she lifted one of his hands. The knuckles were skinned.

'Nothing... Don't worry, Ais, nothing...' Mark was distraught.

'Mark, please, tell me...' she insisted. After all they had been through, she would never let him distance himself from her again, no matter how bad things were. 'Did you find Sean?'

His face told her all she needed to know. 'Tell me.' Her voice was lead.

'I swear, Ais, I just...' He stood and ran his hands through his tousled blonde hair. 'When I saw what he did to you, I...I know I shouldn't have, but I just... I saw red.'

'What did you do?' she asked, dreading his answer.

'I went down there, and there he was in his kitchen with his cashbox, counting his money as if nothing, so I beat him up. But Sam appeared. He saw I was gone and knew where to find me. Before I could do any damage, I swear, he pulled me off him, and the snivelling little weasel was crying, cuddling his moneybox when we left him.'

Relief that her husband wasn't going to be hanged for murder soon gave way to a torrent of other emotions. Fear, panic, disgust, denial and grief all jostled for position. She didn't know what to feel –

all of it, none of it? She was numb. It was as if she were drowning, so far away, falling deeper and deeper into the abyss. She opened her mouth but no sound came out.

She just looked at Mark, wanting him to say something, to make it all stop, to turn the clock back, but he was silent. It was true. Sean Lacey might have killed their baby. The cruelty of it took her breath away. They'd waited for so long, so many years, so many disappointments, month after month. Tests, doctors asking them questions about things that should have been only their business, but they endured it to have their baby. And then it happened. She hadn't believed it – she and Mark were going to have a child of their own. A little boy or girl, who would call them Mammy and Daddy, a little baby to nurse and wash and dress and hold. Aisling started to shiver violently. She felt her teeth chatter in her head, though she knew it wasn't cold.

Mark wrapped one of the blankets that had been spared when she threw up around her shoulders and continued stripping the bed. 'I'll have this ready in one minute, sweetheart. Kate had to go, as she had to do breakfast, but she said she'd be down immediately afterwards. She was managing it all on her own this morning. Well, I'm sure Beau and Sam will pitch in...' His tone was soothing, kind. She knew he was just trying to fill up the space, filling the empty hole with words to avoid having to look into it, see it for what it was.

'Where is Eve?' Her voice didn't sound like her; it was raspy.

'She...' Mark couldn't meet her eyes. Something else was wrong.

'Tell me,' she demanded now, her voice still hoarse. Panic was taking over the maelstrom of other emotions.

'She's fine. She...she went into labour last night. She's having her baby,' he finished.

'Is Doctor Grahame with her?' Aisling asked.

'I'm not sure, darling. Bartley is though, and last I heard, she was doing fine. I'm sure there will be news soon.'

Aisling just nodded.

Within a few minutes, Mark had the bed made up once more and the dirty laundry gathered and placed in the basket. He brought a basin of warm water and a flannel and washed her face, taking care not to press on her cuts and bruises. Then he brought her toothbrush and fresh water. When he'd brushed her hair, he helped her back into bed. Dr Grahame had left some pills and a note saying to take two when she woke, so Mark gave them to her with a fresh glass of water.

Her whole body hurt, everywhere, but it was nothing compared with the profound sadness.

'Will I get you a cup of tea, something to eat?' Mark asked helplessly.

Before she had time to reply, there was a loud knocking on the front door. Mark started as if the sound had startled him, and he stood frozen for a second before leaving to go downstairs.

Aisling heard male voices, two, maybe three. Mark and two others. Was it Eve? Had she had her baby? Surely there would be jubilant sounds by now if she had? Maybe they were keeping it low-key because of her. That was silly; Eve and her baby had nothing to do with this. She was happy for her sister, excited to meet her new niece or nephew.

The voices were still too low to be audible. Then Mark's voice, louder. 'You can't think...'

What was going on? Something was wrong. Was it bad news about Eve? Or about her mother? Aisling fought back the panic and pulled the blankets off. It hurt to move but she could manage. She took her dressing gown from the nail on the back of their bedroom door and pulled it on, shoved her feet into slippers and started down the stairs.

'This is ridiculous...' she heard Mark exclaim. 'He was fine when I left him. Sam Kenefick is a witness...'

As she opened the door, she saw three men as well as Mark. Sergeant O'Connell, another guard in uniform and a man in a suit. The uniformed guard was placing handcuffs on Mark.

'What's going on?' Aisling whispered, feeling dizzy and nauseous. The whole room was spinning.

The sergeant threw her a pitying look before saying, 'Mark Belitho, I am arresting you on suspicion of the murder of Sean Lacey.

You do not have to say anything, but anything you do say can be used as evidence.'

Mark struggled, but the two uniformed guards half led, half pushed him out the door of the cottage. She noticed there were two cars there.

'Mark!' Aisling screamed. 'What's going on? Sergeant O'Connell, please, tell me…why are you taking Mark away?'

The sergeant glanced at her but turned his attention back to Mark. 'Detective O'Rourke will explain, Aisling.'

She moved outside in the lane as Mark was put in the back of a car.

'Ais, I'll be back. I don't know what they're on about, I swear to you, Ais. I never killed him, I didn't…' The younger guard pushed Mark roughly and then sat beside him. Sergeant O'Connell drove away.

The man in the suit, over which he wore a tan trench coat, turned to her. 'Mrs Belitho, my name is Detective Inspector O'Rourke. I'll need to ask you some questions. Can we go back inside please?'

Aisling wanted to follow Mark and Sergeant O'Connell, to get an explanation from the man who'd been the policeman in Kilthomand for the last twenty years, not this man, who she'd never seen before. The car disappeared down the lane and she turned. 'What's this all about? Why have they taken my husband? Is Sean Lacey dead?'

'If we could just go inside?' He was soft-spoken but firm.

'Fine, but this is a mistake. You've made a mistake. Mark didn't….' The blood thundered in Aisling's ears. Sean Lacey was dead? How could that be?

She sat down at the kitchen table, and the detective stood by the sink.

'Mrs Belitho, can you tell me what happened last night?' His grey eyes never left her face, and she felt exposed, vulnerable. There was something about him that was deeply unsettling. He was over average height and stocky, with thinning brown hair brushed back from his face. His face was unlined, but there was a weariness to him or something. He took out a small leather-bound black notebook.

'What?' Aisling felt her face flush. Did they know? Should she say? Would it help or hurt Mark?

'Last night?' he prompted. 'What happened?'

She tried to think. Should she say Mark admitted to beating Sean up? That Sam saw it? What would be the best thing to say? The pills that Dr Grahame had left for her were still making her brain foggy. She remembered – she wished she didn't – but the whole thing was such a jumble of everything, and then getting back here and people coming and going.

'Mrs Belitho, a very serious crime has been committed. It would be most helpful if you could tell me in as much detail as possible your movements last night.' His voice had an edge of insistence now. She stood, her hand on the table for support, her body aching, and she tried to focus.

'Can we do this later on? I...I'm not well,' she said.

'Perhaps if you sat down? I could get you a drink, a cup of tea?' He was not going to just go.

'No... I need to go back to bed. Please, later...' She moved towards the stairs, not caring if it was rude. She didn't want to speak to this man. She needed someone from her family here; she needed to find out what was happening with Mark. If Sean was dead, then could Mark have done it? She prayed not, but she could not say with 100 percent certainty that he could not have done it.

Both she and the detective turned as the front door opened. The key was in the lock, and anyway, they never locked it. Aisling felt a wave of relief. 'Daddy,' she said.

Dermot crossed the floor in two paces and gently put his arms around her. She smelled the warm familiar scent of him and felt his broad chest, his strong arms, everything that signified comfort and safety for her and her sisters since they were born.

'Who are you?' Dermot asked bluntly.

'Detective Inspector O'Rourke. I need to speak to your daughter as a matter of urgency, so if you wouldn't mind...' He gestured with his hand that Dermot should leave.

Aisling felt her father stiffen.

'I will not be leaving,' he said, his voice like steel. 'Do you feel able to talk to this man, Ais?' he asked her, moving back slightly to look into her face.

'No...I...I just want to lie down,' she said. She needed time to figure this out.

'But I'm afraid it is imperative...' the detective began, infusing his voice with as much authority as he could muster in the face of the intimidating Dermot Murphy.

'What is *imperative*,' Dermot said, 'is that my daughter, who is, as you can see, injured, gets back to her bed. Now, unless you have a warrant for her arrest, I'd suggest you get off this property. She will speak to you when she is able, I will ensure that. You can see yourself out.'

Something in Dermot's tone made the younger man stop in his tracks. Perhaps he knew of Dermot's past, or had heard rumours, but either way, it seemed he was not going to defy him.

Aisling felt her father's arms around her as he led her upstairs without so much as a glance in the direction of the detective. They heard his car move off down the lane as Dermot settled her into the clean bed once more. Once she was resting back against the pillows, Dermot pulled the chair up beside the bed and held her hand. 'Tell me,' he said quietly.

'But what about Mark, Daddy? They took him... He went down to Sean last night, he hit him, but Sam arrived and pulled him off... Mark said Sean was crying when they left...' It was all she could think about.

Seeing he wasn't going to get anything out of her until he told her what he knew, Dermot spoke. 'Look, apparently Sean Lacey's body was found in his house this morning. Biddy Cronin does a bit of cleaning or something, and she let herself in and found him on the kitchen floor. He was dead a while by that time.' He paused and watched Aisling's face for a reaction, then went on. 'Your man O'Rourke is from Dublin, but Frankie O'Connell had the good sense to send one of the local lads to find me and tell me what's been going on.'

Aisling didn't know for certain, but she had a feeling Sergeant O'Connell was an old IRA comrade of her father's. 'Mark wouldn't have...' she began.

'Of course he didn't. And Sam is a witness. They can't charge him for this with no evidence. Ais, I know what Lacey did to you,' her father said quietly. 'Kate told me this morning. Don't be mad at her – she had to tell me and I had to know. You might be a grown woman, married and all of that, but you are my little girl and I...'

She heard the catch in her father's voice.

'But you know, Mark has a previous conviction. And he's English, and there are plenty around here who'd love to see an Englishman hang, no matter what the reason. My poor pet. I don't blame Mark one bit if he did do it, but he says he didn't and I believe him. But I might as well tell you they'll probably say he died of his injuries from the beating or something. Look, let's try not to get ahead of ourselves here. Let's see what they say and take it from there.'

'But what if they hang him?' Aisling's voice was strangled. This wasn't happening. It couldn't be. How could she have been merrily going to the pictures with Kate, Mark playing hurling, their baby growing happily inside her, and now this? *It can't be right. It must be a nightmare.* She would wake up any moment, and Mark would be sleeping beside her, his tousled head on the pillow, and he would turn and place his hand on her belly and cuddle her close. That's what would happen. She closed her eyes, willing herself to wake.

'It won't come to that, Ais. No, of course not. This is going to get solved.' Dermot was anxious to reassure his daughter.

'Am I dreaming this? This isn't really happening, is it?' she whispered, longing to hear him say it was just a nightmare.

'It is, pet. I'm sorry to say, it is happening.' Dermot's voice sounded heavy with sadness.

'I wish Mam were here,' she heard herself say. She missed her mother all the time, but now she especially needed her reassuring presence.

'You and me both, love, you and me both.' He rubbed her hair, and they sat together for a few moments, each lost in thought.

Then she remembered. 'Eve! I forgot, how could I? How is she?' She saw a smile pass over her father's face.

'She had a little girl, Bella, after your mam, and they are both fine.'

'Oh, that's great news. Something good happened tonight... She wasn't too small, was she, coming a bit early and everything?'

'I don't think so. I only got it from Beau. I met him as I was coming down here. I left as soon as I spoke to Kate...' He stroked her hair again. 'We'll sort this out, pet, I promise. And you'll be fine. And the baby will too, please God. I remember your mother got a bleed when she was expecting Kate and we got a right fright, but she took it easy after that, rested in bed for a week or so, and she and the baby were fine.'

Aisling longed to believe it. She placed her hands on her belly and prayed.

CHAPTER 17

*H*annah pushed the pram down the avenue, Poppy and Daisy walked behind, and Jack and Austina raced each other to the next tree ahead. Normally she just had the three little ones on the morning stroll as Jack and Austina were at school but they had a day off today so it was lovely to have them all.

They loved school, and though Kate and Lillian had been nervous sending them off, they were universally adored. Hannah often picked them up in the afternoons and to see them rush out, full of news and tales of their friends antics always made her smile.

She looked in on Bella, who was so tiny, so perfect. The young woman found it hard to keep her eyes off the child. She wondered how things would be if she'd been allowed to keep her baby. *Stop*, she told herself. *Do not think about it.* That's what the nun or whatever she was in the place they sent her to told her. The child wasn't hers, she should not think of her as hers, but if Laura wasn't Hannah's, whose was she?

She wasn't Damien's. Damien never even knew she existed. He'd only arrived at St Basil's the summer before, to work in the garden. He wasn't supposed to talk to any of the girls in the home, but he had spoken to her and they became close. He didn't mean to get her pregnant – they didn't really know how it happened. But being with him was nice. He was handsome, and at sixteen, he seemed so much older and wiser. He'd held her hand and hugged her. Nobody had ever done that before. She'd been abandoned and nobody had ever loved her before him.

But once the authorities saw the way she was, her belly getting bigger every day, they sent her off to that place, a horrible place with statues and nuns, and she'd had her baby. She wasn't even Catholic but that was the place for all girls in trouble it seemed. When she went back, Damien was gone and nobody knew where. She'd had no idea what was happening, and one of the nuns had to explain how she got into the situation and how her baby was going to be born. It was so frightening. And that place was awful. She'd had to wash sheets all day long until her hands were chapped and bleeding, and she'd had to pray and go to mass and beg forgiveness for her sins, the biggest of which was allowing Damien so close.

SHE HAD the memory of the day her baby was born burned on her brain. A little dark head, blue eyes, a tiny rosebud mouth. Her little Laura, and they took her away.

Nobody knew. Even the others in St Basil's. The lady that ran the place said it was better that way. She was told to say she was sent to work in a big house for a while. And then she came back. Not one person in her life knew she was a mother, that somewhere was a little girl – she'd be two now – her little daughter. She wouldn't be called Laura, as her parents would have given her a new name, but in Hannah's heart, she would always be Laura.

'Hello there! Is this heaven?'

Hannah was startled. A young man had sprung up from behind the hedge. She'd never seen him before, but she guessed right away he was Bartley's brother. She was in the house full time taking care of the little ones, so she didn't mix with the male students the way the other girls did. But at night in the dorms, she heard them talking about him.

He was beautiful. She felt her stomach lurch. Beautiful was a silly word for a boy, but this boy was that. He had a delicate bone structure, almond-shaped eyes ringed by thick black lashes and lips so red he might have been wearing lipstick.

'I...I'm sorry. I don't know what you mean,' she managed.

'Well, it must be because you're surely an angel.' He leapt the hedge and approached her, his hand extended. 'Isaac Doherty. I've been trying to find a way to meet you since I got here, and I knew you were beautiful from afar, but up close...what can I say? Wow.' He grinned and winked, and she giggled though she shouldn't encourage him, she knew.

'I'm Hannah Woods,' she said shyly, taking his hand.

He inhaled as if breathing in the essence of her. 'I knew it!' he announced triumphantly. 'I told my brother Bartley, she'll have a beautiful name. She'll have a name for an angel, and Hannah is perfect. As are you.' He smiled again and his eyes crinkled.

She blushed. Austina and Jack had come running back to see who she was talking to. All four of the children eyed the exchange with fascination.

'Hello.' Isaac went down on his hunkers and said, 'Have any of you found a farthing?'

Solemnly, they shook their heads.

'Really?' His brow furrowed. 'Have you looked in your ears?'

Austina giggled as Isaac put his hand behind her ear and extracted a shiny coin. Poppy and Daisy checked each other's ears, and Jack looked astounded.

'Do it again,' the twins demanded, delighted with this new game. 'I want money in my ears!'

'Now, children, we must be getting on, and Mr Doherty has work to do, I'm sure. Good day to you.' She nodded and tried to round up the children, but they were not having a bit of it. It was as if Isaac's dark eyes had entranced them; they were completely under his spell.

'Will I tell you a story?' he asked, his dark eyes twinkling with mischief.

'Yes, please,' Austina said, clearly mesmerised.

He sat on the bank. 'Gather round so. And have a seat.'

The children settled on the grass verge, gazing up at him and hanging on every word. Hannah too was captivated but tried not to show it.

'Did you know that my great-great-great-grandfather was the king of the travellers?'

The four little ones shook their heads, never taking their eyes off him.

'Well, he was. And his name was Dingo Doherty. He had hands as big as shovels and long curly hair that went all the way down his back. When he was a young buck like myself, he would fight any man in the whole of Ireland and beat them easily, but he didn't like to fight. No indeed. He would rather sing a song or make a rabbit stew. He was loved by everyone, but he had no wife. All the traveller girls wanted to marry him because he was so handsome and so strong, but he told his father and mother he wouldn't accept any of the girls they found for him. One by one, they were paraded before him, but he refused them all. The whole of Ireland was in tears over him, so they were, because he wouldn't choose. Every traveller girl in Ireland, the tall ones and the small ones, the skinny ones and the chubby ones, not one of them would do him.' He grinned. He obviously enjoyed the rapt attention of his audience.

'But then one day, he was working in a field. Farmers loved him too, you see, because he could lift cattle and pull a plough if the horse had a sore leg, he was that strong. Anyway, one day, he was working away, picking spuds, when he stood up to stretch, and what do you think he saw?'

They were spellbound.

'You can't guess?' he questioned, and they shook their heads once more. 'Right, I'll have to tell you so. He saw there, before his very eyes, the girl of his dreams. But she was no ordinary girl, oh no. No ordinary girl would do for Dingo. This girl was so special, so beautiful... She was like an angel.' His voice had dropped to a whisper.

'Tell us what she looked like,' Poppy demanded, excited..

'Well...' He looked directly at Hannah. 'She had golden hair that framed her face, and when she let it down, it fell almost all the way to her waist, like a lovely golden waterfall. She had hazel eyes that sometimes looked green and other times brown, and she had a smile that would melt an iceberg. Her front tooth was a tiny wee bit crooked, and when she laughed, all the little birds in the trees stopped building nests and came to sit on a nearby branch just to hear her.'

Hannah's cheeks flushed hotly. Her front tooth was crooked and she had blonde hair, but she was not a beauty the way Isaac described. She thought he must be teasing her.

'That sounds like you, Hannah,' Jack said excitedly.

'Does it now? Well, isn't that the most incredible thing?' Isaac pretended to be astounded but gave Hannah a small wink.

'What happened? Did they get married?' Austina asked, anxious that he go on.

'Well, the thing was, Dingo was the king of the travellers but he had no money. And this girl, the one he'd fallen in love with, well, he had nothing to offer her. She was a settled person, and she might not have wanted to have anything to do with a travelling man, especially one with empty pockets. He didn't say anything to her but vowed he would find a way to get a nice house and even a pony and trap and some money to buy her ribbons and petticoats and things ladies like. And then he would ask her father if he could marry her.'

He paused. The children waited expectantly for him to continue, but he remained silent, never taking his eyes off Hannah. She felt her stomach lurch; he was not like any boy she'd ever met. He was lithe and full of energy, and his dark eyes danced with merriment. His hair was so dark it was almost black, and a lock fell over his eyes in a curl. He looked like Clark Gable.

'What happened?' Daisy demanded.

'Well...' Isaac smiled slowly. 'That is the next part of the story, so you'll have to wait and see.'

The children groaned. 'When will you tell us the next part?' Austina asked.

'This day next week, if you all get the lovely Hannah here to this exact spot at this exact time, then I'll tell you the next bit of the story of Dingo and his angel. Now' – he leapt up – 'I must be getting on

159

because I have a brother called Bartley and he's a right slave driver, let me tell you, and if he finds me sitting down here gasbagging with you all, he'll hang me up by my ankles on the old bridge down there and make me catch an upside-down fish.'

The children giggled at the idea, and he tousled their hair. His eyes met Hannah's and held her gaze for a long moment. 'See you soon, Hannah Woods,' he said in a voice that was barely audible, and he hopped the hedge back into the field.

Hannah was flustered. She'd never met anyone like him before. Damien had been lovely, but quiet and shy like her. Isaac was so confident, so sure of himself. She pushed Bella in her pram down the avenue as the children ran ahead, all chat about Dingo and his huge hands.

She was seventeen; it had been her birthday yesterday. But she never said. Birthdays weren't really celebrated in St Basil's anyway. Most of the children there had no idea when their birthday was, but Hannah did. She knew her mother died in 1939, when Hannah was only six years old. Her mother had been a housekeeper in a fancy house, and Mrs Bonnington, who kept the records in St Basil's, told her that there did not appear to be anyone to care for Hannah and her brother Desmond so they arrived at the Protestant children's home. Her mother had visited and met Mrs Bonnington when she was very ill, inquiring about a place for her children. Hannah knew her mother had loved her.

She could remember her. There wasn't a photo or anything, but Hannah had an image of her in her mind, a bit like the angel Isaac had described. She wondered who her father was. Desmond didn't know either. She wondered how he was. She hoped he'd stay out of trouble now, he was a good person, but the world just wouldn't give him a chance. She could see how he and Isaac became friends, they were similar. Jokey and funny on the outside but genuine and sincere underneath.

The children threw pebbles in the little pond and tossed bread for the ducks, and soon it was time to bring them back for lunch. She normally would go back the quicker way through the orchard, but she decided today to retrace their steps, not even admitting to herself it was because she wanted to see Isaac again. She didn't, much to her disappointment.

As she entered the kitchen, she found Bartley and Kate in conversation.

'Ah, Hannah, great! You're back! Hello, my loves,' Kate said as her children ran to her and Bartley picked Bella up out of her pram.

The adoration in his eyes as he gazed at his infant daughter made Hannah sad. Had a man ever looked at her like that when she was a baby? Bella would want for nothing in her life; not only had she adoring parents but also this huge loving noisy extended family and this gorgeous home. She was a very lucky little girl.

'I'll bring her up to Eve. She'll want feeding now, I expect,' Bartley said, cradling the baby in the crook of his arm. Eve was recovering very well, and the baby was the most placid-tempered little person ever, but she had taken to turning day to night and wanted Eve to be up and sitting under her all night.

'Was she up again last night?' Kate asked with a smile.

'Aye, she was, and so was Eve. I offered to take her, but Eve said she could sleep during the day while I had all the students to watch over, so she took her to the sitting room. Poor Eve is exhausted, but she's such an adorable wee girl, we just stare at her sometimes.' Bartley was more animated than anyone had ever seen him. He was normally very quiet and sincere, but now he was positively chatty on the subject of his daughter.

'Well, maybe try to keep her awake during the day?' Kate suggested.

'We do, but she's a little fairy and just keeps dropping off. Your ma wrote and said we should strip her down a little, that we're making her too cosy and she won't sleep if she's not warm, but it seems too cruel so we can't do it.' He smiled.

'Don't mind Mammy, she couldn't do it either. She's soft as butter really,' Kate said, laughing. 'She had all of mine bundled up like little bugs in rugs. She wouldn't be able to keep her cold if she were here either.'

Hannah was serving the children their lunch of homemade vegetable soup and ham sandwiches as Kate drew Bartley away. 'Did she say anything in her letter about her own health?' she asked him quietly.

Bartley shook his head. 'Eve asked, but no.'

Kate sighed. 'We were thinking of going to ask Perry's godson directly, you know, but then everything with Aisling happened and...'

'How is Aisling doing?'

'Distraught. That's the only word. She experienced a horrible thing, her husband is in custody for murder, and if he's convicted he will hang. I...I don't know what to do for her, I really don't. Daddy is going to visit Mark later today – he's in Portlaoise Prison as you know. Only because Daddy knew someone and pulled a few strings was he able to get a visit.'

'And the baby?' Bartley's voice was low.

'So far, so good. Dr Grahame came up yesterday evening, and though it's early in the pregnancy, she hasn't had any more bleeding and she is still nauseous, so that's a good sign. He's made an appointment for her at the hospital for next Tuesday, so they might know more then.'

Bartley looked at her, one of his strange looks that still unnerved her slightly. It was hard to explain. Aisling had said she felt the same. They liked and trusted Bartley completely, but there was something otherworldly about him. Not creepy or dangerous or anything like that, but there was definitely something strange about the man.

'That's good news. I've some tea I make, so I'll drop it down. It helps with the nausea. On the subject of Mark, it's hard to know, isn't it?'

Kate, like everyone at Robinswood, desperately wanted Mark to be innocent, but it was looking very bad. He had a previous conviction, he'd served time for assault... Could the attack on his wife have precipitated a violent outburst?

'Sam and Mark both say he was alive when they left, but maybe something happened afterwards as a result... I don't know. I wish I'd have kept a closer eye on him. He slipped out when I was talking to Sam.'

'Look, we'll just have to wait and see. Poor Ais, my heart goes out to her. And to Mark. Has Sam given a statement?'

'Absolutely,' Kate confirmed, 'but he kind of got the impression that they thought he would say that. They see him as English as well even though he is from here, and he and Mark were in the RAF together and all of that.'

'The truth will come out, Kate. It always does in the end.' He smiled as Bella cooed in his arms.

*

CHAPTER 18

*B*eau stood in the huge room. His wife was in her usual spot by the window, reading a book. Conversation between them had been stilted for weeks, ever since he had walked in on her slapping Kate. They'd had an argument that night, their first real full-blown fight, and she had been very frosty with him since.

She took care of Austina when the little girl wasn't with Hannah, but apart from that remained aloof from everyone. Without ever discussing it, he slept in the small room with Austina now and she stayed alone in their large bed. He hated it, but he didn't know how to get through to her. She seemed so haughty and distant. She deeply resented being there, but he couldn't offer that they leave. He had very little money, though he saved every penny he earned from Sam. Lillian seemed to have a supply of money from her mother, or more likely Perry, but he didn't feel it was his place to ask.

He longed for the days when it felt like it was them against the world. He adored her then; he still did actually, because he could see this was just a shell. She was hurting, and when she felt like that, she grew a hard crust around herself and didn't let anyone in.

Austina had gone on a picnic with Hannah and the other children. It was wonderful to see her interacting with her cousins, and Hannah was lovely to them all. He couldn't bear the idea of people being mean to his daughter because of her mixed race, something that would surely happen if they left Robinswood. How could he do that to his darling child? But staying here was clearly taking its toll on Lillian. She felt unwelcome, she felt trapped, and now she was so closed off from him he had no idea how to reach her.

He had postponed his day to preach; it didn't feel right with everything else going on. Things were so hectic at Robinswood nowadays. Everyone worried about Isabella, who wasn't making the progress the doctors hoped she would. Poor Aisling had been attacked by that local guy, and then he was found dead and Mark probably did it. She was on doctor's orders to rest, so Kate was worn to a frazzle trying to do everything herself. Eve got out of bed and helped almost as soon as the baby was born, but she was overdoing it and the baby wasn't sleeping apparently.

He tried to help in the kitchen as much as he could while Sam and Dermot managed the farm with Bartley and his students, but it was relentless. Dermot desperately wanted to go to Switzerland to see Isabella, but he'd confided in Beau that Sam couldn't cope without him now that Mark was in Portlaoise Prison. News of the hotel was spreading far and wide, and despite the chaos behind the scenes, more and more people seemed to want to come and stay. They were already booked up for most of the rest of the year.

'Good mornin',' he said, and his wife looked up. She was thinner now than she used to be, and she seemed to wear some variation of a cream blouse and a cardigan with a dark-grey skirt and pearls every day. Her hair was tied up; he never saw it down any more. He used to love to run his hands through her hair as he kissed her, but now that all felt like a life that belonged to someone else. He'd barely touched her for weeks, and they'd not made love in months. He missed her like a physical ache. He knew nobody understood them – they were different in every conceivable way – but they never saw what he saw. They didn't know that underneath that hard shell was a gentle, unsure-of-herself woman, who had never really felt wanted. Sam was the precious one, the heir, so once their father had that, he was happy.

Violet doted on her son, and then he served his country so valiantly in the war, and everyone was so proud of him. Lillian was in his shadow always, raised for marriage to some aristocrat. She wasn't educated in anything useful, so she had no skills to navigate the world she was given. But she was brave and strong and fiercely loyal. She was kind and considerate and loved passionately. She adored her child and refused to give her up, even when most women in her position would have done just that. She wouldn't accept that Beau was in prison, so she got him out of Parchman Farm, one of the most notorious of Mississippi's jails. She faced down white men who questioned her audacity. She did it all just for him, and no matter what had gone on, he would not abandon her now.

'Good morning,' she answered, but went back to her book. It was the most conversation they'd had all week.

'Honey, can we talk?' He sat down opposite her. The wingback chair she sat in was facing the window, so he'd pulled a stool over to sit beside her.

'About what?' Her voice was flat.

Gently, he took the book from her and placed it on the table. He took her hands in his. 'I hate this, us being like this. I miss you and I love you and I don't know what's gone wrong, but I want to try to make it right between us...'

She allowed him to hold her hands but would not turn her face to him; she kept her gaze fixed on the faraway horizon.

He tried again. 'We fought so hard to be together. It was so hard. Nobody wanted us to make it, and you fought like a lion for me, and I'm scared, darlin'. I feel like I'm losin' you, and I don't know what to do...'

Still she didn't move, but a single tear slid down her cheek.

'Please, Lillian, please just talk to me. We can fix this, I know we can, for us and for Austina. We're a family, and we need to stick together...'

'*They* are your family Beau, the Murphys. *They* are your people, not me.' Her voice was tight.

'What are you talkin' about? You're my wife. I love you and nobody

166

comes before you, nobody...'

She turned then, a combination of fury and sadness on her face. 'Everybody comes before me. Them, God, the estate – every single thing comes before me with you. I thought we could live here happily together. I know everyone is forever accusing me of living in the past, but I did try to fit in. I did. I even went down to the kitchen and offered to help, but they shooed me out after I made a mess of it. I offered to go to your church, to support you, but you refused. Austina prefers being with Hannah and the other children more than with me, and you fit much better toiling in the fields than in here. It feels like you're ashamed of me, and then when you took Kate's side...well...'

Beau felt a pang of pity for her. He should not have refused her offer; he had thought she was only doing it under sufferance. He never took Kate's side; though he could see how irritating Lillian was being, Kate had a hot temper and was inclined to lash out. And he was definitely not ashamed of her. He inhaled; how he handled the next few minutes would be crucial.

'First, I'm sorry I refused your offer. I was scared, that's the truth. If nobody came, or they didn't think I was good enough, I didn't want to look foolish in front of you. Second, ashamed of you? Are you crazy? I'm a poor black man from Georgia married to Lady Lillian Kenefick, and you think *I'm* ashamed of *you*?' He couldn't help but chuckle. 'Honey, if anyone is slummin' it, it's you. And as for taking anyone's side over you, well, that just didn't happen. You slapped Kate. I dunno what went on before I got there, but I do know it takes two to tango, so I don't think it was all your fault. Anyway, that's between you two, ain't got nothing to do with me. Y'all need to fix that yourselves. But I am on your side, always.'

Her eyes raked his face, searching for something. Then she spoke sadly. 'But you're not, though. You might think you are, but you are much more like them than like me. Everyone thinks it's our skin colour that makes us different, but it's not that. You blend in with servants and tinkers and IRA men. They accept you because you might be a different colour but they see you as like them. I'm always going to be outside – it's how it is.'

167

Beau pulled her to her feet and put his arms around her. It felt good to hold her again, to smell her scent. He was terrified she would recoil, but to his relief, she allowed him to embrace her.

'If you're outside, then so am I, 'cause darlin', I'm wherever you are. But it doesn't have to be like that. Sam is like you, but he copes. And sure, it's a bit different, but he laughs at how we are, and we laugh at him. You're right, I do have more in common with workin' people. I was raised to work, and I had a full-time job when I was twelve years old. But y'know something? They're just like you deep down. I love them, as they're kind and funny and honest, but so are you.' He gazed into her blue eyes and saw a longing for acceptance there. 'You can take that wall down, you really can, sweetheart. You don't want to be up here all on your own, and I want you with me. I hate being away from you. I miss sleepin' beside you. I want you. I want us to be together like we used to be. Please come back to me, Lillian?'

She moved out of his embrace slightly and looked up at him. 'Really? Are you on my side?' she asked.

He sighed but kept his arms around her waist. 'I hate that there are sides, but I'm always on yours. You're my wife.'

A smile, the first he'd seen in so long. He bent his head and kissed her lips. Slowly at first, he felt her respond to his touch. Relief mixed with passion flooded through his body; it was going to be OK. He wasn't going to lose her. To his surprise, he felt her pull his shirt from his trousers, her cool hands on the skin of his back. On and on he kissed her until she led him to their bed.

Afterwards, the linen tousled by their frantic lovemaking, she lay in his arms. The only sound was the ticking of the alarm clock on the bedside locker. The bell in the yard rang to indicate it was dinner time, and Beau relaxed.

'I want to leave here, Beau,' she said, her head on his shoulder and her hand on his chest.

His heart sank. 'And go where?' he asked, trying to keep the disappointment out of his voice. It had been too much to assume everything was all right again.

'England. I hate it here, feeling like we're not welcome, that we're all here at the discretion of the cook's daughter.'

Beau hated to hear that bitchy tone she reserved for talking about the Murphys, Kate in particular.

'But Austina is so happy here, sweetheart. She has her cousins, and she's sheltered from what people might say... Y'know how people are...' He didn't want to start another fight; their truce was too new.

'Yes, I know she is, but I'm not.' She sighed. 'We'll stay at Framington. Perry will be delighted, and Mother will have to get over it. They're hardly ever there anyway, and so we'll have the run of it when they are gone, and it's big enough for us to stay out of each other's way.'

When Beau didn't answer, she sat up, took a cigarette from her ivory case and lit it. He watched the determined set of her chin, the straightness of her naked back.

She must have sensed his reticence because her tone changed. 'Look, Beau, I'm going and taking Austina, and I want you to come with me. You said you were on my side, so if you are, then you'll come.'

'And what would I do at Framington?' he asked, trying not to betray the hurt he felt at being used. He'd thought their lovemaking was a confirmation that they were back on track, but it wasn't; it was leverage.

Lillian laughed, the sound that her mother said was like a braying donkey.

'Do? Why, Beau, darling, we *do* nothing, we just *are*.' She turned to him, stubbing out her cigarette. She kissed his lips again and she tasted of cigarettes. He hated the smell of them. He'd smoked during the war but had quit.

'And if I don't want to go?' he asked, dreading the answer.

She sighed. 'I tried, I really did. I offered to help, I offered to go to your church, I take care of Austina. But you're right. I'm up here all alone, day after day, a stranger in my own home. I can't stand it any more. Please come.'

CHAPTER 19

 ermot waited in the dingy room before his visit with Mark. It was only due to having an old comrade in the jail that he was able to get a visiting order. Mark was being held on remand, his trial set for two weeks' time.

He sighed deeply. A letter from Bella was in his pocket. She wrote every day, as he did to her, and reading between the lines, things were not good. She was not responding to the treatment, and they were concerned at her weight loss. He'd made the decision. He felt bad leaving Sam in the lurch, but he had to go to her. He'd see what could be done with Mark first, but then he was going back to Switzerland.

Why couldn't life be simple? He and Bella had been through so much together, surely now they were entitled to a peaceful retirement. He knew she would be angry with him for coming, as the girls needed him more than ever now. Eve was doing as well as any new mother, but Kate was worn away from work, and Aisling, well, she was in such a dark place, he didn't even know how to reach her. He tried, but she needed her mother.

And Aisling wasn't the only one. Each night, he lay in the bed he'd shared with his wife for thirty years and tossed and turned, imagining the worst in the small hours before the dawn. Even back in the '20s, when there was a price on his head, and in the interrogation room, where torture and execution were a distinct possibility, he wasn't afraid. Not like this. Fear was his constant companion now, day and night, the fear that somehow, in response to all the hearts he had broken by sending British soldiers home in boxes, he was getting his just desserts. God was taking the one person he could not live without, and there was not a single thing he could do to stop it.

He took her letter out again.

DARLING,

How are you? I'm so worried about you all, my poor Aisling, God love her, and Kate working herself into the ground. And I know you said Eve is doing fine, but she's just had a baby and needs to recover, not go straight back into the demands of Robinswood. Sometimes I think that place is a curse, not a blessing.

I know you're doing your best and that it's hard without me, but knowing you are there and helping everyone along gives me great comfort. You say you want to come over to me, and I would love nothing more than to see your handsome face or to feel your arms around me, Der, you know that, but I need you to stay and take care of our girls. They need you more than I do. They have their men, and they are lucky to have them – except for poor Mark – but they need you. Sam can't manage the farm on his own, and the boys are such a help, but Bartley needs to be with them – they're only young lads after all.

Kate is running herself into the ground. I know she is, though she says she's not. She used to have all four of us, and now it's just her and whatever Eve can do. Make sure she rests, and to hell with guests. If she has to close for a week or two to take a break, so be it. But she won't – we know what our girl is like.

Tell Aisling that I love her, that her baby will be fine. I can't even think about Lacey, I can't even allow him into my head because, by God, Der, if he weren't dead already, he would be by the time I was finished with him. May he burn in hell, I curse his soul.

. . .

HER HARD WORDS had shaken him the first time he read them. His wife was a devout woman, more than he was really, and he'd never heard her speak about anyone like that.

I WON'T ASK what you think about the Mark situation. I know. I don't know how to advise you, but just take care of them, Der. It's so hard lying here, looking at stupid bloody mountains and eating, eating, eating constantly like some kind of a suckler when I should be at home with my family. I just want to go home, whatever happens, just sleep in my own bed, with my own husband, and have my girls around me. I know it's not what you want to hear, but I'm starting to think they've done all they can here, that there is nothing left to be done. I want to come home and let it all rest in the hands of God. I'll stay in isolation, but I don't want to waste any more time here. Please don't fight me on this, as I've made up my mind.

I love you, Der, always have.

Your Bella.

HE WIPED HIS EYES. Every letter made him cry now. He had to go there, convince her to stay. If she stood any chance of getting better, it was there. He'd spoken on the telephone to Henry Carlin, and the doctor had been honest. The TB was winning – Isabella was getting weaker, and her lungs were showing no signs of improving – but Dr Carlin wasn't giving up hope yet. Dermot was going to tell the girls a few days ago, but then everything happened with Aisling and Eve had the baby and Mark was arrested… There was no good time.

His thoughts were interrupted by the sound of the metal-plated door opening and Mark being led in by a prison officer. The lad looked dreadful, exhausted and pale. Dermot was invited to sit at one side of a table, with Mark on the other. The officer walked to and stood in the corner of the room.

'Hello, Mark, son, how are you doing?' Dermot asked.

'I'm OK. How's Ais?' he asked. He'd not been allowed any contact, not even a letter, since he'd been arrested.

'She's all right. We're taking care of her.' Dermot wanted to be reassuring but wasn't going to lie to the lad.

Mark paused. 'And the baby?'

At least there was some good news on that score. 'She went up to the hospital the day before yesterday, and they reckon everything is fine. She's still pregnant.'

Mark seemed to slump in the chair, so great was the relief. 'Thank God for that.' He exhaled. 'I keep picturing her losing the baby, and I'm not there.'

'She's all right. She's worried sick about you, and her mother of course, but day to day, she's doing fine. We're keeping her in bed as much as she'll allow, and the doctor pops in very often, so don't worry about that at least.'

Mark nodded. 'Dermot, I didn't kill him. And I'm not saying I didn't want to, but Ais means too much to me to risk everything like that. I swear to you, I didn't. I admit I went there and I hit him, but when I left, he was crying and carrying on. I would have stopped anyway, but Sam made sure all I did was hit him a few slaps. There's no way I could have killed him.'

In his sixty years, Dermot had learned a lot about human nature. He'd grown up in a broken family, and when he met Bella, she became his home. But his years of fighting to free his country from England's tyrannical rule taught him the most and had put him in situations where life was at its most immediate, its most raw. He'd been at the receiving end of brutality and torture, and threatened with execution so often he'd lost count, but it taught him one thing: the difference between truth and lies. And Mark Belitho was telling the truth.

'I believe you,' Dermot said quietly.

'Do the police think I did it?' Mark asked.

'They do, and that's a massive problem. Apart from yourself, and later on Sam, nobody was seen either going into or coming out of Lacey's house that night, and apart from the killer, you were the last people to see him alive.'

Dermot could see the crushing effect his words had on Mark, but there was no point in soft-soaping the lad. He might as well know what he'd be facing.

'And Sam's told the police what happened?'

'Of course he did,' Dermot reassured him. 'Exactly as you describe it. But the thing is, independence is still new, and there's an inherent mistrust of people like Sam, being Protestant English gentry and all of that. It's nothing to do with this case, it just is how it is, and the fact that you and him are friends since the war, well, they seem to think he's lying for you.'

'So what do I do now?' Mark asked helplessly.

'Wait for the trial, that's all you can do. Hope the guards uncover something.' Dermot felt for the man opposite him, but there was no way to see his future as anything but bleak.

'How's Isabella?' Mark asked, changing the subject.

Dermot sat back; this was an even more uncomfortable conversation. Should he lie? 'I don't know. Not great, I suppose. She's still very sick, and they are at a bit of a loss as to what to do next. But...ah... they'll keep trying, I suppose, and we just have to trust...' He tried to keep his voice strong, reassuring, but his son-in-law had got to know him well over the years he and Aisling had been together and saw through him.

'It's all right, Dermot,' Mark said gently. 'You don't have to put a brave face on for me. Do it for the girls, but you can tell me the truth.'

Dermot sighed. He'd never thought anyone would be good enough for his girls, but he'd come over the years to see Sam, Mark and now Bartley as the sons he never had. Although different from each other as chalk and cheese, he would not have hand-picked finer men for his daughters, and each one suited the Murphy girl he chose perfectly. Sam was decent, practical and quiet, the perfect partner for the impulsive live wire Kate. Bartley too was quiet but in a different way; he was a deep thinker, and he was what the generations before would have called an old soul. Initially – he supposed because Bartley was the opposite of Eve's first husband, the jovial, open-hearted Jack O'Neill – he had worried, but there was no need. Bartley and Eve had both had more than their fair share of hardship, and they were grateful and happy to have found love. They cherished it and each other. But of the three, Mark was the one he was fondest of. It was probably because he came from simple people, no Lord of the Manor or traveller hierarchy there, just a decent working lad from a good family. He was a straight talker and adored Aisling.

'I'm losing her, Mark, and I don't know what to do about it...' He choked on the words.

'What are the doctors saying?'

'That she's not responding to the treatment. She just wrote to me. She wants to come home, let nature take its course, but I can't let her. She has to stay and fight it, or at least allow the doctors to fight it. But she thinks what with everything going on, she needs to be here. She's stubborn as a mule, my Bella, and once she makes her mind up, you can neither lead nor drive her.'

'How long has she been there now?' Mark asked.

'Almost five months, and it's felt like five years to be honest. The girls need her. I'm trying to do and say the right things, but they need their mother. But I can't let her turn her back on the treatment! I can't watch her wasting away in front of my eyes and do nothing.'

The prison officer had obviously been tipped off to give Dermot some space, so he continued to stand in the corner, staring straight ahead and saying nothing as the two men spoke.

'But if it's what she wants, and the treatment isn't working anyway? Maybe suggest a compromise, like a sanatorium here, where we could visit? Then maybe she wouldn't feel so cut off and –'

'No, she's adamant. She wants to come home, and if she does, that's the end of the treatment. Dr Grahame said he could manage the symptoms but can't do anything else.' Dermot gazed out of the tiny window. 'I was never scared, not like this. I've been in some situations where, well, things were looking fairly dire and the consequences didn't bear thinking about, but I just didn't let fear in. There was a job to be done and that was that. But now... Mark, I can't lose her. I just don't know who or how I am without her.'

Mark leaned over and placed his hand on Dermot's shoulder. 'I wish there was something I could say. I know how close you two are, and I can't imagine. Aisling is probably facing something similar now...though it won't be a disease will get me but the hangman's noose.'

Dermot was immediately drawn back to the spartan room. 'You are an innocent man. We just need to prove it,' he said with a conviction he didn't feel. Hope was all any of them had now.

* * *

DERMOT PUT A PINT in front of his oldest friend.

'Bit short notice, I know, but I was halfway to Dublin visiting Mark in jail anyway, so I decided to keep going.' Dermot sat opposite him.

'I'm always happy to see you, you know that.' Oskar Metz lifted his pint and sipped.

'Oskar, I need your help,' Dermot said bluntly.

'If I can, I will. What do you need?' The two men had been through so much together, there was no need for pretence.

'Isabella isn't improving. She wants to come home and let nature take its course, but I can't let her do that. She'll die... And I just can't...' Dermot exhaled raggedly.

'I'm so sorry, Dermot, this is terrible news.'

Dermot nodded. 'But as you know from my letter, Aisling's husband, Mark, is being held in Portlaoise Prison for murdering this local shopkeeper. He attacked Aisling and Mark went down there, beat the tar out of him it seems, but Sam arrived and pulled him off. According to both Sam and Mark, the snivelling rat was crying when they left him. He had cuts and bruises they admit, but he was very much alive. But when the housekeeper went in the next morning, he was dead. Nobody saw anyone else around that night, so the guards are putting two and two together and pointing the finger at Mark.'

'Do you think he did it?' Oskar asked. 'Not that it matters.'

'No, I don't, but I can't see how the guards or a judge and jury or anyone else for that matter can come to any other conclusion.'

'So what can I do?'

'Two things actually. Firstly, Aisling is going to need someone to go to court with her. The trial will be front-page news, so she'll need protection. I could ask Bartley or Sam, but I'd trust you with my life, so if you could go to court with her and just keep people away from her, that would be such a relief. I have to go to Switzerland and try to convince Isabella to stay there, or else, if she won't, then I need to bring her home. I know you might not be able, with the shop and everything, but I –'

Oskar raised his hand. 'I'll be there, no problem.'

'But what about the shop?' Dermot asked.

Oskar smiled slowly. 'I have the leather shop to keep me busy, to take my mind off…well, so much. But I don't need the money. I'll just close until the trial is over.'

'Thanks, Oskar.' Dermot was sincere.

'And the second thing?' Oskar asked.

Dermot fixed his friend with a look. 'The trial is happening at Waterford. He'll be held downstairs in the cells before and afterwards.'

Oskar grinned. 'Well, that's something in our favour, I suppose. One last go, eh?'

'Something like that. We wait until the verdict, but if it doesn't go our way – and I have to believe it won't – then we do what we've done so many times before. I've spoken to Barty Sheehan, he's still the court clerk, who assured me that the whole place is exactly the same as it was.'

Oskar nodded. 'I haven't heard of Barty since the days we sprang people out of Waterford courthouse before breakfast. It's amazing they never made it more secure.'

'Maybe the current authorities don't know. It's a long time since anyone had to use the tunnel, I suppose. Anyway, Barty says it's still there and still usable. He'll help. He never forgot how we got his brother away to England and stopped the Tans burning his mother's house that time. So if needs be…'

'Mark'll have to go on the run,' Oskar finished Dermot's sentence for him.

'I know, and leave Ais behind. But at least he'd be alive and not at the end of a hangman's rope. It's not ideal, but it's all we have. I wish I could do both, take care of Aisling and Isabella, but I can't.'

Oskar reassured his friend. 'Look, you go to Switzerland, take care of your wife. I'll look after everything here, and I'll take Aisling to court every day. And as you say, let's have a plan in place to get Mark away if we need to. You never know, if he didn't do it, the police might find whoever did. Truth will always out in the end, my friend, it always does.'

CHAPTER 20

'Nice work,' Bartley said, admiring the rosewood inlay on the polished teak jewellery box his brother was finishing off in the workshop. Isaac was gifted when it came to turning wood and intricate decorative work, only using a small pocketknife he kept in his boot. 'Where did you get that nice timber?'

'In the lumberyard in Dungarvan. Sam sent me in there to get some fencing posts while he was in the bank, and these offcuts were just lying there, so the man said I could have them.'

Bartley chuckled. 'You must be the first person in the world to ever get anything for nothing from Denis Quinlan. He's a notorious skinflint.'

'Ah sure, it's my charm.' Isaac winked and smiled. 'It's for Hannah.'

Bartley felt a pang of something. Sadness, relief, nostalgia?

'Go easy there,' he warned. 'We don't allow company keeping, as they say, between female and male students, and I don't want anyone to think you're getting special treatment because you're my brother.'

'She's going to be a slow burner, don't worry.' Isaac winked again.

Bartley watched Isaac as he opened and closed the lid of the box several times, checking that the tiny brass hinges were doing their job properly. He adjusted a hinge expertly with the tip of his knife, then slipped the knife back into his boot. He looked like their father, sinewy and muscular, and with those dark good looks the Dohertys were famous for.

Since he'd met Isaac, the boy had seemed upbeat and cheerful. He was happy to go back to Robinswood with him and Eve, delighted to have been found by his older brother. They'd had lots of jokey banter, but they had yet to have a real conversation.

Isaac had explained that he was in juvenile prison for a series of minor offences: affray, drunk and disorderly, brawling, petty theft. Nothing very serious, but taken all together and because he was a traveller, the judge had given him six months. It was his first time in prison.

Any time Bartley tried to have a proper chat, ask him about his life or anything meaningful, Isaac skirted around it and avoided the question.

'Where did you grow up?' Bartley asked, looking his brother straight in the eye. He wanted to get some answers.

'Ah sure, you know us, Bartley, here and there, come here. Do you think Hannah would go to the pictures with me on Saturday? Sam gave me wages this week. I wasn't expecting any, room and board was enough, but I'm in the money.'

'In industrial schools?' Bartley persisted.

'Yerra yeah, some of them, and in and out, you know yourself.' Isaac was making to leave.

'Isaac, I want to talk about it all, about what happened to you once they took you away, and I'll tell you about what happened to me too if you're interested.'

Isaac turned, his hands deep in his trouser pockets. 'I'm not.' He shrugged. 'Look, it's over. It's in the past, and I'd just as soon forget about it. You found me, and I knew by looking at you we were related, though obviously I'm better looking.' He grinned and his dark eyes danced with merriment. 'You gave me a start here and I'm happy, but raking over the past isn't going to do either of us any good, will it?'

Maybe he was right but Bartley needed more. 'Did you ever hear from any of the others again?'

'Sure I was only a baby, Bartley, how would I know any of them?'

Isaac was being reasonable, and Bartley had to concede he was right. He had envisaged doing right by his parents and uniting the family once more for so long, but Isaac had no memory of them, or of any one of the clan, that to suggest he should care about them was probably farcical.

'Aren't you even curious? You have a big family, nine boys and five girls, our brothers and sisters. Aren't you interested in finding them?' Bartley asked, wishing Isaac cared more.

'Look, as I said, I'm glad to have met you and all of that, and I'd like to stay here for a bit anyway, but I've lived alone all of my life. I'm used to it, I can fend for myself, and I don't need anyone.' The boy shrugged and smiled to take the sting out of his words. 'It's different for you. You remember them all, and you went back afterwards. I understand that, but I don't go backwards, only forwards.'

'Were you adopted?' Bartley asked, determined to get at least something from him.

Isaac sighed in exasperation. 'Yes, I was adopted, for a while, and then I was on my own again, and then I went from place to place, and now I'm here. Right, is that enough? Will you stop badgering me now and tell me how to get this Hannah to go to the pictures with me?'

Though the words were light, Bartley heard the edge in the tone. Whatever his brother had or had not done, he was adamant he was not going to talk about it.

'All right, I'll let it go, but I do want to know about your life, Isaac. You're the only family I have and –'

'Sure haven't you that gorgeous redhead and that small little girl?' Isaac asked, his face innocent.

'I do. And they mean the world to me, but I want to try to find the others. I wrote to a few places, asking, but nobody responded. When Mammy died, back then there wasn't much in the way of paperwork. They just decided Da couldn't manage and took us all. I just want to make sure they are all OK,' Bartley said quietly.

'They'll be fine, I'm sure. Forget about it.' Isaac examined his face and smoothed his curls with his hands while looking in the glass of the workshop door.

'But they're our family! Don't you think we should be at least trying?' Bartley hated that he was wheedling the boy, but he wanted him to care. He'd spent most of his life alone, as no doubt Isaac had as well, and it was true, Eve and now Bella were his home. But it was like a gnawing pain inside him that refused to ever leave, the sense that out there, somewhere, one or more of his brothers or sisters was struggling for the want of a bit of help.

Isaac shrugged. 'Look, you can if you want, but I… It's not that I don't wish them all the best, I do, but they are strangers. I have no more feeling for them than I do for any of the people here, for example. They seem nice, I wish them no ill will, but I've my own life to live.' He grabbed the box and popped it in his pocket.

'All right,' Bartley conceded. He couldn't force the issue, and maybe Isaac was right that it wouldn't do any good. But he had a brother now, and no matter how blasé the lad was about his family, Bartley knew it was a front. He also knew how children were treated in those institutions, and it was most unlikely that Isaac escaped, so he was dealing with it the best way he could, by putting it behind him. 'But if you ever want to talk about anything, you know where I am. We are in this together now, Isaac. You're not on your own any more.'

His younger brother gave him a strange look, one Bartley couldn't read, before giving a mock salute and whistling his way out.

In a way, Bartley admired him. He was charming and funny, and Bartley saw how the girls reacted to him. He was good-looking for sure, but there was something else about him, something that made him want to protect the boy.

* * *

HANNAH CROSSED the yard between the house and the girls' dormitories. She'd fed and bathed the children and was shocked when Austina announced that she was going to live in England. Hannah had heard nothing about Beau and Lillian moving away, and she hoped it wasn't true. She'd grown so fond of the little girl with coffee-coloured skin, a mop of dark curls and big brown eyes. The child had no idea what the world could be like. Hannah remembered a girl with brown skin in the place where she was sent to have her baby and how cruel they were to her. They said horrible, hurtful things and made the girl cry. Here, Austina was protected and loved, but out in the world, a little girl with a black father and a white mother...well, she was worried about how she would fare.

She'd never even seen a black man before meeting Beau. She tried to call him Mister Lane, but he insisted that Beau was fine. His wife was different though, and Hannah called her Lady Lillian.

She was about to go upstairs – she was exhausted and had planned an early night – when she saw him, leaning on the wall. All week she'd kept her eyes out, but Isaac had been nowhere to be seen. Now here he was, like magic. She tried not to look flustered but failed.

'Hello, angel,' he said slowly, a smile playing around his perfect cupid's bow lips.

'It's Hannah,' she said primly, moving towards the door.

'Hello, Hannah,' he said, more seriously this time. 'I brought you a present.'

'Is it a farthing for my ear?' she asked, sceptical. He was so gorgeous, but all the girls thought so, and several of them had been forthcoming about how far they would be willing to go with him. He could have anyone, and she was certainly not the prettiest, nor was she likely to do anything that would land her in her previous predicament.

'No then, it is not,' he replied, walking in step beside her now. 'Do you want to see it?'

Despite his obvious sophistication compared with her sheltered experience, he looked like a puppy, desperate for play.

'You're going to show me whether I do or not,' she said, but smiled a little so he wouldn't be hurt.

He pulled the little box out of his pocket and handed it to her. It was exquisite; she'd never seen one like it. It was chamfered and oiled and polished until it shone. The hinged lid was inlaid with a lovely red wood, and the design was of a half-open rose.

'Where did you get this?' she gasped. It was the most lovely thing she'd ever seen.

'I made it for you.' She heard the tinge of pride in his voice. 'Open it.'

She did as he instructed and found a little bag of gold velvet. He extracted it and opened the little drawstring. Inside was a necklace, a gossamer-thin gold chain with a tiny golden angel hanging from it. 'Do you like it?' he asked quietly.

'It's beautiful! I've never seen anything like it. It's amazing, but I can't accept it.' She placed the necklace back in the pouch and put the pouch in the box. She handed it back to him.

'Why not? I got it for you.' Isaac looked crestfallen, and immediately she felt a pang of guilt.

'Because I don't know you and it's too much...' She was flustered again.

'Please, Hannah.' He took her hand and placed the box in it once more, gently folding her fingers over its smooth surface. 'I made the box especially for you, and the necklace...well, you're like an angel and I just wanted you to have something almost as pretty as you.' He smiled that smile, the one she felt could light up the whole world.

Hannah blushed. Surely it would be churlish to refuse? She didn't know what to say. He took the necklace from the bag once more. He turned her gently so she had her back to him, and she felt his fingers brush against the nape of her neck while he closed the tiny clasp. It sent a thrill through her.

Hannah's hand went to the angel. 'Thank you, Isaac. I've never had anything so lovely.'

'You're welcome.' He grinned, back to his jokey self. 'Now, will you come to the pictures with me tonight?'

She would have loved nothing more, but Miss Doherty and Bartley had been most adamant about no shenanigans, as they called it, between the boys and girls. But strictly speaking, Isaac wasn't one of the students. Maybe if she asked, Miss Doherty might say it was all right.

'I could ask,' she said shyly.

Isaac's brow furrowed in confusion. 'Ask who?'

'Miss Doherty,' she replied, confused. Who else would she ask?

Isaac took her hand in his and stood before her. 'How old are you, Hannah?' he asked gently.

'Seventeen.'

'Right, so am I. At seventeen, and in the eyes of the law, we are both fending for ourselves now. To say you're here, I assume you came out of St Basil's, right?'

She nodded, ashamed by her lack of parentage or family.

'Well, I came out of someplace similar, and as you know, up until fairly recently I was a friend of your brother Dessie's above in Mountjoy. And will I tell you something?'

'What?' she asked.

'Nobody is going to tell me what I can and can't do any more. I've had a bellyful of their rules and regulations, and I just want to live my life and have some fun at long last, and ideally I'd like to do that in the company of the loveliest girl I've ever seen. So how about we start acting like the grown-ups they keep telling us we are and make our own decisions?'

She smiled. He made it all sound so simple. 'If only it were that easy.' She shrugged.

'But it is, Hannah, it really is. I understand how you feel in a way a lad raised in a family wouldn't. I know the life, bells and timetables and having to feel grateful for the bit they give you out of the goodness of their hearts, but we don't have to live like that. We can be free. We are free. We don't need to ask anyone anything. We can do whatever we want.'

'Maybe you can, but I need this job, the experience I get here, and I'm hoping they might keep me on afterwards if I'm good enough,' she said.

'Is that what you want? To be a nanny here for these toffs?' he asked with a grin.

'They're not toffs. You've got that all wrong. Kate, Aisling and Miss Doherty are the children of the cook and the farm manager. Only Sam and Lady Lillian are toffs, as you call them. They all work really hard, and they're trying to make a go of things. And what's so wrong with being a nanny? For someone like me it would be a really great position!' She was offended that he would belittle her achievement.

'Ah, Hannah, don't be vexed with me. I didn't mean it like that. I just meant that just because you were raised in an orphanage doesn't mean you have to be in service all your life. You could do anything, go anywhere.'

'I don't want to go anywhere. I like it here.' She knew she sounded sullen now and felt a pang of regret when she saw how crestfallen he was.

'Not even to the picture house in the village? Would you venture that far at least?' He stuck his bottom lip out and made a funny face, and she couldn't help giggling. Even pulling faces he was gorgeous. The others would be green with envy.

'Look, I'll ask Miss Doherty, and if she says it's all right, I'll go as far as the village. But not an inch further, do you hear me?' She smiled and was rewarded by his spotlight beam once more, all offence forgotten.

'I'll be here, waiting,' he said.

'Don't you have work to do?' she asked. 'I'm sure Bartley wouldn't be happy if he caught you loitering about here.'

'Ah, but you see, my darling Hannah, no man owns me, brother or not. I'm free as a bird.' He took off, circling her with his arms outstretched while making cawing sounds, and she was half amused, half mortified at the idea that someone would see them. She had never met anyone like him; he was a one-off, that was for sure.

'So you go and ask herself inside if you can spend your own free time with another adult person, and come out and let me know what Her Ladyship decrees.' He winked and held his hands up when he saw her look of disapproval. 'Ah, Hannah, I'm only messing with you! I won't say another word on the subject, I promise!'

Hannah turned back in the direction of Robinswood in search of

Eve. She found her and Kate in the kitchen preparing dinner. It was seven o'clock and the picture started at eight, when they would be in full serving mode. With a bit of luck, Eve would just say yes without too much debate because she was so busy.

Hannah went in the back door and hurried along the passage towards the cavernous kitchen. It was a bad idea to get stuck in the passageway during mealtimes because they were busy serving and there was a stream of people coming and going with tureens and platters – woe betide anyone who got in the way. She ducked into an alcove as Beau, dressed in a footman's uniform now, approached with a large platter, on top of which was a delicious-smelling leg of lamb.

Beau gave her a wink as he passed but said nothing. He was lovely, and to see the sheer joy on Austina's little face when he came to collect her from the nursery would melt an iceberg. Lady Lillian came sometimes, and while she was nice and always spoke politely to Hannah, she wasn't exactly warm.

The kitchen was a hive of activity. Hannah spotted Eve in the corner showing a group of girls how to pipe cream decoratively around the dessert using a bag with a nozzle on it. Kate was supervising the filling of serving dishes full of vegetables and making sure there were no drops of butter or water on the sides. She had several bowls of chopped herbs and condiments on the huge table, which were used to garnish the dishes before they went upstairs.

Eve looked up as she approached. 'Hannah, is everything all right?' she asked.

Eve looked pale and tired, not her usual radiant self, but Hannah knew it was because Bella wasn't sleeping. Hannah did all she could to keep the little one awake during the day, but it was close to impossible.

'I… Could I have a quick word please, Miss?' she asked, reddening at the attention her request had garnered from the other girls.

'Now?' Eve asked incredulously, her gaze taking in all that was going on in the kitchen.

'It…it will only take a second.' Hannah was mortified, and she could sense the other girls were dying to know what was so urgent that she would disturb Miss Doherty in the middle of dinner.

'Well, spit it out.' Eve smiled as she instructed the others to mash the potatoes with more cream and butter.

'In private if you don't mind, Miss?' Hannah gulped as Eve gave her a strange look but led her towards the pantry.

'What is it, Hannah?' Eve asked.

'I'm sorry to disturb, Miss, but I was wondering if it would be all right for me to go to the pictures this evening with...with Isaac Doherty, Miss. He asked, and I told him I'd have to check with you.' She blurted the entire sentence out in one long breath.

Eve's face gave nothing away. Hannah stood there, waiting on her answer.

'Of course you can go, but, Hannah, please be careful. Isaac may be a little more...well, a bit more worldly wise than you, if you know what I mean, so just be mindful of that.'

'I will, Miss, thank you.' Hannah tried not to skip out of the hot kitchen.

Isaac was exactly where she'd left him. 'Well? Are we on?' he asked hopefully.

'We are.' Hannah failed to keep the glee out of her voice.

'Great, let's go so.' He held his arm out to her and she took it.

As they walked down the avenue towards the main road into Kilthomand, he was all questions about her but revealed very little about himself. He deflected every inquiry. He was funny and flattering and completely over the top with the compliments. Once at the cinema, he bought them not just tickets but a big box of sweets and two bottles of lemonade.

The picture was a silly one about aliens or something; Hannah had no idea really. But when Isaac leaned over and took her hand and held it in his, she realised she was happier than she'd been in such a long time. She missed human contact. She had never been hugged or cuddled the way the children of Robinswood were, and then with Damien, well, that was so short-lived but gave her a sense of what it was like to feel someone's arms around her, to feel special to someone.

Once the picture was over, they stood in the tiny foyer, and Hannah noticed the glances of admiration he got from the local girls. Isaac was dressed very fashionably, in wide-legged trousers and a freshly pressed shirt. He had arrived into the yard like that, so he must have assumed he would convince her to go with him. She didn't feel he was presumptuous or forward though; he was just the kind of person who got what he wanted she supposed.

The walk home was chilly, and he insisted she wear his coat. A guard stopped them.

'Where are you two off to?' he asked, a note of accusation in his tone.

'Home, we live at Robinswood.' Isaac's voice was light, but there was a trace of insolence that made Hannah exhilarated and a little nervous at the same time.

'And you are?' he asked, taking out his notebook.

'Did we do something wrong, guard?' Isaac asked.

'What's your name?' the guard repeated.

'I'm Isaac Bogart and this is Hannah Bacall.' Isaac winked at Hannah as the guard began to write but then stopped.

'Your real name, sonny,' he said with a note of impatience.

'Isaac Doherty and Hannah Woods,' Hannah said quickly, not wanting to get them into any trouble.

The policeman wrote their names and looked up. 'Right. Well, see that you go straight home.' He turned to where someone was singing loudly outside the pub.

Hannah walked on quickly, pulling Isaac with her despite his reluctance. He wanted to stay and see what was going to happen.

'Everyone is talking about the murder. It's hard to imagine someone could be killed in this village, isn't it? Sam was saying there were never guards around all the time, but since that man was killed, they're everywhere.'

'Pigs,' was Isaac's only contribution.

'The man they say did it, Aisling's husband, Mark, I didn't really know him or anything, but he seems like a nice person. They say he's going to hang for it.' Hannah shuddered.

'Well, after what that Lacey fella did to his missus, there would be few men who wouldn't do the same. The world is better off without people like him.'

'What did he do?' Hannah asked. She had heard mutterings, and of the middle sister, Aisling, there was no sign in recent weeks, but because she minded the children all day, she was out of the rumour mill.

'He attacked her. Apparently they used to be sweethearts years ago and he's jealous or something. She's a fine-looking woman, so I doubt she'd ever have gone for the little shopkeeper, so he decided he'd have what she was denying him.' Isaac shrugged.

'How do you know all this?' she asked cautiously.

'I was in the car with Bartley and Eve the night we found her, walking the road, her clothes all torn. She was in a right state.'

'Poor Aisling, what a horrible thing to go through. It's so scary. And I think...well, there is a rumour that she's expecting as well.' Hannah's heart broke for the kind and gentle Aisling. 'No wonder Mark went down there, but he's saying he didn't kill him.'

'Well, nobody would blame him if he did. That man deserved what was coming to him. To attack a woman, especially in that way, well, he got his just desserts as far as I'm concerned. The world is better off without the likes of him in it. The jury will hear that, and if he gets a good brief, he'll have every single man imagining what kind of a monster that Lacey fella was and Mark will get a very light sentence. He might not serve any time at all actually.'

He put his arm around her shoulders as they walked. 'But let's talk about happier things, will we? Whatever happens with that, it's not our business.'

She knew she should probably pull away; it wasn't proper to be walking along a dark road with a boy she hardly knew, and for him to be so close. She didn't think the authorities at St Basil's had told Miss Doherty and Bartley about her baby – they would hardly have taken her on if they had – so she was anxious not to do anything that might endanger her reputation. But it was so nice, the nearness of him, the feel of his body close as they walked along. She liked the weight of his hand on her shoulder, the touch of his hip on hers.

'I'm going to America, Hannah,' he said wistfully, looking up at the stars. 'Will you come with me?'

She laughed, thinking it was another of his jokes.

'I'm serious. I'm going, just as soon as I can get passage. America, that's the place to be, not this miserable backwater. I'm going to make a fortune and be a toff myself. Come on, come with me. What craic we'd have, the two of us.' He gave her a squeeze, and she wondered if he was actually in earnest.

'I'd love to go to America,' she said, playing along with the fantasy. 'We might bump into Humphrey Bogart and Lauren Bacall, and we'd eat hot dogs...'

'And go to baseball games, and drink soda, and make a fortune,' he finished, delighted she was playing the game with him. He laughed.

'And how will you make this fortune, Mr Isaac Doherty?' she asked with a grin.

'Oh, it's easy if you know how,' he replied airily.

'And you know how?' She raised an eyebrow doubtfully.

'I sure do, ma'am,' he replied in an American accent. She giggled.

They stopped, and he led her to a felled tree, sat on the trunk and pulled her down beside him.

'Isaac, I'm not going to...' She was nervous and embarrassed.

'Hannah, don't worry, I'm not about to jump on top of you here in the dark. What kind of an animal do you take me for?' He held her hand like he'd done in the cinema. He gazed up at the starry sky. 'When we make love, it will be in a big feather bed, a four-poster, where we can stay for as long as we like, and you will be happy and content and dry and warm. I'm not a fan of outdoor loving, even if you are.' He chuckled and took out a cigarette, offered her one which she refused, and lit it, inhaling deeply and then exhaling a long thin line of blue smoke.

When we make love. The words ran around in her brain. He was so sure that was going to happen, and so sure of her, she didn't know whether to be flattered or offended.

'What makes you think that we'll...' She couldn't make herself say the words and was glad of the dark so he couldn't see her cheeks burn with the shame of the conversation.

He turned and cupped her face in his hands, looking deeply into her eyes. 'I don't *think* it will happen, I *know* it will. Because you and I are meant to be together. You do like me, don't you?'

The question was so direct, so straightforward, she couldn't give a coy answer. 'I do but...'

Before she could go on, he placed a finger to her lips. Almost involuntarily, she kissed it.

'And I like you, very much. More than I've ever liked any girl before, so I just know, don't ask me how. Maybe my brother isn't the only one with the sight.' He chuckled and kissed her cheek.

'Are you serious about America?' she asked.

'Deadly. I've nothing to keep me here, and I've wasted enough time in this backwards place – not just Robinswood, but Ireland generally. There's so much to discover out there in the world. I want to see it, hear it, feel it, taste it, and I want you to do it with me.' He said it so matter-of-factly, like he was suggesting the simplest of outings.

'But don't you have a brother now, and a job?' she asked, and he gave her one of his strange looks.

'I do indeed have a brother, and a fine job. So I'd better get you home because the same brother will expect me at the fine job at cock-crow and I need my beauty sleep.' He leapt up and offered her his hand to help her off the log.

All the way home, they chatted about this and that, but he didn't take her hand or put his arm around her again. She was confused – had she done something to make him go off her? He walked her to the door of the girls' dormitory and without touching her said, 'Good-night, lovely Hannah.' And he was gone.

CHAPTER 21

*A*isling stood at the sink, washing the huge pots they'd used to make the morning porridge and scrambled eggs. Everyone hated scrubbing the pots but she didn't mind. The scullery was behind the kitchen. It had no window, which suited her. It looked like she felt. Cold, empty.

Kate and Eve had tried to convince her to stay in bed, but the days dragged on and on. She wasn't sick – she was pregnant. Her bruises and cuts were all but gone. There was no evidence of what Sean Lacey did left on her body, but it was indelibly etched on her heart.

At least he'd not taken her baby. But he'd managed to do what he'd been trying to do for years – he'd separated her from Mark.

The trial was due to start next week, and she needed to keep busy. At night she tried to sleep, but all she could see was Mark walking towards the hangman's noose. She felt sick. Sometimes she actually threw up at the thought of it. She'd not been allowed to see him, but Dermot said he was protesting his innocence. She didn't care if he'd killed Lacey or not – if he had, she was glad, but she did not want him to pay the price. Mark was a good man, a decent man who loved his wife and his child. Lacey was… Well, there were no words for what he was. Her bitterness grew like a cancerous tumour inside her.

'Ais, can you come in and sit down for a minute? I need to talk to you all.' Her father's voice cut through her thoughts.

She nodded but didn't say anything. She spoke very little these days.

Kate and Eve were already sitting at the table when she dried her hands on a tea towel and sat down. They knew by their father's face it wasn't good news.

'Girls, I've spoken to Doctor Carlin, and he's not happy with your mother's progress. She's getting worse, not better, despite all the treatment.'

Aisling knew from the way her father spoke that he'd rehearsed this many times.

'She knows it too and is demanding to come home. She says she needs to be with you all and let God or nature or whatever take its course.'

The girls exchanged a glance. Letting nature take its course meant only one outcome.

'And what do you think?' Eve managed to ask.

'I want her to stay there, but she is determined and says there is nothing more they can do for her. Henry Carlin says the same. He doesn't have any more medical tricks up his sleeve, only more of the same.'

'Is Mammy dying?' Kate, normally so calm and competent, asked, her voice quivering.

Dermot was grave. Deep despair was etched on his face, and the little lines around his eyes that normally crinkled when he smiled now had the effect of making him look old. Aisling had never thought of her father as an old man, and he wasn't, not really; he was as able as any of the men half his age. But this was killing him, and they could all see it.

He reached across the table. His large hands covered Aisling's on one side and Kate's and Eve's on the other. 'I think we need to prepare ourselves for that possibility,' he managed.

'If she wants to come home, then we should let her. Maybe coming home is what she needs, to be around us... She can move in here, and we can all be around her, and she might recover…' Kate said, but the words died on her lips.

'She's highly infectious, Kate. With the children especially, it would be too dangerous,' her father said.

'So where would she go? A sanatorium in Dublin or something?' Eve asked.

'No. If I can't talk her into staying, then I'm going to bring her home to sleep in our bed and live in our house.' He sounded bone-weary. 'And I'll be with her, right to the very end. And after that, well, I just don't know.'

'But, Daddy, what about us? We need you…' Kate said, tears in her eyes.

'You're grown women, Kate, with your own families. I thought the day would never come, but it has. I'm so proud of you, and so is Bella. You are such wonderful women, but I can't…' To the girls' horror, they saw something they had never seen before. Their big strong father was crying. His shoulders shook as he drove the heels of his hands into his eyes to stem the flow of tears, but it was no good.

The women exchanged looks of anguish. No matter what had befallen the family over the years – and their lives had certainly been eventful – their daddy was the rock. He never wavered, never weakened, and they'd spent a lifetime knowing it was all going to be all right in the end; their father would make sure of it. To see him like this, so vulnerable and so broken, was deeply shocking.

Eve was the first to recover. She put her hand on her father's shoulder. 'Daddy, when Jack died and I was distraught, you promised me that if I could just breathe in and out and put one foot in front of the other, that one day I would smile again. I didn't believe you. The pain was unbearable, and I wanted to climb into the grave with him. But I trusted you and I did what you said, and it felt like years – it *was* years – but then one day I smiled, and a while after that, I laughed. And while a part of my heart will always be his, I'm happy now.'

Dermot looked at his eldest daughter. They'd always had a very special bond. She was the one who looked most like him – Ais and Kate were more like Isabella – and when the other girls took off for

England during the war, Eve remained at home. He looked at her, and it hurt her to see the raw pain in his face.

'We have to do what Mammy wants. If she doesn't want to stay there and wants to come home, then we'll do that. She wants to live, and she's not a stupid woman, so if she thinks nothing more can be done, then we'll just have to accept it and give her the dignity and love she deserves for whatever remains of her life.' Eve's words hung in the air.

'What remains of her life...' Aisling echoed quietly.

'I...I can't, Eve... I can't lose her...' Kate was no longer the capable woman, singlehandedly running the hotel and raising her family. She was the youngest child, and she needed her mother.

'We're not getting a choice here, Kate,' Eve said gently.

'But some other doctor, some clinic maybe...' Aisling was desperate.

'Dr Carlin explained that they were using the most modern drugs and therapies, but it's just not working. I told him if there was treatment anywhere, America even, we'd do it, we'd find a way, but there just isn't.' Dermot sounded defeated.

'All right.' Eve took charge. 'Will you travel to Switzerland and bring her home, Daddy?'

Dermot nodded sadly.

'Do you want one of us to come?' Kate asked.

'No, pet.' He again laid his big calloused hand on her small one. 'I'll be fine. We'll fly from Zurich to Dublin. It's a long train journey from Davos to Zurich, but we can manage.'

'Have you the money for that?' Kate asked. International commercial flying was only for the very wealthy. Most people still travelled by boat.

Dermot nodded. 'Don't worry about that, love.'

When they had all returned to Robinswood after the war, Sam insisted on making the place a profit-sharing venture between him and his father-in-law. Sam gave Dermot the old farmhouse, handing over the deeds so he and Isabella would never again be in a position of homelessness, and over the last few years, they'd ensured that the estate thrived. Kate knew her parents had lived through very lean times and were used to being frugal, so her father had probably saved all the money they made.

'When will you go?' Aisling asked. She'd been drawing strength from her father's presence. He was her anchor in a storm-tossed world.

'I'll leave on Friday. I'm going to try to get her to stay, but I know already that's a waste of time, so I'll most likely be coming home with her. When that will be, I don't know. It really depends on how able your Mam is for travelling. She doesn't let on in her letters, but Dr Carlin said she's getting weaker.'

Aisling nodded. Her mam needed him now. But Mark's trial was on next week, and she didn't know if she could endure that without him beside her. It was as if he could read her mind.

'I know I'll miss the start of Mark's trial, but everyone else will be here. I've asked Oskar to come down too. He'll go to court with you, just while I'm gone, so he'll be here to help as well.'

Aisling felt a wave of relief. Oskar Metz was their father's best friend; they'd served in the IRA together though Oskar was half German, and he was as close as a brother to Dermot. It wasn't the same as having Daddy around, but the girls loved Oskar and he them, especially since he had never had any children of his own.

'That's kind of him,' Aisling said.

'Sure he's heartbroken over your mother as well. Bella was very good to Oskar over the years. He wants to help. He'll go to court with you and help around here if needs be, though between the lads and the students, I think everything will be all right. If you girls can manage the hotel, then that's everything...' Dermot stood, and they knew the conversation was over.

'It's going to happen, isn't it?' Kate asked Eve, knowing what her older sister was going to say but needing to hear it, let it sink in.

Eve's eyes were bright. 'Well, barring a miracle, yes, it looks like we are going to lose our mother.'

They sat, the three of them, holding hands but not speaking in the mid-morning sunshine.

CHAPTER 22

'*L*illian, you cannot be serious, not now, knowin' what we do about Isabella and the trial and everything?' Beau was appalled that she would even suggest it. He'd been up since before dawn to get the milking done and had only just returned for breakfast. Lillian was still in bed, so he had brought her up a cup of tea. That's when she announced the bombshell.

'Oh for goodness' sake, Beau, whether we leave or not will not make one iota of difference.' She got out of bed and pulled a silk dressing gown on over her negligee as she spoke. 'Isabella's health is going to go whatever way it will go regardless, and they have that German, Oskar, here as well now. And that business with the shop-keeper and Aisling's husband, well, he obviously killed that man even if it was an accident. But one thing is for certain, it is not our problem.' She took a seat in her usual spot at the window and sipped her tea.

Beau looked at his wife and didn't recognise her. Had she always been this cruel and unfeeling? Was he blind to what she really was all these years, or had she changed? He could not reconcile this hard woman with the Lillian he'd married.

Normal relations had resumed, and they were back in the same bed, but he couldn't shake off the feeling that he was being manipulated. She was beautiful, and she seduced him regularly, but afterwards, he didn't feel the glow of love he used to; now he felt used or something.

'Not our problem?' He was incredulous. 'They're our family, our friends, Austina's family too! And you want to just walk away from them when they need all the help they can get?'

He was trying to avoid their relationship going back to the frosty way it was before, but it was becoming increasingly difficult. She was determined to go back to England, though when he'd asked her how her mother and Perry felt about it, she'd been vague with her answer. If he knew Violet, she would not be thrilled, and the prospect of living off Perry was a horrible one. He liked working; he earned his wages here and felt independent. Austina was happy with Hannah and her cousins. But Lillian didn't seem to care about any of that. She wanted to go and that was all there was to it.

'They are not my relatives, they are our former servants, and one of them married my brother. In nobody's language does that make us related.' Her tone was so haughty, it grated on him. 'Look, Beau, this place, it's hell for me. I can't stand it. I need to get back to England, to my own people. I've no friends here, I don't have anywhere to go or anything to do, there are no shops, no social life – I'm going out of my mind. Now, we're leaving at the weekend either way.' She raised one eyebrow in a way he used to find endearing but now hated.

Something snapped in Beau. He was raised to be deferential to white people, and he was always polite and courteous, but he couldn't take any more. 'Lillian, you do not get to order me around. I'm not goin' to abandon everyone just because you can't go shopping for more shoes, so no, we're not leaving at the weekend. We are stayin' here, and we're going to pull our weight and try to do something to repay the kindness and hospitality of these people.' He kept his tone even, but he was resolute.

Shocked at his refusal but obviously recognising the steel in his voice, she tried a different tack. 'Oh, Beau,' she said patronisingly. 'Look, I know you feel you owe them, but you don't. This is my home, not just Sam's, and I'm entitled to be here. You're my husband, so my entitlement passes to you. They'll figure this all out – they always do. That family are forever getting themselves into impossible scrapes, but they always work it out. This time will be no different.'

The way she dismissed the huge problems facing the family made him furious. 'Lillian, in case you don't know, the shopkeeper, as you call him, attacked and almost raped Aisling. She could have lost the baby she's carryin', and now her husband is havin' to stand trial for that guy's murder, which he did not do.' Beau tried to stay rational and calm, but her truculence was very hard to take. 'Isabella, the woman who raised you, by the way, is terminally ill, and Dermot, who is the *only* reason Sam and you have a home to come back to from what I can see, is devastated. So do you think you could, for one second, just stop thinkin' about your own self and consider what other people are going through? And maybe, just maybe, you could offer to help?'

A flash of something registered in her eyes. Maybe he was getting through to her. He went on. 'So help me God, I love you, but right about now, I don't think I even know who you are. So here's what me and my daughter are going to do. We are stayin' here at Robinswood. We are goin' to do all we can to ease the burden by me working as hard as I can and supporting the family in any way they need. I'll pray for them all, I'll wait on tables every day, I'll work the land till I can't stand up because you know why?' He stared at her.

She didn't answer but looked mutinous.

'Because, Lillian, these people care about us. They love us. And me and Austina at least love them too. And when people you love are going through a tough time, you stand beside them, you help. We may not be able to do anythin' about Isabella's illness, only the Lord can do that, and we have no influence in the courts to get Mark back with Aisling, but we can be there for them, and that's exactly what *I* will be doing' – he paused and maintained eye contact with her – 'either with you or without you. So make your choice – stay here and be useful, or go. It's up to you, but Austina and me ain't going nowhere.'

'Austina is my child. You can't do that. She will come with me wherever I go.' Lillian stood to face him and her eyes glittered danger-ously. 'You won't stop me.'

'Oh, I can. And I will. You will *not* take my little girl to someplace where she'll be alone, without her little cousins and her family to love her –'

'She'll have Perry and Mother and me...' Lillian interrupted.

'No, she won't. Because she's not goin', and neither am I.' Beau stood before her, quaking inside. Was this the end of his marriage? He prayed to Jesus that it wasn't, but it sure felt like it.

They stood, two feet apart, neither willing to back down.

'You can do what you like, Beau, but I *will* take my child,' Lillian hissed, her rage barely suppressed.

'No, you won't.' His voice was quiet but firm. 'She's happy here. I'm happy here. But our happiness doesn't seem to interest you.'

'And you think you'll stop me, do you? No court will give you custody of her! You're a fool if you think otherwise,' she said in that horrible condescending tone again.

'So we're at the point of courts now, are we? It's come to that?' Beau couldn't believe his ears.

'If needs be. And let me tell you, the daughter of a peer will not be beaten by a...' She stopped. The silence hung between them, poiso-nous and heavy.

'Go on...' he said quietly. 'Say it. We both know what you were going to say.'

'Beau, I...' she began, flustered now.

'Will not be beaten by a nigger, is that what you wanted to say, Lillian?' Beau asked calmly.

'No, of course not... I was just...' Lillian coloured as she tried to wriggle out of it. The conversation had suddenly taken a very uncom-fortable turn.

'We both know what you were just about to say.'

'Beau, you're being ridicul –' But he'd left and slammed the bedroom door behind him before she could finish.

Beau stormed out to the low paddocks and began driving the new fence posts with such violence he could feel the muscles in his back and shoulders stretch and ache. How could it have been that he married someone who only saw the colour of his skin? He'd always thought Lillian was different, that it didn't matter to her, even if it mattered to everyone else.

When he arrived in England, he'd been amazed at how the English girls took to him and his fellow black GIs. They were so used to being shunned by white folks, to have these pretty girls being so forward was a shock. He'd been raised right, he knew it, and he would never take advantage in the way they were suggesting, but the other guys ribbed him all the time about how he was the English girls' favourite. In his mind, he was there to do a job, not to court girls, and besides, he'd always imagined that he'd probably go home, if he survived, and marry someone from his community. But then he met Lillian. There was something about her. She was tough and so British, but there was something behind her eyes, a softness that intrigued him.

She made no secret of how she felt about him, but while he was fascinated by her, she wasn't his type. She drank too much and smoked and went to clubs and had no job. When he discovered she was titled, some of it made sense, but when he was just about to call it off – they'd gone on a few dates – they were stopped in the street. The drunk white GIs from Alabama started going on with the usual stuff, telling her she should stick to her own and not give in to the nigger, but they had no idea what they were in for. He'd stood, astounded, as she verbally tore each of them to shreds in that cut-glass way of talking she had.

'Sergeant Lane is my boyfriend, and I am very proud of him. Our country is forever in his debt. He is more of a man than any of you pathetic little boys are or will ever be, so kindly run along and play with your toys and get out of our way.'

She'd then taken his arm and walked confidently past them. He'd admitted to her afterwards how he'd been nervous. The white officers and men from the Southern states made no secret they wanted to create the kind of segregated society in Europe they were used to.

That night, they'd sat in a Lyons Corner House and he told her the truth about what it was like to be black in Georgia. He described the lynchings, the brutality, the way people from his community were treated – and she'd been horrified. They talked for hours that night, not just about race but about everything, and he felt like he got to meet the real Lillian. She'd told him about how she'd loved her father so much but that he'd not cared about her, or at least he found her slightly ridiculous, how her brother was the apple of their mother's eye and could do no wrong. How she wished she'd been raised for something other than marriage to some 'chinless wonder', as she called men of her class.

He remembered how he'd walked her home and she wanted him to come in but he refused. She'd lived with her mother in a really nice house on Hampstead Heath, though she was disparaging about it. Compared to Robinswood, he guessed, it was pretty modest.

They'd fought so hard to be together. She'd fought like nobody ever had for him, and she risked her own life to get him back from the States. So how did it come to this?

On and on he pounded the fence posts, one after the other, as he poured all of his frustration and hurt into the work. He was startled a couple of hours later by Bartley. He'd not heard the other man approach.

'You never came down for lunch, so Eve made you a flask and some sandwiches.' Bartley handed over a bag.

'Thanks, Bartley. I just wanted to get this finished. Dermot and Isabella will be home, so I want to have it fenced by then.' Beau took a bite of a delicious home-cooked ham and tomato sandwich. He poured some coffee and smiled. Nobody in Ireland drank coffee as far as he could tell, but they kept some just for him.

'It's going to be a tough time ahead once Isabella gets back, and what with the trial and everything,' Bartley said, leaning on the bank beside them.

The flask had two cups, so Beau offered to share the coffee, and Bartley accepted.

'Yeah, I kinda can't believe it. We just thought Isabella would go there and be cured. Comin' home no better, and probably worse, wasn't something we thought about.' He sipped the coffee. 'How's Eve about it all?'

Bartley sighed. 'She's the eldest, so she's keeping it all together for Ais and Kate. Aisling doesn't know if she's coming or going, and Kate is at a breaking point. Having the students is the saving grace though. At least they are able to do most of the work now, but they need supervision.' He yawned and stretched.

'Still no sleep, huh?' Beau smiled.

'Not much. She's a bonnie wee lassie and we are stone mad about her, but she's got a set of lungs on her and all she wants is to be up in arms walking about. We walked the floor last night – she wasn't hungry or wet, she just wants to be up.' Bartley closed his eyes and rested back against the bank.

'I don't know if Austina was like that. I didn't meet her until she was a toddler, and I think there were nurses or something in the place Lillian had her. And then she had a nanny when she was with Perry and Violet, so we don't know,' Beau said with regret.

'We'd not have said no if a nanny showed her face at three o'clock this morning, let me tell you.' Bartley chuckled ruefully.

'Well, if she'd stay with me, I'm happy to walk with her for a couple of hours tonight so you guys can get some sleep,' Beau offered tentatively. After a lifetime of segregation and racism, he still was conscious of overstepping the boundaries, though nobody at Robinswood ever treated him as anything but equal – nobody but his wife at least.

'Ah, we couldn't ask you to do that,' Bartley protested.

'You're not asking, I'm offering. If she's OK with me, I could take her to our room, or downstairs, away from you guys anyway, and you can sleep for a while? I'd like to help. I know I'm not part of the Murphy family, but I want to do whatever I can.'

'You are as much a part of this family as any of the rest of us, Beau, and if you are sure, then Eve and I would be so grateful. Eve was crying this morning she was so tired. Though it might put you off having another one of your own after a night with our wee madam.' Bartley grinned.

'That's not likely, though I'd love nothin' more. I feel like I missed out so much with my little girl, and I doubt I'll get a chance again.' Beau shrugged, put the cup back on the top of the flask and finished the last of the sandwich.

Bartley looked at him. 'Beau, tell me to mind my own business if you like, but is everything all right with you and Lillian?'

Beau knew it was disloyal, but he needed to talk, to try to make some sense of the mess that was his life. 'No, Bartley.' He sighed. 'Everything is not all right, but I've absolutely no idea what to do about it.'

'Well, would it help to talk about it?'

Bartley wasn't like anyone Beau had ever met. He was the kind of guy who marched to his own tune and didn't care too much what anyone thought. Beau knew Lillian thought him kind of peculiar. He didn't do small talk, and he had a way of fixing you with his dark eyes that was a little uncomfortable, like he could see beyond what you were showing to the world or something, but Beau liked him. He was a traveller, and those people were discriminated against – not to the extent a black man was back home – and he understood what it was like to have people judge you based on how you looked rather than who you were.

'I guess. I don't know.' Beau shoved his hands deep in his trouser pockets. He gazed out over the estate, its emerald-green fields separated by hedgerows and ditches, the entire property sloping gently towards the ocean. It was like heaven on earth. 'It's like we don't know who we are any more,' Beau began. 'Lillian is complicated, I get that, but I saw past what everybody else saw, y'know? She let me in, and it was like me and her against the world. You know how people look at you, bein' a traveller, right? Well, multiply that by a thousand for a penniless black man and a woman from the aristocratic end of town. I thought at the start she was just playin' with me, tryin' to shock her mother or her friends, but she convinced me it wasn't that. She really loved me, and man, I was crazy about her. Not was – am. I love her, but it's like she's gone behind this wall, and I'm only seein' what everyone else sees, her bein' all snooty and condescending.'

'Did something happen to bring about this change?' Bartley asked.

'Well, her and Kate don't hit it off, but I think she just feels like she doesn't belong here or somethin'. Like Sam got it all and she's in the way. She doesn't like it here and feels disconnected. She knows the girls don't like her, and that Sam is only toleratin' her. I know she tried to help more, but she's not raised like us, to be productive, y'know? I mean, she risked her life! Seriously, she could have been killed when she got me out of jail – you know that story – but she's like a lioness, not scared of anyone. And this is the same woman who found out after I left that she was pregnant, but she fought to keep our baby girl when every single person in her world was horrified. Carryin' a black man's child is one thing, that's bad enough, but for me to be gone, not knowin' if I was ever comin' back, that took guts. And she's got that, so much guts. That's the Lillian I love, the one who is brave and kind and loves so fiercely. But this woman she is now?' He paused. 'I swear, Bartley, I don't know who she is.'

'So when did everything change?'

'I guess since comin' here. Maybe this was a mistake. So she wants to go back to England and take Austina with her, and I refused. She more or less said she'd be going with or without me.'

Beau couldn't bring himself to tell Bartley what Lillian had almost said. It had shocked him deeply. He was used to being called names – it was the story of his life – but to realise that his wife felt the same as all other white folks was something he was having a hard time coming to terms with.

'Is there a reason you two didn't have any more children?' Bartley asked.

Coming from anyone else, the question would have been impertinent and intrusive, but it was something Beau had often wondered himself.

'Well, we have a normal marriage, if that's what you're askin', or at least we did up until a few months ago. Then after the day she slapped Kate and we had an argument, I was sleepin' in Austina's room. But a couple of weeks ago, well, things went back to normal. I was relieved. I thought if we were back together physically, then we'd get back to where we were in every other way, but it wasn't like that. I feel like she seduced me to get her way, to get me out of here.'

Beau was embarrassed to admit the state of his marriage, but Bartley wasn't judging him or Lillian when he said, 'I think, as you say, it's hard for her. Watching you blend in here, and Austina too, when she doesn't. You might be American and black, but you're a working man, and none of us came from money the way she and Sam did, so we have more in common with you than she does. Before, you were all hers. Maybe she misses you, resents sharing you and Austina. The girls don't like her, it's true, so she's not imagining it. Maybe she wants another baby and it's not happening and she has nobody to talk to about it, or maybe she misses the life she had and the only way she knows how to be. It must be lonely being Lillian.'

Beau was surprised at how understanding Bartley was towards her and was grateful for it. He needed to sort this out, but he couldn't bear anyone to disrespect his wife.

'Well, I did ask a few times – y'know, about us having another baby – but she seemed kind of upset and I didn't want her to feel like I was pressurin' her, or that her and Austina weren't enough. You're right, she must be lonely, but it's just so hard to get through to her, y'know?'

Bartley nodded. 'I do.' He smiled. 'When I met Eve, she...she took my breath away, but I took a full year to ask her out. I saw her every single day in the place we both worked, but I would barely say two words to her. Not only was she beautiful and from a decent family, but her first husband died and it broke her heart. I used to lie in bed at night asking myself over and over what on earth someone like Eve would do with someone like me, no family, a traveller, and how could I measure up to a man who died?'

'So what did you do?' Beau asked.

'To be honest, it was Elena who kind of pushed us together, and I'm so glad she did. At the start, it was a wee bit odd, as she talked so much about her family and I...well, apart from my brother Isaac who I've just found, I don't have any. But bit by bit, she broke down all the walls I'd built up around myself. And now, well, I can't imagine life without her.'

'That's how I feel about Lillian, but I just don't know what to do,' Beau said miserably.

'Tell her. Open up and tell her how you feel. She feels insecure, that you're more with us than her, so show her that she's your priority. You've nothing to lose at this stage now, anyway, do you?'

'And if she says, "If you love me, then come back to England with me," what then?'

'Then you have to decide which you want more, us or her.' Bartley patted him on the shoulder and walked back down the field.

CHAPTER 23

*A*isling took her seat in the courtroom, Oskar's strong, stoic presence beside her. Just as Dermot had promised, Oskar didn't let her out of his sight.

She'd had a meeting with Mark's barrister, and he'd filled her in on the situation so far. Mark's brief was a very distinguished-looking man, with longish silver hair and an imposing manner. He barely spoke to the family at all, but Perry, who'd insisted on engaging him at mind-boggling expense, assured them that Geoffrey d'Alton was the best there was. He was Irish apparently, though one would hardly know that by his accent, but he lived between London and France and his cases were often featured in international media.

He didn't give her false hope, but he explained how Irish law differed from British in that a person could be tried for murder but have a manslaughter charge considered as well.

The judge's face was impossible to read. On and on the prosecution's barrister went, feigning sympathy. Marks's actions were understandable, his wife had been attacked, he was in a blind fury, he lashed out at the man who did it... The lurid details of the case that captured the attention of the country made Aisling's cheeks burn with shame.

Newspaper reporters were in the courtroom daily, their numbers growing as detail after sordid detail was revealed, their headlines getting more and more salacious by the day.

Before he left for Davos, Dermot had told her she didn't have to go, to listen, but that first morning, when Mark's eyes locked with hers as they led him to the dock, decided her. She would be there for him, her darling husband, no matter what she had to endure. They'd allowed her one brief supervised visit in all the time he'd been held on remand, and during it he'd told her he didn't do it. She believed him.

She wasn't called as a witness for the prosecution, and Mark apparently told his lawyer that he didn't want Aisling put on the stand, made to relive the horrible event in front of everyone. Dermot and Oskar agreed it would be too hard. Doctor Grahame's testimony and the police evidence would be enough.

Dr Grahame had to give evidence as to the nature of Lacey's injuries; d'Alton had only just found out upon disclosure that Sean had been stabbed. When the prosecution asked Dr Grahame about the nature of Aisling's trauma, she remained stony-faced beside Oskar.

The rest of the family took turns accompanying them, but she pleaded with them to get on with things as she had Oskar beside her, and she felt better with him there. There was something reassuring about the German man, and his stoic presence ensured nobody approached her as she entered and left the courtroom each day.

Sergeant O'Connell had to take the stand to explain what he discovered when he went into Lacey's house after the cleaner found the body, and of course Biddy Cronin, Sean's cleaner and the biggest gossip in Kilthomand, loved every moment of her time on the stand.

Sam was called, and he described finding Mark and convincing him to leave Sean alone. He testified that while Mark was understandably very upset, he agreed to go back to Aisling, and how Sean was crying and had a cut over his eye but otherwise was fine.

It wasn't until the detective from Dublin was questioned that d'Alton seemed to come alive. They had not recovered the murder weapon and the cashbox was gone, and d'Alton focused on just one line of questioning. 'Detective O'Rourke, did you or your men search the Belitho cottage for the missing cashbox and murder weapon?'

'We did,' the detective answered dourly, knowing what was coming.

'And did you find anything?' d'Alton asked pleasantly.

'No,' O'Rourke admitted.

'Well, Robinswood is an extremely large property. Did you search it?' d'Alton asked.

'Inasmuch as was possible, yes, we searched the house and the outbuildings. But a wide-scale search of the property, an area of over fifteen hundred acres, would require manpower that we simply do not have,' the detective answered.

'So, Detective O'Rourke, there is no murder weapon, and the missing cashbox remains elusive?'

'Yes.'

'So there is no evidence linking my client to either a stabbing or a theft?'

O'Rourke took his time in answering, weighing up how he should respond, but finally said, 'No.'

Aisling believed Mark when he said he didn't kill Sean, but she thought he might have delivered an injury during the fight that later resulted in Sean's death. However, once she found out that Sean had been stabbed, she was sure. Mark wouldn't do that. And as for stealing, well, that was ridiculous. Surely the jury must see that.

The jury heard how the shop accounts were open on the kitchen table and that Lacey must have been doing his paperwork either before or after the attack. It seemed most unlikely that he would come in after such an event and calmly do his finances, but equally unlikely that he was doing them earlier in the day and just left the book open and the money in a cashbox beside it. Also, he'd had the box with him at the time of the incident, so why would he have taken it back out of the house once he came home?

Lacey had been drinking more than his usual amount, and it seemed some unpleasantness went on between him and Mark in Maher's pub that evening. It came as news to Aisling how often Lacey tried to belittle Mark, and it was nice to hear the men who were in the pub that night defend him on the stand. Apparently, Lacey made some remark about Aisling and him being close, trying to insinuate there was something going on, and the Englishman had had enough. He was stone-cold sober, but he stood up in front of Sean, towering over him, and told him that he was pathetic, that everyone knew he had tried to break him and Aisling up and that he wasn't then, and would not be now, successful. That Aisling couldn't stand him, and she and everyone else in Kilthomand knew exactly what kind of man Sean Lacey was. The jury heard how Lacey stormed off in fury.

When Mark was arrested, there were several cuts on his hands and arms. He explained that he may have got some of them from his assault on Sean Lacey but that also in the days before the attack, he had been cutting briars. All evidence was circumstantial, but since he was the only one with a motive and the opportunity, and because he had a previous conviction, the odds were not on his side.

Lacey's assistant, a young man called Timmy O'Flaherty, explained to the court how Sean took the cashbox home every evening once the shop closed. On Saturday nights, he crossed the square with the ledger and the cashbox to do his accounts, ready to lodge the money in the bank in Dungarvan on Monday morning. Timmy always opened up on a Monday, and the boss came back around eleven.

Lacey wasn't exactly popular – the testimonies gave the distinct impression that he was considered a bit of a sneak, and well able to overcharge too, knowing he was the only draper's in the village – but he'd lived his whole life in Kilthomand.

Eleanor Conlan, the woman Sean had been fooling around with when he was supposed to be going out with Aisling all those years ago, was called to the stand. Kate had humiliated her in front of everyone at the dance that night, and Eleanor had hated the Murphys ever since. She was in the pub the night Sean was killed, and her testimony was particularly damning.

'Miss Conlan, could you describe the relationship between the accused and the victim as you understood it?' the wigged and gowned barrister asked.

'Mark Belitho hated Sean Lacey. He made no secret of it,' she said, a self-satisfied look on her face. 'Poor Sean was always at the butt of his jokes' – she nodded in Mark's direction – 'and he was upset by it. Even the night it happened, that Englishman was crowing about how he'd scored the winning point in a recent match, and Sean just pointed out gently how an older local man had done better in years gone by, when Belitho gave him a look of pure hatred. He didn't like anyone undermining the cocky image he had of himself. I think that he was jealous of Sean, who was a well-respected businessman and liked by everyone, when Mark Belitho hardly has a penny to his name and is a convicted criminal. Sean never did anything to hurt him, or anyone else...' She took out her handkerchief and dabbed her dry eyes.

'Thank you, Miss Conlan.'

The prosecutor sat down, and as Eleanor got up to leave, Mark's barrister stopped her. 'If you could resume your seat for a moment, Miss Conlan, I just have one or two small things...'

Aisling glanced at Oskar. D'Alton had been remarkably quiet all through the trial, almost always declining to cross-examine the witness with a mere wave of his manicured hand. On the first day, she was so worried he wasn't doing anything for Mark, they rang Perry in a panic, but he explained how d'Alton had a unique style. He lulled the other side into a sense of false security and seemed almost disinterested in the case until they made a crucial error, which they inevitably did. Then his vague manner disappeared and he swooped like an eagle. Perry was fascinated by him and had gone to watch him in the Old Bailey several times. His cases were becoming a huge spectator sport, it would seem. Perry urged them to trust him. If anyone could get Mark off, it would be him.

D'Alton was fumbling with some papers and seemed disorganised. For the millionth time, Aisling prayed Perry was right.

The lawyer stayed behind his desk, not going into the body of the courtroom as his opposing counsel did. 'How well do you know Mr Belitho?' he asked mildly, his voice only barely audible.

Eleanor smirked. 'Kilthomand is a small place, everyone knows everyone,' she answered cheekily.

'So you just have a passing acquaintance with him?' d'Alton asked, his tone almost bored.

'Yes, I would say so. We're not friends, if that's what you're asking.' She glared at Mark in the dock.

'Hmm.' The sound was enough to cast aspersions on her honesty. He went on. 'And what about you and Mr Lacey, how would you describe your relationship with him?'

Eleanor looked uncomfortable now, and the gathered crowd almost slid forward on their seats to hear what she would say. Everyone in the village knew she'd had her eye on Sean Lacey for years, but apart from that one night at the dance, he'd never looked in her direction again. It was widely accepted that Lacey's heart was only for one woman, and that was Aisling Murphy. Eleanor threw herself at him, but he never took the bait. When Aisling came home after the war, Lacey tried to break her and Mark up. Kate made sure everyone knew what he did by mentioning it to one of the town gossips. Eleanor was still sniffing about Sean at that stage, and she'd lost out to Aisling again.

Eleanor decided to bluff it out. 'We're both from Kilthomand, we've lived here all our lives...' she began.

'So you had the same relationship with the deceased as you would have with, say, Mrs Cronin, or the postmaster...' d'Alton smiled innocently.

Eleanor blushed. 'Well, we were friends, I suppose...' she began.

'Close friends?' d'Alton pressed her.

'Well, not really. Well, yes, I suppose so...' She was flustered now.

'Is it not true that you would have liked to have had a romantic connection with the deceased but he wasn't interested?'

'Objection, Your Honour, irrelevant.' The prosecutor was standing now.

'Please clarify how this line of questioning is relevant, Mr d'Alton,' the judge said warily. D'Alton's reputation preceded him, and Oskar had overheard one of the junior barristers remark that this judge was going to have to watch his Ps and Qs. There was absolutely no aspect of law, no matter how obscure, that the famous barrister could not quote or twist to his advantage.

'Well, I am merely establishing bias on the part of the witness in favour of the deceased and against my client, Your Honour.' D'Alton smiled once more.

'Overruled,' the judge said. 'Carry on, Mr d'Alton.'

'So it would seem there is considerable history between the dead man and my client, but I cannot find any evidence to suggest there was any ill will on the part of Mr Belitho – it would seem Mr Lacey was the one with a grudge. It cannot have escaped your notice, Miss Conlan, that nobody else in the bar that night heard my client speak disrespectfully to Mr Lacey apart from yourself. In fact, it was Lacey who goaded Mr Belitho, and he responded, I think in everyone's opinion, in a calm and measured way. How can you explain that?'

'Well, I know what I heard,' Eleanor said belligerently, but refused to meet the barrister's eye.

'And is Maher's a large public house?' he asked.

'No, not really,' Eleanor muttered.

'So you expect this court to believe that in a very small pub, you overheard harsh words between Mr Belitho and Mr Lacey and not one other person did? In fact, according to several witnesses here today, it would seem that if anyone was needling anyone else, it was Sean Lacey. He had tried to break up my client's marriage, he tried to blacken Mr Belitho's name around the village, he even tried to have him dropped from the local hurling team, which I understand is enjoying unprecedented levels of success since my client joined the club?'

There was a murmur of assent from the locals in the packed public gallery.

D'Alton went on. 'If there was hatred, I would put to you, Miss Conlan, that the only person who felt that was Sean Lacey. He had feelings for my client's wife and was unwilling to accept that she had chosen someone else. On the night in question, Sean Lacey did a terrible thing, a criminal thing, for which he should be standing trial.'

The silence was palpable as everyone hung on d'Alton's words.

'Gentlemen.' He stood now and addressed the jury. 'My client has confirmed that he assaulted Mr Lacey. He's never denied it. The man brutally attacked his wife.' He paused and gazed calmly at the jury for a long second before going on. 'And after he attacked her, he went home calmly and began to do his weekly accounts at the kitchen table. Gentlemen, somebody else committed a murder. That person or persons will be brought to justice in due course, one would hope, but what you must consider is that it was not my client. There is no murder weapon, the money and cashbox were never found, and Mark Belitho is not, as we heard from so many local people, known as a hothead or a violent, dangerous man. True, the men did not like each other, everyone in Kilthomand knew that, but not liking someone doesn't mean a person is capable of murder. He explained how he left the house, understandably upset, while the doctor examined his wife, and how he walked to the village. He described the route he took. He went to Sean Lacey's house, and yes, he did assault him. But when my client left Mr Lacey, Mr Lacey was very much alive. Not only that, but you have heard evidence from Samuel Kenefick, who was there that night, to corroborate that fact. And that, gentlemen, is the currency we must deal in, not supposition or hearsay or anyone's surmising, but in cold, hard facts. Sean Lacey was alive when my client left him, and there is a witness to confirm that.'

Aisling guessed he decided to make this speech with Eleanor Conlan, who was clearly biased, still on the stand.

He sat down and one could hear a pin drop. He went back to his notes, and after what felt to Aisling like a very long time, he looked up at the stand as if he'd just remembered that Eleanor was still there. 'No more questions,' he said with a pleasant smile.

Court was adjourned for the day, and Aisling and Oskar waited as the crowds filed out. Aisling watched as they took Mark back down, and they managed to exchange a glance for a moment. *I love you*, she mouthed, and he gave her a small smile.

To her surprise, Geoffrey d'Alton remained in his seat as well. She wanted to talk to him, to see how he thought it was going. She'd spoken to him two or three times, always brief exchanges, and he seemed a bit peculiar, if she were honest. He was clipped and bordering on dismissive, but there was something deep about the man; it was hard to describe. He had an assistant who had given them platitudes but no guarantees, but he did deliver a letter from Mark saying how much he liked d'Alton and how he had great faith in him, so that had to be enough.

Once the courtroom was empty, the barrister stood up and approached them. 'Mrs Belitho... And this is your father, I assume?' He extended a hand.

'Er...no, this is a family friend, Oskar Metz. My father is caring for my mother, who is very ill,' Aisling said. 'Mr d'Alton, the detective said Sean was stabbed and his money stolen. Mark could not have done that, I know he didn't...'

The barrister's face was unlined and tanned, and he was clean-shaven. It was impossible to say what age he was. He had perfectly straight teeth and eyes the colour of sapphires, and he smelled of some expensive woody cologne.

'It's a pleasure to meet you,' he said to Oskar as he perched on the table recently vacated by the prosecution team. 'Yes, that was a shock, and it should have been made clear to our side in disclosure, which I will be having words with the judge about. The lack of a murder weapon or the cashbox will help, but as the detective said, the estate is enormous. Mark could have thrown them anywhere.'

Aisling was shocked. He was talking like Mark had stabbed Sean. 'But there's no way Mark could –' she began.

He interrupted her. 'Perception is reality.' He seemed angry. 'I do not wish to alarm you or to cause you undue distress, but we must prepare for a guilty verdict.'

Aisling felt like a block of ice was churning around inside her. She couldn't speak.

'But there is no evidence... You said yourself...' Oskar began.

'Yes, that's the case, but discovering that the victim was stabbed in the middle of a trial is not ideal from my point of view. I wish someone would have told me.'

Aisling was furious now too. 'Mr d'Alton, there is no chance Mark stabbed Sean Lacey or stole his money. I guarantee it. They can search every inch of Robinswood, and they won't find the knife or the box. My husband did beat him up, and even if he hadn't admitted it, I would believe him capable of it, but stabbing and stealing? No...he just wouldn't do it. He lashed out because of what Sean did to me, which is understandable in the circumstances, but stabbing and murder, he just wouldn't, I know he wouldn't.' Her eyes pleaded with his. 'You have to believe that, otherwise he doesn't stand a chance.'

D'Alton observed her, and she could feel her cheeks flush. 'I'll need you to take the stand,' he said.

'But Mark doesn't want me to, and my father –' she began, but again he interrupted her.

'With respect, you are employing me – or Lord Goodall is, at any rate – to get your husband out of this mess, so please, listen to *me*. I know they want to spare you the ordeal, and it will be an ordeal I assure you, but you are a very convincing young woman, and if you can give just as good an account of yourself on the stand as you just did to me, then I think we can at least secure a manslaughter verdict rather than a murder charge.' He stopped and looked at Aisling and then Oskar. 'The fact that you didn't make a statement to the guards at the time is not helpful, so the prosecution will argue either that it never happened or that it was consensual. But as I said, you're convincing, so if they hear it from your mouth, there is a chance they will believe you. It's his only hope.'

Aisling turned to Oskar. 'What do you think?'

'If Mr d'Alton says it will help, I think you should do it,' he said slowly. 'But it's up to you in the end.'

'How graphic would I have to be?' Aisling asked, dreading the answer.

'As graphic as it was, and more if you can. Aisling, if Mark is found guilty of this murder, and I believe at the moment that will be the verdict, then all I can do is try to ameliorate that by going hard on what Lacey did to you. The men of this jury will, by the time I am finished, be picturing their own wives in such a situation and imagining themselves taking precisely the course of action of which Mark is accused. The goal here is an acquittal, of course, but failing that, a manslaughter conviction, which does not carry the mandatory death penalty. The judge may even go easy on him, and he could be looking at only ten years.'

Aisling opened her mouth to speak but no sound came out. She tried again. 'But he didn't do it, Mr d'Alton.' She knew she sounded like a child. That wasn't how the law worked, but it was so hard to hear.

'Possibly not, but without any other suspect… And Mark had a significant motive as well as a previous conviction for violent assault. All fingers point to him, I'm afraid. Your testimony will be crucial. I will of course press for a "not guilty" verdict, but I have to tell you that I cannot see it happening. I will, however, give you my word that I will do everything in my power to commute it to manslaughter and a lighter sentence. So will you do it?'

'I will,' Aisling said, the ice water sloshing about inside her. 'Can you tell Mark, and explain why?'

'Of course.' He nodded. His demeanour suddenly changed. 'What you've been subjected to, Aisling, well, nobody should have to endure it. Sean Lacey should be the one facing years behind bars, not Mark, but this is the best I can do.'

She blinked back the tears. His kindness was the final straw. She'd remained dry-eyed throughout the entire trial, Oskar telling her not to give the satisfaction of seeing her cry to the photographers, but now she couldn't hold them back any more.

'Thank you, Mr d'Alton…' she began.

'You're welcome, Aisling. And by the way, it's just d'Alton. No Mister. I use my surname all the time.'

She heard a slight Cork accent, and she wondered how she'd ever thought him aloof and unapproachable. He was kind.

'Take her home, Mr Metz. I'll be in touch.' The barrister shook Oskar's hand and left.

CHAPTER 24

The following day, Kate looked up, stunned to see Lillian at the kitchen door. Hannah had taken the children upstairs to play. It was getting too cold now to take them outside in the mornings, and anyway little Bella had a bit of a cold, so they were in the newly converted playroom. Bartley and Beau had worked every evening on it, and now the room that had once been a draughty bedroom was a bright sunny place with a big open fire for heat and lots of toys. Perry donated an old rocking horse and a collection of tricycles and scooters, and Sam found his old train set in the attic for Jack. It took some painstaking work from Beau to get it going, but now it puffed happily around the perimeter of the room. There was a table and four little chairs where they did artwork and ate lunch sometimes, and they loved it there.

'Good morning, Kate.' Lillian's tone was neutral. There had been nothing but the most perfunctory of exchanges between the two women for weeks now, and frankly, at the moment, Lillian was the least of Kate's worries.

'Yes, Lillian?' Kate asked wearily. She didn't have the energy for round two of the battle.

'I wondered if I could help.'

Kate thought she must be hearing things. Lillian looked different, she noticed, not so dolled up and not wearing make-up.

'With what?' Kate asked.

Lillian looked awkward. 'Well, the hotel, or the children, whatever needs doing really.' Lillian flushed red but continued. 'This is a very difficult time for you all, for us all really, and it seems stupid my sitting upstairs doing nothing if you need help.'

Kate didn't know what to say.

Lillian mistook her confusion for reticence. 'Look, we've not exactly seen eye to eye, but can we just bury the hatchet so to speak? I'm sorry for the way I behaved, and I'm genuinely devastated about your mother. Beau told me the news is not good from Davos.'

Kate couldn't speak. She clenched her jaw tightly to stop the tears and just nodded.

Lillian crossed the big warm kitchen and put her arms around Kate. 'I'm so sorry, Kate. I really am. Your mother was more of a mother to me and Sam than our own ever was. This is a very hard blow. Please let me help?'

Kate allowed her body to relax, and she melted into her sister-in-law's embrace.

'You were right. And I didn't see it. But Beau, well, suffice to say he's made it clear that I was being selfish and that I should change. You were there for me when I needed someone. When I was pregnant, when I had to leave Austina to find Beau, you were the one, as you rightly pointed out to me, that I came to for help. I'm sorry I didn't appreciate you fully, but please, let me return the favour now?'

'Thanks,' Kate managed.

Giving Kate a last quick squeeze, Lillian took an apron from the back of the kitchen door. 'Look, you know from the last disastrous attempt to help out that I'm fairly useless, but I can wash pots or peel potatoes?'

Despite her heartbreak, Kate giggled. 'What's brought this on?' she asked.

Lillian thought for a moment. 'Two things. First, my husband made me realise I was being a complete witch. Last night, he came home and we had a long talk. Apparently Bartley gave him some good advice. Anyway, I realised that he was in fact right and I was wrong. The only thing stopping me being as happy here as he and Austina are is me. He told me he loved me but that he couldn't go on the way things were between us. I can't be without him, and I want to be happy. My brother can muck in with the rest of you, and if he can do it, perhaps I can too. Sitting up in that room seething all day wasn't doing me or anyone else any good.'

'And the second thing?'

'Austina. She wanted to bake a cake for your mother for when she gets home and asked me to help her, but I told her I didn't know how. She asked me why I can't make a cake like you and your sisters, and I had no answer for her. Her little face... She looked so disappointed! And I realised then and there I want to be useful, not an ornament, and anyway I wasn't even a very beautiful ornament. So I'm here, and I'm willing, but how able I am, well...that's anyone's guess.'

'It was brave of you to admit that. And look, maybe I'm a bit... Well, I know I'm only playing pretend that I'm the mistress of this place...and you're the real thing, so I probably resent that a bit or something.' She sighed. 'To be honest, none of it matters to me at the moment. I'm losing my mother, and I'm not ready. I can't...' She broke off, unable to continue.

'This is so hard, Kate, for all of us, but for you girls and Dermot, well, you're the closest family I've ever seen, so I can't imagine. But lean on us. We all want to help. And yes, the coming days or weeks or whatever are going to be cruel, but we all want to help.'

Kate nodded, wiping her eyes with the linen handkerchief Lillian offered. 'Thanks.'

Lillian smiled, pure relief. 'Well, how about I make lunch for the children and bring it up to the playroom? Hannah is taking care of all of them up there, so she has her hands full.' Lillian smiled. 'I think I can manage that.'

'Great, thanks.' Kate went to the oven to take out the roast chickens for the evening supper. Then she realised her sister-in-law had not moved.

'And what do they eat?' Lillian asked.

Kate groaned inwardly. Lillian being helpful, she suspected, was going to be ten times harder work than Lillian in a mood upstairs, but her mother would have welcomed her into the kitchen and shown her patiently what to do, and Kate would do no less.

The morning flew by. Eve changed all the linens with the new group of students that had arrived last week. Hannah was due to leave as well but she'd asked to stay, and the children loved her so they'd agreed. Hannah did love the children too, but they all knew it was the rakish Isaac that was keeping her at Robinswood.

Isaac was a good worker and very pleasant and charming. Eve had confided to Kate that Bartley liked him but found him a bit of a mystery. Isaac had no interest in finding their family and refused to even discuss the past or the future. Bartley had hoped that Isaac would make his home with them, but the young man shied away from any conversations beyond the next few days.

Beau's beam of delight at seeing Lillian stirring a pot of stew when he and the others came in for lunch lit up the room. He washed up and immediately gave Lillian a hug, which made her blush with pleasure. Kate and Aisling exchanged a look. One up to Beau. Good for him; he'd stood his ground and played her at her own game.

They served lunch to all the farmhands. There were over fifteen full-time workers on the estate now, as well as the students, so feeding the staff was a huge task. Kate and Sam suggested refusing any new bookings – it felt wrong to carry on with Isabella so ill and Mark on trial – but Dermot insisted. They'd all worked so hard; throwing it all away now would not be right. In fact, he said it would be an insult to all the work Mark and Isabella had done to get the ramshackle old ruin back to the glory it once enjoyed.

Lillian was clumsy and disorganised, but they tried to be patient, and Kate deliberately stepped back, though why her sister-in-law brought cutlery to the table in ones rather than grabbing a handful of soupspoons or whatever was a mystery. Lillian's hair was stuck to her neck and she was going as fast – if not as efficiently – as she could. It was lovely to see the smile on Beau's face as he helped her ladle Irish stew and slice bread, and there were stewed apples and custard for dessert.

Kate had everyone trained to bring his or her own cup and plate to the large sink in the scullery. She washed as Lillian dried all the tableware and replaced it in a jumbled order in the cupboard. Kate itched to rearrange it. Could Lillian not see that bowls had their own section, not on top of side plates, which had been placed on top of dinner plates? She took a deep breath.

Eve came in and helped Lillian, unobtrusively replacing everything in the right order, and by the time they were cleared up, the place was its usual ordered self. 'Now let's have our own lunch, and then we'll get started on tonight's dinner, will we?'

'Shall I lay the table?' Lillian asked. 'Do the female students come in now?'

'Great, do please.' Eve smiled. 'No, it's just us. The girls are eating in their quarters.'

Bartley had built a sitting room and kitchen for the girls so they could cook and clean for themselves and begin the process of deinstitutionalising. It was lovely to see these timid young women, only ever used to life in a children's home, suddenly blossom into adults. They loved cooking and relaxing in their little sitting room. Oskar had fixed an old wireless that had been abandoned in one of the rooms upstairs, so they sat at night, listening to the radio, reading or knitting.

Eve sighed and sat down. 'I've spent the morning showing the students how to make a dress from a pattern. There's great excitement, as they're planning on wearing the new dresses to the village dance at the end of the month. For almost all of them, it's their first dance.'

Lillian looked a little uncomfortable now that it was just them, but she seemed determined to be useful. She cut bread, refilled the butter dish, dried the stew bowls and placed four on the table. As she worked, she said, 'I remember the excitement of dances during the war. I'd only ever been to coming-out balls, which were heavily chaperoned and deathly boring, so the freedom of going dancing was so much fun.'

'I remember we used to dance at the Palais on Tottenham Court Road. Seeing all the men in uniform, it was such a thrill. It might as well have been a million miles from Kilthomand. Ais and I used to feel so sophisticated.' Kate rolled her eyes and smiled at her naïve self of those days.

'Well, I don't know how exciting the Kilthomand parish dance is going to be, but they are looking forward to it anyway,' Eve said as she took the tureen of stew from Lillian with a smile of thanks. 'Thanks for the help, Lillian.'

'It's fine,' Lillian answered. 'I want to help. I'm not much good at most things yet, but I'll get the hang of it I hope.'

'Well, we're happy to have you here. With Mam being sick and Daddy and Mark not around, we are in need of all the help we can get.' Eve reached for a slice of bread, stifling a yawn. Bella still wasn't sleeping. The child was adorable but seemed to only need about twenty minutes sleep. She and Bartley were shattered. She had tried taking the baby to another room so at least he could sleep, but the baby yelled so loudly, they were afraid she'd wake the whole house. Their quarters were the most isolated.

'Still no sleep?' Kate asked sympathetically.

'No. She's a little demon.' Eve smiled. 'She fell asleep on Bartley's chest last night, and he was almost afraid to breathe in case he woke her up, but that only lasted for a few minutes. It seems she only needs a catnap and then she's full of beans again. I wish Mammy were here – she'd know what to do.'

'Beau and I could take her overnight tonight?' Lillian offered, and instantly reddened. 'I mean, if you would like. I know Beau did a night or two before. He really is remarkable with babies, and they seem to relax with him. But our rooms are quite a way from the guests, so even if Bella did cry, she wouldn't wake anyone. Perhaps Austina could sleep in with yours, Kate?'

The Murphy girls tried to hide their astonishment. Lillian barely took care of her own child let alone a screaming baby. Beau had been wonderful, and they knew the offer was there, but they'd felt bad about keeping him up all night when he had a long day of work ahead.

'Ah, thanks, Lillian, but...' Eve began, but Kate put her hand on her sister's.

'That's a great idea. Austina can have the spare bed in Jack's room, and that way little Bella won't disturb her and you and Bartley get a full night's sleep together.' Kate gave Eve a glance that said, *Let her do it. Don't throw it back in her face.*

'Well, we'd be happy to help, so if it's all right with you... As I said, Beau is great with babies and I'll do what I can...'

'You had Austina and took care of her on your own, Lillian. I know Beau is good, but you're a mother and a very good one too, so don't run yourself down,' Kate said kindly.

Lillian looked unsure of how to respond. 'Well, I had a nursing home, and a nanny at Framington, but...'

'You're a great mother, Lillian. Bella will be fine with you,' Kate said certainly.

And Lillian rewarded them with a genuine smile, something they rarely saw. 'Thank you, Kate. That means a lot coming from you. I know I've been a bit...well...difficult. My own mother has berated me on more than one occasion and Beau too, but I promise I'll make a serious effort this time. You are all so capable, but then you learned at the expert's knee. Isabella did so much for Sam and me, she really did, and we love her. I wish she'd have taught me to be useful as she did you three girls, but I'll do my best to catch up.'

'She loved you and Sam like her own,' Eve said, covering Lillian's hand with hers. That wasn't strictly true; their mother loved Sam but found Lillian to be a stuck-up madam, but that was hopefully all water under the bridge. Lady Lillian was finally trying to fit in, and the Murphy girls would respond as they had been taught to do, with grace and gratitude.

CHAPTER 25

*H*annah felt very forward as she walked down the potholed lane behind the house that linked the old converted barns where the boys lived with the stable yard. The main avenue had been filled in and covered with gravel, but the funds did not stretch to the other lanes around the estate, so she had to hop from one dry bit to the next. She pulled her cardigan around her. She should be wearing a coat really, but her only one was so shabby and she wanted to look nice. Not all dressed up like she was going to a dance nice, but nice all the same.

Since the weather had turned colder and wetter, her opportunities to see Isaac were curtailed, and she longed to meet him again. They'd gone to the pictures twice more, and on the last occasion, he had kissed her under the elm trees before seeing her to the door.

She found herself thinking about him all the time, resenting it when the other girls spoke about how good-looking he was. They all seemed to like him, and he had time for everyone. Hannah hoped she was special; he certainly gave her that impression, but then maybe he did that with everyone? After that first night, he never mentioned America again. Isaac Doherty had something that she'd never experienced before. Not that she'd had a lot of experience with males, but even she could tell there was nobody on earth like him. It wasn't just his good looks, with his black curls, sallow skin and flashing eyes, but he was just bursting with life. Nothing scared him, and he never seemed to second-guess himself or wonder if he should do or say something. He sang if he felt like singing, no matter who was listening, and when he sang, he was like a linnet. He was as dexterous as a monkey, and when his eyes fixed on hers, she could feel the butterflies dancing in her stomach.

She'd dressed carefully. Kate had given all the girls material for dresses, but she'd given Hannah a beautiful scarlet-red dress that she said she would never wear again. It had a sweetheart neckline and cinched in tight at the waist but smoothed down over her hips. It was the most beautiful thing that Hannah had ever owned. She'd put a white cardigan she'd knitted over it, and even though the October evening was chilly, she was determined not to spoil the look.

She had no idea what she would do or say if she found him, nor indeed did she know where to start looking. The estate was huge and he could be anywhere. The last thing she would want was for Kate or Miss Doherty to hear she was loitering around the boys' dorms looking for someone. She would have to look like she was nonchalantly out for a walk.

The new group of girls seemed nice. The last lot had 'graduated' from the course a few weeks back, and she and Isaac were the only two who'd stayed on. But she didn't let on that she had anything special going on with him.

A group of boys were lifting bags of firewood and carrying them back to the dormitory. Hannah knew they had a large stove in there to keep the place cosy. They waved hello and she waved back, scanning to see if Isaac was among them. He wasn't. She felt foolish. What should she do now? The lane was a dead end, the big barn where the boys lived at the end, so she would have to turn around. But if she did that, it would appear as though she'd been looking for someone.

'Can we help, miss?' one of the boys asked, a cheeky grin on his face.

Hannah thought quickly. She knew Bartley was up at the house –

she'd seen him go into the kitchen as she left – so she called, 'I'm just wondering if Bartley is about?'

The red-haired boy that had called to her ran over, dropping his bag of logs. 'He's not, I'm afraid. Can I help you?' His green eyes danced merrily. 'I'm Joseph Browne, at your service.' He bowed theatrically and she laughed.

'No thanks. I just had a message for him.' She turned to go, and as she did, a voice called out from the nearby barn, which Bartley had converted into his own workshop.

'You could give it to his brother.' Isaac sauntered out, smiling laconically, wiping his hands on a dirty rag. 'On your bike, foxy,' he said to Joseph, who reluctantly returned to his logs.

'Oh, it's nothing... I can just... It was just that dinner is ready...' Hannah finished lamely, her cheeks burning.

'I'd say he knew that when he heard the bell ringing in the yard like it does every evening, but thanks for coming to find him in case he starved to death.' Isaac laughed gently. 'I'd hate my long-lost brother to be hollow with the hunger.'

'Well, I actually...' Hannah began, but thought better of it and quickly turned on her heel and tried not to run back up the lane.

Isaac ran after her. 'Now that you're here, can't you stay for a bit?' He looked like a puppy wanting to play.

'No, I'd better get back...' she mumbled, totally mortified now. She cursed her stupidity. What kind of girl goes looking for a boy like that? Didn't she get herself into enough trouble before? Maybe she was just bad to the core, like that nun who'd delivered Laura said she was.

'Hannah, please. I'm so happy to see you. I was only teasing you! I'm sorry, I shouldn't have. I was just hoping you might have been looking for me...' He stood before her, pleading now. Out of nowhere another shower split the heavens, and without asking, he took her hand and ran towards the workshop from where he'd emerged. He wrenched the door open and drew her inside. It was warm and dry and smelled of oil and wood shavings. They were alone.

'I shouldn't be here...' she began, panicking now.

'Hannah, it's only me. Bartley is up having his dinner, and the lads are all over in the barn having theirs. Let me make you a cup of tea, please, to say I'm sorry for being a clown and upsetting you.'

She was looking at the floor, a dirt one, covered in a dusting of sawdust. She felt him reach over and lift her chin, bringing her eyes level with his.

'Please, lovely Hannah? A cup of tea? And my sister-in-law made Bartley some truly delicious fruit cake that I'll throw in to sweeten the deal?'

Hannah had to smile. 'Won't he mind?'

'Nah, he's very generous, my brother. He wants me to be happy, so making you happy makes me happy, which will make Bartley happy, and a happy Bartley is the goal here, isn't it?'

Hannah was confused. Was Isaac being sarcastic or not? It was hard to know with him. She had tried to get him to talk about his family or even about how it felt to be reunited with his brother, but he only ever made jokey remarks. She understood it – she didn't enjoy conversations about her origins either – so she didn't push it, but still, it would be nice to talk to him properly.

'All right, one cup so,' she conceded, and he punched the air in delight.

'Yes! Victory.' He winked at her as he filled the kettle and lit the little gas stove.

They sat sipping their tea and nibbling on the fruit cake as they chatted easily. She told him about her days, about funny things Jack or Austina said, or how incorrigible Daisy and Poppy were, and he told her about a newspaper report he was reading about a famous robbery that had happened back in January in America.

'It was amazing, Hannah! These lads – they reckon there were eleven of them, led by a fella called Anthony Pino – all dressed up in Halloween masks, robbed an armoured car and got away with 2.7 million dollars.' His eyes glittered with the excitement of the story. 'They were only caught because one of the robbers, a fella called O'Keefe – wouldn't you know he'd be Irish – was picked up for something else and he threatened to squeal on his mates. The rest of the gang got wind of it and tried to do away with O'Keefe, but it was a botched job. The Irish boy sang like a canary, and the cops got the whole lot of them.'

Hannah didn't really know how to respond. 'My goodness, that's a bit frightening, isn't it?' she said. 'Though after what's been happening here in the last few weeks, even little old Kilthomand isn't safe.'

'Your man below, do you mean?' Isaac asked. 'The shopkeeper? Sure they got that fella, Eve's sister's husband, for that?'

'Yes, but he says he didn't do it.'

'Well, if he didn't, who did? It's not like mad murderers are roaming the fields battering people to death every day, are they? The shopkeeper hurt his missus, and she seems like a nice woman. As I said to you before, I don't blame him. He's no loss to the world, a man that can do that to an innocent woman.' Isaac took another sip of tea.

'Except that he didn't die from being hit. Apparently he was stabbed. One of the girls read about it in a newspaper. If he's found guilty, he'll hang for it.' Hannah shuddered. There had been no news-papers at Robinswood for weeks, but one of the girls managed to pick one up in the village; the story of the murder was just too tantalising. If any of the family found out, there would be trouble. They'd all been warned by Bartley and Miss Doherty not to speak to anyone about life in Robinswood. It was all right to talk to Isaac, surely though?

She went on. 'There was money taken too, all the cash for a week, it seems, but they've searched Aisling and Mark's house and it's not there. Apparently it was an unusual tin box with a hunting scene on the lid, according to the man's shop assistant. He used it for years, and his mother before him, so all the locals know the box. So if the thief just discarded it, someone would recognise it surely?'

Isaac shrugged. 'Yeah well, even if he's found guilty, he won't swing.'

Hannah was shocked at his casual use of the word.

'He'll get manslaughter and be out in a few years. It's worth it, and the man who attacked his wife is dead, so that will keep him going.'

Hannah was a little surprised at his words but didn't want him to think her unsophisticated or innocent. 'I suppose so, but poor Aisling is so sad. It's so hard to watch her. And their mother is dying as well.' Hannah sighed. She'd grown so fond of the kindhearted Murphys.

'If anyone hurt you, I'd do what Mark did,' Isaac said quietly.

They sat in silence for a moment, and Hannah didn't flinch when Isaac reached over and took the cup from her hands, placing it on the table beside them. He then crouched down in front of her, his face only inches from hers, and gently tucked her hair behind her ear. 'You're lovely, Hannah. I've thought so from the first moment I saw you.' He was whispering now as the rain lashed outside. 'Did you come looking for me?'

Hannah couldn't help herself – she nodded and he smiled. It was the most radiant smile, and she basked in its warm glow. He wasn't like this with other girls; he couldn't be.

'I'm so glad. I really like you,' he said, tracing her face with his finger.

'I...I like you too,' she replied, her voice husky.

Then he kissed her, but it wasn't like the time under the tree, sweet and romantic. This was urgent and hot, and he held her close to him. She knew she should pull away – it was wrong – but she felt like she was falling down a deep hole and nothing she could do would stop it. She wanted him, and more than that, she wanted him to love her.

He stopped and moved back, placing his hands on her shoulders. 'I don't want you to do anything you don't want to, Hannah. I'm not that kind of person. But I want to be with you, so much.'

She knew what he was saying. She knew what she wanted, but was this going to be another Damien? She couldn't go through it again. She couldn't find herself in that position.

'I had a baby.' She heard the words before she'd even realised she'd spoken.

He looked confused. 'What?' he asked.

'I had a baby, a little girl. I called her Laura, but the nuns took her away. I can't...' She felt her throat constrict.

'Oh, Hannah, my darling girl.' Isaac drew her into his embrace, and his arms felt so good around her. He rubbed her back and kissed the top of her head, making soothing sounds as silent salt tears ran down her cheeks.

He led her up the rough stairs to the loft, where he had a mattress on the floor. Fully clothed, he lay down and patted the space beside him, inviting her to join him. She couldn't resist. He drew her head onto his chest. He made no move to touch her other than to hold her. 'Tell me,' he said quietly.

The entire story tumbled out. Damien, how he was as lost and alone as she was, how she didn't know what had happened, she didn't really understand how babies came to be, the pregnancy, the nuns, the birth, her little baby and then how they took her away.

'You poor thing. That's so hard. No wonder you're so good with the little ones.' He sat up and looked down into her face. 'Laura is being loved, Hannah, I'm sure of it. She's probably in one of those big fancy houses in Dublin, with a rocking horse and a tricycle and a wardrobe full of fancy dresses. And you'll have another baby one day, one of your own that nobody can take away from you.'

She hoped he was right. 'What if she's in an orphanage, only barely tolerated like we were?' she said, voicing her deepest fears.

'She's not. She'll look like her mammy, and the posh people only want to adopt pretty babies. Honestly, she'll be fine. Trust me,' he said, and she found that she did. Completely.

They lay in silence for a while, and she wondered if he was sleeping. The rain drummed on the tin roof of the workshop, and the sound was strangely soothing. It was as if nobody in the world existed but her and Isaac.

'Why were you in borstal?' she asked, hoping she wasn't overstepping the mark, but it was something he never mentioned and she wanted to know.

He sighed. 'Because I was a very bold boy.' He chuckled, but something in his tone told her not to take it further, and they fell into silence again.

'I'm going to America,' he said quietly at last. 'I've had enough of it here.'

She fought the panic. Isaac was leaving. He couldn't. 'When?' she managed.

'Soon. There's so much opportunity there, so many places to go, things to see. A man can make a new start there. In America, you can be whoever you want to be, you know? Not like this miserable hole.'

She was surprised at the passion in his voice. 'This place isn't so bad.' She tried to lighten the mood. Maybe she could talk him out of it.

'Oh, it is, Hannah. It really is. I'm always going to be the tinker's son who was shoved from pillar to post, a worthless knacker. That's what people see.'

It was her turn to be passionate. 'That's not what I see. I see a lovely person, a kind lad who all the girls love...'

He smiled. 'They do, aye, but they'll not bring me home to their fathers.' He shrugged.

'I don't have a father to take you home to,' she said shyly.

'We're cut from the same cloth, Hannah.' He reached over for a pouch of tobacco and rolled a cigarette, which he lit as he lay back on the straw ticking that was his bed. He looked at her for what felt like a long time, and she could see he was deliberating. 'Come with me,' he said.

She inhaled. Was he serious? 'To America?' she breathed.

'No, to Kilthomand. Of course to America, you goose!' He was back to being his funny self once more, his dark mood gone.

'But I couldn't...'

'Why not? What's keeping you here?' He shrugged. 'Up to you. I won't force you, but it's an opportunity you may not get again.'

'But I've no money for the fare or anything.'

'Is that all that's stopping you?' he asked. His question felt like a challenge.

'Well...' She wondered what *was* stopping her. She had nothing to lose; she was going to ask the question. 'Would I be going as your girl?' She felt shy again.

He chuckled. 'Well, you're not like some mad old Aunty Biddy with whiskers, so yeah, if you like.'

It wasn't the best answer he could have given. She would have liked a protestation of love, but Isaac wasn't like that. He played his cards close to his chest.

'How much is the fare?' she asked.

'Don't worry about it,' he said calmly. 'Will you come if I get you a ticket?'

'But I can't let you do that...'

But before she could go on, he raised his hand. 'Call it a loan if you want.' He made a funny face and did a bad American accent. 'It's you and me, kid.'

She giggled as he drew her into his arms and kissed her; this time there was no reason to stop.

CHAPTER 26

*A*isling and Oskar waited for d'Alton in a little room he'd managed to procure off the main courthouse. She wished her father were there. Though Oskar was like a guard dog, she still longed for her father's reassuring presence. Mammy was too ill to travel it seemed, so the doctors were trying their best to build her up and get her a little strength for the journey home.

Oskar listened intently and didn't say much, but he was always there. He told her to stop thanking him, that after all her family had done for him, it was an honour to be able to help in some way. He asked pertinent questions of the legal team when she couldn't, but mainly he just protected her. He could do nothing for his old friend Dermot, whose world was disintegrating, but he could fill his shoes as a parent until he was once again able.

D'Alton swept in, robes and wig impeccable, and Aisling raked his handsome face for a clue as to how things were going. He pulled out a battered tubular steel chair and sat down. 'So the bright side first.' He gave her a small smile. 'Your testimony convinced the jury that Lacey was a ruthless monster, so they have not a shred of sympathy left for him. That will help Mark. I apologise if I came across as unfeeling the first few times we met, but I needed you to see how dire the situation was – still is, to be honest. I have also tried to make them realise that without a murder weapon or a witness, a conviction would be on very shaky ground, so even if it goes against us, we can appeal. The fact that neither the money nor the tin in which it was held has ever turned up is also in our favour. The guards have searched your house and the buildings on the Robinswood estate and found nothing. There are no fingerprints matching Mark's, nor footprints – all of that is good.' He drummed his manicured fingers on the tabletop, thinking as he spoke.

'And the not-bright side?' Aisling asked, dreading what she was about to hear.

'Well...' He paused. 'As you heard, the jury has been sent to deliberate. The judge did not direct to acquit, but he did direct them to consider a manslaughter charge. The jurors are' – he pulled a small notebook out of his pocket and read aloud – 'five former IRA, two landowning farmers, one man who has a brother in jail, two more are Protestant, one is only recently back from England and the last one has not been convicted but is known to beat his wife.' He flipped the notebook closed.

Ignoring Aisling's look of dismay, he went on. 'The IRA men will most likely vote to convict based on Mark's British military record. The landowners too, a group not generally very pro-British, and Mark's previous conviction might sway them against him. The man with the brother in jail – he visits him every month – could go with a not guilty vote. The Protestants – both had family members in the British forces during the war – will probably acquit, the man back from England too, maybe he'll be more pro-British. And the wife beater could go either way.'

Aisling was aghast. 'But it's not about whether they like Mark or the British or whatever, it's about whether they think he did it or not!'

D'Alton looked sympathetic. 'I know. That's how it should be, but it doesn't work like that. The law would be so much easier if it did, I assure you. In cases such as this, people vote with their hearts more often than their heads.'

'How do you know so much about them?' Oskar asked.

D'Alton replied silkily, 'It's my job to know. But' – he changed the subject – 'even if Mark is found guilty of murder today, and that is a distinct possibility, then we can appeal, and I'm confident we can reduce it to manslaughter next time. It's unfortunate that we have such an anti-British jury this time.'

'So now what?' Aisling asked.

'Now we wait.'

'Will they take a long time, do you think?' Aisling asked.

'Impossible to say.' He stood. 'I know how difficult this is, to wait, knowing that the fate of your husband lies in the opinions of twelve strangers, but I will tell you that time drips slowly here. I won't advise you to leave, as they don't give much notice when they are about to come back in after their deliberations.'

'Thank you, d'Alton,' she whispered. 'I know they won't let me see him, but can you give him a message?'

'Of course.'

'Tell him that I love him. That I will wait for him no matter how long it takes, and that I believe in him. And that I'm all right.'

'I'll relay that message word for word,' d'Alton said sincerely.

The rest of the day passed by as slowly as d'Alton had predicted. They drank tepid tea and ate the sandwiches Eve had wrapped up for them that morning. They telephoned Robinswood to let them know that there was no news, and at four thirty, d'Alton's assistant, a prissy man, came to tell them that the judge had instructed the jury be taken to a hotel for the night and not to speak to anyone.

Wordlessly, Oskar put his arms around her, and she leaned on him for support. This nightmare was going to end soon, one way or another. She was exhausted, physically and emotionally. Doctor Grahame was able to hear the baby's heartbeat now with a stethoscope. He checked her regularly and assured her all was well. Now she just wanted to be with Mark.

'Let's go home. We'll come back in the morning. Some dinner, a bath and a night's sleep will do you good.' Oskar led her out the back way to where the car was parked. He'd found that route on the first

238

day, and it spared her being asked horrible questions by overzealous journalists.

Oskar drove her up to the big house and delivered her into the waiting arms of her sisters.

Eve looked so much better, and Aisling remarked upon it.

'Beau and Lillian have taken Bella for a few nights,' Eve explained as she linked her arm with Aisling's and led her up the steps and in the front door. She lowered her voice. 'And incredibly, Lillian has found a way of getting her off to sleep. It was entirely by accident, but Lillian and Beau apparently had been taking turns walking with her on that first night when Lillian started singing her an old song her father would sing when he'd been on the whiskey. It was an old song of the trenches of the Great War, and despite the dreary images, the melody seems to do the trick for Miss Bella Doherty.' She grinned. 'Listen.' Eve pointed in the direction of the drawing room, where Lillian was carrying the baby and gently crooning.

Sing me to sleep where bullets fall,
Let me forget the war and all;
Damp is my dug-out, cold are my feet,
Nothing but bully and biscuits to eat.
Over the sandbags and helmets you'll find
Corpses in front and corpses behind.
Far, far from Ypres I long to be,
Where German snipers can't get at me,
Think of me crouching where the worms creep,
Waiting for the sergeant to sing me to sleep.
Sing me to sleep in some old shed,
The rats all running around my head,
Stretched out upon my waterproof,
Dodging the raindrops through the roof,
Dreaming of home and nights in the West,
Somebody's overseas boots on my chest.

. . .

AISLING WAS ASTONISHED. Lillian caught their eye and gestured to the pram parked in the hallway. Eve wheeled it towards her, and Lillian placed the sleeping baby in it and tucked her in.

'Thank you.' Eve smiled and Lillian winked.

'Tea?' Lillian mouthed as Eve rolled her sleeping daughter towards the kitchen.

The sisters and Lillian sat and had tea as Aisling explained all she knew.

'I'm glad that Perry was able to get d'Alton at least,' Lillian said. 'He's quite a celebrity, you know. People talk about him all the time. If anyone can get Mark off, it's him.'

They didn't have much time to discuss it, as they had a large group of guests in for dinner, and everyone got into their positions. Beau was in black tie as usual, serving at table, and Lillian dressed to the nines to make the guests feel like they were dining with the aristocracy. Nobody ever guessed that Lady Lillian was married to the dark-skinned footman. Sam sat at the head of the table, carving meat, as his sister regaled the gathering with tales of the Keneficks through the ages. Eve, Aisling and Kate manned the kitchen. They'd done it so often now, everyone was in tune.

Aisling was glad of the distraction. She helped all evening despite Kate's objections and eventually fell into bed, totally exhausted.

CHAPTER 27

*H*annah crept out as the clock on the landing ticked. It was two o'clock in the morning. They were going to walk to the main road and hitch a lift to Cork and then on to Cobh, where they would board the *Christabel* for New York. She'd left her suitcase at the bottom of the lane. She'd have preferred to be honest and just tell Kate and Miss Doherty she was leaving, but Isaac insisted she not. He said he didn't want a scene with Bartley. She'd always got the impression that Bartley wanted more from the relationship with Isaac than the other way round. It seemed cruel to just take off without telling anyone, but it was how Isaac wanted it to be. He said he didn't like big emotional scenes.

The whole family was distracted. Miss Doherty's mother was due back in the coming days. And the jury was deliberating now so the moment of truth for Mark was coming. Poor Aisling was drawn and pale, and everyone was trying to be positive, but Hannah could tell it wasn't looking good.

Lady Lillian popped in to the nursery on and off all day, and she was marvellous with baby Bella. Lillian seemed to work on the estate now rather than just sit in her room all day. Between everything that was going on and all of the guests, they were all run ragged. Hannah thought her secret might have been written all over her face, but Lady Lillian never noticed.

Hannah had hugged each of the children as they went to bed, and it almost tore the heart out of her. She'd come to love them so much in the five months she'd been at Robinswood, but she loved Isaac more.

Since the rainy night in the barn last week, they'd been inseparable, and when he told her he'd got them two third-class tickets on a ship bound for America, leaving the next night, she'd hardly believed him. She was doing it, going to America with Isaac Doherty, the man of her dreams. He made it sound so exciting. They would land in New York, and he'd even booked a hotel there for them until they could find work. He was right; here in Ireland they would forever be nobody, kids out of orphanages, no family to stand behind them. But over in America, the whole world was gathered. Nobody cared who your family was. It was a place for young adventurous souls like herself and Isaac.

She lifted the latch gently, praying nobody would hear her, and she escaped undisturbed. The cold night air stung through her thin coat as she navigated the avenue, keeping to the side just in case someone was watching out of the windows of the big house. The cattle stood in the fields, sleeping presumably, and a fox startled her by fleeing past. She stifled a scream.

Her case was where she'd left it, near the main gate behind the big stump of a tree, felled last winter because Kate's father said it was rotten and in danger of falling. She'd stowed the case in the base of the pram when she took the children for a walk earlier.

She looked around, but there was no sign of Isaac. Perhaps she was early, but he did say two o'clock and it must have been ten past. She hugged herself to stay warm, the biting wind cutting through her. She had a hat on her head and was wearing her best dress and cardigan under her coat.

Time ticked on. Surely he was coming? Panic gripped her. Maybe it was all a cruel joke? Stupid Hannah, falling for a lad who was only making a fool of her? *Stop it*, she admonished herself. Isaac loved her.

Well, he'd not said those exact words, but it was obvious that he did. He was taking her to America for goodness' sake. If that wasn't love, she didn't know what was.

She didn't have a watch, but she was sure she'd been waiting for half an hour at least. Maybe he'd slept on. That must be it. She replaced her suitcase behind the tree and moved in the direction of the barn and the workshop. The entire place was in total darkness, but she moved stealthily towards where Isaac lived. The door creaked loudly, she knew from previous visits, but luckily it was slightly ajar and she managed to slide in silently. The familiar smells again, sawdust and oil. She stood still. There was sound coming from behind the lathe. Her eyes adjusted to the light and she could see him there, hunched over something, a single candle burning beside him on a shelf.

She felt a flood of relief. He hadn't left without her. He was unaware she was there, so she crept up behind him, placing her hands over his eyes playfully. 'Hello, sleepyhead,' she whispered. 'I thought you'd forgotten about me.'

He leapt up, springing back from her, and she was startled by the look on his face – haunted, hunted.

'Don't creep up on me like that! You nearly gave me a heart attack,' he hissed.

Instantly, she regretted her earlier mischievousness. 'Sorry, I just...' Her eyes were drawn to the corner. His bag was packed, but on top of it, where he'd been hunched, was a box, open and full of crumpled banknotes.

'What's that?' she asked.

'Nothing,' he said in a dismissive tone, and went to push her away. 'Let's just go.'

She shook him off and went to the box, flipping the metal lid closed. The pale candlelight was just enough for her to see the picture on the tin box; it was a hunting scene.

'Isaac...' she said, hardly breathing. This couldn't be right. How could Isaac have Sean Lacey's money box? It made no sense. 'Where did you get that?'

'It doesn't matter. Let's go.' He grabbed his bag and stuffed the notes into his trouser pocket.

'No… But that's the tin with the money, Sean Lacey's money…' She wanted to scream. How could this be happening?

He stopped, dropped the bag and held her by the shoulders.

'Hannah, it doesn't matter. He's dead. And his money is going to give us a new life. Now, we can stay around here and discuss with the guards and whoever else you like how his tin came to be here, or we can walk off into the sunset, the two of us, and never look back.'

She longed for him. The future he offered her, a home, a family of her own was all she ever wanted.

He waited and then said, 'I love you, Hannah. I want to marry you. I want to have children with you, a house, something neither of us has ever had. And our kids will be well loved and fed and looked after, and we'll live happily ever after. But we need to go now. This is our only chance.'

He loved her. Isaac Doherty loved her and wanted to make a life with her. Her heart sang. She'd known he loved her, or at least she'd hoped he did, but hearing him say it out loud was music to her ears. He put his arms around her and kissed her, and she melted into him. She closed her eyes, wanting to lose herself in his kiss.

'So are we going?' he asked as he released her.

She nodded and was rewarded with one of his smiles. He picked up his bag once more, kicked the tin under a load of old sacks, and took her hand.

The walk to the main road took about an hour, and they walked mostly in silence, holding hands. He had his own bag on his back and her little suitcase in his other hand.

As they reached the main Cork to Waterford road, they turned in the direction of Cork. The port at Cobh used to be called Queenstown, and it was the last point in Ireland so many emigrants saw. It was outside of the city, so they would need to get to Cork first, about sixty miles away, and then down to Cobh, but Isaac was confident. There was a train from the city if they couldn't get a lift.

No vehicle passed them as they walked.

'Once the delivery vans start coming, someone will pick us up, don't worry,' Isaac said cheerily.

He was right. At around five thirty in the morning, a bread van stopped in response to Isaac putting a hand out. The man was happy to take them all the way to Cork. Isaac sat beside the man, who introduced himself as Teddy O'Mahony, and Hannah took the edge nearest the passenger window.

Teddy liked to chat, so Isaac kept him entertained in his own inimitable way while Hannah stayed quiet, just looking out of the window.

'I'm actually going to the city, so I can drop you to the train if that would suit?' Teddy said kindly.

'That would be great altogether. Thanks very much.' Isaac's smile was warm.

'And ye're off to England, is it?' Teddy asked, and Hannah was surprised to hear Isaac answer in the affirmative.

'Yes, I've a sister in Liverpool, so she's going to put us up until we get ourselves sorted out. We sail on the *Innisfallen* tonight.'

'God bless the sisters. I've one myself and I'd starve only for her.' He patted his round belly. 'Neither of us ever married, so we live happy as Larry, the two of us, Nora and myself. I envy the two of you heading off. Sure maybe you won't stop there, you might strike out for America after that? Nora would love to see America, she's always saying it. But sure we never had the money or the time or anything, and now that we have, sure I only drive a few days a week and they're only keeping me on out of pity. But we're too old for gallivanting now.'

'You're never too old. Sure you can't be more than sixty?' Isaac asked.

'I am indeed sixty, and Nora is fifty-eight. But sure we might go sometime. Our parents left us a few bob and 'tis sitting in the bank, but yerra 'tis hard to get organised to go. I'll tell you what I'd do if I went there though, I'd walk across the Brooklyn Bridge. An uncle of ours sent us a postcard one time, and it was of the Brooklyn Bridge, and I thought 'twas the nicest thing I ever saw. Nora loves the musicals – she's always stuck in one of them in the local dramatic society,

My Fair Lady was the last one – so she'd love to go to Broadway, to see a show. But sure, 'tis only pipe dreams we have.' He sighed.

'And what part of the country do you come from, Teddy?' Isaac asked.

Teddy was off again, explaining the wonder that was the village of Ballymacarrick.

Hannah waited for him to take a breath before she interrupted. 'I'm so sorry, but I wonder if there is somewhere we could stop, just for a moment. I...' She coloured. 'I need to go to the ladies.'

'Oh, I'm sorry, girleen, I never thought. Sure 'tis easy for us, isn't it?' He nudged Isaac conspiratorially. 'We will of course stop. There's a hotel in the next town – we can stop there.'

Hannah smiled at his kindness. It struck her as a pity that no woman had the gentle Teddy as her husband.

Isaac squeezed her hand. 'Not long now,' he whispered, and she nodded, returning his smile.

The hotel was a beautiful ornate building on the seafront. She walked in, and there was nobody about. The reception desk was unmanned, and it was too early for guests to begin appearing for breakfast. She hurried to the ladies' powder room.

Within a few minutes, she was back at the bread van. Isaac was having a cigarette and looking out to sea. Of Teddy there was no sign.

'All right now?' he asked with a smile.

'Fine. I don't think I'd have made it all the way to Cork.' She giggled, and he put his arm around her, pointing out to sea with the other hand, the smoke from his cigarette swirling around his fingers as he pointed.

'Can you see it?' he asked.

'What?'

'The statue,' he said, as if it were the most obvious thing in the world.

Hannah peered. All she could see was navy blue sea all the way to the horizon, where the sky was brightening to welcome a new day. 'I can't see a statue.'

'You're not looking closely enough.' He pulled her closer and whispered in her ear, 'The Statue of Liberty. Out there, waiting to welcome two young Irish people with the whole world at their feet.' He chuckled and kissed her cheek.

'I can't wait.' She turned her face to his and kissed his lips.

Teddy's whistling interrupted their moment, and they released each other and walked back to the van. The rest of the journey into Cork passed as Teddy prattled away, only needing the odd interjection from Isaac. He told them about his greyhound, Doris, named after Doris Day, and how she was a beauty. He waxed lyrical about her trusting eyes, her glossy coat and his secret additive to her food, poitín, the illegal alcoholic spirit made from potatoes. Teddy swore by it, and Doris apparently loved it. He rubbed her down with it after races as well, as it was excellent for muscle fatigue. Isaac told him of an old traveller trick with greyhounds involving ginger or something, and both men were engaged, so once again she was left alone with her thoughts.

As the sun rose, Teddy pulled in outside the railway station in Cork and let them out. He got out himself, retrieving their bags from underneath the trays of fresh-baked bread, and shook hands with them.

'The best of luck to ye, son, and I'll remember the trick with the ginger.' He pumped Isaac's hand.

As he took Hannah's hand, she locked eyes with him. He looked confused for a moment, then smiled his broad beam once more. 'Best of luck to you too, girleen, and say hello to the king for me.' He winked at her and let go, shoving his hand in his pocket.

They stood on the pavement as he drove away, giving them a cheery wave and a toot of his horn.

'Shall we?' Isaac offered her his arm theatrically, and she took it with a giggle.

They entered the enormous railway station with its glass roof. The air was cool in the early morning, not yet filled with the clambering odours of steam, coal, humans and food she had come to associate with railways.

'Over here.' Isaac indicated a ticket office, and together they approached the window. A clerk sat inside, his moustache oiled and his sleeve garters showing. His railway company jacket was slung over the chair behind him.

'Two tickets to Cobh, please,' Isaac said.

'One way or return?' he asked, not looking up from his ledger and barely registering their presence.

Isaac smiled as Hannah said with certainty, 'Just one way, please.'

She felt the reassuring warmth of Isaac's hand on her back. She'd noticed that his confidence slipped a little whenever he was dealing with anyone in uniform. She presumed he'd not had much good experience with people in authority.

They settled into their seats, as the train would leave in half an hour.

'We're doing it.' He grinned. 'Really doing it.'

'We are.' She looked deeply into his eyes. For all his bravado and charm, she saw vulnerability there. She understood better than most what a childhood spent in captivity did to a person. He'd built up a hard shell, and to virtually everyone it was impenetrable, but she got glimpses of the frightened little boy inside the body of this man opposite her and her heart ached for him.

'They'll be waking up now in Robinswood, realising we're gone,' she said with a sigh. She hated the idea of Daisy and Poppy calling for her and not being there for them. They had taken to rushing to her in the mornings as she reported for duty, all four of them. It was a race to see who could get the first hug. They really were four bundles of love. Her sadness must have been evident on her face.

'Regrets?' he asked, his face impossible to read again.

'Some,' she said truthfully, placing her hand in his. 'But I'm doing the right thing.'

CHAPTER 28

$\mathcal{A}$isling was stirring the rancid tea that was now tepid into the bargain, when d'Alton's assistant stuck his head round the door. She, Kate and Eve all looked up expectantly. The barrister had managed to secure this little room for them to wait in while the jury deliberated. The case was garnering huge media attention now, not just because of the salacious nature of the crime or the presence of the enigmatic d'Alton, but also because the jury was on their third day. The longer the trial went on, the more column inches it warranted, and by now, every paper was full of it. The family tried to insulate themselves from it as much as they could, but it was close to impossible. Everyone read the reports, and only a few people mentioned Mark's name. Aisling felt hurt; they'd loved him when he was winning cups for the village hurling team, but the mistrust of the English ran deep, and Sean Lacey, no matter what else he was, was one of their own.

Doctor Grahame, however, seemed to be on her side. He'd said he hoped his testimony helped but wasn't sure.

She'd managed to smile at their old family doctor. 'You told the truth, Doctor Grahame, what more could you do?'

His old face looked tired, she thought. All of this was taking a lot out of him, like them all.

Oskar had gone outside for a smoke; one of the court clerks knew Oskar from years ago, so they often enjoyed a cigarette together. Aisling was glad he had someone other than her to talk to.

'The jury are in,' the secretary said, and was gone.

Just as Eve was about to go and find Oskar, he appeared. Nobody spoke. Lillian and Violet were manning the hotel, though there were no guests so it was just them and the staff that needed to be cared for. Kate had insisted on cancelling any bookings for two nights – she and Eve needed to be with their sister, and while Lillian was willing, she certainly wasn't able.

Perry and Beau had taken over the estate and were overseeing the animals and the things that were vital, allowing Bartley and Sam to be in court too. The girls had to admit they would be lost without them. The irony that the Kenefics of Robinswood were once again in charge, but this time as caretakers for the former servants, was not lost on them. In that peculiar way that life has of turning everything on its head, the Kenefics and the Murphys were now family. In the long hours in that little airless room, the girls talked, they cried a little, and mostly they sat, in silence, each thinking their own thoughts.

'Let's go,' Eve said, putting her arm around Aisling's shoulder and giving her a squeeze.

'I don't know if I can…' Aisling suddenly panicked.

'You can. Keep your eyes on Mark. Nobody else matters,' Eve advised as they filed back in to the packed courtroom. Bartley and Sam were already sitting in the public gallery.

The jury took their seats to the right-hand side of the judge, and Aisling did as her sister suggested. Though Mark was sitting in the dock, she sat on the far left so he could see her. The rest of the family filed in behind her. She locked eyes with him and refused to break the contact. She tried to not even blink.

I love you, she mouthed.

I love you too, he mouthed back.

He looked exhausted, the way he'd looked back in the bad days

250

immediately after the war when he couldn't sleep and drank too much. She'd really thought their marriage was over then. The sunny happy-go-lucky man she'd married had gone, replaced by a dark, angry person she didn't recognise.

He finally told her why, how he couldn't forget the sight of the bodies in the water when he and his fellow RAF men bombed some passenger ships in the Baltic Sea. The intelligence said they were hiding senior Nazi officials, but what they did not know was the ships were full of concentration camp survivors. They were given orders to bomb the ships and then strafe the waters for survivors. It was too late when the pilots realised what they had done.

It had impacted Mark so badly at the time, he couldn't function. He questioned all he was, all he'd fought for. He sought solace in the bottle, and took his anger out on walls usually, but on two occasions drunk men who had nasty things to say about the Jews.

She remembered the horror she felt when he was sentenced to serve time in Dartmoor for the second assault, but in fact, it saved his life. He'd stopped drinking, got himself together and managed to regain her trust. Her love was never in doubt. He'd been a model citizen ever since, so this was so unfair. It felt like the universe was conspiring against them.

She would not break eye contact. Mark was her husband, her only love, and she would be with him in his hour of need no matter what.

D'Alton sat in his usual spot, in the body of the court below the dock, the prosecution occupying the table opposite. She longed to look at him, to try to ascertain from his face any clue as to what was likely to happen next, but she could not take her eyes from Mark's. She wondered if d'Alton got nervous. He seemed to always exude almost disdainful boredom when he was in court, but he was a very different person outside of it. He was a mystery really.

The elderly judge with a surprisingly gentle voice and a west of Ireland accent came through the door behind the bench and took his seat. He'd not said much during the course of the trial, and even when instructing the jury, he was sparse in his words. Once he was settled and all eyes were on him, he spoke and it was quiet enough to hear a pin drop.

'Chairman of the Jury, please rise.'

A heavyset man in his sixties with a grey beard and a balding head stood.

'Have you reached a verdict?' the judge asked.

'We have, Your Honour,' the man replied.

'Is it a verdict on which you all agree?'

'It is, Your Honour.'

'Very well. Would the defendant please rise and face the jury.'

Mark stood, dragging his eyes from Aisling's.

The clerk of the court addressed them then. 'Members of the jury, in the case of the state versus Mark George Belitho, charged with the murder of Sean Lacey at an address in The Square, Kilthomand, County Waterford, how do you find the defendant, guilty or not guilty?'

Aisling dug her nails into her palms and felt the perspiration prickle her back. She was holding her breath. *Please God, anyone, please help*, she pleaded.

'Guilty, Your Honour.'

Blood thundered in Aisling's ears. The crowd in the courtroom erupted. The judge banged his gavel, demanding silence.

Finally, the noise died down. The judge placed a square of black fabric on his head before addressing Mark directly. 'Mark George Belitho, you have been found guilty of murder by a jury of your peers. This crime carries the death penalty. You will be taken to the place of incarceration from which you came, and you will be hanged by the neck until you are dead. May God have mercy on your soul.'

He paused, then addressed the guards who had appeared beside the dock. 'Take him down.'

There was stunned silence for a moment before it gave way to a cacophony of cameras clicking and voices talking. Aisling didn't notice Oskar slip out of the end of the pew where they sat.

Mark was being led away, and she felt hands propelling her. She was being moved, but she was screaming... Was she screaming? Was it inside her head? She pulled away from the hands – she wanted to get to Mark. She heard the banging again, and the judge calling, 'Order, order, or I will clear the court!'

Aisling looked up. Someone was speaking to the judge, and he bent his head to hear what was being said above the din. He shook his head. His brow furrowed as he listened again to what the man was telling him.

He banged his gavel once more. 'Clear this court!' he bellowed.

Immediately, the uniformed officers began shepherding everyone out. Cameras were shoved in Aisling's face. Going out the back way was no longer possible. Kate and Eve flanked her either side, with Sam and Bartley taking positions before her and behind her, but it wasn't enough to insulate her from the incessant questioning and the flashes going off left and right. The court officials continued to drive the crowds back through the two double doors at the rear of the courtroom. Suddenly, the scene was swimming before her eyes. She was so hot, being crushed by the crowds... She tried to focus but it was no good, and everything faded to black.

CHAPTER 29

a s Mark was led into the courtroom and the entire courthouse awaited the verdict, Hannah marvelled at the number of people milling about the quayside. Some were rushing about, others stood, embracing their loved ones; trunks and suitcases were everywhere. Babies wailed and harassed-looking parents did their best to soothe them. The *Christabel* looked resplendent and impossibly high as her white hull gleamed in the winter sunlight. Smartly dressed crew issued instructions about ticket checking and suitcase storage, but the gangplank remained roped off.

'Embarkation will commence shortly. Tourist and third class to the right, first and second class to the left please, ladies and gentlemen!' a purser shouted at intervals.

Hannah looked around anxiously, but Isaac was in fine spirits. He placed his bag on the ground as he took in the scene.

'I need to find the gents. Can you just hold on here?' he asked. She nodded. He kissed her cheek and made off in the direction of the toilets. Hannah quickly leaned down and removed two envelopes from Isaac's bag, stuffed them quickly under the clothes in her bag and closed the buckles on her case. Within a few moments, Isaac was back.

'Are you hungry? We could get a cup of tea and a bun over there.' He indicated a makeshift stall where an elderly woman was selling drinks and snacks.

'That would be lovely.' She smiled at him.

'Our last Irish cuppa.' He grinned and trotted off with a wink, slinging his bag onto his back.

She saw Teddy making his way through the throng, and instantly he caught her eye. Her heart thumped in her chest. Behind him were two uniformed policemen, and their sudden arrival caused the gathered passengers to part like the Red Sea.

Hannah nodded in the direction of the stall where Isaac stood with his back to her, paying for their tea. Teddy said something to the police, and like lightning, they moved. Isaac spotted them bearing down, and he bolted, almost knocking bystanders into the sea on the open quayside.

'Stop that man!' bellowed one of the Gardai, pointing at Isaac, whose getaway was hampered by the throng of passengers awaiting embarkation. Hannah watched in horror as he struggled to get away, frantically pushing through the crowd. The police were almost on him now, and she saw him reach into his boot and extract a sharp knife. The crowds parted in terror, some people screaming. He brandished the knife in one hand, throwing his bag into the sea with the other, but it was too late. A large policeman jumped on him and wrestled him to the ground, disarming him of his knife and forcing his head onto the rough stones while sitting on his back.

The crowd were all agog now; a public arrest was always interesting.

'What the hell do you think you're doing?' Isaac roared. 'Let go of me!'

'Isaac Doherty, I am arresting you on suspicion of the murder of Sean Lacey at Kilthomand, County Waterford. You do not have to say anything, but anything you do say may be taken down and used in evidence. Do you understand?' The younger but slighter of the policemen read Isaac his rights as the other, a burly man in his forties, clipped handcuffs on him.

Hannah stood, frozen, praying he would not turn and see the guilt on her face, but the policemen pushed him right past her.

'Hannah, I...' He stopped. 'It was you.'

He was so certain. She couldn't deny it. She looked down at her feet. Before she had time to reply, the guard pushed him forward towards the road where the police car waited. The crowd parted, still agog at the action unfolding before them. Isaac stared at her for a long moment before being shoved in the back by the policeman, which forced him forward. Within seconds, she'd lost sight of him; he was swallowed up in the throng on the quayside surging forward as the purser declared the gangway open. Embarkation was beginning. Hannah stood stock still, her heart pounding in her chest, her body prickled with sweat. The tickets were in the envelope along with the money he stole and the confirmation from the hotel in New York.

'Miss Woods?' A policeman stood before her.

'Yes,' she confirmed.

'I'm Detective Inspector O'Shaughnessy. I want to thank you for your quick action.'

Hannah nodded.

'You are not under suspicion because as you explained in your note, once you realised what sort of a man Doherty was, you contacted the authorities. But my officers will be in touch to take a statement in the coming days. Your address will be at the Robinswood estate, I assume?'

Again, Hannah nodded, unable to form words. Had she just betrayed the only person who'd ever made her feel safe in the world?

Teddy waited at a distance until the detective moved on. Then he came and stood beside her. 'Have you the tickets or did he have them?' he asked kindly.

Some other officers were now on the quayside trying to retrieve Isaac's bag, but it was long sunk beneath the waves.

'I have them,' she said quietly.

'Well? Are you getting on, girleen?' Teddy asked kindly, his huge bulk protecting her from the crush as people tried to embark.

Hannah looked up into his big kind face, suddenly glad he was there. There was only one other time in her life she felt this bereft – when they took Laura away.

'I...I don't know. The guards need to take a statement, and well, without him, it... It was Isaac's idea, you see.' She fought back the tears. She was the reason Isaac wasn't by her side; she could blame nobody else.

'You did a brave thing. When you pressed that note into my hand when I left you in Cork, I had no idea what it was about, but sure the minute I went to the guards and gave them the instructions to contact Sergeant O'Connell in Dungarvan, they acted quickly.'

'I didn't know if they would make it in time. To be honest, part of me hoped they wouldn't.' Her voice caught as she tried to quell the tears.

'Sure, it must be very hard to give up someone you love, but you did the right thing,' Teddy assured her. 'Will we have a cup of tea? They'll be loading these people up for ages yet. Maybe have a think, see what you want to do?'

'Thanks, Teddy, I'd like that. The ship won't sail until tonight actually, but I suppose people are anxious to get on. They'll be on it long enough.' She smiled ruefully, glancing up at the huge ship.

They walked into the railway station beside the port, and Teddy ordered tea and toast and marmalade. She extracted one of the envelopes as he balanced their drinks on a small tray. She didn't really feel like eating – she was heartbroken – but she nibbled some toast so as not to appear ungrateful.

The ship's horn sounded.

'Do you live far from here, Teddy?' she asked as he drank his tea.

'Not really. Ballymacarrick is only about five miles away. Why?' he asked.

'Why don't you go and get Nora, pack a small bag and go to New York?' She pushed the envelope across the table. 'Take these tickets. I know they are only one way, but this way you'd only need to buy one leg of the journey. We found a cheapish hotel in Brooklyn, so you could stay there. We paid in advance for a week just to get ourselves settled, so you might as well use it.' She noted the look of incredulity on his round face, a mixture of excitement and terror.

'But these are your tickets! You're a young woman. Why not go, see what America has to offer you?' he said.

'No. I won't go. It wouldn't be any good to go without Isaac. Anyway, there's someone here I need to find. So if you don't use them, nobody will. Please, it's a shame to waste them. And you said you and Nora would love to go.' She pushed the envelope across the table. It contained two tickets and a letter from the hotel confirming a room for seven nights.

Teddy looked down at the envelope, then up at her. 'And you're sure you can't use them? Bring someone with you? There would be time if she doesn't sail till tonight.'

'No, there's nobody.' She smiled at this big kind man. 'I had a baby, you see. Laura. And they took her away from me, but I want to find her. So no, I won't be going to America.'

Teddy placed his big rough hand on hers. 'Well, Hannah, I hope you find Laura, and when you do, bring her to Ballymacarrick for a visit. Nora loves babies, and we have a pond with ducks and everything, so she'd love it there.'

Hannah smiled. 'Thank you, Teddy. I will.'

'You're a good girl, Hannah, a really good person. Your parents would be proud of you for what you've done. Will you go home to your mother and father now?' he asked innocently.

'No. I don't have anyone. I'm an orphan... But there's a house, Robinswood, and the people there have been very good to me. I'm hoping they'll take me back. That's why I had to give him up. Someone there was being tried for what Isaac did. I couldn't let that happen.' She sighed.

'Well, you're a great girl, very selfless. And I'm sure they'll appreciate it. And sure, don't be stuck anyway, myself and Nora are rattling around in our big huge place, so...' He looked embarrassed. 'Well, don't be stuck. If you just ask in Ballymacarrick, everyone knows us.'

Teddy's kindness threatened to undo her stoic resolve. Instead she changed the subject. 'So you'll go, have the holiday in America you dreamed about?' She hoped he would; there had to be some good to come out of this situation.

'Well, 'tis the maddest idea I ever heard to be totally truthful with you, but I'll go up and see what Nora says. She's a right one for skites is Nora, so I'd say we'll take you up on it, if you're sure? Thanks very much, Hannah.'

Teddy went to pay for the tea, and she thought about the envelope of cash, the money he'd stolen from Sean Lacey. That would help her find her daughter. She'd never stolen anything in her life before, but she was sure the guards would assume the money was in the bag, and that was at the bottom of the harbour by now. Even if they did manage to retrieve it and discovered the money was gone, they would never assume she had it. She felt no guilt. It wasn't like Lacey had children who needed it. It would just go to the government, and it was the government that had stolen her child.

Teddy returned and together they walked back out onto the pier. He fell into step beside her as she headed for the train back to Cork. As she bought a ticket, he held her bag. He walked her to the door of the carriage, and she turned and stuck her hand out.

'Goodbye, Teddy, and thanks for everything. I hope you and Nora have a wonderful time in New York. Send me a postcard of the Brooklyn Bridge. My address is Robinswood, Kilthomand, County Waterford.'

'I'll do that, Hannah, to be sure I will. And well, the offer is there if you ever need...' He reddened again.

She nodded, her eyes bright with tears as she shook Teddy's hand and stepped onto the train with her little bag.

CHAPTER 30

*B*ack at Robinswood, Perry had placed some of the heftier of the students on the gate with strict instructions to allow nobody but family up the avenue. There had been some newspaper people sniffing about the village, and while the family couldn't stop people talking to the reporters, Beau had gone to the pub and the post office and asked in that gentle, respectful way he had that people didn't.

Father Macintyre made a similar plea from the pulpit, and so far, nothing had come out. They could never be sure though. The history between Aisling Murphy and Sean Lacey was common knowledge. What Sean did, and his end, were the talk of the place since it happened, but the people of Kilthomand were loyal to their own, and like Sean Lacey, the Murphys were locals.

Sam drove past the boys, who watched wordlessly. He pulled up to the front door, Oskar's car immediately behind. Kate jumped out and opened the back door, but Mark and Aisling were wrapped around each other, seemingly unable to move.

'Well, are you getting out or what?' Kate asked.

Eve and Bartley had driven with Oskar, and now everyone fussed over Aisling and Mark as they emerged into the cold sunshine. Eve went into the house, but Bartley walked away, his hands deep in his pockets.

Lillian and Violet shepherded them into the drawing room and gave each of them a brandy. It burned Aisling's throat but warmed her. Mark could not let her go. He sipped his drink with one arm around his wife.

'I just can't believe it,' Lillian kept saying.

Beau arrived, and hugged Mark and clapped him on the back. 'Welcome back, buddy.' He grinned.

'Thanks, Beau. I can't believe it myself... I just...' Mark was at a loss for words.

'So tell us everything,' Violet demanded, her face suffused with delight. 'Oh, Perry, surely there's some champagne somewhere? This really is most wondrous.'

Realising neither Aisling nor Mark was able to relay the events of the past few hours, Eve explained how there had been a telephone call made to the court, relaying that Isaac was arrested and charged with the murder of Sean Lacey. 'He had a knife in his boot that the Gardai are sure was the murder weapon, and they sent someone to the place above the workshop where he slept and found the cashbox. Isaac arrived the night Lacey attacked Ais and heard it all in the car. He must have gone there after Bartley asked him to get out. I suppose we'll know for sure once he's tried, but...'

'Where is Bartley, Eve?' Mark asked.

'He said to tell you he'd speak to you later. He's so relieved you are out, but he's devastated obviously about his brother,' Eve responded.

Mark nodded and hugged Aisling closer to him. Oskar took a glass from Perry, who somehow had managed to find some champagne, and stood beside Mark.

'How are you doing?' the German asked quietly. All around, voices chattered excitedly. Aisling was telling them how she came to on a bench, having fainted, to d'Alton telling her Mark was free to go.

'I'm so overwhelmed, to be honest, Oskar. I can't really take it in. When they came down to the cells and told me I was free...I just couldn't believe it. It was all so surreal. But I don't understand... Why were you down in the cells, Oskar?'

The German shrugged and smiled. 'I'll tell you some other time. Today is not the day.'

Mark looked bemused, but everyone else was so relieved and thrilled that he was free at last they didn't notice.

The four children, hearing the noise, burst into the room. There was lots of hugging and kissing. They were delighted to see their Uncle Mark, and he spun them in the air one by one. Eventually, after they got drinks and a biscuit each, Lillian stood and gathered them.

'Now, bath time, you lot.' She lifted Bella from her high chair. 'You too, little poppet.'

Bella giggled and Lillian cuddled her close. Violet shepherded her grandchildren after Lillian.

Kate and Sam stood close together as Eve and Aisling hugged, silent tears of relief sliding down Aisling's face.

'I think we'll leave you two alone. You need some time to adjust. But I'm jolly glad to have you back, Mark.' Sam patted him on the shoulder, then left, his arm around Kate.

'I'll go too. I need to find Bartley,' Eve said sadly.

'Poor Bartley,' Mark said. 'I... Look, tell him he couldn't have known.'

'I will.' Eve leaned up and kissed her brother-in-law on the cheek. 'Welcome home, Mark.'

CHAPTER 31

The large bathroom was filled with steam as the water poured into the large enamel bath. All four of the older children fit in it, which was useful, and Beau and Violet washed them as Lillian washed Bella in the sink. Within twenty minutes, they were in pyjamas and tucked in.

Eve and Bartley appeared, him looking wretched, and took Bella back to their quarters, Eve having thanked Lillian profusely for taking such good care of her. Kate and Sam took their three back to their rooms to read them a story.

Austina sat on Beau's lap as Lillian combed her hair in sections. Beau's cousin had sent a special comb which could just about tame her curls when Lillian added a little olive oil, and Lillian had bought some silk pillowcases – another tip she'd heard – to stop her daughter's hair getting frizzy and dry overnight. She'd sent a parcel of them to Beau's cousins, and they were really pleased with them. She hoped she'd done the right thing, as she didn't want to offend anyone, but Beau assured her they were very touched by the gesture.

She smiled at him. Things were so much better between them now. That awful conversation, during which he'd told her he would not leave and that if she wanted to go to England it would be without him or Austina, was deeply shocking but in a way made her grow in respect for him. He was a gentle, loving man, but he knew his own mind and would not be bullied.

He'd preached twice at his church now, and she and Austina had gone. He was so proud of them both, and she found to her surprise that she enjoyed the whole experience. Church for her was usually a dry affair to be endured at Christmas, but the warmth and welcome of the Baptists, and their message, attracted her. She told Beau she wanted to look into converting. He was so thrilled that she wished she'd done it years ago. His faith meant so much to him that having her and Austina to share it would be wonderful.

Her first few days in the kitchen had been tough. She wasn't used to working so hard and the Murphys were powerhouses of activity, but they helped her and taught her, and now at night she fell into bed beside her husband, exhausted but happy. She found they accepted her, and now they were friends. She'd never had real friends before, women she could talk to about life, children, men, and it was lovely. They sat together in the kitchen after dinner was served and all the clearing away done, drinking tea and chatting. They had given her so much. She was glad to be able to support them now.

'Isabella and Dermot will be here tomorrow. Perry has sent the car for them to fetch them back from Dublin. Isabella is very frail, it seems,' Lillian said, genuinely sad.

'At least Mark bein' free is some good news for her. It will be an ease to her to know Aisling and him and the baby will be fine.' Beau soothed her, gently rubbing her back. 'I'm so proud of you,' he whispered as Austina's eyes batted slowly, her long dark lashes resting on her cheeks.

'Thanks. I'm learning, but it's slow,' she whispered back.

She and Sam had even begun to get along a bit better. He had called her the Queen of Puddings the other evening, and he seemed to mean it. Beau was of course right, Robinswood was the best place for them, but she had been too busy being a snob and hankering after a life that didn't exist to realise it.

Austina fell fast asleep as she finished brushing her hair. Lillian and Beau looked down at her in total adoration. She really was the sweetest child and loved them both so much.

Beau stood and gently lowered the child into her little bed in the room off theirs. They kept the door open, so most nights she crept in sometime in the early morning to sleep between them, something they all loved. They tucked her in together, and Lillian bent to kiss her cheek. As she rose, Beau put his arms around her. 'I love you,' he said simply.

'I love you too,' she whispered back, wrapping her arms around his neck.

He led her back to their huge bedroom and sat on the bed. He took her hand in his but kept his eyes on the floor. 'Lillian,' he began, 'we don't talk about it, and I haven't brought it up because I thought, well, maybe it was hard for you to discuss, but I was wonderin'...'

She knew it was coming, the conversation she'd been dreading.

'Is there a reason we only have one child?' He turned to face her, and she knew she couldn't lie.

She tried to avoid sex in the times when she was most fertile – the doctor in London had explained all of that to her – and on those occasions when she couldn't avoid it or didn't want to, she slipped into the bathroom beforehand and inserted her diaphragm. She was sure he'd never noticed anything.

Her face must have registered something – shame, guilt, she wasn't sure – but he didn't let her hand go. 'It's OK, you can tell me the truth. We'll be OK whatever it is.'

'I...I use a device to stop falling pregnant. I just didn't want another child. I was afraid, I suppose. Things were so horrible here, and we had no money, and things between us weren't exactly wonderful, so I just couldn't cope.' She wished she didn't sound so selfish, but it was time they were honest with each other.

'I can understand that,' he said to her surprise.

She turned to face him. 'Can you?' she asked.

'Sure. This hasn't been easy for you. It's weird, but I fit in here better than you and I'm a black American and it's your home. But at least it used to be like that. I'm so proud of you. You're a wonderful mother and a wonderful wife, and now you're takin' part here... Well, I'm as happy as I could be, so if you don't want another child, then that's OK with me.' He reached out and smoothed her hair from her face. 'But no more sneakin' around, OK?'

'Did you know?' she asked.

'I'm a man, but I'm not blind, Lillian. I guessed you were doin' somethin', but I thought you'd tell me in your own time. And like you said, things weren't so good for a while there, so it was one more thing I didn't need to deal with.'

'I'm sorry. I should have been honest. I just thought you'd want another one and you're such a natural father –'

'Hey, you're the only one in this house that can get little Bella to sleep, and there's Austina, and Kate's three adore you, so don't run yourself down, sweetheart.'

'Bella is gorgeous, isn't she?' Lillian smiled. 'I can't believe Austina was ever that tiny, but I think when she was little, I was so worried about the future, not knowing where you were or if you ever intended to come back...' She sighed, thinking about those days.

'She's a cutie, all right,' Beau agreed, lying back against the pillows and pulling her beside him.

Lillian cuddled up to him, resting her palm against his chest. There was a long pause and then she said, 'So maybe, and it's only a maybe, having another baby wouldn't be such a terrible idea?'

He chuckled, and she felt the rumble deep in his chest. 'You are one complicated lady, Lady Lillian, but sure, whatever you want.'

'Actually, I'm dropping the "Lady" thing. I'm either just Lillian or Mrs Lane from now on. I told the last intake of students that they could call me Lillian, and I caught Eve and Kate exchange a glance over my head, but everyone will get used to it.'

'You don't have to. I don't mind,' Beau said, but she knew that wasn't strictly true. It hurt him a little to hear her introduce herself by her maiden name and play Lady of the Manor while he waited on tables, but he had learned how much titles meant to people of her class so didn't expect her to give it up.

'You do mind, and you should. It wasn't right. And anyway, Kate is the lady of the house now, not me.'

'OK, Mrs Lane.' He grinned. 'So are we goin' to see about that brother or sister for Austina?' he murmured into her neck, kissing her sensuously.

'Well, it might take some practice...' she whispered back. 'So best get cracking.'

CHAPTER 32

*I*sabella lay back against the pillows and gazed at her husband. 'I'm so happy to be home, Der. Thank you.'

Dermot could tell she knew without looking in the mirror on the dressing table opposite the bed how the TB had ravaged her. She could see her twig-like wrists, could feel how heavy her head was when she tried to sit up. He'd stopped saying 'when you're better'. Isabella knew that day was never going to come.

'How's everything above?'

They'd arrived back to Robinswood in the early hours of the morning, Perry's luxurious Bentley making the final stage less arduous than the rest of the journey.

Bella had been weak when he got to Davos two weeks previously – he got such a shock when he saw her – but the long train ride from Davos to Zurich, then the flight, and then the journey by car home had depleted her even more. She was slipping away before his eyes.

'I spoke to Oskar last night – everyone else was in bed. He's been so good, Bella, to take care of Ais the way he did. She even testified, and according to him, she was brilliant.' They knew Mark had been acquitted, as Perry had got word to the driver who brought them home, but Dermot filled Isabella in on the details.

'I might as well tell you now, myself and Oskar hatched a plan. We sprung loads of our lads out of Waterford court back in the day. It used to be the British military barracks, so it was there they took our lads when they picked us up, and Barty Sheehan – remember him?'

Her brow furrowed.

'He was with us, part of the Dungarvan flying column?'

'Oh yes,' she said, knowing exactly what he meant, that the man was an IRA volunteer. 'He had a limp?'

'The very man. Well, he's a court clerk, and he never forgot a turn I did for him when the British were after his brother, so he agreed to help Oskar bust Mark out if the verdict went against us. There are tunnels under there, closed for years now but usable all the same. Mark would have had to go on the run, but it was better than the alternative. Thanks be to God it didn't come to that.'

'I'm so relieved,' she said, every word an effort.

She hadn't the strength for long conversations any more; even short exchanges seemed to take it out of her. She needed her energy, what was left of it.

'Bring the girls down, Der,' she said, hating how raspy her voice was now. The medicine the clinic sent her home with made her drowsy, but her breathing was so laboured, it was hard to sleep. Strangely, she slept better during the day. 'I need to see them. Give them the masks they gave me in Davos.'

The clinic had provided her with some disposable masks that they suggested she give to visitors. Also advising that keeping the windows open and using fresh handkerchiefs that were disposed of in the fire after use would mean she could stop the infection spreading to her family.

He had lain beside her night after night on the journey, rubbing her back, filling basins with hot water and friar's balsam so she could inhale the steam, making her tea and bringing food she couldn't eat.

'You're too tired, Bella love. I'll ask them to pop in tomorrow for a minute or two.' He soothed her, and stroked her hair. He'd barely left her side since she came home, and she loved him for it, but she needed to see her daughters.

'No, I'll sleep later.' She could only rest sitting up; lying down it felt like she was drowning. Before she could go on, another cough overtook her, her lungs screaming for air as she spewed bloody phlegm. Dermot's eyes showed agony, but he remained calm and soothing. He gave her fresh handkerchiefs and helped her stay upright.

'Bring them...' She paused to catch her breath, then lay back once more. The effort of speaking and coughing had depleted what little energy she had. It wouldn't be long.

* * *

SHE WOKE to gentle tapping on the door, and the faces of her three girls appeared. She smiled. How she loved them. They were grown women now, but to her they were her little girls and always would be. They were each wearing the masks, and the window was wide open, allowing air to circulate. She had a pile of fresh cotton squares beside her and a bag to place them in when used. On the bed was her box that Dermot had placed there for her.

'Come in, girls.' She beckoned them weakly.

'Hi, Mam.' Eve sat on one side of the bed, Aisling on the other, and Kate sat on the bed. 'How are you?' Eve tried to keep her voice light, but Isabella could see from their faces how her appearance shocked them. She'd not seen them in months, and she longed to hold them close.

She didn't answer, but tried to smile. She opened the small mahogany box her father had given her for her sixteenth birthday; he'd handcrafted it himself. She extracted her wedding ring, long ago too big for her skeletal fingers.

'Eve, I want you to have this,' she said. 'I had the happiest marriage, and I love your father with all of my heart. I know you have your own, but this is for you.'

Eve took the gold band wordlessly. She looked into her mother's eyes. Bella shook her head and closed her hand over Eve's. The little band was nestled in her daughter's palm.

Then she took out her engagement ring. It was a solitaire

diamond, the most expensive one Dermot had been able to afford. There were times over the years when money was tight that she'd considered pawning or even selling it, but she hadn't been able to do it. She loved it.

'For you, Ais...' She handed it to Aisling.

'Oh, Mam...' Aisling slid the ring onto her right hand. 'Thank you.' She leaned in and kissed her mother's withered cheek.

'And this is for you, my lovely Kate.' Isabella took out her locket. It was an heirloom from her own mother, a little golden ball that opened into three little photo frames. In it were pictures of her daughters as babies. For as long as they remembered, their mother was never without it.

'Put your own babies in it, that way they'll always be close to your heart like mine were for me.'

Kate took it, unable to speak.

Isabella had refused to take her medication that morning and everything hurt, but she wanted to be alert and the tablets and powders made her sleep. She inhaled as best she could, trying to gather her strength.

'I don't have long, my loves. I don't want to leave you or your dad, but God has other plans for me. I'm so proud of you, how you've turned out. I could not have wished for a better family.'

'Mam, please don't, I can't...' Kate begged her.

'Let her talk, Kate,' Eve said, holding her youngest sister's hand.

Isabella reached up and stroked Kate's hair. She took as deep a breath as she could and spoke again, glad that her voice sounded a little stronger. 'I love you girls with all my heart, and I'll watch over you and yours for the rest of your lives. I want you to mind your daddy, all right? He's not one for opening up, and he only talks to me, but don't let him wallow for too long. And if you can, help him to find someone else maybe...' She stopped then, needing to rest once more.

'We love you too, Mam. You're the best mother anyone could ever have had. Everything we are, it's down to you and Daddy.' Eve's voice caught but she remained dry-eyed. 'When Jack died, I thought I'd never recover, and when we had to leave here, it was you who kept us strong. We'll be strong for you now.'

Aisling and Kate nodded, their eyes bright.

Isabella nodded and patted the space on the bed beside her. Just like when they were little, they lay down and cuddled up to their mother, each one knowing that this was goodbye.

CHAPTER 33

*D*ermot put the poetry book down. Bella liked him to read to her, and she especially loved Yeats, but he could see she was asleep. The visit with the girls had really taken it out of her. They were devastated, as he was, but they would survive.

He couldn't say the same of himself.

He stood and stretched, easing the tension out of his muscles. He tiptoed across the room in his stockinged feet. The darkness had fallen, and the winter was definitely on the way. Bella liked the curtains to be open so she could see out, but the sunlight woke her early, so he'd keep them shut for tonight. His stomach grumbled; he couldn't remember the last time he'd eaten. The girls had dropped by plates of food, but he couldn't eat them. Maybe he should go down now and get something. He didn't care what. He went as far as the door, his hand on the handle, when he looked back. The small lamp beside the bed threw a pool of yellow light across her face. Bella was awake again. Her brown Spanish eyes had never dulled, even as the TB ravaged her once curvaceous figure. He could lift her now like he lifted the girls when they were small, she weighed so little.

Doctor Grahame had warned him it wouldn't be long. He'd been very good. Everyone had. They were all trying to help, trying to ease the pain for him and his daughters, but there was nothing to be done.

He couldn't think about it, what it would be like, a life without his wife. One day, one minute at a time was all he could do. Taking care of her, being with her, that was all. He let the handle go. All thought of food vanished, and he went back to her.

'Can I get you anything, love?' he asked.

She shook her head, even that small effort causing her to sigh deeply, which in turn led to weak coughing. He helped her sit up and held the cloth to her mouth as the now-constant blood-streaked phlegm filled it. Her dark curls were grey now, fanning out on the pillow, but even the sickly pallor of her skin could not hide her beauty.

The coughing fit subsided, and he eased her back onto the pillows.

'You'll be all right, Der,' she whispered. 'After...' She tried to gesture with a hand but it was as if it was too heavy for her to lift. 'Open the curtains.'

He sighed and went to the heavy drapes and opened them once more. The inky black night was starless.

'Bella, don't try to talk...' he began as he sat beside her.

She patted his hand and ignored him. 'Mind the girls, and let them mind you.' The words came out individually on her laboured breath.

There was something about the way she said it. Fear, pure unadulterated panic gripped him. It felt like there was a band of ever-tightening steel around his chest. *No!* He wasn't ready, it was too soon, he couldn't, not yet! Despite his promises to himself to be strong, he heard himself plead with her.

'Bella, please, don't leave me. I can't go on without you... I can't...' Dermot wiped his eyes with the sleeve of his jumper, one she'd knit for him years ago.

She placed her hand on his. He looked up then, straight at her, his beloved wife, and saw the pain there. She wanted to stay, she knew he needed her, that they all did, but something told him she was holding on for him and he was being selfish.

'Let me go, Der...' she said slowly. 'I...' She coughed again.

He summoned up the strength he'd never needed before. Nothing had prepared him for this. He knew it was over. He'd faced enemy fire, interrogations, harsh conditions, he'd worried about his daughters, he'd held Eve up when Jack died, he'd pulled Robinswood out of the ashes with Sam and Kate... But nobody knew that all of his strength came from her, the knowledge that no matter what life threw at him, at his side, for better or worse, for richer or poorer, was Isabella – that's what gave him the power he had. Now he needed to dig deep.

'In sickness and in health,' he said quietly.

She nodded and a small smile formed on her chapped lips.

He lay beside her on their bed, taking her frail and ravaged body in his arms. How often had he lain there, in this room, with this woman beside him? It was their first home. It was where their girls had been born, him out of his mind with worry downstairs each time, wishing he could do something to stop the pain. Then seeing her radiant face as she sat up, a new tiny bundle in her arms, so proud to show off her baby to him. He remembered vividly each one, Eve, Aisling and then Kate, and the bursting pride and love as those tiny fingers gripped his thumb. And as they grew up, the various childhood illnesses... Bella would put them into this big bed and look after them tenderly and with such love. So many Christmas mornings, the girls rushing in to show them what Santa Claus had brought, their little faces alight with joy.

It was here he and his wife made love so often, never diminishing in frequency or passion as the years went on. She responded to him as ardently as he approached her; it was one of the many things he adored about her. It was in this bed they talked about their children, their problems, their worries. He wasn't a man who found opening up emotionally easy, but in this room, in this bed, he felt safe. Isabella was his safe harbour. He'd never for a moment considered there would come a time when he would be without her.

She turned to face him as he spoke.

'I loved you the first day I saw you, up in Galway. You and your sisters on the pier in Salthill. You shone, Bella, like an exotic bird in a flock of crows. I had to make you mine. I'd no idea how, but I had to make it happen. And when you agreed to walk out with me, even though your whole family thought you could do better, I was the proudest man in Ireland. And I still am. I love you, Bella, in a way I never knew was possible. You've given me everything I could ever want. Your love, our daughters, our home... You are an angel. We've been through so much, not all of it good, and I'm sorry for those times – risking you and the girls, deliberately provoking the British, putting you in danger. But there were more good times than bad, weren't there, pet?'

She nodded and smiled again. 'I've loved...every...minute,' she managed. 'Say my poem.'

He knew exactly what she meant. He didn't need the poetry book, so often had he recited this one for her, but she loved to hear it. It was from Yeats.

Nobody knew, not even the girls, that he had read poetry to his wife all their lives.

He began, trying to keep his voice strong and steady.

WHEN YOU ARE *old and grey and full of sleep,*
and nodding by the fire, take down this book,
and slowly read, and dream of the soft look
your eyes had once, and of their shadows deep.
How many loved your moments of glad grace,
And loved your beauty with love false or true,
But one man loved the pilgrim soul in you,
And loved the sorrows of your changing face.
And bending down beside the glowing bars,
Murmur a little sadly how Love fled,
And paced upon the mountains overhead,
And hid his face amid a crowd of stars.

. . .

HE MANAGED to get to the end, and the silence when he stopped was golden. They breathed as one, same inhale, same exhale, their hearts beating in unison. He knew.

'But now it's time to say goodbye, my darling. I'm going to have to let you go, aren't I?' His eyes were filled with tears that blinded him, and he could see that hers were too.

She nodded.

He inhaled, praying he would have the strength. 'All right.' He swallowed. 'Isabella Murphy, my beautiful wife, our girls' beloved mother, you can go. And we'll be fine, I promise you. We'll take care of each other, and we'll be fine. I'll watch over our girls and our grandchildren for as long as I can, until the day comes that God brings me home to you. Because, Bella, my only home is where you are.' He gazed into her eyes. 'It's all right, my love, you can go.'

He kissed her forehead, and his hands cupped her face. Then he kissed her lips.

'Goodnight, Der...' she said, resting her head on his shoulder as she'd done almost every night for thirty-five years.

He woke as the dawn streaked the sky, for a moment disorientated. He was still dressed, but he must have fallen asleep. He was stiff and cold but didn't want to move in case he disturbed her. He turned his head and looked down at his shoulder, where Bella's head rested. Her long hair fanned across the pillow, and her face was serene. He reached over to move a lock of hair from her face and knew. She was cold. His darling girl was gone.

CHAPTER 34

*D*ermot stood at the corner of the front pew of the church. St Patrick's in Kilthomand had been the site of their children's christenings, First Holy Communions and confirmations, Eve's wedding to Jack, and various funerals and weddings of friends and neighbours, and now it was where Father Macintyre would say some nice things about Bella before leading them all through the village and up to the cemetery overlooking the sea.

Bella died on a Tuesday, and it was now Friday. She'd been laid out in their bed, and friends and neighbours called, brought food and offered comfort. Though Dermot had often thought it might have been awful for the bereaved, when he was the sympathiser, he found it strangely comforting. Oskar, Perry, Violet, Elena and all the students were invaluable, as they took care of everything. Dermot was managing during the day, but he couldn't get into their bed without her. He hadn't slept since the night she died. He dozed off on the chair now and again but that was all. People had so many stories of her, most of them funny or showing her deep depths of kindness. Bella had helped anyone she could. The tinkers came to town specially for her funeral because she'd always been so good to them. Her friends

278

from the church flower-arranging committee made the most beautiful wreaths; she'd have loved them.

The morning she died, Dermot had waited until the girls would be getting up anyway before going up to tell them. He'd laid beside her, cradling her in his arms for a long time. He didn't want the fuss, the people arriving, the food, the undertakers and priest, the mechanics of the funeral, the age-old process where everyone knew what to do, what their place was in the whole production.

Eventually, he knew he couldn't hold off any longer. He would have to face the world without his wife beside him for the first time in so many years.

The girls had been distraught of course. Though they expected it, it was still a shock. The guests had been relocated to other hotels. Everyone had been very kind, Sam said.

The girls sat beside him, their husbands in the row behind with Beau, Lillian, Violet, Perry, Elena and Oskar. The Hamilton-Brooks children, Georgie and Arthur, now almost grown, were inconsolable. Isabella was the grandmother they never had.

Hannah was looking after Austina, Bella and Kate's three. A funeral was too sad for them, and Isabella had asked that they be kept away. She'd wanted them to remember her as living, not dead.

The local women had done a great job. Isabella looked like herself lying in the casket. She looked like his darling girl but without the lines of pain that had marred her beautiful face these past months. Her hair was loose, at his request, and she wore her favourite green dress, the one she'd bought in Dublin for Eve's wedding to Bartley. The girls had made her buy it, though she confided in him it was the most money she'd ever spent on a frock in her life. She'd looked like something from a storybook in that dress. She had danced with him after the wedding, and he could remember the feel of her in his arms. The dress was silk, and he had been afraid his rough hands would catch on the fabric. She slipped it off that night, in a hotel room in Dublin, and he'd caressed her creamy skin. She was cross in the morning that in their passion she never even hung her dress up, but he'd laughed at her, delighted that even after all those years, their attraction to each other was as strong as when they were young.

He ran moments of their lives in his mind, like a film reel, the funny moments, the sad, all of it, as he sat in the church.

On and on the people came, each one wanting to sympathise. They shook his hand and then each of the girls' and said they were sorry for their trouble. He nodded his thanks, not trusting himself to speak. The girls too were stoic, but he could tell that, like him, they were broken inside.

D'Alton turned up, which was nice of him. Apparently, young Isaac had managed to escape custody while being transferred to prison from the police station where he was charged and was still at large. Bartley and Hannah had been questioned by police, but neither had any idea where the lad was.

Old school friends stopped to have a word with the girls. All the workers from the estate, the students, the people of Kilthomand were genuinely sad. Bella was universally loved.

A family of travellers came and pressed paper flowers into the hands of the girls – Bella had always bought them from the traveller women – and they vowed they would pray for her soul, not that she needed it.

'Missus Murphy went straight up, God be good to her,' a tinker woman assured Dermot. 'She was a grand woman, your wife.'

'She certainly was,' Dermot agreed with a smile.

The priest finally stopped the lines of people and began the mass. He spoke of Bella's soul being with God, how such a dedicated and devoted wife and mother could not be anywhere now but at the right hand of the Lord. He told the congregation what they knew, that Isabella Murphy was a wonderful woman and would be sorely missed.

The church choir was in fine voice, singing Bella's favourite hymns. Father Macintyre explained how Isabella had picked out her hymns weeks ago and asked him to have them sung at her funeral mass. Though it was almost November, the choir sang her favourite as the procession left the church, 'Queen of the May'. Through their tears, Eve, Kate and Aisling sang along, as they had done with their mother so many times.

BRING FLOWERS OF THE RAREST, *bring flowers of the fairest,*
  from garden and woodland and hillside and vale.
  Our full hearts are swelling, our glad voices telling,
  the praise of the loveliest rose of the vale.
  Oh Mary we crown thee with blossoms today,
  Queen of the Angels and Queen of the May,
  Oh Mary we crown thee with blossoms today,
  Queen of the angels and Queen of the May.

ONCE THE PRIEST had done the final blessing in the church, swung the thurible with its pungent incense and sprinkled the coffin with holy water, it was time to take Isabella to her final resting place.

Dermot and Beau, being the tallest, walked to the head of the coffin, Sam and Mark to the middle and Oskar and Bartley to the rear. With the help of the undertakers, the men hoisted Bella's casket onto their shoulders, each placing his arm around the shoulder of the man opposite for stability.

Dermot pushed his face to the pine, wanting for one last time to lay his head beside her. Together, the six men carried Isabella to her grave.

Aisling, Eve and Kate, supported by Lillian, Violet and Elena and her children, walked behind the men to the graveyard, linking arms, and behind them the extended family and all the people of Kilthomand walked in sad silence.

As they approached the freshly dug grave, Isabella was taken from the men's shoulders and her coffin placed on a low scaffold beside the grave. Father Macintyre began the final decade of the rosary, and the crowd answered in the age-old tradition.

Dermot felt as if he was not in his body; instead, it seemed as though he was looking down on it, observing the proceedings from above. He was numb. He couldn't feel the cold, though everyone was wrapped up warm as the priest droned on about the five sorrowful mysteries. Dermot watched as Dan O'Sullivan and his son Henry, the local gravediggers, approached the timber trestles on which Bella's coffin rested. They slung some rope around the coffin and then, with practised ease, lowered her into the dark hole. The ropes holding the pine box creaked as they gently and expertly laid her to rest, taking care not to bump her off the side.

Father Macintyre sprinkled yet more holy water on the coffin, and each of the girls, followed by Lillian, Violet, Georgie and Elena, threw in a single rose. Then they handed the shovel to Dermot. He knew he was to throw a scoop of the deep, rich brown earth on his wife's coffin, but he was frozen. He couldn't do it. He just stood there, the eyes of the parish on him.

Then from behind he felt someone pass him and take the shovel. Oskar dug into the soil and threw the earth in the grave. Each of the men – Sam, Mark, Beau, Bartley and Perry, followed by the men of Kilthomand – followed suit. Throughout it all, Dermot stood rigid and unmoving.

Father Macintyre spoke again. 'Lord Jesus Christ, by your own three days in the tomb, you hallowed the graves of all who believe in you, and so made the grave a sign of hope that promises resurrection even as it claims our mortal bodies.

'Grant that our sister Isabella may sleep here in peace until you awaken her to glory, for you are the resurrection and the life, that she will see you face to face, and in your light will see the light and know the splendour of God, for you live and reign for ever and ever.'

The gathered crowd said, 'Amen.'

Eventually, it was over. Those in the crowd blessed themselves. Some people approached the family once more to sympathise, but eventually they began to shuffle out of the graveyard. There was tea and cake and whiskey in Robinswood, and the family were expecting the whole parish, if for no other reason than to get a glimpse inside the iconic local mansion.

Sam, Bartley and Mark took care of their wives as Beau helped Lillian, Elena and Georgie over the uneven ground, leading them to the waiting cars. But still Dermot stood. Several people patted him on the shoulder, and some of the women squeezed his hand. Perry gently shepherded people out; he seemed to know Dermot needed to be alone.

Oskar came and stood beside him, saying nothing. Together, side by side, as they had done since they were little older than boys, they waited as the voices and engines faded away and it became still and silent.

'I want to crawl in there with her,' Dermot heard himself say, his voice unrecognisable to his own ears.

'I know you do. But she needs you to go on, to look after the girls, so you'll do as she asks like you always did.' Oskar lit two cigarettes, handing one to Dermot, who drew on it gratefully. He'd not smoked a cigarette for ages, but today he needed it.

'She was one of a kind, Oskar, she really was.' Dermot allowed the tears to fall.

'She was, my friend. You're a lucky man to have known such love.'

'But what do I do now?' He turned to Oskar. 'I don't know who I am without her, how to be. Nothing makes sense to me without my Bella.'

Oskar drew on his cigarette, and then spoke. 'Eve told me that when Jack died, you gave her advice – to just breathe in and out, put one foot before the other and not to expect too much of herself. That one day she would smile again. Maybe it is time to take your own advice.'

Dermot shook his head sadly. 'She was young, she had her whole life to live. She'd find someone else. I knew that she loved Jack but that she'd get over it. But Bella and me, we are intertwined over decades. She's wrapped around me like a vine, and we can't be separated at this stage. I'm too old. I don't want to smile again. I should want to stay, for our girls, our grandchildren. I know I should, but I don't, Oskar. I want to go with her.'

'Not today, my friend, not today.' Oskar patted him on the back. 'I envy you, you know,' the German said suddenly.

Dermot looked at him. 'Why?'

'Because you're so sure. You know that Bella is in heaven, that you will be with her when you die. I have no such faith. My Brigitta died, so many years ago now, but I don't think she is anywhere. And I won't see her again.'

'Maybe I'm right, and maybe you will, whether you believe it or not,' Dermot responded. They'd often talked about faith, God, heaven and hell over the years. And though Dermot wasn't a very demonstrative Catholic, preferring to keep to himself, he went to mass and had a deep, quiet faith.

'Maybe. Who knows?' Oskar shrugged. 'But you knew great love, my friend, and that is a gift to be cherished, even after it's gone. You have your memories, so Isabella for you, like Brigitta is for me, is in here' – he pointed at his temple – 'and in here.' He laid his palm on his chest.

Dermot nodded and took the last pull from the cigarette. 'Thanks for taking care of Aisling. I wouldn't have trusted anyone else, and I couldn't...' he said, quenching the butt under his foot.

'I was happy to help,' Oskar answered. 'And we didn't need to go back to our old tricks.'

Dermot sighed, suddenly so weary. 'Probably just as well. Our jail-breaking days are behind us.' He turned to Oskar. 'And that young fella, Bartley's brother, gave the guards the slip, I heard?'

'He did.' Oskar smiled. He had no love of law enforcement of any kind. 'He's a smart boy, that one. He'll be fine. And Sean Lacey is no loss anyway, he got what he deserved, so if young Isaac manages to get away, more power to him, I say. That girl Hannah did the right thing – she got Mark off, and she did it when she had an opportunity few could resist, a new life in America. She's as brave as your three.'

'She is. And the girls will look after her for it. Eve told me she's heartbroken, as she was mad about him, but she couldn't face knowing Mark was being tried for something he didn't do, and with poor Aisling carrying his child, it was too much.'

'There's not many would do it. I'd say young Doherty is halfway to America now, well out of the clutches of the Gardai.'

Dermot was now lost in thought again, just staring down at the half-filled hole.

'See you outside. I'll wait in the car.' And Oskar walked away, leaving him to say goodbye to the love of his life.

CHAPTER 35

'Any sign of him?' Kate asked as she popped the cake in the oven and sent the children to wash their hands.

'Not yet.' Eve sighed. Bartley was being questioned by the Gardai once more about the whereabouts of his brother. It was a source of embarrassment to the police force that Isaac managed to escape, seemingly without a trace, and they refused to accept that Bartley had no idea where he might be. 'It's like he's vanished into thin air. I don't care that he killed Sean Lacey. I know that sounds awful, but I don't. But he would have let Mark hang, can you believe that? Thank God for Hannah being so brave and selfless.'

'I know,' Kate agreed. 'She's a great girl, she really is. I'm so glad she came back. Apart from the fact that the children adore her and we badly need a nanny, I'm happy she felt she could come back, that Robinswood was her home.'

'I'd say it broke her heart – she really loved him.' Eve felt so sad for the lovely blonde girl. When she'd arrived back that night, carrying her suitcase up the driveway – she'd walked from the village – she told them everything. How she loved him but couldn't stand by and watch Mark pay for something he did, how she passed the note to

Teddy, who contacted the guards who arrested him, and subsequently the court secured Mark's release. She was afraid they would reject her, but they didn't. In fact, they were so grateful for what she had done that the girl felt comfortable telling them about Laura and her plans to get the child back. Everyone knew of girls who'd been sent to the nuns after getting in trouble, but nobody had ever heard of anyone getting a child back. But Hannah was determined, and that night the three Murphy sisters promised they would do all they could to help her, to repay her kindness in telling the police about Isaac.

'She did. He seemed convinced Mark wouldn't be found guilty of murder, according to what Hannah said. I feel for Bartley as well though. He wanted to make a connection with his brother, but it's all ended like this.' Kate was circumspect.

'Exactly. Isaac is his brother, and he wanted so badly to be close to him, but Isaac is an odd fish. Maybe it was his upbringing, who knows. He was all charm and nice on the surface, but he's icy under it all. It's tearing Bartley's heart out, to be honest.'

Eve picked Bella up and cuddled her. 'Poor Daddy is sad, isn't he darling? So we'll have to be extra lovely to him.' The baby cooed and Eve kissed her cheek. 'I wish Mam was here,' she said, her eyes bright with unshed tears.

'I know. I can't believe she's gone,' Kate replied. 'It's all so horrible, passing the house, knowing she'll never be there again, never bake a loaf of bread or mind her flowers for the May altar. Daddy said he'd come in for dinner, but I made Sam promise to force him if he makes any excuse. He's working like a man possessed, and he hardly eats. I know it's his way of dealing with it all, but he's going to fade away in front of us.'

Aisling and Mark had moved back to their cottage. Mark and Bartley had a conversation the night Mark was released, and Mark assured Bartley that he felt no animosity towards him. But Eve's husband felt guilty nonetheless. He'd brought Isaac among them and felt responsible.

The sisters watched out of the window as Lillian showed the

students how to select winter blooms for a centrepiece. The girls were gathered around her as she stood, secateurs in hand, showing them how to cut the holly and the variegated laurel, and adding the flame-coloured heuchera to bring a splash of colour to the dining room.

The rain began, and the sisters watched in amusement as Lillian's first thought was for the tablecloths drying on the line. She ran and pulled them down, saving them from a soaking. The old Lillian would have only worried for her hair.

'Mam is gone, but what would she make of Lady Lillian suddenly becoming the housekeeper of the year?' Kate murmured.

'Just Lillian now, Kate.' Eve winked. 'She'd probably say she knew she had it in her, and isn't it great for us and for her that she's finally fitting in?' Eve smiled, remembering her mother's calm pragmatism and optimistic outlook on everything.

'That's exactly what she'd say. And Lillian and Beau seem so much better, don't they?'

'They do,' Eve agreed. 'And I'm so happy for them. During the trial and all the time Mam was sick and over the funeral, we'd have been lost without them. And Violet and Perry too – they were so good taking care of things here and helping with the children and everything. It's hard sometimes when I think back to the days when we used to hide on the back stairs watching all the gentry arrive for the hunt balls and we were just the servant's kids, to be seen and not heard. I look at Lillian and Violet sometimes and wonder – are they the same people or are we?'

'I know. Life is strange, isn't it?' Kate sighed.

They turned as they heard the kitchen door open. Aisling stood there. She'd regained some of the weight she lost through anxiety and morning sickness and now radiated happiness and health. Her bump was beginning to show too, and the doctors were confident that all was well with the pregnancy. She had Mark home and that meant the world.

'Hi, Ais, how are you feeling?' Eve asked.

'Great.' She smiled. 'Mark is gone up to the top acre with Beau and

Sam ages ago. There's a lame cow up there. Poor thing had twins last week and it nearly killed her, so they are gone up to see if they can move her down nearer the house so she doesn't have to walk so far. The trek to the milking parlour is killing her. They'll have to dry her off anyway. They should be back soon.'

'Sam was up at five this morning. Without Daddy for so long when he was in Davos and caring for Mam, Sam was worrying he'd done things wrong. Sam works so hard, but he was used to checking every single thing with Dad. Managing the place on his own was good for him in a strange way, learning to trust his own judgement.' Kate sighed. Her husband was not a natural farmer, he was a pilot and a scholar, but he was so determined that Robinswood could be resurrected and he was going to make it happen.

'It's not easy. There is so much to do. But Mark is back now and so is Daddy, so between them all, they'll get everything running smoothly,' Aisling reassured her sister.

'It's been a hard year,' Eve acknowledged. 'Mam being sick and then losing her. Daddy is working morning, noon and night at the moment, but it's best just to let him cope in whatever way he can. After Jack died, I was useless, literally useless for the longest time. Mammy and Daddy just kind of propelled me along. And I know my marriage compared to theirs wasn't anything as long, but Daddy convinced me I'd be all right, and I am. It takes time, and he'll never get over it, but he will be able to live with it eventually.'

As they stood watching, the car appeared. Bartley was back. Mark, Sam and Beau must have seen him turn in the avenue as well because within a few minutes, they appeared also. Everyone congregated in the kitchen. Lillian must have sent the girls to do something because a moment later she arrived as well and moved to stand beside Beau.

Eve went to Bartley, putting her arm around his waist, and he hugged her.

'Well, any word?' Sam asked.

Bartley shook his head. 'He escaped custody as he was transferred from the van to the courthouse it seems. They've scoured the country for him, but not a sign.' He edged closer to Eve, needing her strength now.

Dermot passed the window, and Eve beckoned him in. He took his mud-encrusted wellingtons off at the back door and came in in his socks. He looked exhausted. Deep lines were etched on his face, and it broke his daughters' hearts to see him so profoundly sad.

Kate poured tea from the enormous teapot and handed around cups and some gingerbread fresh from the oven. Even Beau had been converted to tea at long last.

'I'm glad we're all here.' All eyes were on Bartley as he addressed them all. 'Could someone get Hannah? I'd like her to be part of this too.'

Immediately Lillian volunteered. 'She's playing with the children in the nursery. I saw them through the window. I'll run for her. My mother is in the drawing room, and she can step in.'

'Thanks, Lillian,' Bartley said.

The group passed milk and sugar and complimented Kate on the cake as they waited. Hannah appeared with Lillian moments later.

Bartley looked around before speaking. 'I...I just have something I want to say.' The hubbub of chatter quieted down and he had their attention.

'My brother Isaac is wanted now for the robbery and murder of Sean Lacey. Frankly, I doubt they'll find him. He's clever, so he won't allow himself to be caught twice, I'd imagine. I thought I'd come to know him, a bit anyway – it turns out I didn't. Only that Hannah found it in herself to alert the guards, Mark would have been hanged for something he didn't do. I'm so...' He paused. 'I'm so proud of you, Hannah. I know how you felt about him. What you did was brave and selfless, but you did the right thing, and I know everyone here feels the same way. We've had a hard year, individually and as a group, but I wanted to say this. I'm so sorry for bringing him here, for putting you all through this on top of everything else, when the family were suffering the most awful loss of Isabella. To have this piled on top of it was just horrible, and I'm so sorry.'

Mark spoke. 'Nobody blames you, Bartley. You were just trying to do right by your brother. There's nothing wrong with that.'

'Maybe, but it caused such pain...' he protested. 'Until I met Eve and came here, I never had a home, I never belonged anywhere. And now I feel like I betrayed that...'

'What happened was not of your doing,' Sam agreed. 'Mark's right. Nobody blames you. And look, Sean Lacey is dead and good riddance. There won't be any tears shed for him in this house.'

It was Sam's turn to take the floor. 'This year, everything that's happened could have broken us. We were under so much pressure, in every way imaginable, almost to the breaking point several times, but we came through it because we stuck together. Kate and I don't see this as our house any more. Robinswood is home for all of us now. We all share in the work, we all share in the successes, and we pull together in the tough times. Losing Isabella was the hardest thing I've ever had to deal with, let alone Dermot, Eve, Ais and Kate. She was such a special woman, and she gave us all so much. I think she'd be proud of us. We are making something here, a safe and happy home for us and for our children. We're providing a chance for Eve and Bartley's students. Life hasn't been kind to many of them so far, through no fault of theirs' – he looked at Hannah – 'and we are providing employment in the area, so fewer families are torn apart by emigration. Kilthomand is an unusual village in that only the people who want to emigrate do, as there's work here if they want it. We belong here in Robinswood, all of us.' He looked straight at Lillian, who smiled. 'The road wasn't smooth to get us here, and no doubt there will be more trials and tribulations ahead, but we can face them together.'

Mark put his arm around Hannah, drawing her into the group as Sam went on.

'We are a family, me and Kate, Lillian and Beau, Mark and Ais, Eve and Bartley, and now Hannah, the children, and of course Dermot, who will always be the boss of Robinswood no matter what title I have' – his little joke was rewarded by a smile from his father-in-law – 'and nothing will ever change that. We loved Isabella and we'll miss her every day, but she died knowing we were all together. And I could not wish for a finer group of people with which to share our lives.

'To Robinswood and Isabella.' Sam held his mug aloft.

'To Robinswood and Isabella,' they echoed, clinking mugs, tears shining in their eyes.

THE END.

THE BEAUTIFUL HOUSE featured on the cover of this series is in County Sligo and is called Temple House. It's a spectacular place complete with lake and Knight's Templar castle on the grounds. It is the family home of friends of mine and is a fabulous place to stay, host a party or even a wedding. If you ever get the chance you should visit and walk among my imaginings of the Keneficks and the Murphys, you'd love it.

www.templehouse.ie

I SINCERELY HOPE you enjoyed this series, it's always hard to say goodbye. For me as the writer it is anyway!

I thought you might like to know about another series of mine, which follows the life of two German Jewish children who through a series of both fortunate and unfortunate events end up in Ireland.

It's called The Star and the Shamrock and you can get it here:

https://geni.us/TheStarandtheShamrocAL

Her is a sneak preview to get you started:

THE STAR AND THE SHAMROCK.

Liverpool, England, 1939

Elizabeth put the envelope down and took off her glasses. The thin paper and the Irish stamps irritated her. Probably that estate agent wanting to sell her mother's house again. She'd told him twice she wasn't selling, though she had no idea why. It wasn't as if she were ever going back to Ireland, her father long dead, her mother gone last year – she was probably up in heaven tormenting the poor saints with her extensive religious knowledge. The letter drew her back to the little Northern Irish village she'd called home...that big old lonely house...her mother.

Margaret Bannon was a pillar of the community back in Bally-cregggan, County Down, a devout Catholic in a deeply divided place, but she had a heart of stone.

Elizabeth sighed. She tried not to think about her mother, as it only upset her. Not a word had passed between them in twenty-one years, and then Margaret died alone. She popped the letter behind the clock; she needed to get to school. She'd open it later, or next week... or never.

Rudi smiled down at her from the dresser. 'Don't get bitter, don't be like her.' She imagined she heard him admonish her, his boyish face frozen in an old sepia photograph, in his King's Regiment uniform, so proud, so full of excitement, so bloody young. What did he know of the horrors that awaited him out there in Flanders? What did any of them know?

She mentally shook herself. This line of thought wasn't helping. Rudi was dead, and she wasn't her mother. She was her own person. Hadn't she proved that by defying her mother and marrying Rudi? It all seemed so long ago now, but the intensity of the emotions lingered. She'd met, loved and married young Rudi Klein as a girl of eighteen. Margaret Bannon was horrified at the thought of her Catholic daughter marrying a Jew, but Elizabeth could still remember that heady feeling of being young and in love. Rudi could have been a Martian for all she cared. He was young and handsome and funny, and he made her feel loved.

She wondered, if he were to somehow come back from the dead and just walk up the street and into the kitchen of their little terraced house, would he recognise the woman who stood there? Her chestnut hair that used to fall over her shoulders was always now pulled back in a bun, and the girl who loved dresses was now a woman whose clothes were functional and modest. She was thirty-nine, but she knew she could pass for older. She had been pretty once, or at least not too horrifically ugly anyway. Rudi had said he loved her; he'd told her she was beautiful.

She snapped on the wireless, but the talk was of the goings-on in Europe again. She unplugged it; it was too hard to hear first thing in the morning. Surely they wouldn't let it all happen again, not after the last time?

All anyone talked about was the threat of war, what Hitler was going to do. Would there really be peace as Mr Chamberlain promised? It was going to get worse before it got better if the papers were to be believed.

Though she was almost late, she took the photo from the shelf. A smudge of soot obscured his smooth forehead, and she wiped it with the sleeve of her cardigan. She looked into his eyes.

'Goodbye, Rudi darling. See you later.' She kissed the glass, as she did every day.

How different her life could have been...a husband, a family. Instead, she had received a generic telegram just like so many others in that war that was supposed to end all wars. She carried in her heart for twenty years that feeling of despair. She'd taken the telegram from the boy who refused to meet her eyes. He was only a few years younger than she. She opened it there, on the doorstep of that very house, the words expressing regret swimming before her eyes. She remembered the lurch in her abdomen, the baby's reaction mirroring her own. 'My daddy is dead.'

She must have been led inside, comforted – the neighbours were good that way. They knew when the telegram lad turned his bike down their street that someone would need holding up. That day it was her...tomorrow, someone else. She remembered the blood, the sense of dragging downwards, that ended up in a miscarriage at five months. All these years later, the pain had dulled to an ever-present ache.

She placed the photo lovingly on the shelf once more. It was the only one she had. In lots of ways, it wasn't really representative of

Rudi; he was not that sleek and well presented. 'The British Army smartened me up,' he used to say. But out of uniform is how she remembered him. Her most powerful memory was of them sitting in that very kitchen the day they got the key. His uncle Saul had lent them the money to buy the house, and they were going to pay him back.

They'd gotten married in the registry office in the summer of 1918, when he was home on brief leave because of a broken arm. She could almost hear her mother's wails all the way across the Irish Sea, but she didn't care. It didn't matter that her mother was horrified at her marrying a *Jewman*, as she insisted on calling him, or that she was cut off from all she ever knew – none of it mattered. She loved Rudi and he loved her. That was all there was to it.

She'd worn her only good dress and cardigan – the miniscule pay of a teaching assistant didn't allow for new clothes, but she didn't care. Rudi had picked a bunch of flowers on the way to the registry office, and his cousin Benjamin and Benjamin's wife, Nina, were the witnesses. Ben was killed at the Somme, and Nina went to London, back to her family. They'd lost touch.

Elizabeth swallowed. The lump of grief never left her throat. It was a part of her now. A lump of loss and pain and anger. The grief had given way to fury, if she were honest. Rudi was killed on the morning of the 11th of November, 1918, in Belgium. The armistice had been signed, but the order to end hostilities would not come into effect until eleven p.m. The eleventh hour of the eleventh month. She imagined the generals saw some glorious symmetry in that. But there wasn't. Just more people left in mourning than there had to be. She lost him, her Rudi, because someone wanted the culmination of four long years of slaughter to look nice on a piece of paper.

She shivered. It was cold these mornings, though spring was supposed to be in the air. The children in her class were constantly sniffling and coughing. She remembered the big old fireplace in the national school in Ballycregggan, where each child was expected to bring a sod of turf or a block of timber as fuel for the fire. Master O'Reilly's wife would put the big jug of milk beside the hearth in the mornings so the children could have a warm drink by lunchtime. Elizabeth would have loved to have a fire in her classroom, but the British education system would never countenance such luxuries.

She glanced at the clock. Seven thirty. She should go. Fetching her coat and hat, and her heavy bag of exercise books that she'd marked last night, she let herself out.

The street was quiet. Apart from the postman, doing deliveries on the other side of the street, she was the only person out. She liked it, the sense of solitude, the calm before the storm.

The mile-long walk to Bridge End Primary was her exercise and thinking time. Usually, she mulled over what she would teach that day or how to deal with a problem child – or more frequently, a problem parent. She had been a primary schoolteacher for so long, there was little she had not seen. Coming over to England as a bright sixteen-year-old to a position as a teacher's assistant in a Catholic school was the beginning of a trajectory that had taken her far from Bally-creggan, from her mother, from everything she knew.

She had very little recollection of the studies that transformed her from a lowly teaching assistant to a fully qualified teacher. After Rudi was killed and she'd lost the baby, a kind nun at her school suggested she do the exams to become a teacher, not just an assistant, and because it gave her something to do with her troubled mind, she agreed. She got top marks, so she must have thrown herself into her studies, but she couldn't remember much about those years. They were shrouded in a fog of grief and pain.

Chapter 2

Berlin, Germany, 1939

Ariella Bannon waited behind the door, her heart thumping. She'd covered her hair with a headscarf and wore her only remaining coat, a grey one that had been smart once. Though she didn't look at all Jewish with her green eyes and curly red hair – and being married to Peter Bannon, a Catholic, meant she was in a slightly more privileged position than other Jews – people knew what she was. She took her children to temple, kept a kosher house. She never in her wildest nightmares imagined that the quiet following of her faith would have led to this.

One of the postmen, Herr Krupp, had joined the Brownshirts. She didn't trust him to deliver the post properly, so she had to hope it was Frau Braun that day. She wasn't friendly exactly, but at least she gave you your letters. She was surprised at Krupp; he'd been nice before, but since Kristallnacht, it seemed that everyone was different. She even remembered Peter talking to him a few times about the weather or fishing or something. It was hard to believe that underneath all that, there was such hatred. Neighbours, people on the street, children even, seemed to have turned against all Jews. Liesl and Erich were scared all the time. Liesl tried to put a brave face on it – she was such a wonderful child – but she was only ten. Erich looked up to her so much. At seven, he thought his big sister could fix everything.

It was her daughter's birthday next month but there was no way to celebrate. Ariella thought back to birthdays of the past, cakes and friends and presents, but that was all gone. Everything was gone.

She tried to swallow the by-now-familiar lump of panic. Peter had been picked up because he and his colleague, a Christian, tried to defend an old Jewish lady the Nazi thugs were abusing in the street. Ariella had been told that the uniformed guards beat up the two men and threw them in a truck. That was five months ago. She hoped every day her husband would turn up, but so far, nothing. She considered going to visit his colleague's wife to see if she had heard anything, but nowadays, it was not a good idea for a Jew to approach an Aryan for any reason.

At least she'd spoken to the children in English since they were born. At least that. She did it because she could; she'd had an English governess as a child, a terrifying woman called Mrs Beech who insisted Ariella speak not only German but English, French and Italian as well. Peter smiled to hear his children jabbering away in other languages, and he always said they got that flair for languages from her. He spoke German only, even though his father was Irish. She remembered fondly her father-in-law, Paddy. He'd died when

Erich was a baby. Though he spoke fluent German, it was always with a lovely lilting accent. He would tell her tales of growing up in Ireland. He came to Germany to study when he was a young man, and saw and fell instantly in love with Christiana Berger, a beauty from Bavaria. And so in Germany he remained. Peter was their only child because Christiana was killed in a horse-riding accident when Peter was only five years old. How simple those days were, seven short years ago, when she had her daughter toddling about, her newborn son in her arms, a loving husband and a doting father-in-law. Now, she felt so alone.

Relief. It was Frau Braun. But she walked past the building.

Ariella fought the wave of despair. She should have gotten the letter Ariella had posted by now, surely. It was sent three weeks ago. Ariella tried not to dwell on the many possibilities. What if she wasn't at the address? Maybe the family had moved on. Peter had no contact with his only first cousin as far as she knew.

Nathaniel, Peter's best friend, told her he might be able to get Liesl and Erich on the Kindertransport out of Berlin – he had some connections apparently – but she couldn't bear the idea of them going to strangers. If only Elizabeth would say yes. It was the only way she could put her babies on that train. And even then… She dismissed that thought and refused to let her mind go there. She had to get them away until all this madness died down.

She'd tried everything to get them all out. But there was no way. She'd contacted every single embassy – the United States, Venezuela, Paraguay, places she'd barely heard of – but there was no hope. The lines outside the embassies grew longer every day, and without someone to vouch for you, it was impossible. Ireland was her only chance. Peter's father, the children's grandfather, was an Irish citizen. If she could only get Elizabeth Bannon to agree to take the children, then at least they would be safe.

Sometimes she woke in the night, thinking this must all be a nightmare. Surely this wasn't happening in Germany, a country known for learning and literature, music and art? And yet it was.

Peter and Ariella would have said they were German, their children were German, just the same as everyone else, but not so. Because of her, her darling children were considered *Untermensch*, subhuman, because of the Jewish blood in their veins.

To continue reading click here:

https://geni.us/TheStarandtheShamrocAL

ABOUT THE AUTHOR

Jean Grainger is a USA Today bestselling Irish author who lives in a stone cottage in Mid Cork, Ireland. She writes contemporary and historical fiction with an Irish twist. She lives with her husband Diarmuid and the youngest two of her four kids, the older two come home with laundry and to raid the fridge.

f

ALSO BY JEAN GRAINGER

To get a free novel and to join my readers club (100% free and always will be)

Go to www.jeangrainger.com

The Tour Series

The Tour

Safe at the Edge of the World

The Story of Grenville King

The Homecoming of Bubbles O'Leary

Finding Billie Romano

Kayla's Trick

The Carmel Sheehan Story

Letters of Freedom

The Future's Not Ours To See

What Will Be

The Robinswood Story

What Once Was True

Return To Robinswood

Trials and Tribulations

The Star and the Shamrock Series

The Star and the Shamrock

The Emerald Horizon

The Hard Way Home

The World Starts Anew

The Queenstown Series

Last Port of Call

The West's Awake

The Harp and the Rose

Roaring Liberty

Standalone Books

So Much Owed

Shadow of a Century

Under Heaven's Shining Stars

Catriona's War

Sisters of the Southern Cross